the book of *Rachel*

the book of Rachel

sandra *goldbloom*

ALLEN & UNWIN

First published in 1998 by
Allen & Unwin
9 Atchison Street
St Leonards NSW 2065
Australia
Phone: (61 2) 9901 4088
Fax: (61 2) 9906 2218
E-mail: frontdesk@allen-unwin.com.au

National Library of Australia
Cataloguing-in-Publication entry:

Goldbloom, Sandra, 1943– .

   The book of Rachel.

   ISBN 1 86448 757 7.

   I. Title.

A823.3

Set in 10.5/l2pt Goudy Old Style by Bookhouse Digital, Sydney
Printed and bound by Australian Print Group, Maryborough, Victoria

10 9 8 7 6 5 4 3 2 1

With gratitude, for my mother and father.

'We have not stopped trembling yet,
but if we had not loved each other
none of us would have survived.'

James Baldwin, *The Fire Next Time*

Klayn kint, klayn tsures, Groise kint, groise tsures.

Timeless Jewish wisdom

PRELUDE

'Hullo, Mum. Anything to eat?' Ruby drops her schoolbag in the middle of the kitchen floor. Irritated, Rachel glances at the bag; she makes no remark.

'Hello, Ruby.' Rachel walks to where her daughter is standing and kisses her. 'What a question. When is there never something to eat in this house?' She smiles. 'How was school today?' There is a note of expectation in her voice.

'Oh, Mum,' Ruby moans, long-suffering, 'you always ask me that. School's school.'

She opens the door of the refrigerator and inspects its contents.

'And?'

'Get off my case.' She relents. 'Oh, all right.' Ruby returns her mother's smile. 'I got an A plus for my painting. Mr Parry wants to put it in the Year 10 exhibition.'

Rachel radiates pride.

'Of course.' She sighs, satisfied. 'And what else would my brilliant artist get but an A plus?'

'Cut it out, Mum', Ruby retorts, flushed with irritation.

'We'll get it framed. The framer in Brunswick Street. They do beautiful work. I'll take it down—'

Ruby bristles.

'I found some pieces of timber in the woodwork room', she interrupts, not looking her mother in the eye. 'I'm going to make my own frame. Parry said he'd help me.'

'Oh.' A tense silence hovers between them . . . 'Sandwich?' . . . and is sent packing.

1

'No thanks. May I finish off this apple strudel?' Ruby *returns* to her mark. 'It's not bad though, is it?'

'It's fantastic. Excellent. I'm very proud of you, Ruby.'

'Oh, Mama.'

Nudging the strudel with her fingers, Ruby slides it off the baking dish onto a small plate and places it in the microwave. In a series of deft movements, she sets the time and temperature. Using her index finger, she scrapes the remains of the cold, buttery strudel pastry and flecks of caramelised apple from the dish. She puts each scraping into her mouth, languidly sucking the scraps from the tip of her finger, savouring each morsel. Watching her, mesmerised, Rachel shivers.

'Where will you hang it?'

Ruby does not miss what is unspoken in Rachel's question, the covetous desire.

'Don't know yet. Maybe my room.' Ruby makes no attempt to disguise the impish look—or is it sly?—that lights her face. 'I might even sell it', she adds as she peers into the black window of the microwave oven.

The electronic ping does little to dispel the renewed tension.

Ruby removes the steaming strudel from the oven and serves herself two generous dessertspoons of cream. The smell of cinnamon fills the room.

'Got a stack of homework, Mum. I'm going to my room. See ya.'

As Ruby departs she scoops up her schoolbag by its straps and heaves it over her shoulder. Rachel smiles when Ruby bobs her head to lick some cream off the plate. She admires the long, thick auburn braid that hangs between her daughter's shoulders, the round womanliness of her hips and the shapely turn of her ankles.

What a jewel you are, Ruby. We named you well.

— o —

Rachel sighs as she looks around the kitchen. She sniffs the air, as if, six years later, this act of sniffing will recapture the tang of Ruby's oil paints, the congestive fumes of turpentine. What comes to her are the fragrances of the fresh herbs from her potting shed: lavender, rosemary, borage, sages, the many thymes and others. Warm sunshine has followed a light spring rain, released the aromatic herb oils into the moist air, heightened their bouquets. Perfumes of spring flowers in the household garden come—freesias, wisteria, climbing roses, peach and citrus blossoms, the mock orange. Sweet, yes, almost cloying; that is how they seem to her. She doesn't want their sweetness; she wants oil paint and turpentine.

It has been many years since the pungency of Ruby's artwork has graced her home.

Rachel steps out through the double doors to the wisteria-covered patio. She walks along the gravel path of the cottage garden to the potting shed where, as neat as a battalion of soldiers, hundreds of black and green plastic pots—three, six and eight inches in diameter—planted with the herbs she grows for sale, stand on tier upon tier of trellises awaiting her fastidious attention.

BE'RESHIT

Why art thou angry? and why art thou crestfallen?
If thou doest well, shalt thou not be accepted?

Be'reshit (Genesis) 1:6

'Papa, Papa! Where are you going? When will you come back? Mama, is Papa coming back? Papa?'

Rachel hears her childish voice, whimpering and uncertain, as she watches Nate pack a suitcase. Her parents argue. Rachel is too young to understand their argument, knows only that their voices are raised and her father is going away again.

'. . . always leaving . . . misses you', she hears, and '. . . Rachel . . . naughty . . .' and '. . . I supposed to do . . .?' Nate's suitcase, as Rachel recalls these incidents, is removed from its place under her parents' bed when they fight. He packs his clothes and departs. Rachel believes his departures occur as a result of her being naughty. They are her punishment. Didn't she hear them speak her name, toss it between them like a ball? She tugs at her hair. She weeps.

'Stop that!'

Rivka's grip on Rachel's shoulder is sharp; Rachel squirms. Rivka mutters to herself in Yiddish, a sure sign she is angry. It is a language

4

Nate barely understands; beyond a few words, a commonplace phrase or two, Rachel will never learn it, a fact of her life she grows to regret.

'Every time the same question.' Rivka tsks with impatience. 'What do I know, Rachel? I'm just his wife.' She glares at her husband. 'Go to your room now. Papa will come to say goodbye when he is leaving.' Followed by more Yiddish.

Rachel cringes from the force of the bitterness in Rivka's voice. Nate refuses to acknowledge Rivka's sarcasm, her face flushed with impotent rage; he continues to place his neatly folded clothes into the suitcase.

'Rachel, you know I always come back', he says, irritated by her anxiety.

Rachel will not be mollified.

Of Nate's work, Rachel understands little. He sells things, she thinks, or fixes them. Aeroplanes. Propellers that turn around and around. She knows Nate enjoys his work. He takes pleasure in travelling from one big country town to another, going bush to call on farmers, tinkering with their aircraft. These men know he was a pilot during the war and trust him to fly their planes. When Nate returns home he delights Rachel with descriptions of the magic feeling, the freedom of flying. He describes to her what he sees on his travels: the flocks of brightly coloured birds, the native animals—kangaroos, koalas, echidnas—which Rachel has only seen at the zoo, encaged. She stares, wide-eyed and sombre, her toes scrunched up in her slippers, when Nate gives an account of the numerous rabbits and possums and snakes he sees strewn along the Hume Highway, a ragged-edged, two-lane country road, not yet the smooth ribbons of divided black-topped highway it is to become. Dead animals, spellbound by the headlights of oncoming cars and trucks, flattened before they could gather enough wits to scuttle out of the path of immanent death.

'Is there blood, Papa?'

'Yes, Rachel, there is blood.'

'Much blood?'

'Yes,' he pauses to contemplate, as if surprised, still, 'for such little creatures, there is much blood.'

Father and daughter shudder.

Nate describes, with a loving gentleness, the colours of the land he travels. Rachel imagines it a broad, soft-hued rainbow stretching to *infinity. She is fascinated by his description of the lives of country children: the harshness, the vast emptiness and grand beauty of their environments. Years later, she will drive through these landscapes with her own children. In adulthood they will be familiar to her as the shapes and colours her father painted for her in her childhood.*

— o —

Alone in her bedroom the child Rachel sobs, feels her stomach tighten with fear; the sickness rises, making her dizzy. Her vision blurs. In her consternation she tries to remember what it was she did wrong. Was she naughty enough for him to stay away forever this time? Didn't she put away her toys before going to bed? Perhaps he is angry because she didn't finish her drawing for school. That she came home last week with muddied shoes.

She is afraid of his anger; it is loud with shouting.

The child Rachel's brow is knotted with concentration. All of a sudden her eyes light up. The prayers! It must be the prayers. That's it. I said the prayers incorrectly on Shabbat. Last Friday. Or was it the Friday before?

'Barook Adonoy, Elhainu meleck alom . . .' she had intoned.

'No, Rachel,' Nate had corrected her, stern in the matter of her Jewish education, which by the time she is twelve the family has abandoned and by fifteen she has all but forgotten, 'Barukh ata Adonai, Elahainu melekh ha-olam. And what does it mean, hmm?'

'Um,' she stammers, 'um, Bless you . . . um . . . bless God . . .'

Her translation is halting, not from faulty memory, but for fear of making a mistake and Nate's subsequent disapproval. If she gets it wrong, he may leave again.

Recollection brings a flood of relief, a temporary end to her search. Now she can remedy her ways. I will practise harder, she resolves. So much to remember. So easy to slip, to make an error.

Nate comes to her room and draws her to him, hugs her and strokes her hair. 'Don't cry, Rachel, Papa will come home soon, I promise. You know I always come back. Don't you worry.' He kisses the palm of her hand. 'You'll look after Mama for me while I'm gone, yes?'

From the earliest years of her life, Rachel becomes a shwitzer. Adults are amused by her. To Rivka they say, 'What a little worrier, such a shwitzer, your Rachel. So serious.' They pronounce 'worrier' as 'warrior'. 'One so young shouldn't worry this much', they chuckle.

'A tense child, your Rachel', others observe.

Rachel overhears their remarks and ignores them, forgives them their foolishness. They are old, she thinks. They have forgotten how well a girl must behave in order to win her father's affection. What would they know? Their fathers didn't go away all the time.

No one has told her what happened to their fathers.

— o —

Does he write while he's away, or phone? Rachel doesn't remember. It will be some time before she realises that Nate leaves home but twice a year on his trips and that this employment lasts a mere two years, that the arguments between her parents are about his leaving and about money; they have nothing to do with her behaviour. Older still before she comprehends her mother's desire. During the war Rivka worked, proud and cheerful, in a factory where trucks were made. She longs to return to work, to earn her own income, to be in the company of other working women. Her need is desperate. If Nate didn't roam the state tinkering with aeroplanes, Rivka insists, she could get a job too; life would be easier.

— o —

Is there a pattern to his leave-takings, his homecomings? Rachel the child is unable to tap a rhythm, senses only an erratic sequence: the crescendo of her parents' voices, Nate's departures, Rivka's Yiddish mutterings, the periods of Nate's absence.

And his homecoming. On his return he is greeted by Rivka not so much with pleasure as with relief and a hostile acceptance.

— o —

It is a minor irritation to Nate that while he is away Rivka does her best to find him other employment. She buys newspapers and circles job advertisements; by the time he reads them the vacancies will be filled. Rivka enquires, too, through friends and acquaintances in the community. She makes a list of the possibilities.

Nate presents Rachel with tokens of his travels: a miniature dog on a tuckerbox, a branch laden with fresh oranges from a citrus grove in Mildura, a stuffed toy kangaroo. 'Made from real kangaroo fur',

7

he boasts. On one occasion his gift is a little painting of a fully armoured Ned Kelly standing by his horse. On another the smooth, dry skin of a dead snake.

Rivka presents Nate with a home-cooked meal of roast chicken, fresh peas and baked potatoes; for dessert she serves him the past and current weeks' 'Situations Vacant' advertisements together with her list. Nate runs an accommodating eye over the columns of newsprint, scans her neat, handwritten prospectus of offers from clothiers in Flinders Lane, manufacturers in the suburbs, an office here or there, then places the newspapers in the rubbish bin; the slip of paper he sets beneath the rose-glass bowl on the mantelpiece, or carefully folds before sliding it into the inside pocket of his suit jacket. An observer might be fooled into believing Nate will consider Rivka's agenda a little later. Not Rivka: she knows he never enquires.

'Thank you, Rivka,' Nate says each time, a matter of courtesy.

'Who will you ring?' she asks.

'There is nothing here that interests me.' He sighs. 'I don't want that work. It's the planes I love, and the outdoors. The bush.'

'Feh! The bush.' She shakes a finger at him. 'You barely looked', she snaps.

'I looked. There's nothing.' He becomes irritable.

'No, you didn't. You never look.' Rivka pauses and draws a deep breath. Her turn for the baton has come around: she clutches it, commences her lap. 'You don't want me to work, that's what it is, isn't it? That's why you keep on with this job of yours, travelling all over the damn country to those Godforsaken towns, flying those bloody planes.'

'Rivka, mind your language in front of the child.'

'That's all you have to say? "Mind your language"?'

Little more than hour after Nate arrives home they are arguing. Rachel is banished.

'Rachel, Mama and I have things to discuss. Go to your room, there's a good girl.'

'But Papa, I want to stay.'

'Rachel,' Rivka orders, 'do as Papa says. Go to your room, now.' Nate's voice is firm. 'I'll be in to see you soon.'

'I hate you, Papa! Why won't you talk to me now? You always go away and then you won't talk to me when you come home.'

'That's enough, Rachel. To your room. At once!'

Rachel drags herself to the solitary confinement of her bedroom.

There she opens one of her many storybooks containing colourful pictures of happy families—people, dogs, goats, hens, other farmyard and jungle animals. Tonight she chooses a human family. Cross-legged, she sits on her bed, sucking her thumb, as she pores over the pages. Here is a pretty, smiling mother who has bobbed, blonde hair. Father, too, is cheerful. Watched by the delighted mother, he plays with two laughing children, a boy and a girl, bright-eyed and pink-cheeked, the girl fair-haired like her mother, the boy and father with matching sandy hair and light-brown freckles. These children are never naughty; their father seems always to be at home, their golden mother is ever smiling. A spaniel romps in their garden.

The child Rachel drools with envy. She imagines herself into their lives, the fifth member of their family, transporting herself to a state of rapture where the knots in her stomach and the creases between her coppery brows disappear. She looks like—she becomes—a carefree little girl, bubbling with delight.

— o —

Rachel's childish comprehension that her parents' love should have a different shape does not come solely from her storybooks. It comes, too, from the tender moments they have together, the times of laughter and joy and fun, and from the calm times, reading books, sitting beside the piano while Rivka plays Chopin, Schubert and Gershwin; it comes from the evenings when they huddle together around the radio. She loves the occasions when Rivka or Nate whisk her into their arms and dance her around the loungeroom to the tunes of Rivka's collection of Duke Ellington records. There are family picnics, and walks in the hills or on the beach after bumpy drives in their blue Morris convertible. When Nate is home he takes her to the swings at a local park. 'Flying is like this, Rachel', he says as he pushes her high into the air. 'Can you imagine a feeling more glorious?'

'No, nothing, Papa. Higher! Higher!'

— o —

Once Nate has departed on his travels, Rivka calms down. On Saturday afternoons she dresses Rachel in her best frock, a white lawn affair with short puffed sleeves; it has hand-stitched red and blue smocking on the bodice and pale blue flower buds embroidered on the cuffs of the sleeves. On her feet, white socks and a natty little pair of red leather shoes fastened with a silver-buckled strap across the instep. 'Mary Jane shoes', Rivka calls them. In her hair, a ribbon tied in a large bow. Before they leave the house, Rivka stands before the long, oval mirror in the hallway: she smooths the skirt of her cotton floral-print dress and makes sure her shoulder pads are even. After one last look to ensure that the seams of her stockings are straight, she pats her curly, chestnut-brown hair, then, with a nod of satisfaction, takes Rachel by the hand. Off they go to Hillier's soda fountain and chocolate shop in Collins Street, there to sit in a padded, red-leather booth, sipping hot chocolate fudges topped with whipped cream and melting marshmallows from tall, ribbed glasses.

'This is what people do in America', Rivka explains.

Rachel dreams of the fairyland America and tells Rivka, 'When I grow up, I will go to America to live forever.'

Rivka smiles and kisses the top of Rachel's head.

They finish their drinks, noisily slurping the last of the sweet, now-cooled milk through waxed-paper straws. Rivka buys four chocolates—dark chocolate, hard centres, each sitting in its own crimped paper cup—then helps Rachel down from the stool and leads her into the darkened cavern of the Plaza or the Regent, grand and elegant picture theatres. They sing at the top of their voices, following the bouncing ball: 'Here we are again / happy as can be / All good pals / and jolly good company.'

Holding hands, their teeth glued tight with toffee, they watch the first serial of the day—Roy Rogers or Hopalong Cassidy—then a cartoon: Mickey Mouse (Rivka's favourite), Donald Duck (Rachel's), or Bugs Bunny. After which comes the film—an American musical, or a Shirley Temple, a cowboy adventure, or Lassie.

In the flickering half-light of the theatre, Rachel steals a look at her mother and considers her more beautiful than any of the stars on the screen, or in Screen Gems, the film gossip booklet they buy before entering. If there is time after the film, Rivka takes her to Regent Place for a look in the window at Tim the Toyman.

Every Saturday.

But Rachel the shwitzer dwells on the arguments, the leave-takings. She cannot help herself. She wishes Nate would never go away again and dreams herself a family like the ones in her storybooks, families she imagines every child—at kindergarten, primary school, high school and beyond—everyone has but her.

— o —

Nate ceases travelling the countryside. To Rivka's satisfaction, he finds employment in a factory manufacturing Bakelite light switches and three-pin plugs. He rises through the ranks, eventually becomes a partner in the business.

Life seems settled.

— o —

Once a year, on the day before his birthday, Nate disappears for the day. He leaves the house at dawn, does not go to work, and returns home well after dark.

At around dinnertime on the evening of the first of these disappearances, Rachel enquires, tremulous, 'Where is Papa? Isn't he coming home for tea? Is he going away again?'

'Only for today, Rachel, only for today.'

'Will he come back tonight? Where is he? He's coming back, isn't he?'

'Always shwitzing, Rachel', Rivka sighs. 'Papa will be here when you wake up in the morning.' She smiles. 'He's gone to the airport at Essendon to fly an aeroplane. It's his birthday present to himself.'

With an intensity that exceeds the bounds of hobby, Nate collects books and cuts pictures from magazines featuring Second World War planes: aloft and grounded, flying formation and solo, pristine, battered and crashed. His interest in the development of postwar craft is perfunctory. A wooden filing cabinet is purchased. Here, in meticulous arrangement, he stores his cuttings. In the spare room of their suburban home, Nathan Grinblatt builds miniature aircraft against a background hum of Rivka's despair about the overwhelming smell of glue and this, a revised version of his absence.

Talk of planes becomes incessant.

'Look at this . . .', and 'Did you know that the Wirraway . . .?'

One evening, Rivka and Rachel are startled by the roar of an aeroplane bellowing through their game of Snakes and Ladders and the delicacy of a Chopin étude playing on the gramophone. They glance at each other and hasten to the room where Nate is ensconced cutting and gluing. There he is, leaning back in his chair, the sound of a fighter plane emanating from deep in his throat. Mother and daughter look at each other and giggle.

'Papa is clever', Rachel says proudly.

'Very clever', Rivka agrees, smiling.

Admiration is short-lived. Nate's guttural roaring develops into a disturbing idiosyncrasy.

For example.

Reading in the chintz-covered armchair after dinner, or seated at the table playing canasta with Rivka, a board game with Rachel, suddenly Nate begins to vroom. Lancasters, Hurricanes, Avro Ansons, Spitfires, B-52s, Messerschmitts, Wirraways, DC3s: Nate has learnt them all. He shapes his broad hand into a make-believe plane—pinky finger and thumb splayed out, three middle fingers squeezed tight together—and swoops his hand-plane through the air, giving it life with a throat engine, which follows in perfect synchronisation the movements of his hand.

During Sunday afternoon tea, family friends sit around the table in lively conversation when—there he goes! Nate takes off.

Rachel overhears people calling him 'eccentric'. While she is uncertain what eccentric means, she recognises the tone reserved for it.

One Sunday guest attempts to connive with her. 'A bisl mishuge, your papa. A bit nutty, eh?' he chuckles, tapping his temple with a forefinger.

Rachel considers the friend disloyal; she refuses to yield, but, in truth, she secretly agrees.

Which sets off a chain of feelings, each inextricably linked:
anger with those who mock him
embarrassment at her father's behaviour
shame and guilt induced by her embarrassment.

Schoolfriends are no longer invited to stay the night. When they come to play after school, Rachel is helping them pack their satchels and hastening them out the door before five.

For days in advance of parent–teacher nights, Rachel lives with the dread that, no matter how many times Mama tugs on his coatsleeve or hushes him, Papa will erupt into planesong. Then, all the children will laugh at her. And the teachers. Oh, she would die! She would have to die.

Each year, parent–teacher night passes uneventfully.

— o —

With Nate established in the city, it is agreed that Rivka will seek employment. What she would most enjoy is to return to the work she did during the war. But the war is over, the staff managers point out. These jobs are only available to men now. 'Go home, love,' they tell her. 'Have yourself a couple of kids.' Defeated, she applies for a job in a factory where sequins and beads are made. As it transpires, Rivka enjoys the work. At night she reads Rachel Ali Baba and the Forty Thieves.

'Aladdin's cave, filled with jewels,' she beams at her enraptured daughter, 'this is where I work.'

At the end of the working week, together with her pay, Rivka brings home presents: little Cellophane packets filled with glittering, brightly coloured sequins and beads—many sizes, many shapes. Rachel sprinkles them into her dolls' hair, licks them before sticking them in decorative patterns on her face; she brushes Clag onto sheets of paper then sprinkles the sparkling jewels over the paste. Rivka helps her make fish scales using the gelatinous green and blue sequins.

'Look at my picture, Mama!'

'It is a beautiful picture, Rachel. Look, Nate, look at Rachel's beautiful fish.'

Nate makes a soaring Spitfire. 'Very nice, Rachel', he remarks between swoops. 'Very nice.'

Rivka sews elaborate patterns of sequins onto blouses, dresses and cardigans. Nate gives in to her pleading and allows his wife to fashion a design on two of his ties, neither of which he wears again.

Rivka is not perturbed.

Life is good.

JACK

Should he deprive her . . . she will leave a free woman.

Exodus 21:11

Wild or demure, one boyfriend or ten, virgin or fallen woman, bookish or sporty, nurse, teacher, factory or office worker, in the Australia of the early nineteen-sixties, girls were expected to marry. Not to be excluded were those who had shown promise at art school, completed their course with distinction and who, while working in a design studio to earn a living, dreamed of becoming a full-time artist.

Thus, after a brief and intense courtship, Rachel Grinblatt, illustrator, aged twenty-one, married Jack Brigg, advertising account executive, aged twenty-seven, in a simple ceremony at the Registry Office. Nate walked Rachel down the short aisle between rows of refurbished church pews and handed her over to Jack, or, as was said in those days, Nate gave Rachel away.

Solid but lean, Jack Brigg in his stockinged feet stood at five feet eleven inches, exactly two inches taller than his bride. He was a pleasant-looking man: his broad face was crowned with a shock of straight, sandy hair that flopped into his eyes, creating in him the habit of constantly brushing the hair away with splayed fingers. For the occasion of his wedding, Jack had slicked it into place with a light application of Old Spice pomade, but the habit of brushing away was so ingrained that his right hand kept rising from his side like a nervous tic, or the beginning of a salute.

Jack's ears stood out a little from the side of his head, which fact made him self-conscious. He remedied this by growing his runaway hair somewhat longer than was yet considered proper for men. Colleagues and friends teased him, suggesting he was trying to look like a rock star. In the street, those of meaner spirit snarled 'Ya girl' as he walked past.

The tuxedo makes him look handsome, Rachel observed as she moved slowly towards him, leaning into Nate. Suede shoes! Very smart. It felt strange, seeing him standing there so quietly: no matter what he was engaged in, Jack Brigg seemed always to be in a hurry.

If his smile was not always ready (there was a tendency to brood), when it did occur, it was wide and generous, giving a feline-like glow to his light-brown eyes.

He was smiling now, revealing the small chip in his right incisor (result of a cricket accident). When Nate deposited Rachel beside him, Jack beamed gloriously, took her by the arm and together they faced the celebrant.

— o —

There had been a moment of uncertainty, of which only the bride and her father were aware; they'd discussed it two nights before the wedding.

'He loves you, Rachel', Nate had said, exasperated. 'What more do you want?'

'I don't know.'

'There, there.' He had held her in his arms. 'Everything will be all right. You'll see. Jack's a decent man and he earns a good salary. You'll have a comfortable life.'

'Papa, I'm only twenty-one.'

'Only twenty-one', he scoffed. 'Your mother and I, we were barely twenty when we were married. Twenty!'

'What about my painting?'

'Painting? There's plenty of time to paint, Rachel. You can paint before the babies come. Or paint later, when they go to school.'

Rachel groaned.

'Babies! Isn't there more for girls than getting married?'

'More?' Her father was puzzled. 'What more? You're almost over the hill, Rachel. Soon you'll be so old no man will want you.'

Nathan Grinblatt had chuckled at his daughter's indignation, then he'd released her from his embrace. Standing in the doorway, he made one of his more joyous aeroplane simulations, blew her a kiss and left the room.

'*Nu?* Is everything all right?' Rivka asked when he returned to the livingroom, her brow knotted with worry.

'It's nothing. Pre-wedding jitters.'

They smiled knowingly at each other. They kissed, then seated themselves, he in the armchair, she on the couch, in front of the television.

After Nate left the room, Rachel looked at herself in the dressing-table mirror.

'It'll be all right', she said to her reflection.

— o —

Outside the Registry Office, in the late afternoon sunshine of spring, family and friends bustled around throwing rice and confetti, chatting as they waited their turn to kiss or shake hands with the newlyweds. Annalise took photos. At the Grinblatt family home a spectacular spread, made entirely by Rivka, awaited the guests on two groaning trestle tables. In the middle of it all, the supreme highlight: a white three-tiered wedding cake, at the top of which stood a pink-faced bride and groom holding hands.

As the hour approached midnight—late for a wedding reception, everyone agreed—Rachel, Esther, Caroline, Annalise and Grace removed themselves to Rachel's bedroom, where the bride changed into her going-away outfit.

'I'm going to miss you!' Rachel wailed to her friends.

'Bloody idiot!' Grace laughed.

'What are you talking about, Rachel?'

'I don't know', she wailed.

'You're only going away for three weeks.'

'I know.'

'We'll be here when you get back.'

'I know. I don't know what I mean. I'm going to miss you.'

They burst out laughing.

'Here, have some more champagne', said Grace.

Esther, Annalise, Caroline and Grace told Rachel not to be a dill and left her to redo her makeup. So done, Rachel returned to the arm of her beaming Jack and an admiring chorus of oohs and ahs.

'Who's next?' she called. Turning her back to the crowd, she tossed her bouquet of gardenias and asparagus fern over her shoulder.

'Me, me, me!' squealed Grace, as she shamelessly elbowed her way to the front of the group of single women.

The flowers landed squarely in Grace's outstretched arms. Six months later, Grace Ryan and Pete Devlin, her lover for the past year, were one.

Imagine that.

They were the last generation of women who would dutifully follow the postwar domestic pattern of marriage, childbirth and obligatory housewifery.

— o —

After a romantic honeymoon in Sydney, they returned to Melbourne, Jack to work at the agency, Rachel to the design studio. The two-bedroom Carlton flat where Jack had been resident for three years was to be their home. Wedding presents were unpacked, the flat redecorated. The second bedroom, which had served Jack as a junk-cum-ironing room, was cleared out and repainted; it became Rachel's studio.

The bohemian life of Carlton suited them well. Two or three nights a week they ate at the University Hotel or walked to The Legend or Florentino Bistro Bar in the city. In Lygon Street they found an Italian cafe which they frequented on Saturday morning. Here they sat reading newspapers and drinking coffee until it was time for lunch: a bowl of rigatoni and a glass of red. They visited galleries and jazz clubs, attended screenings of European films at the Savoy and at the Australia, they met their friends.

On week nights, when Jack was at cricket practice, and on Saturdays when his team played, Rachel went into the studio to paint. Caroline suggested they have a group exhibition with two other artist friends in a small gallery nearby, to which end Rachel worked feverishly.

— o —

Jack was a man who liked surprises. From the start he enjoyed buying Rachel special gifts, gifts not tied to birthdays or anniversaries. Soon after they began going out together, over a period of six weeks, he brought her a present every second Thursday, drawing her in so that she came to expect one again on the eight week. But he didn't have one that week: he spiced the surprises further by choosing random days in random weeks from then on.

During his lunch hour, Jack scoured the city for objects bold and delicate; his taste was impeccable. He found beautifully sculptured pieces of wood, elegant abstract glass birds, handcrafted papers, expensive paint brushes, Venetian-glass ashtrays, modern ceramic vases, Chinese figurines and bowls. Once, a pair of blue-and-white chopstick holders in the shape of fish and a set of intricately carved chopsticks. Many lovely gifts.

One Friday night at Florentino, when Rachel returned to the table from the ladies' room, she found a long white envelope balanced on top of her wine glass.

'What's this?' she asked as she sat down.

'Why don't you have a look?'

Rachel's squeal was involuntary. Inside the envelope were two airline tickets to Sydney and a reservation slip confirming two nights at a swank hotel overlooking the harbour.

It was the best surprise yet.

— o —

Eighteen months after their wedding, at the end of the second trimester of Rachel's pregnancy, the Briggs moved out of Carlton. They bought well in the leafy suburb of Hawthorn, four blocks from the river. A white, freestanding nineteen-forties cottage with a front verandah, the house was sunny and flooded with light. A back wall of floor-to-ceiling, wall-to-wall glass with a sliding door looked out on a large back garden of lawn riddled with clover, a few plants growing along the fences—rhubarb, tomatoes, balsam, calendula, petunias and nasturtium—and a hotchpotch of trees: a prunus, a lemon, an ancient fig, a hideous dark-pink camellia and a scrappy wattle.

Their issue: Ruby and, two years later, Eli.

In the seventh month of her first pregnancy, Rachel quit her job. Jack insisted. Rachel knew he would; she knew she would comply. Who among them, once they'd started a family, remained in their job?

The Briggs followed the child-rearing advice of one Dr Benjamin Spock, whose book they read avidly, choosing his wisdom over that of their respective mothers, whom they considered old-fashioned and interfering.

Children's teeth came in, potty training was completed. By the time Eli was crawling, Ruby was running; she was talking in comprehensible sentences long before Eli gurgled his first words. Rachel and Jack proudly recorded these events in a large family album: photographs, cards, small paintings, hand-drawn notices and collages, which Rachel constructed with precision and care.

They were a typical family of their class and time.

— o —

Rachel and her housewife friends painted rooms, made curtains, darned socks, sewed on buttons, let down hems, hung out washing and ironed; they tidied away toys, despairing when their children scattered them asunder within minutes of waking from their naps. They dealt briskly with dishes that needed to be cleaned almost, it seemed, as soon as the last pile had been put away. There were beds to be made, floors to vacuum and polish, shopping to purchase and put away, cakes to bake, flowers to arrange, lunches to prepare and clean up after, new recipes to learn for evening meals and entertaining, gardens to be weeded, lawns to mow.

Children were taken on outings to the zoo, to Station Pier to watch the ships tie up or depart, Essendon Airport to see aeroplanes land, Catani Gardens for Shetland pony rides, the Botanic Gardens to feed the swans, playgrounds to be pushed on swings and caught at the bottom of slides, for rides on trams and, twice a year—once in autumn, once in spring—to the Dandenong Ranges for a ride on Puffing Billy.

Mothers became adept at picking up a conversation's threads—face to face or on the phone—no matter at what point or how long ago the break had taken place: it could have been days.

One afternoon when their offspring were being particularly persistent, Esther moaned, 'I have become a mistress of the fractured conversation.'

— o —

All Jack's previous surprises were exceeded the night Rachel opened an envelope (Jack had found a special one—hand-made Chinese ricepaper— for the occasion) and discovered they were to spend ten days in Fiji.

'But the children—' she grinned and spluttered at the same time.

'It's all arranged', he smiled. 'Esther said she and Shimon would mind the children.'

'You lucky bugger', Grace said. 'Esther told me.'

'I suppose I am', Rachel replied, laughing.

Three weeks later Rachel and Jack were lying on the white sands of Fiji surrounded by the turquoise water of the Pacific Ocean.

I suppose I am.

— o —

Ruby began her first year at school.

'Rachel,' Esther's voice at the other end of the phone was excited, 'I've found a creche in the city that takes the children of non-working mothers!'

'Non-working mothers, my arse!'

Utilising this service once a week, Esther and Rachel booked those of their children not yet at school for four hours of childcare: they dawdled around Victoria Market, devoured apple strudel and coffee at Pellegrini's in Bourke Street, went to the art gallery, or to see a film, where, because she was so tired, Esther frequently fell asleep.

Grace joined them on the creche days when she could. She had recently turned her hand to publishing an art magazine from a room in the mud-brick Devlin home, built on an acre at Eltham. Though its circulation barely covered the production costs, Grace was optimistic for the magazine's future. She took pride in her achievement. The hard work, which included juggling the demands of her family, was small price to pay for the pleasure it afforded her and the convenience of working from home. In fact, as Esther pointed out to Rachel, Grace seemed to have more energy than the two of *them* put together.

Occasionally they met Annalise during her lunch hour. A barrister specialising in divorce, Annalise was the only woman any of them knew who continued in her profession after the birth of her two sons: Jean-Luc and Paul. Rachel and Esther spoke of Grace and Annalise with admiration that disguised— somewhat thinly—a deep-seated envy, which each did her best to conceal. As much as Rachel and Esther adored their children, loved their husbands (to greater or lesser extent), took pride in their comfortable and stylish homes replete with the latest gadgets, comfortable furniture, modish crockery and colour-coordinated Manchester, each secretly felt the disquiet of an inexplicable emptiness, a longing, as though something undefinable were absent—or lost—from their lives. Each woman, believing herself to be the only one who bore her shameful secret of ingratitude, the only one who was unable to find contentment, occasionally found herself repressing an overwhelming desire to scream.

'What did we do before we were married?' Esther said one afternoon as she and Rachel sat in the Briggs's backyard keeping an eye on their children. 'Can you remember?'

'Damned if I know', Rachel replied. 'Come,' she beckoned Esther, 'look at this.' She led Esther to the spare bedroom where, tucked into a corner near the window among discarded baby furniture, cartons of old clothes, and Jack's cricket gear and carpentry tools, her easel stood. 'I've been trying to finish this painting for months. The kids go to sleep and I tell myself, Now. Go and do some now. But my thoughts are completely scattered,

I'm so exhausted. I come in here and all I can do is dabble. After half an hour I leave the room and collapse on the bed.'

'Painting!' Esther exclaimed. 'What's painting? All my creativity goes into designing the most enticing way to arrange peas, potatoes and a little lamb chop on a bunny plate so Zev and Henry will eat them while I nurse Jake.'

They laughed until their sides ached.

'Is this all there is for the next fifteen years, Esther? Is it?' Rachel's despair burst through their laughter. 'Jack is so sweet. He buys me presents, and flowers every Friday night, he's fantastic with the children and generous with his money, but whenever I tell him I want to work, a bit of freelance at home, anything, he gets furious. He insists that he's the provider and there's no need for me to work.' She scowled. 'It's not about the money.'

'I know what you mean', Esther said quietly. 'Shimon and I talked some more last weekend. I told him that unless I did something with my days other than look after children and do housework, I would go crazy. I must have sounded desperate. I think I frightened him.' She smiled shyly. 'I've applied for a job, two days a week, at the gallery as a tour guide.'

Fortified by Esther's courage, Rachel again broached the subject with Jack.

'You have a very easy life, Rachel. Why do you want to work?'

'Jack, I love the children, I love my friends, but I need to be out in the world, at least for some of the week.'

'No, Rachel.'

She burst into tears of frustration.

'Now, now.' He patted her on the cheek. 'In twelve months Eli will be at school and we can talk about it again. All right?' He didn't wait for her answer. 'I know!' he exclaimed. 'What about the garden? Nothing very exciting has happened there since we moved in. Why don't you turn some of that artistic talent of yours onto the garden? That will give you something useful to do.'

The next evening, Friday, Jack arrived home with the customary one dozen long-stemmed white roses. This time they were accompanied by an elegant bottle of Madame Rochas perfume.

Rachel could have killed him.

'I hate him', she yelled over the phone to Esther.

— o —

Rachel succumbed and bought plants that she added to the strag-gly collection she had inherited from the previous owner. Nothing seemed to match particularly well, but once she had them in the ground, she dutifully tended them, surprised to dis-cover she enjoyed the work. As things turned out, the roses were the only flowers she liked enough to pick. The roses, the rhubarb and the figs. Rachel's baked rhubarb with lemon rind and caramelised sugar, and her rhubarb and apple crumble brought her high praise. Her fig jam, it was universally agreed, was sublime.

— o —

Jack worked longer and longer hours, a cause for increased bick-ering. It was not uncommon for him to arrive home well into the night—ten, eleven o'clock, even midnight. 'Don't think I enjoy these long hours, Rachel', he said bitterly. 'I work hard so you and the children will have a good life.' And with that, he dumped the weekly roses on the bench and strode from the room.

Was this the good life? What did she have to compare it with? Her friends' lives? Her parents'? It was true—as Jack reminded her, often—there was nothing in the way of material goods she could possibly have needed. Yet she felt thoroughly dissatisfied. She missed Carlton. Jack, with his compulsive drive for the good life, was beginning to get on her quince.

— o —

Both children were now attending school, and Rachel missed them. Though her energy to paint returned, she was still unable to settle into it. Passion was lacking, the requisite concentration. She blamed it on the phone calls.

Three, four, sometimes five times a day, Jack phoned.

'Just wanted to say hello, see how you are', he'd say.

'Rach, be a darling and collect my shirts from the laundry, would you?'

'Did I mention I'd be home late tonight? I couldn't remember if I phoned this morning or not.'

'What's on tonight's menu? Roast chicken? I hope I can get home in time.'

'Please, please, Jack,' she would beg, 'don't ring so often. It's impossible to concentrate on my painting with you ringing all day.'

'I thought you'd like my ringing you. I didn't want you to feel lonely.'

'I'm not lonely. There's no need for you to ring so many times.'

'Rachel, I know I said I wouldn't call, but I didn't remember until after I left the house. Do you remember the cricket gloves I misplaced? Would you mind picking me up some—'

'Couldn't it have waited, Jack?' Rachel sighed. 'Can't you get them in the city?'

'Hello, Rachel. How's the painting coming along?'

What's the point of continuing?

She wandered around the house, looking for the children, as if they were playing a game of hide and seek and any moment now would roll out from under a bed or leap from a wardrobe, giggling at her. She imagined, in the middle of the day, that she heard their voices as they played.

Rachel joined the school's parents' committee for something to do. Next she volunteered to work a day a week in the tuckshop. Then to read once a week to the grade twos. It was all pleasant enough, and Jack approved, but it provided little satisfaction.

— o —

Rachel volunteered her services as an artist to the organising committee of the Vietnam Moratorium Campaign, in which capacity she designed badges, posters and leaflets. They were sold at the huge demonstrations held in the city, and from street stalls by members of suburban, country and interstate antiwar groups.

'Red ragging now, are you, Rachel?' Jack sneered.

On the desirability of Australia's disengagement from the south-east Asian war Jack and Rachel did agree, but their views diverged on the necessity (Jack) or otherwise (Rachel) for an alliance with the United States. Of protest, Jack believed that the ostentation of chanting and waving flags in the street was embarrassing and to be avoided: petitions, letters to the newspapers or one's local member of parliament were what he preferred.

'If you choose to see what I do as red ragging, Jack, then yes, I am.'

'And what about the children?'

'What are you talking about? I am here for the children. All my red ragging is being done from home.'

During the early nineteen-seventies, Rachel Brigg's artwork was to be seen on walls, lamp-posts, lapels and T-shirts throughout the land.

She cleared a corner in the spare room and began to paint: large, dark canvases implying warfare and battle.

— o —

'Where were you this afternoon?' Jack demanded. 'I tried to ring three times. You didn't tell me you were going out.'

'Checking on me, were you, Jack? Hello, Jack.' Rachel sighed. 'Do I have to report my every move?' Unable to maintain her irritation, she grinned. 'Jack, let's not argue tonight. I had a fabulous day.' She looped her arm through his and danced him to the garden. Ruby and Eli, arms similarly linked and giggling, followed their parents outside. Jack's curiosity was aroused; a grudging smile crinkled the corners of his mouth, until Rachel said, 'I was at the agency arranging some part-time work.'

The smile slipped from his face; he loosened his tie with a vicious tug, brushed the hair from his eyes and stood before her, rigid with anger.

They argued, of course, but this time Rachel stood her ground.

'My mind's made up, Jack. There is no good reason why I can't spend a few hours a week in the office.'

'Children,' he commanded, 'go inside and watch television. Your mother and I will be in shortly.'

'I want to stay here', Ruby pouted.

'Me, too', cried Eli.

'Inside! Now!'

Jack returned his attention to Rachel. 'And what,' he enquired, tight-lipped, 'constitutes a few hours? What is to become of the children?'

'The children? Why, they're going to live on the street, Jack. They'll eat scraps they scrounge from rubbish bins. The Salvation Army will give them blankets so they'll be comfortable on their bus-stop bench.' He was not amused. 'Ease up, Jack. The agency agreed to ten until two, two days a week.' Rachel tickled him under his chin. 'I'll be home in plenty of time for the children.'

A cold light shone in his brown eyes as he pulled his head away from her teasing fingers. 'Your friends talked you into this, didn't they? Bitches! How dare they interfere in our lives.'

'Jack! That's not true and it's not fair. You and I have talked about this for years.'

'You've known my attitude to you working once we had children.'

'Yes, I have, and I agreed. But now the children are at school. There's no point in my being here all day. I feel trapped, Jack. I need to work, to be among other adults.' Rachel softened her voice. 'Jack, this is exciting. A job, and it won't impinge on my caring for the children.'

He ran his fingers through his hair.

'You're never satisfied, are you Rachel?' he sighed.

'What are you talking about?'

'No matter how much I give you—'

'It has never,' she shouted, '*never* been about money, Jack.'

For the following fifteen minutes they glared and shouted.

'At least let's give it a try Jack.'

He stared at her, finally saying, 'One month.'

'One month! That's hardly enough—'

'One month or—'

He didn't get a chance to say or what. Their argument was brought to a halt by the children, who had become fractious. Ruby and Eli refused to stay inside, demanded that Mummy and Daddy stop being mean to each other and whimpered that they were hungry.

Jack squatted down and hugged the children to him. He soothed them, watching over their shoulders as Rachel disappeared into the kitchen to prepare the evening meal.

'We'll see', she muttered. 'We'll see.'

— o —

Jack took to sleeping on the couch. His late nights at work and his absences from their bed became so frequent that one morning after shaking him awake it suddenly occurred to Rachel to ask, 'Are you having an affair, Jack?'

'Yes, Rachel, I am.'

Well! Couldn't be more straightforward than that!

Without pause or ceremony, Jack outlined the pertinent facts. 'Her name's Dorothy. She's twenty-eight, she's pregnant and we're getting married. I'm leaving you, Rachel. I would have told you sooner—'

'Or later, Jack? Or never? You bastard!' she shrilled. 'Just that she became inconveniently knocked up so it had to be sooner, eh?'

Rachel was as much upset by his deceit and his long-held post on the moral high ground as she was by the fact of his affair. All those years of it.

'I'm sorry, Rachel.'

'No you're not, Jack. If you were sorry you might have tried to work things out. How long has it been going on?'

'Twelve months.'

'Twelve months! A whole year!' Rachel was too shocked to cry. 'Why didn't you talk to me?'

'The situation was unresolvable.'

'What situation?'

'Your insistence on having a job. So, now you have a job. There is nothing more to discuss.'

'You are a prig and a hypocrite, Jack, and you're inconsiderate', Rachel shouted. 'You think that flinging some money about for a new kitchen appliance, a bunch of roses, those same fucking roses every Friday night, and a quick roll around the sheets once every two or three weeks is enough to keep your wife happy and our marriage intact.'

'Dorothy doesn't think I'm a prig, nor does she think I'm inconsiderate', Jack said slyly. 'Dorothy thinks I'll make a marvellous provider.'

Jack's parting shot as he strode to the bedroom to commence his packing?

'This time I'm marrying a woman who is delighted, *delighted*, Rachel, to stay home to be a real mother, and a real wife.'

'Fuck you, and fuck Miss Dorothy', Rachel yelled after him,

as the tears began to gather. 'I hope you'll be perfectly fucking happy together.'

— o —

Three nights later, Rachel delivered the children into the care of a concerned Nate and Rivka in order to avail herself of an invitation, secured by Grace, to an opening at an art gallery.

'Don't worry about me', she said breezily, fobbing off her parents' questions when she caught them darting worried glances at each other. 'I'll be fine. Honest.'

At the gallery she met Eric and was instantly attracted to him. She had no idea who he was, how he came to be there, what he did. Nor did she care. Eric. They eyed each other off for an hour, brushing past and up against each other at every opportunity, making small talk about the art. At nine-thirty, Eric suggested they go to his studio.

See, Papa, thirty-three and still not too old.

At Eric's studio, Rachel was surprised to see a piano, two saxophones and a music stand. Sheet music was everywhere. She had expected him to be a painter, or a sculptor.

Little effort was required from Eric to coax her into trying a tab of acid. In less than an hour the drug had taken hold, after which they fucked and dozed until three in the morning. Rachel thought it inappropriate to refer to what they did as making love. There was no love; there was only desire and the need to be wanted. It was fucking.

Early in the morning they woke. Tingling with the shivers of coming down from the acid, they fucked again. Eric pleasured her and teased; his movements were unhurried. When it was all over, Eric held her in his arms and stroked her hair.

'I would like to see you again', he whispered into her neck, his breath warm against her skin.

Unexpectedly, Rachel began to weep. She could not stop.

'What's wrong?' Eric said, startled. He drew her to him and cradled her head in his hands, wiping away her tears with the corner of the sheet. 'Ssh, don't cry. What's the matter?'

'I hate you, Jack Brigg', she sobbed into Eric's chest. 'You are a treacherous prick.'

She shook herself free of Eric, fell out of the bed, stood up, dressed and left.

Rachel told Esther that the acid had been a lot of fun and that sex with Eric—whom she declined to see again, despite his many phone calls—was the best she had ever experienced.

When Jack phoned to see where she and the children had been the night before, claiming he had phoned to say goodnight to the children, Rachel felt buoyed enough to tell him it was no longer any of his damned business where she'd been.

So followed a continuum of squabbles and disdain. Once the children were old enough to make arrangements with their father themselves, Rachel spoke to him only when necessity required it.

CROSSING THE RIVER

spread your wings
come on fly

Van Morrison, 'Ballerina'

Twelve months later, Rachel decided it was time to return to Carlton, whose long-held designation as Melbourne's bohemian quarter had not changed. On the contrary, it remained populated by university students and academics, the politically active, artists and writers, performers and musicians: in increasing numbers they continued to arrive—as did single mothers and their children. Remnants of what was once a large Jewish community were still to be found along Lygon and Elgin Streets. Friends and acquaintances would be close at hand.

Rents were cheap: gentrification had barely commenced, and if the price one had to pay for low rent was an outhouse at the far end of the back yard and a hot-water heater that made a loud and startling bloomph each time it was lit—well, these were minor enough concerns. Community was what life was about and Carlton had it in abundance.

Following a series of calls on local real estate agents and the successful procurement of a house—she decided to rent for the time being—Rachel and the children crossed the river and moved in.

— o —

Ruby and Eli came slowly to accept that their parents would never be reunited. Their tearful demands for reconciliation diminished, their confusion subsided. They readily made friends at the local school and soon settled into their lives. Routines were established, which included Jack driving up to the front door every second Friday evening, tooting the horn of his spanking new car and driving away with the children until Monday morning.

— o —

Rachel's announcement that she was changing her name back to Grinblatt was cause for considerable—albeit brief—consternation.

'No! I don't want to be Grinblatt!' Ruby stamped her foot.

'Me either. I'm a Brigg. Eli Brigg.'

'You don't have to change your names.'

'People won't know you're our mother. No one will know who we are', Eli wailed.

'Daddy will be really sad.'

Rachel pressed on with it: to her friends she became Rachel Grinblatt; at the children's school and to their friends she remained Mrs Brigg or, simply, Rachel.

— o —

Rachel's spirits soared. She strode the world a woman of purpose. The studio kept her on the same hours; before too long freelance work began to trickle in as well. In a corner of her large bedroom she set up a studio. Here, as well as executing the commissions that came her way, she approached her painting with renewed vigour.

Earning her own wage gave her satisfaction beyond measure. Less money was available to her than when she was with Jack, but she managed. Both children sought and found afterschool jobs to help pay for some of their own entertainments and indulgences.

The weeks when there was no freelance work, or when its

delivery was behind schedule, when an unexpected expenditure stretched her budget, these were times she worried.

There were days—weeks—when raising two children, working and attempting to maintain a social life got the best of her. Exhausted by the end of the day, she stretched out in the bath, there to doze until the water became cold and she was too tired to run more hot. In bed she smoked a joint and soon after fell into a deep sleep.

— o —

Carlton had Professor Longhair's record shop, Readings Books, a film cooperative and, around the corner, two experimental theatres. The Carlton Theatre, affectionately known as 'The Bug House' since the days when Rivka was a child and attended with her sisters, continued to screen films and accommodate bugs. Street life was lively.

Bands played in pubs on Thursday, Friday and Saturday nights. What did it matter that licensing laws meant the gigs ended at ten? There was usually a party at someone's house to go to after the gig, or a select group of friends could be invited home.

Trattorie, gelaterie, pasticcerie: the aroma of coffee and garlic permeated the air. An endless variety of places to have coffee, pasta and pizza had gradually replaced the kosher butchers, Polish and Russian cake shops, tailors and other elements of Jewish life once abundantly evident along Lygon and Elgin Streets. *Gefilte* fish and *kreplekh* no longer were. For these, you went south of the river, usually to your mother's, or to Acland Street in St Kilda.

Rachel and the children availed themselves of the reasonably priced cafe and pub meals: they enjoyed eating out one night a week, two if she was flush.

'What's for tea, Rachel? I'm starving.' Eli rubbed the flat of his hand in circles around his stomach.

'Me too', Ruby joined in. 'Famished. Let's go out.'

Eli and Ruby glanced at each other. He cued her with a subtle movement of his head. 'Pizza, pizza, pizza!' they chanted.

'Hey, Ruby', Eli snapped his fingers. He marched around in a tight circle, changed rhythm and began clapping his hands, cheer-squad style. 'Pi-zza'—clap clap clap, 'pi-zza'—clap clap clap. Ruby fell in with his parade; they laughed uproariously at their own joke. Ruby whooped.

'Not pizza again!'

'Please, Mum. You don't have to have pizza. Please?'

Deep-fried whitebait mounded on a plate appeared before her eyes and she began to salivate. 'I'm starving too. Let's go. Now! Give me five minutes to scrub up. Clean T-shirts please, everyone.'

Ruby and Eli rolled eyes at each other. Rachel showered, put on a fresh linen blouse and a pair of black jeans. They headed off to Del Monico's Pizzeria and Ristorante, the children bounding ahead like antelopes.

'Pi-zza, pi-zza, pi-zza!'

I will hate it when they grow up and leave home. Hate it.

— o —

'See that big house down there?' Rachel pointed to a double-storey Victorian as they strolled home along Lygon Street. 'Grace, Caroline, a bloke called Gully McGuinness and three others shared that house when we were students. Pete lived there for a while too.'

'You too?' Ruby enquired through a slurp of strawberry gelato.

'I wasn't allowed.' Rachel made a dour face.

'Why not?' asked Eli.

'Mama and Papa wouldn't let me. They used to say people would talk.' The children looked at her quizzically. 'They were afraid their friends would think they weren't good enough parents if their children wanted to leave home. Our parents were afraid we'd fool around with boys. Get pregnant. Bring shame on our families. In my day nice girls stayed home until they married.'

'Did Esther's parents let her?'

'No.'

'How come Grace's parents let her? Wasn't she nice?'

'Not everyone's parents thought like mine and Esther's.' Rachel grinned. 'Esther and I snuck off there as often as we could. We'd tell our parents we were going to each other's house, or to another girlfriend's for the night, someone who still lived at home, and we'd nick off and stay there.' She indicated with a toss of her head. 'Shimon romanced Esther in that very house.'

'Did you ever get caught?'

'Many times.'

'What did they do, Nana and Zaider?'

Rachel smiled at them.

'What do you think?'

Eli and Ruby turned to each other, their faces clouded with uncertainty. The light of recognition sparked in their eyes at the same time. 'Grounded!' they chorused and hooked pinky fingers high in the air.

'Exactly.'

They walked on in step.

'Did you like going there?' Ruby asked.

'It was worth every grounding they gave me. It was worth the month I wasn't allowed to go to the jazz club, it was even worth the time Papa locked my records away for a week.'

Eli and Ruby gasped at so heinous a punishment.

'Being at the house was exciting', Rachel continued. 'They seemed so grown up. I was very envious of them. I hated Mama and Papa for not letting me go.' She laughed.

'Why didn't you just go?' Ruby and Eli said at precisely the same moment.

'Go?' said Rachel, puzzled.

'You know,' Ruby said, 'why didn't you just go?'

'Leave', Eli said.

Flabbergasted, Rachel replied, 'Because they said I couldn't', as if that explained everything, which, when she thought about it, it probably did.

As they turned into their street the children sprinted away from her, rattling their keys at each other, laughing as they went. They were still laughing when Rachel reached the house. Eli held the gate open for her, Ruby the front door. She lingered at the fence for a moment, looking out over the rooftops.

'I hope you enjoy living here as much as I do', Rachel said to them. Eli closed the gate and she followed her children inside, reminiscing about Gully McGuinness.

— o —

Gully McGuinness. A gifted sculptor, two years ahead of the others at art school. Tall and physically strong, he had a craggy face topped with dishevelled dark-brown hair. Intelligent, laughing eyes peered through his owlish spectacles. Women—Grace and Rachel included—adored him, men wanted to be his friend. Grace invited him to move into the vacant room in the student house.

It soon became apparent that of Gully's domestic habits there was much to criticise; however, when he deigned to prepare a meal all was forgiven: among his many talents, Gully excelled at curries. He volunteered to enhance and maintain the garden, an activity his housemates had neither a skerrick of interest in nor any aptitude for.

One Saturday night Gully acquainted the householders and their visitors with marijuana.

'Where did you get it?' Esther enquired.

He recounted a tale of his three-month holiday in India. India? No one they knew had been to India. Overseas meant England, Europe. It meant Israel. India? They looked at him with renewed respect. This was exceptional sophistication. It was exotic.

'Everyone smokes marijuana or hashish in India', a blasé Gully told the wide-eyed innocents around the kitchen table.

'Isn't it illegal?' Esther asked, fascinated. The others awaited his answer with bated breath.

His reply was a withering gaze.

They felt diminished by his daring. A little childish.

'Who's for a try?'

A little afraid.

They cast nervous looks at one another as he rolled the cigarette, took a deep drag and held the smoke in his lungs for so long that the onlookers' nerves began to jangle. When, at long last, he released his breath, the others, who hadn't realised they too were holding their breath, exhaled with him.

A gentle wave of self-conscious laughter flittered around the table.

'Your turn', Gully offered the long, fat cigarette to Rachel, who sat next to him.

A little curious.

What would Mama and Papa say . . .?

A little bold.

Rachel mimicked his performance. Unpractised, she was able to hold the smoke for a mere few seconds before she began to splutter and cough; her eyes turned red and began to run.

Seeing the alarm on her face, Gully chuckled. 'You'll be all right', he soothed, rubbing her back. 'Now pass it to Esther.'

Grace rose from the table and placed a Charlie Parker record on the turntable.

Music and the resinous aroma of marijuana filled the kitchen. A feeling of wondrous good will seemed to emanate from everyone and everything in the room.

The cigarette—'It's called a reefer', Gully explained—was passed from one to the other, each participant's attempt marked by the onset of coughing and spluttering. Except Grace; she seemed to manage okay.

'How come Grace isn't choking?'

Grace was a study in nonchalance. 'Gully let me try it a few times. I'm used to it now.'

Gully rolled another.

'Nice smell', Esther observed, which set off a round of uncontrollable giggling.

'I'm starving', said—who said it? No matter.

Caroline, who also seemed to take smoking the reefer in her stride, whipped up a cinnamon butter cake with apple. Forty-five minutes later she removed the cake from the oven and placed it on the table; in an instant it was devoured.

They listened to music and danced, or sat quietly talking. One or two dozed off. They laughed and laughed. In the morning, Gully cooked toast and eggs, Grace made strong coffee. Together they served each resident and guest in turn in their beds.

After breakfast, assembled in the garden, one and all agreed that it had been the most fun they'd had on a Saturday night ever.

— o —

Restless soul that he was, Gully soon moved on.

Two Saturdays later, though it was not his turn to cook, Gully volunteered.

'What's the occasion?' his housemates remarked upon seeing a splendid banquet arrayed on the table. There was no birthday coming up for weeks, was there? Aha! A gallery must have offered him a show.

'All will be revealed', Gully replied mysteriously. 'Please be seated.'

Without delay they took their places around the table, eager to receive his news. 'Fellow artists, students of lesser disciplines and our one industrial worker, you are the honoured guests at Gully McGuinness's farewell party.' They gasped. 'It's time to move on.'

As one, in involuntary response, the householders turned to Grace, who they suspected was having an affair with him. Grace sat impassively, but when she phoned to tell Rachel he was leaving, she cried.

'I hate him!' Grace screeched. 'I hope I never see him again.'
Nothing to worry about on that score.

Reefers didn't cross their paths after he left. Rachel never gave it another thought.

— o —

By the mid seventies, it seemed whoever Rachel came in contact with in Carlton was smoking dope. And why not? It was more pleasant than alcohol; it was gentler. Some grew their own supply in the small patches of garden at the back of their rented Victorian cottages.

Yes, yes, it was illegal, but in this, consensus went, the law was an ass. Gully, who had never left Carlton, dropped in from time to time and shared with her what he now called a joint. Grace and Pete, who also enjoyed a smoke, introduced Rachel to a man called Spike, from whom she bought a deal once a month. Each night, before going to sleep, Rachel soaked in the bath and smoked her joint for the day.

— o —

The move to Carlton was the commencement of a four-year period which became known in the family's history as AJ, BJ— After Jack, Before Jerry. Just the three of them: Rachel, Ruby and

Eli. There was a magic quality to this time, a sense of solidarity, carefree spirits.

Rachel taught the children to cook. Ruby's potato chips were beyond compare—'The best in the whole world', Eli pronounced them. On this they were unanimous. Her second speciality was butterfly cakes. Sunday mornings saw the three of them crowded into Rachel's bed eating Eli's pancakes, which he served with maple syrup. From a book, he taught himself how to prepare vegetable curries with rice, which became their Wednesday night dinner. These curries were worth every long minute required to clean up after him. That was the deal: you cook, you don't wash up, a rule useful for the barter of favours.

If there were times Rachel felt frustrated, overwhelmed or restricted by her role as a single parent, these feelings were more than compensated for by the good times.

Times they had laughed until they had the stitch and Rachel's eyes ran with tears.

'Owee owee owee', Ruby howled as she rocked back and forth on the couch, clutching her ribs.

'Ruby, look!' Eli pointed at Rachel's streaming eyes, gasping his words through his laughter, 'Rachel's leaking laughs.'

They read to each other from books, conjured stories from their imaginations. Together they sat in the livingroom or sprawled across Rachel's large bed, reading their individual choices to themselves. There were long sessions of painting with Ruby. Peaceful sessions painting alone after she had kissed the children goodnight. Watching Eli's concentration as he produced a comic strip for the school newspaper. The exertion of playing baseball with them in the park. Picnics, walks, bicycle rides.

Birthday parties.

'Mmmm,' Ruby said as she licked the mixing bowl clean, 'green marshmallow! None of the other kids had that on their birthday cakes, Mama. You're clever.' Together they decorated it with fresh violets, tiny silver cachous and white birthday candles. Proud as could be she was, until her schoolfriends arrived and made jokes about Ruby's mouldy cake, for which humiliation Rachel was not forgiven for weeks.

Eli suffered his birthday embarrassment the year they were

trying to live healthy. Rachel had put out a spread of dried and fresh fruit, nuts and sunflower seeds, clunky dark bread spread with a suspicious looking semi-sweet paste (no sugar), carob-coated sultanas and the like. Eli's friends howled their dismay.

'Hey, Eli, when's your mum going to bring out the chocolate crackles?'

'Where's the hundreds-and-thousands?'

'Yuk, Mrs Brigg, what's this stuff?'

'Mrs Brigg, where's the lollies?'

'Eli, didn't your mother get any Coca-Cola?'

Eli could have killed her.

'I'm so sorry, Eli', Rachel whispered to the blushing and infuriated Eli. She fetched her purse and ran—*ran*—to the local milk bar. 'Hang on, kids,' she called as she fled out the door, 'I'll be back in ten minutes.'

Four large bottles of Coke and four flavours of lemonade, licorice blocks, raspberries, mint leaves, bananas, snakes, black cats, honey bears, milk bottles, traffic lights, musk sticks, sherbet bombs, packets of Twisties, peanuts and potato crisps, chocolate-coated biscuits, cream cakes, sliced white bread, hundreds-and-thousands—anything, oh, anything at all there was to be had in the shop. She slapped her money on the counter, filled her shopping bag and sped back to the house, where she tipped all that healthy rubbish on top of the untouched quartered chunks of fresh fruit and distributed the sugary, salty collection among the bowls and plates in the middle of the table. A cheer filled the room as six salivating ten-year-old boys and three girls surged forward in noisy, ravenous delight, their wormy little fingers grasping for the bounty.

Eli alone remained stone-faced. 'I'll never forgive you for this, Rachel', he hissed through a mouthful of licorice blocks. 'Never.'

After his guests had departed, Eli lay on the couch, his stomach bloated, his head snuggled into Rachel's lap, a picture of contentment.

They celebrated other milestones: Ruby's graduation from primary school to high school, and the day she began to menstruate (this shyly, a more sedate occasion). Eli's voice breaking was good for a night out, as was Rachel's paintings (two) being selected for hanging in a group show in a Fitzroy gallery, and the day the agency gave her an extra day's work and pay rise. They proclaimed Ruby becoming their first teenager, Eli their second.

Their front door was ever open to friends who dropped in for meals, cups of coffee, a drink and a chat, a joint. Eli and Ruby's friends stayed the night.

Arguments ensued over the length of skirts, the tightness of jeans, all the matter of housework. What was a reasonable hour to go to bed during the school week and to stay out on weekends consumed considerable discussion time, as did whether it was more desirable to do homework before dinner or after, and whose turn it was to choose what to watch on television.

Once a week, at six o'clock, the three of them went to see a film. On weekends there were gigs in neighbourhood parks, church halls and pubs, to which all the parents of their crowd brought their children. Benign publicans laid in extra supplies of raspberry lemonade and Twisties. To the church hall gigs and those held in parks, revellers brought a plate. Food, drinks and joints were shared by all. Hordes of children, from babes in arms to teens in jeans, danced their Friday and Saturday nights away along with everyone else.

— o —

Rivka and Nate lent Rachel money to buy a Kombi, third-hand. Gully built the van a mezzanine of sweet-smelling pine. Rachel and the children covered the platform with mattresses, blankets and pillows; underneath they stashed milk crates filled with games and books, clothes, art materials, camping gear and food. Music tapes were stacked in a specially crafted box fitted between the front seats.

Off they went—weekends and school holidays: into the bush, along the coast or to the desert. Along highways playing tapes of current pop singers, singing along to their hearts' content. It was on these trips that Eli and Ruby learnt to appreciate classical music. Try as she might, Rachel was never able to induce in them a love of jazz.

They played 'I Spy' until Rachel could stand it no longer and left the children to tire of it themselves.

The year she turned thirteen, Ruby said, 'I Spy is for little kids.' She condescended to a brief round with Eli, 'just to keep him happy'. Then she brooded for the next fifty miles.

How long will it be before she doesn't want to come any more? Before going on holidays with your younger brother and your mum is only for little kids, too?

— o —

As might be expected, Rachel worried.

When Eli rode his bike to school the first time, and the first few times he went to the football on his own. When Ruby went to her first night-time party. When they were injured or ill. Whether they were doing well at school. How irritable and distressed they became before exams. If they were getting their homework in on time. When a teacher had been unkind or unjust. When they were late home from school. That she had no ability to help them with their maths and science homework. When their feelings were hurt on the weekends Jack couldn't see them. Who their friends were. Where they went. What they got up to when they were there. When Ruby's breath smelt of cigarettes. Whether they tried alcohol. Smoked pot. When Eli . . .

She worried.

'Stop worrying!' the children grumbled.

Rachel's greatest worry? That she was not a good enough mother. That she was unable to satisfactorily fill the absence of Jack from their lives. That she was too lenient, or not lenient enough. That she didn't have enough money to buy them all the things they would like to have had.

'Rachel,' Esther admonished, 'you would need a bottomless purse for that!'

She observed her children watching television shows, *The Brady Bunch*, *Eight Is Enough*, believing she detected a wistfulness in their faces as they stared at the screen. Was that the type of family they wanted? How could she ever provide them with *that*?

'Why couldn't we have been like one of those television families?' she said to Esther. 'Everything so perfect.'

Esther was incredulous.

'You can't be serious.' She laughed without restraint. 'Who has a family like that?'

Rachel was no fool: she knew that few, if any, such families existed, that perfection—whatever it might be—occurred in moments as fleeting as vapour.

Ruby and Eli's doleful faces as they watched these shows, their laughter, aroused in her a streak of guilt. When Rachel suggested they might long for such a family, the children mocked her with sputtering laughter. Eli curled himself up like a slater and rolled around the floor.

'Don't be silly, Mama. *Nobody* has a family like that.'

'Really?'

'Really.'

'You don't want to be like them?'

Her breath is bated.

'Oh, Mama, they are so boring. We like us, don't we, Eli?'

'Yes, us', Eli concurred.

Their reassurances, which she sought often, never completely persuaded her.

Thesis, antithesis . . .

Rachel prevaricated, torn between her desire for the wholesome simplicity and unscarred community the family sitcoms trotted out, half hour after half hour, night after night, and a bitter mindfulness that they were myths, fantasies of the writers who created them, many of whom, in all likelihood, had lives and families as messy and confusing as her own. Along with her yearning, Rachel reserved for these cheerfully bland fairytale families a scorn as searing as white heat.

This much she could admit.

This she would not.

She had grown fearful of the void that would be created by the children's impending departure, of a vacuum in her soul she would never be able to fill.

When she offered them continued domicile after they completed high school, they turned her down.

'Mama, everyone would laugh at me', Ruby protested. '*Nobody* stays with their parents when they leave school. I don't want to hurt your feelings, but . . .' Her voice trailed away.

'Thanks, Rachel,' Eli said, 'I'll be right. Might drop my washing off every fortnight though.' He winked at Ruby, who giggled. 'You could do it for me.'

'Or give us a feed', they chorused, and burst into loud laughter.

'All right, all right. I just thought . . .'

They looked at each other again; their laughter was uncontrollable.

'Poor Mum,' Ruby wheezed. 'I thought you'd be glad to get rid of us.'

'I'll miss you.'

'We won't be going far!' Ruby shrieked. Rachel could hear irritation growing in her voice, see the squint forming around her eyes.

'You'll be fine, Rachel', Eli consoled. 'You've got Esther and Grace. We won't be that far away.'

It probably wouldn't matter if you were at the other end of the street.

'Why are we talking about this now? I'm only thirteen', Ruby said. 'I'm not going for years.'

'Me either', said Eli. 'Even more years.'

It probably wouldn't matter if you were not going for another twenty.

'Come on', Rachel sighed. 'Dinner's almost ready. Someone set the table please.'

'You set the table, Ruby. I'll dry the dishes.'

They shook on it, one of those soul brothers' handshakes they'd learnt from television shows, then went about their chores.

— o —

Gully dropped in. She had not seen him in months. Now, here he was, as appealing as ever. There were rumours he was messing around with heroin. Today he seemed fine, so Rachel invited him to stay for lunch. They ate in the garden, quiet, relaxed.

Rachel made coffee. When she returned to the garden she found him squatting near one of the beds, his strong fingers crumbling the tacky clay soil; a joint dangled from his lips. He stood up, rattled a branch of the spider-infested camellia. 'Botanical clichés', he pronounced. 'Small as it is, you could do something exciting here.'

Rachel recalled his efforts in the student household.

'Where did you learn so much about gardens?'

'Under the tutelage of my mother, whose girlhood dream was to have a huge family, to live on a farm near a river, and be mistress of a garden she could spend her days in. Her dream came true. I grew up in Euroa, the adored youngest of six. The farm has a beautiful garden, the most productive garden in the district. A paradise. Mum has more varieties of flowers and trees growing than you can imagine. She and Dad never want for fruit or vegetables. What with the cows and chooks, it all but feeds them. Yabbies, too, from the dam, and trout from the creek.' A tender smile softened his face.

'Mum taught me gardens. Dad taught me art. Every Sunday after breakfast, he'd call out, "Who's coming to make pictures?" He'd tuck his easel and a sheet of Masonite under his arm, chuck his paints, some sandwiches and a Thermos of tea into a Gladstone bag and we'd head off to some part of the block or down to the creek', Gully explained. 'He was never brilliant, but he had talent and a good eye. He turned out some lovely pieces.' He grinned. 'Not a bad beginning for a young bloke, eh?'

So, what went wrong?

Gully encouraged Rachel's interest in plants, introduced her to a vast range beyond hybrid roses, jasmine, cineraria, marigolds and zinnias. 'Gardening can be as creative as painting', he said. 'Colour, texture, light, form. Same thing, my sweet.'

He suggested books and magazines she might read, named nurseries for her to investigate.

Rachel scoured newsagents and nurseries and began to teach herself about flowers and herbs, vegetables and fruit trees. She went to the Botanic Gardens with a box of pastels and a sketch pad and began to draw flowers.

An idea put down roots and began to grow.

I shall become a nurserywoman.

— o —

From their first meeting at the design studio, Claudine Perlman, a copywriter, and Rachel Grinblatt became friends. Claudine, who also lived in Carlton, was a shy and often serious woman. This was not to deny her lively humour, readily observed when she relaxed among friends. Politics, Italian clothes, reggae and Motown music were Claudine's passions. Rachel and Claudine discovered they enjoyed similar books, the same films, little of the same art.

It was the tearoom session that sealed their friendship. Among the staff gathered for the mid-morning coffee break a heated debate broke out. Though the war in Vietnam had been over for some years, it continued to arouse passions. Claudine, Rachel and Ralph, another copywriter, found themselves united: Australian troops should never have been sent. The crescendo of voices brought curious staff from all directions to see what was going on. With their arrival, the number of supporters for the three protagonists' views increased.

The discussion turned into one of those rare occasions that occur in an office: no one returned to their desks or drawing-boards for over two hours. With a weather eye on the boss—an opponent of the war and Australia's involvement in it—they argued the South-East Asian war, and American and Australian foreign policy until well into the lunchtime.

— o —

Eli and Ruby took to Claudine immediately. She went with Eli to the football one Saturday a month.

'It's very kind of you to go with him, Claudine. I always feel I should go, but I can't stand football.'

'I love going to the football with Eli. His knowledge is vast.'

'It's the pies she really loves!' Eli exclaimed.

Ruby adored Claudine; Claudine reciprocated her affection by taking Ruby to a film, sometimes to a cafe. Or they would take the long tram journey to St Kilda where, Ruby later reported to Rachel, they screamed into the wind, thrilled by the terror of plummeting through the canyons of the Big Dipper at Luna Park.

During Ruby's turbulent pubescence, after one or other of their particularly fierce arguments, Ruby escaped from Rachel to sleep the night at Claudine's, an occurrence that became regular, in the good times as well as the bad.

Claudine took Ruby shopping for her birthday: a garment or a pair of sunglasses—Italian, of course—and to Pellegrini's.

'I had an espresso', Ruby boasted proudly.

'Aren't you a little young to be drinking coffee?' Rachel

admonished. 'I think hot chocolate should remain your drink for a while yet, Ruby.'

'Mum,' Ruby protested, 'hot chocolate's for kids. I'm fourteen now. *Everyone* my age drinks coffee.'

For Eli's birthdays, Claudine purchased football cards, new Fitzroy Football Club jumpers and matching pairs of socks.

— o —

Sniffing. Claudine's sniffing was the one thing about her that drove Rachel to distraction.

'Have you got a cold?' Rachel once ventured when Claudine was visiting. 'Here, have a tissue. What if I make you a hot toddy?'

'Hayfever.' Claudine smiled.

Grace mentioned it.

'Can't your mate Claudine afford a hanky?'

'Hayfever', Rachel repeated, defensive. 'Claudine's all right.'

'Probably putting something up her nose she shouldn't be.'

'Grace!'

Grace shrugged. 'You always want to believe the best about people, don't you, Rachel? Ah, you're a good soul. Or gullible. In all the years we've known each other, I've never been sure which.' She smiled affectionately, then tapped the side of her nose with her finger. 'Me, on the other hand, I think Claudine's nasal passages are irritated by more than plain pollen and dust.'

— o —

Claudine began going out with Danny. Rachel did not warm to him; he was uncommunicative and, she felt, furtive. Being around Danny was like being in the presence of a ghost. Esther and Rachel referred to him as Claudine's *éminence grise*.

'Jealous', Grace declared to Pete. 'That's why Rachel doesn't like him. She wants Claudine back as her hang-loose friend again.'

'Maybe she doesn't like him because he's a creep. You called him that yourself, Grace', Pete reminded her. 'A sleazy creep.'

'Jealous *and* because he's a creep.'

Pete chuckled.

'What does she see in him?' Rachel demanded of Esther.

'Who knows? He seems a bit dull, he so rarely says anything.'

'There's something unpleasant about him, Essie, something dark. He never looks anyone in the eye when he speaks. It's disconcerting.'

'I've noticed, but,' Esther shrugged, 'who are we to judge? Claudine seems happy enough with him.'

Rachel harrumphed.

— o —

When did things turn irrevocably sour? It was more drift than snap, so Rachel was unable to fix a precise date.

'Claudine hardly ever comes around any more. Why doesn't she?' Ruby pointed an accusing finger. 'You had a fight with her!'

'Will Claudine be coming to the football this Saturday? Is she going to have dinner with us this week?'

Sadness was etched in the downturned corners of Eli's mouth.

'I don't know,' Rachel replied, hugging both of them to her, 'but we didn't fight. It's probably because she's spending more time with Danny.'

'Doesn't she like us any more?'

'Did we do something to upset her?'

Rachel had no answer for them. Just as the children missed her company, so Rachel missed it. But unlike the children—how could they know of such things?—Rachel's pain was tinged with suspicion. Her goodwill was diminishing. If she was unwilling to give full voice to precisely what concerned her, she did know that all was not right.

— o —

The children were in the loungeroom watching *The Brady Bunch*. Rachel was pottering in the kitchen when Grace dropped in to confirm what Rachel had not wanted to acknowledge: Claudine had been using heroin since long before Rachel met her.

Heroin. As art students Rachel and her friends had read Kerouac, Bukowski and Burroughs, of course. Rimbaud, too. But really, in the late fifties and early nineteen sixties, what did they know about heroin? They knew it was illegal. They knew from reading magazines that American jazz musicians used it, and that some of them landed in jail or died as a result. That, and what

Jennifer Davis told them. Jennifer had been three years ahead of Rachel at high school. Rachel had not seen her since, until one day, when she was in the city with Grace and Esther, they met Jennifer wheeling her toddler. Jennifer had relished their attention to the details of her protracted and painful labour, information she was only too eager to impart.

'Finally,' Jennifer beamed, wrapping it up, 'when those fools could see I was unable to push a minute longer, they gave me a shot of heroin. Girls,' she simpered, taking in the three of them at a glance, 'now I know why people become hooked on that stuff. It was the most sublime feeling. Sublime.' Jennifer Davis sighed and, for a moment, seemed to have gone somewhere very far away. 'I couldn't have cared what happened to me after they gave me that shot. I would have died happy.'

That's what they knew. Beat books, the lives of a few poets and American jazz musicians, and Jennifer Davis's parturition.

Now we know more.

— o —

'Are you using serious drugs Claudine?'

There, she'd said it.

'Don't be ridiculous. Why do you ask that?' Claudine squinted suspiciously. 'Who's been talking about me?'

'Grace said something.'

'Fucking busybody. I have never been particularly fond of Grace Devlin.'

'I notice things too, Claudine. Ruby and Eli feel as if you've deserted them because of something they've done. They don't deserve that sort of treatment.' In an attempt to give extra weight to her concern, she added, 'There are rumblings about the quality of your work, you know. There's talk of sacking you.'

'I'm thinking of quitting. I'm sick of that place. Don't you worry about me, Rachel. I'm all right. Danny's been giving me a hard time lately, that's all.'

'You didn't answer me, Claudine. Are you using heroin?'

Claudine laughed.

'Stop worrying, Rachel, I have it completely under control. I never inject it. I have a snort once or twice a week. So what?'

Rachel forbade Ruby and Eli to see her. They were furious.

'Why can't we see her? Why not?' Ruby demanded to know.

'I don't want you around her.'

'Why?' Eli this time. 'She's our friend.'

'Not any longer, she's not. She's . . .' How to explain? 'Claudine is . . . she's sick.'

'You're mean. If she's sick, we should be allowed to see her! She might need us to look after her.'

'You may not see her.' Rachel spoke sternly. 'Claudine uses heroin.'

'So what!' Ruby cried, enraged. 'She doesn't do anything to hurt us. She only hurts herself.'

Panic. Swirling fear. Panic. **Panic.**

'You knew! How did you know?' Rachel gasped. 'You've been there when she's using it!' Shouting now. 'What do you know about this?'

A *lightning flash.*

'Did she ever offer any to you to try? Did she?'

'Of course not. I've never seen her use it. Never. But I go there sometimes after school and she's in this funny state, nodding off to sleep, and she can't talk properly. She sniffs all the time. I went around to Jason's after school a couple of times. His brother was like that. It was creepy. I never went back.' She shuddered. 'Jason told me what it was.'

'No more! I don't want you around that stuff. Ever! Do you hear me? Not ever. There will be severe punishment if I find out either of you have been there, or have been out with her. So severe that you will wish all I'd done was to ground you. Is that clear? There are to be no more visits with Claudine, and that's final!'

Later that night when Ruby came to say goodnight she found Rachel in her bedroom, weeping.

'What's the matter, Mama?'

'I'm worried about what will become of Claudine.' She blew her nose and sighed. 'I miss her.'

Ruby sat next to Rachel on the bed and placed an arm around her mother's shoulder.

'Me too. There must be something we can do. We can't just desert her.'

'She doesn't want to see us.'

'How come?'

'I think that's what happens. Heroin becomes their whole life. They only want to be with other people who use it. It makes them feel more . . . I don't know. More comfortable.' She hugged Ruby tight. 'I'm sorry I yelled at you, Ruby. I was frightened by what you said. Don't you ever touch that stuff, Rube. It would be unbearable if my children became . . .'

The remainder of the sentence was too terrifying to hear out loud.

— o —

Eli and Ruby fought with her relentlessly over the ban. Rachel suspected rebellion.

'Ruby, did you go to Claudine's after school?'

'You said we weren't allowed.'

'That is not an answer. Did you go?'

'No', Ruby snarled through clenched teeth. 'You said we couldn't.'

Rachel peered at Ruby.

'I'll ground you!'

'What are you staring at? I said no, didn't I?'

'If I find out you're telling me lies . . .'

Ruby turned on her heel and marched out of the room.

Rachel was certain Ruby continued to drop in on Claudine from time to time, but, short of picking her up after school each day, a mortification she knew Ruby would resist by any means possible and an impracticality as far as her own work was concerned, she felt there was little she could do about it.

'Talk to her calmly. Ruby's a sensible kid. She'll be all right.'

'I'm frightened, Grace.'

'Keep talking to them. Stay calm. You're going to have to ride it out.'

— o —

Claudine came to visit Rachel only when she needed money. At first sight of her standing in the doorway, Rachel felt a rush of pleasure, which dissolved with the sound of Claudine's sniffing, the vision of her scratching at her face, the uncharacteristically untidy sight of dandruff on the shoulders of her rumpled linen jacket. Rachel's heart became tight and her eyes would dim.

The sound of Claudine's voice brought Ruby and Eli running from their rooms to greet her; apart from a feeble smile, a curt nod, Claudine ignored them. Puzzled and hurt, the children left the two women to engage in halting conversation, as if this . . . this *thing* wasn't between them, both of them awkward in their discomfort. Why couldn't Claudine ask for the money outright and leave? Why didn't Rachel simply give it—or not—and both of them be done with it? Why?

Guilt—for what? Rachel wondered each time—feelings of loss and sadness combined to make her give Claudine whatever money she could, or was prepared to give. She became confused and resentful.

Claudine stayed long enough to have a polite conversation and a cup of tea (holding the cup in trembling fingers) then, after saying she would phone Rachel in a day or two (which she never did), she hurriedly departed.

— o —

Two months after the imposition of the ban, Ruby arrived home from school crying.

'I hate Claudine', she'd sobbed. 'I wish we'd never met her. I'm sorry I was ever her friend. I hate her.'

Rachel attempted to console her, to ascertain what had happened. Ruby remained tight-lipped. She threw everything Claudine had ever bought her—with the exception of one pair of sunglasses—into a rubbish bag and tossed it into the bin.

'Would you like to talk about what happened, Ruby?'

'No! Don't ever ask me again.'

Rachel refrained from further enquiry. Neither Ruby nor Eli mentioned Claudine again. The argument about not being permitted to see Claudine, which had continued unabated, came to an end.

— o —

Claudine came to ask for money. The children did not leave their rooms to greet her. Coins clanked against the fruit bowl as

51

Rachel held her purse aloft and shook and pulled nearly forty dollars from it.

'That's it, Claudine. It's all I've got.'

As Claudine rose to leave (no cup of tea offered this time), Rachel said, 'Don't come around any more, Claudine. It causes us too much heartache. And,' she gulped, 'no more money. I can't afford to keep giving you money.'

'You work. You have plenty of money', Claudine sneered.

Rachel's voice cleared of pain and turned to ice. 'You are not welcome here, Claudine. Do not come back.'

She never did.

Rachel never ceased from missing her.

— o —

A different ride, the same merry-go-round.

Six months after the break with Claudine, Grace and Esther were talking on the phone.

'Did you know Rachel's seeing Gully?'

'You're kidding! How long has that been going on?'

Grace knew that Rachel had been sweet on Gully McGuinness since their art school days.

'About five weeks.'

'Why did she tell you and not me?'

'She didn't tell me, Grace. I saw them at Caffe Roma, very lovey-dovey over cups of coffee. I asked her.'

'She could have told me.'

'You know why she didn't. You would disapprove.'

'What's that got to do with anything?'

When Rachel confirmed that she and Gully were seeing each other, Esther had moaned, '*Mayn Gott*, ever since Jack, you can't leave the bohemian types alone. Gully McGuinness is trouble, Rachel. A lovely man, but trouble.'

'And?' Grace's question interrupted Esther's thoughts.

'She said they'd been seeing each other for—'

Grace exploded.

'Seeing each other! You mean he's moved in with her. You mean fucking.'

'Cut it out, Grace. I'm telling you what Rachel said. Her

words were "seeing each other", okay? He's not living with them.'

Grace fell silent.

'What?' Esther said.

'She's always said she won't bring blokes home. She worries that the kids might get upset. She worries that *they* might get upset that *Jack* will get upset. So where's she doing it with him? I'll bet he never takes her to his place.'

'At her place when the kids are at school. They're out of bed by the time the kids get home from school. They all have dinner together then he leaves. Sort of back to front.'

'Back to bloody front', Grace shrieked. 'Esther, you are priceless!'

'Don't be mean, Grace.'

'I'm not. Don't you remember him, Esther? Unless he's had a major character change, Gully will only tolerate that crap for so long. You either take Gully McGuinness in for the duration or you don't have him. Women look after Gully McGuinness, Esther, they feed him, fuck him and nurture his art while theirs goes down the toilet. They nurture *him*.' Grace sighed. 'Does Rachel want a bloke so badly that she's prepared to play Muse?'

'I always thought he was a nice man.'

'Oh, spare me, Esther', Grace groaned. 'Anyway, what about the other thing?'

'What other thing?'

'You know what I'm talking about, Essie.'

Grace had reported to Esther who mentioned to Rachel that Gully had a habit.

'He smokes joints. He's off heroin.'

'That's not what I heard.' Grace became suspicious. 'Who told you that, Esther? What's Rachel heard?'

'She says he's clean.'

'*She* told you! Holy Mary, mother of Jesus! That means he told her.'

'Why are you so down on him, Grace?'

'Why do you think, Esther?' Grace waited.

Esther thought for a moment.

'You didn't! How did you manage to keep it a secret from us? Why did you?'

53

'We wagged classes and did it in the afternoon.' She laughed. 'Back to front. I don't know why we kept it a secret. He seemed to think it was a good idea, so I went along with it.' Grace grinned. 'To tell you the truth, I always suspected he was having it off with Caroline at the same time. Doing it with her at night when I was working in that pub.'

They laughed.

'Was he using heroin then?'

'He dabbled, a Saturday night taster.'

How their language had changed.

Grace waited for Esther to break her silence. 'Well?' she said finally. 'Ask me.'

'Did you ever use it?'

'Once. I puked all night', Grace said dryly.

Another silence followed.

'No, Esther,' Grace responded to the silence. 'The vomiting was enough to put me off it forever. I didn't even smoke another joint for years.'

There was finality in Grace's voice: the subject of her involvement with Gully was closed.

'Is she going to let him move in?'

'She says not.'

'One of us should say something to her. She shouldn't let him live there.'

'It's none of our business.'

'Yes it is. She's our friend.'

'Okay, you do it. You're the one who seems to know all about it.'

'Blunt-mouthed Gracie to the rescue. Thanks, Esther.'

A few minutes more were spent talking about their work and their children, then, with Grace promising she would talk to Rachel about Gully at the first available opportunity, they said irritated goodbyes and hung up.

— o —

To Grace's warning, Rachel replied, 'Had a habit, you mean.'

'No, Rachel. I mean has one. Now.'

'He says he's finished with that stuff. He swore to me.'

'Junkies always say that, Rachel. They always tell you they're clean.'

'How do you know he's not?' Rachel was becoming angry.

'Because people talk. Because of who I see him hanging around with. Because I see him stoned, and it's not on grass. I don't believe you're not aware of any of this.'

'In all the times I've been with him, Grace, I have never seen him stoned on heroin. We smoke joints together. That's all.'

'Rachel,' Grace said gently, laying her hand on her friend's arm, 'would you want to know? You seemed to be enjoying your life. Why is he so important to you?'

'He makes me laugh. I like his company. I've always liked him.' She grinned. 'I like the sex.'

Grace smirked. 'Make the most of it. It won't last long.'

'Meaning?'

'Blokes can't get it up after they've been using for a while.'

Rachel shrugged. 'He's not using', was all she would say.

'Be careful, Rachel. Think seriously about allowing him to move in.'

Rachel became frosty. 'Thank you for your concern, Grace. I must go. See you soon.'

Each paid for her coffee and left.

Rachel had no use for Grace's advice.

— o —

'Mum's got a boyfriend', Eli teased happily.

Ruby was more subdued.

'What's the matter, Ruby?' Rachel asked, tousling Ruby's hair. 'Don't you like Gully? You're not very friendly towards him.'

'Don't love Gully, Mama,' Ruby pleaded, showing more wisdom than her mother, 'he's a junkie.'

'What do you know about Gully? Who told you that?'

'Oh, Mama. *Everyone* knows Gully's a junkie. You know it too.'

Rachel tensed.

'How do you know about junkies?'

'Have you forgotten Claudine already? Mum, anyone who goes to the movies or watches television or reads a newspaper knows about junkies. Just because we're kids doesn't mean we don't know about things.' She held Rachel's hand. 'Most people who live around here know what a junkie is.'

'I hope you don't know people—'

'I know Gully', Ruby replied tartly. 'I knew Claudine.'

'Gully used to, Ruby, that's true. But he doesn't any more.'

Ruby was disgusted with her.

'Mama, can't you see? Don't be with him.'

No use for Ruby's advice either.

— o —

Now that the children knew Rachel was seeing him, Gully stayed for the night on the evenings he came to dinner. In the morning he walked the children to school on his way to his studio in West Melbourne. Still, the warnings made Rachel nervous. She decided to keep him at arm's length for a while, fobbing off his persistent suggestions that he move in.

'Rachel,' Eli asked, 'why can't Gully move in with us? He makes the best curries.'

'That's not enough reason for someone to move in.' Rachel chuckled. 'Besides, you make the best curries.'

'No, Mama, don't let him.'

'Shut up, Ruby', Eli snapped. 'Please, Rachel. He helps me with my maths homework.'

'Even being able to help with maths homework is not enough reason.'

'Then what is?'

Ruby observed her closely.

'I'm not sure that I want to live with him, Eli. Let's see how things go for a while, hey?'

Rachel hugged the disappointed Eli to her. Ruby moved into the circle of Rachel's other arm and hid her face in her mother's chest, though not before Rachel saw a look of intense relief wash over her daughter's face.

— o —

Was Gully's decline as rapid as it appeared to be, or was it that the conversation with Grace made the fact of his using undeniable? At first, each sign alone could have been construed as a growing lack of interest in their relationship, the well-known

Gully McGuinness penchant for moving on. But heroin use was becoming a more common fact of life and Rachel had come to recognise the behaviour she observed for what it was.

The signs.

A pendulum of hitherto unrevealed spite and unbearable obsequiousness. Long-sleeved T-shirts worn on the hottest days and in bed. Unexplained and lengthening absences. Arrangements broken without notice or apology. A growing number of requests to borrow ever-larger amounts of money. Lies, lies, lies. Scratching. Sniffing. Perspiring. Forever perspiring from clammy skin. A diminishing capacity to make love.

Filled with trepidation, Rachel asked, 'Are you seeing someone else?'

He laughed. 'Someone else? There is no one but you, sweet.'

'What's going on, Gully?'

'Nothing, sweet. Tired. Working on a difficult piece, that's all.'

His reply was spoken softly.

'I don't believe you, Gully.'

'Don't you, Rachel my sweet?' He gently stroked her cheek and said, in the same soft voice as he smiled into her eyes, 'You're a bloody nag, Rachel. You think I don't notice the way you look at me? That maternal, worried frown on your face. Always worrying about something. Nothing's going on. All right? Get off my back.'

'I'm not what's on your back, Gully. Are you using again?'

'This seems to be the perfect moment for me to leave, eh sweet?'

'Moving on again, Gully? Running away? Adored youngest son who could never grow up?'

'Fuck you!'

'You don't seem quite capable these days.'

Gully went into the bathroom. 'It's been charming, Rachel', he said, shaking his toothbrush at her as he walked past on his way to the front door. 'Bid your children goodbye. See you around, sweet.'

That was the last conversation she had with him. Gully would not be moving in. First, she informed the children, then Esther, who told Grace, who told Annalise, who told Caroline. Annalise remarked that the act of a lover walking out with his toothbrush had a greater sense of finality to it than any words.

'God,' Grace moaned, 'I hope you're right.'

In fact, Gully did return. Once. During the day, when Rachel was at work and the children at school, he entered the house and stole her treasured record collection. In exchange, he left a note:

> Mea culpa, sweet, but you know how it is.
> Why wouldn't you let me move in?

and on top of the note a punnet of lupin seedlings.

The theft of her records enraged her. The last sentence of his note more so. She threw the lupins against the back fence.

Eli, who had continued to insist how much better their lives would be were Gully to have moved in, turned against him.

'Good riddance.'

'Good riddance.'

'Good riddance.'

If Rachel heard that phrase one more time from her children or her friends ... Well, at least they didn't say 'I told you so'. Not in as many words.

With his departure Rachel was forced to concede what she had known from the moment she returned to Carlton and clapped eyes on him: Gully McGuinness was a heroin addict.

— o —

Rachel's friendships with Gully and Claudine gave her pause. In spite of what had come to pass, whatever Claudine and Gully had become, Rachel could not help liking them, or at least liking the people they had been before they became so devious, so driven.

'Such a waste of a life', she lamented.

Grace said: 'You're wasting your sympathy, Rachel. Scumbags, the lot of them.'

Esther said: 'You are too generous towards him. He stole your records.'

Shimon said: 'Thank God *he's* gone.'

Annalise said: 'Don't you think your sympathy is a little misplaced, Rachel?'

Eli said: 'That bastard.'
Ruby said: 'Good bloody riddance.'
Rachel said: 'Shut up, the lot of you.'

— o —

The Grinblatt Briggs returned to being just three and got on with their lives.

JERRY

A voice is heard in Ramah, lamentation and bitter weeping!
Rachel is weeping for her children,
refusing to be comforted for her children . . . they are gone.

Jeremiah 13:15

Immediately upon leaving university, Jerry Bradman deferred his working life and set out to follow the hippie trail. He journeyed first to Nepal, eventually reaching India, where he lived for a time in Goa. Amoebic dysentery precipitated his return to Australia, where he settled in the small coastal town of Byron Bay. Together with a group of like-minded people, he farmed a property close to town: mangoes, avocadoes, strawberries, bananas and an assortment of vegetables.

One member of their tribe worked casual as a chef in one of Byron Bay's busy macrobiotic cafes, one was a potter, another tooled leather, a fourth—a woman with whom he was to have a long-term relationship—made jewellery from beads and feathers. Handicrafts and produce, including pavlovas made from eggs laid by their own hens, their homegrown strawberries and cream from the neighbour's cow, were transported to a local market stall in their collectively owned Kombi.

Their meagre household income was supplemented by the sale of a small amount of grass cultivated on a concealed part of the block, just enough for their own use and for sale to a select group of regular customers, netting a $200-a-week top-up to their household income, which meant none of them had to work in nine-to-fives or go on the dole.

After leaving Byron Bay (and the jeweller), Jerry completed a twelve-month postgraduate course and worked now as an engineer in the Melbourne office of a London-based mining company.

Jerry Bradman's attitude to heroin use was quite benign, which, in the Carlton of the late seventies, was both unusual and, considering he had lived in share houses over a period of five years with individuals whose Saturday-night party treat had become their seven-day-a-week obsession, somewhat surprising.

At a New Year's Eve party given by Grace and Pete, Rachel listened with interest as he explained to a group of guests with whom he was chatting that ripping off household members was in the nature of the beast. If one chose to continue living in households with users, having one's goods and money stolen was to be expected, even after the users had been kicked out. He made no moral judgement of their behaviour: he simply moved further out of their reach, to a small, well-secured Edwardian cottage in Clifton Hill, there to live alone.

— o —

Rachel was surprised when, two nights after the Devlins' party, Jerry phoned to invite her out. There had been an enjoyable conversation at the party, but she had not felt particularly attracted to him. Nor did she think he had been to her. Just a pleasant party conversation.

What impressed her most was his suggestion that it might suit her to go somewhere she could bring the children. They decided on South Melbourne Beach for a picnic lunch. Eli nagged him all afternoon to play Frisbee, Ruby flirted outrageously with him, competing with Rachel for his attention. Rachel, who had phoned Grace for some details, wondered if he was still in love with the bead-and-feather woman. The woman—Maureen, or

Mary, or Margaret; something like that—had left Byron Bay to live in London. Grace had heard they still kept in touch.

At four o'clock Jerry drove them home, saying he would call again soon.

— o —

The aroma of garlic, fresh bay leaves and rosemary drifted up the hall from the kitchen and curled around the open door of the bathroom where Rachel stood inspecting herself before the oval mirror. She turned her head to sniff the air as the casserole smells wafted in and began to overlay the scent of soap and shampoo.

Rachel paused in the application of her kohl.

'Smells good', she remarked to her reflection. Stepping into the doorway, she called, 'Jerry, give the casserole a stir, would you?'

Jerry turned momentarily from the football replay towards her voice. He nodded and moved absent-mindedly backwards through the large open room towards the stove.

Turning back to the mirror, Rachel composed her face into what she considered its best repose, immodestly pleased with what she saw. 'Not bad for forty', she murmured. She licked her forefinger and smoothed her eyebrows, whose ragged shape had never satisfied her.

A pair of mock tortoiseshell combs lay on the bench. She raised them to her thick, wavy, chestnut-coloured hair, and secured them. Next she slipped the stems of a pair of gold stud earrings through her earlobes. A new amber necklace sat just so on her black jumper. One last nod of approval, a glance at her watch—'Oh, dear', she said, flustered—and Rachel hurried from the bathroom. In less than an hour their visitors would arrive to celebrate Ruby's acceptance into art school.

'Eli, Ruby,' she addressed them as she swept down the hall into the livingroom, 'set the table please.'

Jerry placed Miles Davis's *Cookin'* on the record player. Rachel smiled at the appropriateness of his choice. 'Thanks.' He strolled to the table where she stood straightening the profusion of Iceland poppies in a tall glass vase and began massaging her shoulders.

'Relax', he soothed. 'Slow down. There's plenty of time.'

She turned to him.

'How do I look?'

A cheer blared from the television. Eyes on the screen, he muttered, 'Give me a look.' Once the football fracas was over, he turned to appraise her and chuckled. 'You never get those eyebrows right, do you?'

'Do you like this blouse?'

'It's fine.'

Irritated, Rachel pulled away. She checked the serviettes, ensuring they were laid out in perfect linear arrangement. Harried now, Rachel turned her attention to the stove. Lifting the lid off the pot, she stuck her head into the rising cloud of steam and inhaled. 'Delicious.' Just as she had turned her attention to preparing the salad dressing, the doorbell rang.

'I'll go', Jerry said. 'Sounds like everyone's arrived at once.'

— o —

They had spent a year prancing around each other like mating lyrebirds, each tentative about committing themselves.

For stretches of two or three months they would go out together, stay overnight at each other's houses, then Jerry would get cold feet. It wasn't that he ever said outright he wouldn't be seeing her again; he simply didn't call, or return her calls. He stopped coming around, stopped inviting her to stay. Each separation disappointed her. Each separation, she announced to her friends, was the last. She'd had enough. Trouble was, she liked Jerry Bradman. It had been years since a man had made her laugh as much as he did. And he did love to talk.

Was that enough? Jerry Bradman and his cold feet were becoming tiresome. On the occasion of one of his return bouts, Rachel presented him with a pair of thick woollen socks. Jerry enjoyed the joke, but not enough to stop him disappearing again four weeks later.

Rachel left a message on his answering machine. 'If you come back again, make it permanent or don't come back at all.'

On a Sunday evening soon after Rachel left the message, he dropped in, a sheepish look on his face.

'Would you like a drink? There's some beer—'

'No thanks.' He shuffled from foot to foot.

'Have you come for dinner?'

'Uh, no. No, thanks.'

'What is it, Jerry? What do you want?'

'Let's get married', he said. He was looking directly into her eyes
See! No man made her laugh as much as Jerry Bradman did.

'Can't you see I'm cooking dinner? I'm too busy.'

'Until when?'

'Until you've made up your mind whether it's me you want or
whatsername in London.'

Eight weeks later, they married.

After much gentle cajoling, Jerry convinced Rachel to have
what the children laughingly called their hippie wedding.
Shimon and Esther offered their back garden.

Rachel insisted she retain her own name: Jerry was happy to
accommodate.

— o —

'Ruby, would you like to come shopping with me? Help me buy
the dress?'

They scoured the Indian shops in Chapel Street and found
just the thing: a cream, ankle-length cheesecloth frock with
fitted sleeves, full skirt, and tiny covered buttons down the back.
Ruby insisted Rachel purchase the emerald-green silk scarf with
gold threads running through it.

'Buy it, Mama. It's beautiful.'

Jerry's parents drove to Melbourne from their home in Wol-
longong for the occasion. It soon became apparent that the
senior Bradmans felt uncomfortable with such unorthodox proceedings; Nate didn't look much happier. On his arrival, he took
in the scene and began to make a B-52. Rachel reproached him
with a stern, 'Papa!' For the remainder of the afternoon, he
behaved himself. Thank God. Rachel took his bomber as a sign
of disapproval (the larger the bomber, the larger the disapproval?), though whether of her marrying at all, whether that it
was Jerry she was marrying, or whether he disapproved of the
form of the ceremony, Rachel had no idea. Nate would never
have said. Rivka commented on how soft and pretty they all
looked. 'I don't understand any of it', she said, but she seemed
pleased all the same.

Jerry wore a purple silk vest, delicately embroidered with gold thread and small turquoise beads, over a white *kurtha*. His loose-fitting trousers were made from Indian cotton.

Eli and Ruby pooled some of their earnings and bought Jerry and Rachel a gardenia each to wear in their hair.

Pretty as pictures, they looked.

Ruby and Eli did the honours: with Rachel in the middle and the three of them holding hands, the children led her through Esther and Shimon's livingroom into the garden to where Jerry (barefoot) and the celebrant sat facing each other on the lawn. Henry and Jake, and Linda Devlin strewed rose petals onto the path. Zev refused to participate in the ceremony. 'Sissy hippie shit', he'd growled. He was severely reprimanded by Shimon for his foul mouth and mean spirit.

— o —

By now, real estate in Carlton was out of their price range, so the Grinblatt-Bradmans put a down payment on a house in North Fitzroy and obtained for themselves a mortgage. 'Lovely' was perhaps too generous a description of the house but, as the salesman insisted, it had potential. They chose it because they liked it: it was cheap, had the requisite number of bedrooms (including one for a studio), a roof that didn't leak, floors that were stable. Best of all, it was built on a large block.

'All this land', Rachel swooned. 'I could start a small nursery here. There's enough room for it, you know.'

'One day', Jerry said. 'There's plenty of time for that.'

Haven't I heard something like that before?

'It feels more pressing to me.' She sighed. 'I wish I could give up design altogether.'

'You can't just garden all day.'

'I could, you know. Garden and paint. That would be my idea of heaven.'

'What about money? My income isn't enough to keep us.'

She didn't want to hear mortgage talk, weekly budgets. Not now.

'I know.' She turned to face him, hiding her irritation behind a smile. 'What I'd really like is to earn my living propagating and selling herbs.'

'How would you manage that?'

Rachel described her fantasy: where a shed would be built, how stacking shelves would be constructed, the way in which she would propagate, the labels she would design, who she might sell to.

'That's a nice idea, Rachel. But don't let any of your design clients know. You don't want them giving their work to some other freelancer because they think you're walking out on them to dig in the dirt all day.'

Jerry's attitude served to firm her resolve.

With quiet determination, she began to draw roughs of her fantasy garden and stuck them on the wall of her studio.

— o —

The Devlins contributed a loaf of wholemeal bread and a glazed fruit tart from the local bakery to the meal. Esther, Shimon and Jake (Zev and Henry were out with friends) brought Ruby's favourite desert: golden syrup dumplings and a tub of thick cream. Annalise and Marcel brought champagne, a bunch of flowers and their two boys, Jean-Luc and Paul.

'Pete, you beaut!' Eli exclaimed, plucking a piece of fruit off the tart.

'Hands off!' cried Grace and Esther in unison.

'Congratulations, Ruby!' A chorus went up as she entered the room. Ruby became shy, blushing with discomfort and pleasure at being the focus of so much attention. Caroline, who was only able to stay long enough to have a drink and pick at the hors d'oeuvres, gave Ruby a painting.

'Thanks, Caroline. It's beautiful.'

'Look after it, kiddo. It will be worth its weight in gold one day.'

The doorbell rang again.

'That'll be Rhea!' Ruby said. 'I'll get it.'

She disappeared up the hall to greet her friend.

Rachel announced dinner. Amid conversation and laughter, they all sat down to eat.

At nine-thirty, Ruby and Rhea excused themselves.

'Where are you off to?' Rachel asked, surprised. She glanced at the clock. 'It's late to be going out, isn't it?'

Ruby and Rhea glanced at each other then looked away.

'It's nine-thirty! We're eighteen, Mum.'

'Only just eighteen.'

The guests chuckled.

'We're going to the pub to listen to a band. Our friends are waiting for us.' She turned to Rhea, who nodded.

'Off you go then', Jerry said, shooing them out of the room. 'I'll calm your mother down.'

'Thanks, Jerry', Ruby grinned, kissed him, then kissed Rachel.

'Hey, Ruby! You're leaving me with the dishes', Eli protested.

'I'll do them for you when you finish high school', she laughed. 'Bye.'

'Have you got your key?' Eli taunted. 'What time will you be home? Don't be too late, please. Don't get into a car with boys who have been drinking. Do you have some ID in case—?'

'That's enough, thank you Eli', Rachel warned.

At eleven-thirty, Esther and Rachel stood at the front door waving goodbye to Annalise, Marcel and the boys. Inside again, Esther peered at her friend.

'You look miserable, Rachel. What's the matter?'

Rachel stuck out her bottom lip. 'I don't want her to leave home.'

Esther laughed. 'Yes you do.'

'What's going on?' Grace joined them.

'Rachel says she doesn't want Ruby to leave home.'

'Of course you do. You just think you don't.'

Esther nodded.

'Why do I feel so sad then?'

'Because it is sad. Big milestone. End of an era. She's grown up now. So,' Grace patted Rachel's cheek, 'you'll grieve and you'll get over it.' She opened the front door. 'God, it's cold.'

'Damn you, Grace, you can be so brisk.'

'I know', Grace replied with a smug grin. 'That's why I'm such a good friend for you to have, you old worrier. Goodnight, love. Thanks for the lovely meal. Bye, Esther. See you soon. Come on, Pete, Linda. Let's go home.'

Eli announced he was going to stay the night at Angelo's.

'Oh,' Rachel wailed, 'all my children are gone.'

'Cut it out, Rachel.' Eli was gruff. 'I'm only going to Angelo's.'

'Yes, but soon you'll be gone forever.'

Exasperated, Eli stood in the doorway between the livingroom and the hallway, muttering.

'Go on, Eli, away you go.'

'Thanks, Jerry. I'll see you tomorrow. Goodnight, Rachel.'

'What time will you be home?'

'Good*night*, Rachel.'

'Why are you giving the kids such a hard time?' Jerry asked after Eli had gone. 'Ease up, Rachel.'

Rachel glared at him.

'I don't expect you to understand', she retorted.

'How can they become adults if they don't go out into the world to make their own way?' He slipped his arm through hers. 'They're going to go whether you want them to or not. You might as well make it as easy on yourself as you can. On them, too, if it comes to that. Don't make them feel guilty about moving out, Rachel. It's not fair.'

'Fair! What's fair got to do with it? I'm going to miss them.'

'Ruby's not exactly going to the North Pole.'

'She might as well be, Jerry.'

'What rubbish, Rachel. Don't be silly.'

Unfair. Silly. He could call her what he liked. The fact remained: she didn't want the children to leave. Rachel would willingly accommodate almost any arrangement just to have Ruby stay a while longer; Eli, too, and he still had two more years of high school to complete.

Close on twenty years of her life had been spent devoted to her children. How on earth, she wondered as she straightened the poppies and brushed crumbs from the table, how shall I satisfy this yawning sense of loss?

INTERLUDE I

Time passes. Two years.

— o —

On a midweek evening, Esther and Shimon are at the cinema when they see Ruby in the company of a friend. Esther's first response is one of pleasure; she raises her arm to wave, moving forward to greet the younger woman. She turns to Shimon to tell him that the man with Ruby is her new boyfriend, but does not commence the sentence. Ruby's demeanour, the way the young man comports himself, alerts her: something is awry. Esther steps back, closer to Shimon. Ruby and her companion appear unusually pale, heavy lidded. Black semi-circles smudge the area beneath her eyes.

'Shimon,' *Esther whispers,* 'she looks terrible. They look like they're on something.'

Shimon peers at the young couple.

'I think you're right', *he says thoughtfully.* 'She doesn't look at all well.'

Coins and notes drop to the foyer carpet as the pair fumble their money. Esther decides she doesn't want Ruby to see her and Shimon; she senses the embarrassment it will cause. She steps back further, dragging Shimon by his coatsleeve into the anonymity of the crowd. Unobtrusive now, they continue watching.

'Shimon, this is appalling. Do you think Rachel knows?'

Shimon frowns. 'I have no idea.'

Ruby's lover stands in the queue to buy the tickets while Ruby waits on a nearby banquette, a styrofoam cup of coffee in her hand.

Aghast, Esther observes as Ruby's head lolls onto her chest; the cup tilts as her grasp on it loosens. Coffee begins to dribble onto the carpet.

Suddenly, Ruby snaps awake. She straightens the coffee cup. Blinking rapidly, she focuses her vision and begins to survey the throng. Her eyes settle on Esther and Shimon before the couple have time to duck her gaze. Seeing them, Ruby blushes, runs her fingers through her hair, brings a smile to her lips. With a hesitant step, she moves towards them, dropping the cup into the bin as she passes it.

'Oh my God,' Esther whispers to Shimon, 'here she comes. What will we say?'

Before he has time to reply, Ruby reaches them.

'Hi, Esther. Hi, Shimon.'

She stands before them, hunched into her black leather jacket, her fists jammed into its zippered pockets. Her eyes are shifty.

'Hello Ruby.'

'How are you?' Esther asks nervously.

'Great. How about you?'

Shimon takes a firm grip of Ruby's elbow and steers her to the least-occupied corner of the foyer. Esther follows. Ruby, more than a little annoyed, attempts to free herself from his grasp.

'What are you doing, Shimon?'

'You don't look so good, Ruby. You look like you're on something. Are you on drugs of some kind?'

Esther nudges him. 'Shimon, not here. This is not the place.'

Ruby looks around furtively.

'What's it got to do with you, Shimon?'

'We care about you. You are the daughter of our dearest friend. Are you on drugs?'

'Don't be silly, Shimon.' *Her laugh is hollow.* 'Mum'd kill me.'

Shimon and Esther do not smile.

'Ruby, are you in trouble?' *Esther enquires softly.*

'What's the matter with you two?' *Their lack of response makes her edgy. She blathers.* 'I had a joint. Just a joint. What's the big deal? You smoke joints. So do Mum and Jerry.'

Esther is not convinced.

'Ruby, are you sure you're—?'

Ruby's eyes are darting hither and yon, seeking a path of escape, or rescue.

'Oh, look', she cries. Relief floods her dulled, pinned eyes; it alters her demeanour. 'Greg's got the tickets. Got to go.' In turn, she kisses Esther and Shimon on the cheek. 'You must meet Greg. He's gorgeous. You'd really like him.' She lowers her eyes. 'Don't look so glum, you two. I'm not on anything. Really. A joint, that's all. I'm fine.' With a breezy wave of her hand, Ruby departs. 'Enjoy the movie.'

Over the hubbub of the crowd, Esther hears Ruby's voice: 'Fucking hell!'

Too disturbed to concentrate, Esther and Shimon agree to leave the cinema and repair to the nearest cafe.

'What are we going to do?' Esther asks Shimon when they are seated at the table.

'I shouldn't have done that.'

'We'll have to tell Rachel.'

'It's none of our business.'

'Shimon! Rachel is my best friend. How can we witness Ruby in that condition and not tell Rachel? How could I keep that knowledge to myself and ever look Rachel in the eye again? It would be a betrayal of our friendship.'

Shimon's eyes are sad. 'Poor Rachel', he says.

'Poor Rachel', Esther echoes. 'Poor Ruby.'

They sit in the cafe, silent, staring at the table, each lost in their own melancholy thoughts.

— o —

First, Esther tells Grace. This is the worst nightmare they have for their children. What if . . .? What if . . .? The prospect is unthinkable.

'Poor kid.' Grace shudders. 'Still, you never know, Esther. It might not have been heroin, and if it was, she might not be too far gone. What do you think?'

'How would I know, Grace? I smoke about two joints a month. I knew Gully. I was probably the last person to know about Claudine. I've got no idea what she was on or how far gone she might be.'

'Well, there's only one thing to do. You must tell Rachel.'

Esther envisages the scene with Rachel. 'It's going to be difficult, Grace.'

'Yes, it is.' Grace considers. 'Did she mention to you that things have been a bit tense between them lately?'

'Yes.'

'Maybe she knows.'

They know Rachel doesn't know.

They hang up. There is nothing further to say.

— o —

The telling proves to be as difficult as Esther anticipated. Rachel cringes as if she has been bludgeoned. Esther sees the fear in Rachel's eyes. Its onset is instantaneous. It is accompanied by pain, disbelief, self-doubt.

Then comes anger.

'Esther, what would you know about heroin? She probably had a joint. She would never touch heroin.'

'I didn't say heroin', Esther replies, overlooking Rachel's insulting manner. 'I said she looked as if she were on something stronger than grass.'

'It was probably strong grass', Rachel responds. 'I'll kill her if she's on heroin!'

Esther remains quiet; she holds her friend's hand. Some minutes pass before Rachel whispers, 'Essie, what if it's heroin? What will I do?'

Tears well in her eyes.

'Talk to her. Maybe it isn't. If it is, you can get her to some counselling.'

Esther doesn't believe her own words.

— o —

Jerry tells her she's overreacting.

'For God's sake, Rachel, don't panic. Shimon and Esther wouldn't know the first thing about drugs.'

'Why shouldn't I panic? I'm worried sick.'

'Typical Jewish mother', he laughs.

It is the first time since meeting him that she doesn't like him.

'You bastard. It has nothing to do with being a Jewish mother, Jerry. Am I so different from Mrs di Pieri across the road? Or Mrs Katzanzakis who never lets me out of the shop before she's gone on for quarter of an hour about her what her children are getting up to on Saturday nights and how she's afraid they're getting into drugs? What about that McAuliffe woman whose son's been using heroin for years? Are you telling me she doesn't worry? Hey? And Grace, Grace with her darling Linda always dieting and puking herself into the shape of a twig? Do you think Grace doesn't worry about that? So tell me again, Jerry, how different I am!'

She is shouting.

He does not reply.

'I'm no different at all.'

She glares at him and leaves the room.

Jerry's shoulders droop. He is filled with a sense of dread. First with housemates, now with his wife. He begins to regret not having kept the house in Clifton Hill.

— o —

Rachel invites Ruby to dinner. She insists her daughter come alone.

'Are you using heroin, Ruby?'

Jerry keeps to the background.

'Esther and Shimon been telling tales?' There is something new, barely recognisable, in her voice, in her eyes. 'I knew they'd think that. I could tell from the way they looked at me. Greg and I had a joint. That's all.'

Rachel wavers. What mother would not want to believe this story?

'I want the truth, Ruby.'

Everything about Ruby shouts: This is none of your business.

'Honest. We only had a joint.' She picks a lettuce leaf from the salad. 'Is that all you wanted to talk to me about?'

'All! This is a serious matter, Ruby.' She pauses. 'Tell me, Ruby. Tell me if you're in trouble with heroin. We can get help. There are clinics, rehabilitation centres—'

'Heroin!' Clouds of tumultuous anger are billowing on Ruby's horizon. Rachel has never heard such scorn.

'I'm not using. Okay?' The tone in her voice is beginning to identify itself: belligerence, and a hint of contempt. 'Okay?' She looks at her watch. 'I have to go.' Ruby is shutting down.

'Go? You just got here! We haven't eaten.'

'I told Greg I'd meet him. He didn't have to work tonight after all.'

'But I prepared for you.'

'Sorry, Mama. I meant to let you know I'd only have time to drop in. I forgot.' The apologetic look is faked. Ruby is almost out the door when: 'Oh, by the way, I'm moving.'

'Where are you off to?' Jerry's entry into the conversation is amiable.

'Kensington. Greg and I are getting a place together. It's nice over there, cheaper. We're moving on the weekend.'

What is going on here? Why is Ruby moving out of the neighbourhood?

'Won't that make it difficult for you to get to school? What about your job?'

'We're near the station.'

'I'll give you a hand to move.' It is more than an offer.

'We can manage, thanks Mum.'

'What's your new phone number?'

'We haven't got one yet. I'll call you and let you know.' She turns. 'Bye, Jerry.'

'Bye, Ruby.' He drags on his cigarette. 'Look after yourself. Be careful.'

Ruby softens. 'Mama', she says tenderly, 'I really am fine', and smiles. 'I'll be twenty in two weeks. Isn't it time you stopped worrying about me?'

Didn't I say those very words to my own parents? Don't I still?

Perhaps Jerry is right about her overreacting. Ruby seems as fine as she says she is. A little bit tired, perhaps, but otherwise fine.

'Got to go. I love you, Mum.'

Ruby kisses Rachel and Jerry goodbye and leaves, promising to call with her new phone number as soon as it is allocated. Minutes after her departure, Rachel realises she forgot to get the Kensington address.

'See?' Jerry says, grinning. 'She's fine. Esther and Shimon panicked, that's all. She probably had a wild night the night before.'

He pats her on the shoulder and turns his attention to the television.

Rachel looks in his direction but doesn't see him. An unpleasant twitch irritates her arms; it runs along her spine like a dull electric current. Something has transpired here. She's not sure what it is, but she knows she doesn't like it. A sense of foreboding finds a place in her and settles in.

— o —

And another year.

— o —

'I'm in trouble, Mama.'

Ruby is curled up on the couch, foetal position.

'What's the matter, love? What trouble?'

'I've got a habit.' Ruby confirms Rachel's worst fears. She is twenty-one.

Rachel sucks in air. Reels. 'Oh, God. Oh, you poor baby.' Steadies herself. Firms her resolve. 'What can I do to help? I'll do anything.'

'I don't know if there's anything you can do. I think this is something I have to take care of myself.'

Ruby begins to cry. Rachel seats herself beside Ruby, strokes her with a trembling hand.

'How did this happen? I asked you. You said no.'

'That time Esther and Shimon saw me at the movies? I'd smoked some the night before, partied all night. I was wrecked that day, but I didn't have a habit. I wasn't even using regularly then.'

'How did you start? I warned you never to touch that stuff.'

'Someone offered me some at a party.'

'And?'

'It was fun for a while.' A small smile of remembrance.

'Fun?'

'Yes, fun. I started using it on weekends, not every weekend, but only weekends. Euphoric, gentle, not a worry in the world. I loved it. Then it got to be every weekend. Suddenly—it seemed like suddenly—it was every day. I couldn't stop.'

'What happened, Rube?'

'I thought I had it under control.'

'Tell me what I can do', Rachel repeats. 'Let me help you beat this thing. We'll do it together.'

'I have to do it on my own, Mum.'

'I want to help. Let me help you.'

Ruby looks up from where she lies on the couch. Rachel recoils from her disdain.

'Okay, Mama. Let's do it together.' She becomes truculent. 'You give up the speed, I'll give up the smack. We'll have a great time, coming down together.'

'Speed? Me? What are you talking about?'

'You know, Mama. Those zippy little diet pills you love to pop. The ones the friendly family doctor gives you scripts for.'

'How dare you! How dare you compare that to what you do. Besides,' she is defensive now, 'I haven't used them for years.'

'Yeah, Mama, that's what we all say.'

'We? We? Who do you think you're talking to? It is not the same—'

'Yeah? It is the same. Women everywhere munching away on Valium for their nerves, popping Duramine to get thin. Downers, uppers. It's all the same. More genteel because you score from the chemist.' She rolls on, an angry express train. 'What about the hash? Will you give that up too?' She cackles. 'You hypocrite.'

'There's no comparison. Besides, the hash helps me get to sleep. Otherwise I'll be awake all night worrying about you!'

Could have bitten her off her tongue for that one.

'That's right,' Ruby yells, 'blame me! You self-deluding bitch! At least I admit my addiction. You lay yours off on me and—'

'My addiction! Ruby, where are you going?'

'Away. Away from here. Away from you and your prying. Away from your suffocating interfer—'

'Now who's blaming?' Ruby is striding out of the room, Rachel is in pursuit. Each is as mad and as maddened as the other. 'Are you saying you use because of me? How dare you! Ruby, you come back here! Don't you walk away when I'm speaking to you!'

Ruby returns, almost at a run. She stands so close that Rachel is frightened.

'No, I'm not saying that. But I am saying I'm sick of you treating me like a child. Sick to death of you trying to control my life, of spying on me. You think I don't know you go through my things when I'm here? Read my journals? Peer into my eyes? Ever since Esther and Shimon saw me at the movies.'

'I do not!'

'You do!' She grabs Rachel's hand, catching her off guard. 'Come on', she insists. Rachel tries to pry her hand loose from Ruby's iron grip. 'Come on. You want to do this together? Let's do it together. Do you still keep the hash in the tampon packet? Does Jerry still roll up the grass inside his socks? Think you're clever, don't you?' Her laughter is driving Rachel mad. 'Let's go! Let's flush it all down the dunny. We'll do it together. Just like you said.'

'You're mad', Rachel screams. 'Mad.'

'Sure, Mama. Sure.'

'Let go of me! You're hurting. What do you think you're doing? Keep away from my cupboards. You have no right to go through our things. Let me go.'

'And you have a right to go through mine? Come on, Mama, aren't we going to kick this thing together? That's what you said, isn't it? Let's go. Let's go! Let's kick it. Flush 'em, now. You do yours, I'll do mine.'

'That's not what I meant.'

'Too bloody right, it's not.'

Tears are streaming down both their faces. Ruby releases Rachel's hand as suddenly as she had taken it up, the slackening causing Rachel to stumble. Ruby's laugh is hysterical.

'See, you don't really want to either, do you? Not on your own, not together. I might be hooked on heroin, but you better believe you're hooked too, Mama. Tell me the last time you went to sleep without the help of one of your elegantly rolled joints?' She doesn't bother to wait for an answer. 'You can't, can you? I'm telling you, Mama, we're not as different as you'd like to think. No way.' She wheels around again, strides up the hall. There is finality in her step.

'There is no comparison', Rachel shrieks after her. 'None. Do you hear me?'

Ruby calls back down the hall in a sing-song voice, 'Oh yes there is. Don't you kid yourself. The only difference is that the hash you love so much doesn't give you the stigma of dirty junkie, and the pills are legal.'

Does Rachel hear her sigh from up there in the hall?

'No more, Mama. I've had enough of this. I'm leaving.'

'Ruby!' Rachel cries out.

Ruby walks out and slams the door.

'I'll show you. You'll see.' Rachel mutters the words over and over again. She goes through tampon packets, unrolls socks and searches the other place she remembers she secreted hash and grass. One after the other, she dumps them into a plastic bag.

But when she stands in front of the lavatory, hand poised to throw the drugs into the still, clear water, her hand freezes.

Tomorrow, she decides. Ruby has upset her too much today. I'll roll a joint, have a few tokes, settle my nerves.

Quite a few tomorrows are to pass before Rachel gives up the dope.

Is it possible that giving up is not merely a matter of will?

— o —

Ruby phones. She is weeping.

'Help me, Mama. Please help me.'

Jerry urges Rachel to find a clinic. Rachel advises him that Ruby will come home to get well. Her decision is not negotiable. She, Rachel, will nurse her daughter through the shakes and sweats, the vomiting and aching joints of cold turkey. Gladly.

Which she does.

The worst is over in nine days.

Ruby settles in to being a member of the household again. Though subdued, she is amiable and considerate. She tidies the house, picks flowers, arranges them in vases and places a vase in every room. Delectable meals are prepared for dinner. When Rhea comes to visit, they sit in Ruby's room, talking quietly, listening to music. Most of her days are spent walking, drawing and writing in her journal.

The first week.

'Time to start my life again', Ruby announces on the fourteenth day. 'Rhea said I could move in with her until I find a job and some-where to live.'

She expresses her appreciation of Rachel's offer to stay on, but declines; the invitation is neither approved of nor extended by Jerry.

The second week.

Ruby finds a job and joins a gym.

The third week.

The fourth week appears to pass uneventfully, though Rachel is a little concerned that she does not hear from Ruby, nor does her daugh-ter return her calls.

By the fifth week, the lull is over. Breaking a ten-day silence, Ruby phones to borrow money. Her voice is slurred, she sounds depressed. When she comes to collect the cash, Rachel notices that the black smudges under her eyes have returned. Ruby is in a hurry to leave. Jerry and Rachel neither see nor hear from her for weeks.

— o —

Picture a slide. A spiral slide. It stands in the midst of a barren landscape. Rachel is perched at the top. With a flick of her wrists, she pushes off. The wind caresses her face. Slowly, slowly, slowly, she begins her descent and enters the first loop of the spiral.

Madness has commenced.

ADDICTION

The thing women brood on for years – it's the bed their thoughts flow along while the children are still small – is how to keep [their children] from harm. They usually brood in vain.

Marguerite Duras, 'House and Home', *Practicalities*

Rachel gave herself over, completely, and with an abandon such as, in another circumstance, she might to a new lover. Not that this was a new lover. No. Nor was it Jerry. Jerry ceased to exist for her. Rachel cast him loose, emptied her soul of him, until nothing remained but their bodies, living—if you could call it that—under the same roof.

The gulf widened.

Into this void she poured the life of another. Ruby. Aged twenty-one, twenty-two, twenty-three . . . The years crawled by.

Ruby, with a soft and generous heart, a shell grown hard as flint.

Ruby, with the laughing eyes as dark as bittersweet chocolate.

Wild Ruby. Restless, sensitive, angry Ruby. Loving, and lovable.

Talented Ruby.

Ruby of the high cheekbones, the skin as smooth as silk.

Ruby, my *maydele*. My heroin addict.

— o —

Was it me? Was my mothering unwise? Inadequate? Impatient? Too lax? Too strict? Should I not have gone out to work? Should your father and I have stayed together? Did I set a bad example, smoking joints, drinking whisky?

'No', Ruby answered whenever Rachel asked. 'You were a good mother.'

'You say that only to be kind.'

'It has nothing to do with you. I chose this.' Ruby waved her arm through the air in an arc to encompass the world of her life.

Mother and daughter would fall into each other's arms and sigh, sometimes to weep.

Yes, was Rachel's answer to herself.

And who was to say? Either way.

Rachel fantasised becoming a housewife once more, to devote her time to waiting—as if waiting were something she did not already do—to make herself available if and whenever Ruby dropped in or came to stay.

She fantasised leaving Jerry and considered suggesting to Jack (for whom she cared not one jot), years after their separation and he with another wife and three more children, that they have another go at their marriage.

She gave up smoking joints and gave up drinking, in the belief—too late—she could set a good example.

She gave up the fantasies about remarrying Jack.

She abandoned all consideration of life as a housewife.

Guilt, self-pity, remorse, sorrow, mistrust, anger, recrimination and fear. They became the patina of Rachel's life, her faithful companions. She was leaden with the exhaustion of fear, uninterested in her work, remote from her son, her friends and her parents.

She was unable to paint.

She retreated from activities which had once made her life rich and interesting.

She retreated from life.

'I have nothing left to give.'

To Ruby she gave: meals, a bed for the night (the night often stretching into weeks), time (whether or not she had it to spare), the loan of jewellery (not returned), the loan of clothes (not returned), the loan of the car (returned, with little or no petrol in the tank), and money whenever Ruby asked for it, because, Ruby said, her money was lost on a bus, a tram, in a taxi or in a phone booth (choose one or invent another), her money was stolen by someone in her house, someone on a train, or by a stranger at a party, her wages were short this week (she forgot she had taken an advance the week before), her money was withheld by Social Security (when they realised they had over-paid her on some previous fortnight).

Choose one or invent another.

To Ruby she gave: sympathy, compassion, encouragement, reassurance, consolation and solace.

To Ruby she gave: loyalty, no matter how misplaced, no matter how little she believed Ruby's stories, no matter how much she wanted to believe them—and did.

To Ruby she gave: a pain in the neck.

She believed: it was her fault (the addiction), that if she allowed Ruby to return home whenever she asked, she could keep an eye on her and control it (the addiction), that if she was loving, trusting, available, generous of her time, money and per-sonal belongings, her physical and emotional time and space, she could cure it (the addiction).

She became: the quagmire of her own life.

She mourned: the diminution and, finally, the loss of trust.

She despised: the complicity between them (for how could one continue to perform on this stage if the other refused to play her part?).

She rehearsed: scene upon scene in which she spoke kindly but firmly to her daughter, telling Ruby of her concerns, her fears, and in which she set some limits as to what was accept-able behaviour.

She loathed: the absence of courage to tell her daughter to do whatever was required to get herself clean, to get a life that was worthy of being so called.

Rachel feared that if she told Ruby she was no longer prepared to give her succour, that it was time she put her life in order, Ruby would feel so hurt, become so enraged, that she would storm off and have a hit of heroin damaging enough to overdose and die.

And Ruby, in divine, stoned bliss, had not so much as a clue.

Or so Rachel thought.

— o —

To see her daughter diminishing before her eyes—in body, spirit and self-respect—was a pain almost more than Rachel could bear. Nevertheless, martyrdom was a stripe that ran wide through generations of women in her family, so bear it she did; she thought she had no option.

Rachel was convinced that all that was needed to get Ruby clean was the right key to a tricky lock, a key that would allow her to say the right words, to reassure Ruby of her love, to give encouragement in the appropriate form at the correct time.

She never managed to get it right.

Ruby grew thinner and paler, sadder and angrier, more and more cunning.

'Cunning as a shithouse rat', Rachel snarled.

She thought of the people she had known who had become addicts. Mark Wallace, she'd heard recently. And his girlfriend. Gully. Claudine.

Now? Now Claudine was dead.

'Ruby,' Rachel floundered, 'I have something to tell—'

'Who?' Ruby asked, abrupt, alert, her body instantly tense. She began to chew her bottom lip, biting off her skin. In that moment, Rachel realised death was news Ruby had come always to expect.

'Claudine.'

'Claudine,' Ruby spoke her name softly, without surprise. 'I loved her so much.'

Rachel held Ruby in her arms and they wept. As they held each other, Rachel thought, Now she will stop. Dear Claudine, I've missed you for so long. I am angry that you are dead, angry that you went this way, that your life became such a miserable pile of shit. But if your death will bring Ruby back . . .

Claudine's death did not bring Ruby back.

Her soul—indeed, her entire life, it seemed to Rachel—was lost to the chase, the never-ending quest for money to buy heroin. Whatever that involved. Rachel didn't care to know the finer points; they scared her. It was enough to know there were three main ways to sustain a habit: dealing, stealing or on your back.

— o —

Where might Ruby be, and with whom?
What sort of people were they?
Was she stoned or straight?
Is she lonely?
Is she eating well, sleeping well, dressing warmly?
Has she been caught breaking and entering? Doing a deal?
Is she in jail?
Does she . . . (here Rachel shuddered) prostitute herself?
Is she in good health?
Does she still have a job, a comfortable place to live?
Has she kept up her artwork?
Does she have enough money for food?

— o —

In a rare moment of frankness, Rachel confessed her fears to her daughter. It was still early days. Ruby grinned; her brown eyes lit up with mirth.

'Oh, Mum, don't be silly. You've watched too much television.'

'What do you mean?'

'My life's not all awful, you know. What do you imagine I do?'

If only you knew what I imagine. Jail. Infection. AIDS. The alpha beta of hepatitis. Death.

'That you score then sit in dark rooms using heroin and nodding off all day.'

'You're mad. Not even the worst junkie does that! If you weren't so pathetic, that would be laughable.'

'What do you mean?' Rachel repeated, feeling foolish, feeling her anger rise.

'I'm still holding down a job. I have friends. We go out.'

'What job? Which friends? Where to?'

'I'm twenty-two, Mama. It's time this third degree came to an end.'

Ruby refused to elaborate, leaving Rachel to wonder if all

Ruby's tales, her cries for assistance, were fabrications. That she might be gullible in believing Ruby's stories, to admit to herself that these dramas were invented to wangle money out of her for another score, was too humiliating a prospect for Rachel to dwell on. Not to mention the fact that the stories usually worked.

'I probably support her habit as much as she does', she said ruefully to Jerry.

'Stop giving her money, Rachel.'

She dismissed him with a puff of air exhaled through pursed lips.

It was easier to dwell on the horrors—potential, imagined or real—of her daughter's life. Confronted with Ruby's miseries, Rachel chose to believe that her daughter suffered more than one individual's fair share of rotten luck. Believing this enabled her to maintain a loving sympathy, a despairing wish, an ardent yearning that Ruby would get her life right one day soon.

— o —

If Rachel was aware that her own life was lost to a chase that differed from Ruby's only in the form of the prize and the degree of danger in obtaining it, that attached to itself none of the illegalities of heroin addiction, she spoke little of it. This was a domain in which she cared not to linger. She masked her chase with a more benign description: motherly concern. Jerry and Eli had a different description for it: 'Mothering Above and Beyond the Call of Duty'.

To anyone else who cared to notice—and many did—it was clear that Rachel was too involved with her daughter's life. They knew, her family and friends, that they were helpless in the face of Rachel's obsession. More courageous friends tentatively suggested—once—some counselling, therapy perhaps.

'You don't have to do this alone, Rachel', said Caroline. 'Go and see someone. Talk about it.'

'If you don't get help, you'll go mad', Esther predicted. 'You must let Ruby go, Rachel.'

'Have a few sessions with a professional, someone removed from the problem', Annalise pleaded. 'I'll give you the name of someone.'

'What are you talking about? I don't need help. I'm fine.

Honestly. Fine', Rachel responded through clenched teeth, her smile brittle, her eyes dull. 'Ruby's the one in trouble, not me.'

Despite her protestations, Rachel did toy with the possibility that she was obsessed with Ruby. Then dismissed it. Then wondered about it again. It became a tug of war.

A memory, fleeting.

A story she read the children when they were very young. Push-me, Pull-you. Something like that. Details eluded her.

Another.

The innocent fortune-seeking of a lover plucking petals off a daisy. He loves me, he loves me not, until one last petal, the petal of fate, remains. I'm obsessed, I'm not. I'm obsessed, I'm not. What fate does the last petal hold in store for me? Will I believe it? Only if it tells me what I want to hear.

Rachel did her best to obliterate these thoughts, shunting them into the deepest recesses of her mind. They reasserted themselves, often in dreams, the details of which she had frequently—though not always—forgotten by morning, when all that remained of them was the chill embrace of fear and the sluggishness of waking from a night of disturbed sleep. Refusing to be denied, the dreams lingered, gnawing away at her soul.

Friends waited in faint hope for Rachel to concede: I am hooked. I too am addicted.

Rachel was not forthcoming.

And why would she be? For, just as an addict will say, 'I'm not hooked; I can stop any time I want to', delusional regarding the depth of their engagement, so too was Rachel delusional. Just as Ruby could not give up heroin, Rachel could not give up Ruby.

A drug by any other name . . .

— o —

Blame became a useful tool. Rachel apportioned blame to whomever, at any given moment, she believed was responsible for leading Ruby astray.

And just where is astray? Rachel scoffed at her own enquiry. And answered: astray is a place your mother doesn't want you to be, with people she doesn't want you to be there with.

It was unimaginable that Ruby had volunteered in her own seduction. In her search—which inevitably ended back on her own doorstep—for the definitive answer to the interminable questions, 'Why?' and 'How?' and 'Whose fault?', everyone she had ever known fell victim to her accusing scrutiny. Claudine, there was always Claudine. Then there was Jack, and blameless Rhea. That crowd Ruby used to hang around with at art school. Yes, and Gully. Gully came in for his fair share of abuse.

It was the miscreant Gully, Rachel was convinced, who introduced Ruby to heroin. That is, of course, when she wasn't convinced it was someone else.

'I'll kill that bastard', she would mutter, making particularly brutal snips at the plants with her secateurs. 'Kill him.' Not that she would ever get the chance: Gully, long since departed for the warmer climes and easy scoring of the Queensland coast, was already dead.

'What are you muttering about?' Ruby, who had come for a visit, raised her eyebrow in amusement.

'Nothing', Rachel snapped.

'Who are you going to kill?' She grinned at the thought of it.

'Gully, if you must know.'

'Good grief, are you still thinking about him? He's dead. You're damned lucky he left you.' She frowned. 'Why are you still angry with him?'

'You know very well why.'

'No. Why?'

Rachel paused for a moment, then blurted it out.

'Gully is the one who gave you a taste for heroin, isn't he? He's the one who got you started.'

Ruby's peals of laughter were completely without guile; she was so thoroughly entertained by her mother's remarks that Rachel began to prickle with discomfort.

'Oh, Mama. You take the cake, really you do. Gully? I would never have done drugs with that old fart. Is that what you've been thinking all these years?' She could not stop laughing. 'Don't you think I have my own friends? I told you, someone gave it to me at a party.'

'Who?'

Ruby became wary, though not enough stop her laughter.

'No one you're likely to know. My only friends you'd know

these days are Rhea and Josh, and neither of them use. Anyway, it's a bit late in the day to worry about that, isn't it?'

'Was it Claudine?'

Might as well throw in the lot.

Ruby strolled from the garden into the livingroom, chuckling in wonder at her mother's foolishness.

— o —

Look at her slipping away. She comes and she goes, in and out of her haze. Wired. Ready to pounce should a tone of voice hint at displeasure, if a look is awry, a body movement suggest disapproval. Alert to every nuance.

'What's the matter?' and 'Is something wrong?'

The perennial questions.

'Nothing. Nothing's the matter,' and 'I'm fine. Fine. Really.'

The perennial answers.

Look at the damage she does to her body.

Overeating and starving. Two sides of the same coin.

Chain-smoking. The air foggy, acrid-smelling, hazy grey with cigarette smoke. Smokescreens. Clouding the issue. Sucking for succour. Sucking, sucking, sucking.

She burnt herself on the iron.

Cut herself while chopping food.

Fell off her bike.

Fell down the walkway at the railway station.

Gashed her skin on the thorns of the lemon tree when picking fruit.

Scored her flesh with the tip of a steel nailfile, just to punish her body, just to feel . . . something, anything. Anything but this interminable fucking flatness.

At the supermarket or the convenience store late at night, confused. 'Why am I here?' Buying anything—pet food (she had no pets), tins of creamed corn (the smell and texture of which made her gag), chocolate, detergent, cigarettes—anything, so as not to be conspicuous in her bewilderment.

Passing entire weekends in pyjamas grown rank with use: not bathing, not brushing her hair, her teeth, not dressing, nor putting on makeup.

Sleeping. Hour upon hour of sleeping. Sleeping away the dread, the self-loathing. Sleeping away her life.

Wait! Stop. Stop! Who are we talking about? Rachel or Ruby?

Why, both, of course. Watch them. Look at them go. Plummeting. Spiralling down, down. The one as out of control as the other.

Is there no difference between them? No difference at all?

Only in the substance of their addictions.

Only that? That is all?

All right. All right, then. Ruby's addiction is potentially fatal; she might die.

Might not Rachel also die?

In spirit, yes. In this she is already dead. Such is the nature of addiction. For many years the death of the spirit will go unremarked, be ignored. There is so much rationale or dope available to fill the chasm created by the loss of spirit that the addict need neither acknowledge nor confront its absence. Not that one goes looking. The territory of loss is too painful, too dangerous. On this terrain is found the ineluctable obligation to examine behaviour, to survey cause.

If one were to search this landscape, one may be required to ask, 'Why?' Why is my life permeated with unrequited longing? And ask, 'What?' What was it I wanted for my life that seems always to elude me? And ask, 'How?' How did I arrive at this desolate place?

Unthinkable to search, impossible to question.

Too painful.

Too dangerous.

— o —

Which didn't mean she didn't have some answers.

Rachel yearned for a normal relationship with her daughter, whatever that might be. If pressed, she would have said she imagined it to be like a good friendship: confidants, laughing at jokes, sharing secrets, being wry about the vagaries of life, gossiping about members of their family, ironic about their men. To enjoy shopping together from time to time, an afternoon spent painting, or seeing a film, perhaps discussing books they had read or comparing the music they were listening to that week. Once a week, a coffee in Brunswick Street, for a change at Pellegrini's, or somewhere in St Kilda, followed by a walk along the beach.

Did she not have that?

Some; she wanted more.

You want more? Tell us, Rachel, what more do you want?

Nothing. Only that.

Only that?

I want my daughter to have a good life.

Is it for you to decide what her life will be? Come, Rachel. What is it you want?

I want her to be happy.

Happy?

Forget it. Nothing. Really. That's all.

That's all? What of your own life?

That's all.

Say it, demonic voices whispered. Squealing voices, rapid. Rewinding tape of a telephone answering machine. Fast backwards. Insistent screech of a Vinyl record pushed back and forth on a turntable. Background rhythm. Backbeat. Integral elements.

Whispering voices of her own need, they cried out to her, yowled and moaned; they craved fulfilment.

It was not yet time.

ELI

'A man ain't nothing but a man', said Baby Suggs. 'But a son? Well now, that's somebody.'

Toni Morrison, *Beloved*

Jack stands at the gate holding a piece of paper torn from a book. He looks hurt and is crying.

'Why didn't you tell me you felt all these things about me?' he asks, waving the piece of paper in the air. 'Why did you pretend to love me? I'm taking the children away. I won't permit them to live with you any more.'

Jack starts bundling two young boys dressed in Melbourne Grammar uniforms into a large, silvery-gold Volvo.

Rachel is embarrassed that Jack has found what she wrote about him and upset that he has misinterpreted it. She puts her arms around him to give him a hug, difficult to do as he's wearing a very thick, metallic-grey overcoat, beautifully cut and made of fine-quality wool. But Jack is very angry; as Rachel tries to hug him, he shakes her off.

The older of the boys is already in the car. The other, Eli, is indecisive; he doesn't know whether to get into the car or not.

'Get into the car, at once', Jacks commands.

'Jack, please, don't take the children. Please', Rachel beseeches him.

Eli is crying. He looks from one parent to the other as they argue.
'Mummy, Daddy says I have to get in the car and go with him.'
'Do you want to go with him?'
'Yes', Eli snivels. 'But I want to stay with you, too.'
Rachel becomes angry and slaps the boy in the face.
'Then go, you snivelling little shit, you traitor.'
Eli yowls.

Jack steers him into the back of the car, as commodious as a London taxi, where the older boy is sitting upright, staring straight ahead, his hands clasped on his lap.

As Jack closes the car door, Rachel thinks spitefully, You look like a bloody hotel porter in your long coat.

She watches as the car pulls away. Eli's tearful face is pressed up against the back window where a patch of condensation formed by his warm weepy breath surrounds his head like a halo.

— o —

Eli. As handsome as could be and on the tall side. Thick curly hair the colour of burnished copper. Pale ginger-brown freckles liberally sprinkled over his face and hands; they spanned his shoulders.

Eli never called her Mum. Or Mama.

'Rachel,' he would say, 'what's for tea?' or 'I'll do my homework after *Dr Who*, Rachel.'

'Your son should show more respect,' Nate disapproved with a short burst of Spitfire.

'I don't mind, Papa', Rachel replied. 'In fact I rather like it.'

'It wouldn't have happened in my day, Rachel. The child would have been given a thick ear.'

'Papa, this is no longer your day. Besides, he could call me Mum and still be disrespectful.'

'It's not right.' Nate made a Messerschmitt. He considered his daughter's response impudent and unwise; he let her know his feelings by rarely missing an opportunity to question her authority.

— o —

At the age of eleven, Eli became a vegetarian. Following a rationale sophisticated for one so young—'Just because humans think they are the highest form of life, it doesn't give them the right to kill animals and eat them'—he refused to ever again eat his fellow creatures. Neither fish, nor fowl, nor beasts of the field.

The year he turned fourteen he secured new employment. Rachel offered to pay him to work as an odd-jobber in her burgeoning nursery and in the household garden.

'I might as well keep it in the family', she said. 'Have a think about it, Eli. Let me know by the end of the week if you would like the job.'

'How much will you pay me?'

She offered a reasonable hourly rate.

'How many hours a day?'

'One and a half. No more. You'll have homework to do, and friends—'

'I'll take it', he interrupted.

'Are you sure? You wouldn't like to think about it a bit longer?'

'No. I'm sure. I'm sick of the greengrocer's and I'd rather do gardening than a paper round. Spiro does one. He has to get up at five o'clock every morning. Even in the winter. Brrrrr.' He hugged himself against the imaginary cold. 'This'd be good.'

Rachel was pleased. She had offered the job to Ruby, who remained happy with the work she had been employed in for more than a year: after school, Ruby spent two hours a day, three days a week, and an occasional Saturday morning at an art supplies shop in Fitzroy. 'Let's begin on Monday. We'll give it a one-month trial. How does that sound?'

She started him off scrubbing the plastic pots in the stainless-steel trough. When he finished washing them, she showed him where they were to be stacked.

'Keep an eye out for redbacks,' she warned, 'they seem to like it around here.'

Rachel taught him the herbs: how to identify them by their shapes and colours, by the textures of their leaves, their smells. Breaking off a leaf, she squeezed it until its juice ran, then held it under his nose. Reticent at first, he put his nostrils to her fingertips to sniff.

'Oh, that's not too bad, is it?' became his most frequent response. As he became less tentative Rachel invited him to taste as well.

She imparted information about therapeutic uses, taught him when and at what angle to prune with secateurs, and the best way to build up the compost with the clippings.

'Nothing need be wasted', she instructed.

When she felt Eli had a grasp of what had to be done in the nursery, she introduced him to the greater complexities of her cottage garden: how to mulch with a combination of peastraw, old newspapers and the compost he'd built up in the brick boxes that stood along the fence, the difference between weeds and seedlings, when to dig up bulbs, how to store them and when to replant, when to collect, dry and store seed from flowers and vegetables. She taught him recipes for non-toxic sprays.

'And when to pick flowers,' he said one spring afternoon. 'Here, Rachel, these are for you.'

He handed her a small bunch of freesias.

In the daylight-saving hours, Ruby brought her art materials out to the shed or the garden table when she came home from work. Some evenings, Rachel downed tools and joined her. Sitting quietly on a bench, Ruby sketched Rachel and Eli as they worked in the nursery or the garden. Some of the sketches became a series of oil paintings which she called *Familia botanica*.

'I didn't know you knew any Latin.'

Ruby raised her eyebrows. 'There are probably lots of things you don't know about me, Mum', she said, chortling at her mother's frown.

Rachel's early trepidation that Eli would come home one day and say he'd found another job, that he no longer wanted to work for her, soon evaporated. Eli proved to be a stayer, diligent in performing his tasks and broadening his knowledge about the finer points of tending and propagating plants.

Rachel enjoyed working with him. He gossiped about children at school, praised or complained about teachers, boasted of his scholastic achievements and sporting prowess. They groaned at each other's choice of music, and settled on a day-on, day-off arrangement. If the days of Eli's turn coincided with Ruby's presence, Rachel and Ruby could sometimes cajole him out of his selections. Not often. He became obstinate, forcing them to suffer the heavy metal or punk he favoured. It seemed little enough to pay for his company.

Eli worked in Rachel's employ until he turned eighteen, by which time the pleasure had gone out it for both of them; they performed their tasks mechanically, the silences lacking the companionship of the early days. By the time Eli had turned eighteen, Rachel had disappeared into another world, a world in which there was no place for him.

— o —

Eli developed a passion for football memorabilia. His bedroom became a storehouse of collectables: cards, posters, every issue of the *Football Record*, and the newspaper teasers displayed in wire frames in front of the newsagent's, which Spiro collected for him.

Each night after dinner, Eli shut himself in his room, there to cut from newspapers and magazines anything to do with his team, Fitzroy, and any of his second-string heroes. He joined the Fitzroy Football Club Cheer Squad, and went to the clubrooms on Friday nights to help make the banner that the squad held aloft in all its primary coloured glory for the players to burst through on wintry Saturday afternoons.

Eli was undecided about joining a team; playing on Saturday afternoons meant he would be unable to attend Fitzroy's matches.

'What do you think I should do, Rachel?'

'What about baseball? They play on Sundays.'

'I'll give it a go.'

A local team gave him a tryout and signed him up. Rachel rearranged his work schedule to enable him to attend practice twice a week. The Sunday games freed him to ride his bicycle to all corners of the city to watch his beloved Fitzroy play on Saturday afternoons.

— o —

One of their most memorable arguments was over a handful of football cards. Annoyed at how untidy his room had been for so long, Rachel asked him to clean it up.

'It's my room, Rachel. You always say our bedrooms are our own spaces and that we can keep them how we like.'

'Indeed I do, Eli, but this has gone too far. There is an orange rotting somewhere in here. It stinks. Your baseball boots are smelly, too, and your clothes are all over the place. I want you to clean up your room.'

'I'm sorting my footy cards. I'll do it later.'

'Now, please!'

'Why does it matter when I do it, Rachel?'

'Because I can smell the mouldy orange in the hall. You can't even see the carpet in here for all that football rubbish.'

He muttered under his breath.

'What did you say?' Her voice rose.

'Nothing.'

Rachel bent and picked up a handful of cards.

'This seems to be all you have time for, Eli', she said, waving the cards at him. 'These and baseball. I want you to clean up this room, and find that stinking orange. Put your socks into the wash, get those smelly boots out on the back porch, and tidy up all this football crap. Now!'

'It's not crap!'

'It is crap!' With that, she tore the cards she was holding into little pieces and threw them up in the air. Even before she finished destroying them, her heart was sinking, but it was too late to turn back. 'See! Crap. Rubbish.'

Eli stared in disbelief, his gaze following the pieces as they fluttered to the floor.

'You bitch!' he yelled at her, tears welling in his eyes. 'They were my best ones. They were the most valuable ones.'

'Don't you *dare* speak to me like that! Apologise.'

'No. I'll never be able to replace them. I hate you!'

'Tough. Now do as you're told.'

Rachel slammed out; Eli locked himself in.

'I quit!' he shouted after her. 'I'm not going to work for you any more.'

'Fine with me', she called back, hoping he didn't hear the

disappointment in her voice, hoping it was only his anger speaking.

True to his word, Eli did not return to the nursery. He left his room only to go to school and baseball practice. When Rachel called him at mealtimes, he refused to come. Eli's red plastic lunchbox, which Rachel packed with two sandwiches, a slice of cake and two pieces of fruit for his school lunch (a task he usually performed himself), was left untouched on the kitchen bench. Rachel worried that he was starving himself just to punish her.

'What do you think I should do about this?' she asked Jerry.

'Leave him be. He'll settle down.'

At dinnertime, Rachel called Ruby and said, 'Ruby, tell Eli dinner is ready, please.'

'He won't come.'

Ruby was enthralled by the proceedings; her grin was devilish.

'Tell him anyway.'

When Ruby knocked on Eli's door, Rachel realised they had a code. From behind the closed door she heard muffled giggles.

Cheeky buggers.

It did not take long for her to realise Ruby was slipping food to Eli.

'Mum, may I have some more dessert?'

Ruby was dieting this week ... 'Sure, Rube. Yoghurt?' ... which meant she was off cream.

'Mmm. Cream. Heaps, please. May I eat it in my room while I do my homework?'

'Very well. Remember to bring the plate out when you've finished.'

'Okay.'

Rachel heard bedroom windows being raised; the thud of shoes and knees knocking against windowsills was followed by a loud, 'Ouch!' then by rustling in the garden outside their rooms and choked laughter.

Time to end the impasse.

Three days after the argument Rachel bought a postcard she happened upon in a bookshop on Rathdowne Street. On the front was a naive watercolour painting of a group of Fitzroy foot-ballers at play, one of whom was marking the ball. On the back of the card she wrote an apology, told Eli she missed him and dropped the card into the letterbox at the local post office. When the postman delivered it back to their house the next day she slipped it under Eli's door, hoping he would find it. That night, Eli joined the others at the dinner table.

'Welcome back, Eli. It's a pleasure to have you at dinner with us again.'

'Aha. The return of Babe Ruth', observed Jerry, smiling his welcome.

'Yes, Ee, welcome back', echoed Ruby, grinning at him.

'I'm sorry I tore your cards, Eli.'

'You said that in your card, Rachel.'

'Well, I wanted to say it to you personally.'

'Thanks.'

'Can I replace them for you? Is there anywhere I can buy them?'

'No. I told you when you tore them up, they were special. There's nowhere you can buy them.'

Stinker.

'Then all I can say is I'm sorry again.'

Ruby watched them, her head moving from left to right and back again, an expectant look on her face. Her gaze settled on Eli. A smile played on his lips, crinkled the corners of his eyes.

'What you could get me instead . . .' he drawled, looking up from under his long lashes.

The unfinished sentence floated in the space between them for a second or two, then, all eyes on Rachel, everyone burst out laughing, Ruby loudest of all.

'Yea, Eli!' she whooped, clapping her hands above her head. 'Go, Ee!'

'Well done, Eli', Jerry approved.

Rachel spent more than was necessary on some additions to his collection and the dust settled. But the argument—or, more particularly, her part in it—never left her. Tearing up his cards became one of the many misdemeanours with which she lacerated herself during the nights when guilt overtook her ability to sleep.

After school the next day, Eli sauntered into the garden. 'What's to be done around here?' he asked. 'Looks like you need a hand.'

Rachel looked up from her task and pointed him in the direction of the scarlet runner beans.

'Why don't you pick us some beans for tonight's dinner', she suggested.

He nodded and went into the kitchen to fetch a colander, fully aware, Rachel felt sure, that a contented smile lit up her face as she watched his departing back.

— o —

At about the time Eli was seventeen he began to withdraw his affection from her. Puzzled, and hurt, Rachel queried his silence.

'Is something the matter, sweetheart?'

His reply was always the same.

'No. Nothing.'

There seemed to be little Rachel could do to please him. In an attempt to ingratiate herself, she suggested she come to one of his baseball matches.

'You don't have to come, Rachel', he'd said, annoyed. 'I know you're not interested.'

'No, I want to come.'

'You do not!'

He rode off to the match without her.

'Want to come?' she asked Jerry.

'No thanks. Baseball's boring.'

'Thanks, Jerry.'

Now she had committed herself she felt obliged to go. Not knowing any of the other parents and too reserved with strangers to make their acquaintance, Rachel stood alone against the perimeter fence, shivering in the blow of the southerly, resenting Jack for never being available to go to Eli's games, and ruing the lie that brought her to this cold and windy field.

After the game, Eli ignored her; he remained in a state of mute hostility for the rest of the day and into the night.

'What about a nice cup of hot chocolate?'

'No thanks.'

'Are you angry because I don't come to your baseball matches often enough? Is that what it is?'

'No. I told you. It's nothing.'

— o —

'I'm not going to uni next year', Eli announced one night before the last of his final-year exams.

'What will you do?'

'Take a year off. Muck around. Angelo and I have been talking about going bush together. I think I'll defer for a year.'

'That sounds like fun. After twelve years at school, having a year off is a good idea. Where will you go?'

'Follow the coast west and stay south during the wet. Around April we'll drive north and after that head into the desert. Probably finish up in the Alice, then come home through Mildura and the Wimmera.'

He had saved enough money to buy a serviceable station-wagon. After one month of intense tinkering with the motor, Eli and Angelo loaded the car with food, clothes, cassettes, a football, a Frisbee and Angelo's dog Moosh, and went bush where, for ten months, they took on whatever work was offered them: they jackarooed, pulled beers, served petrol, oil, food and soft drinks at a general store, picked fruit, and laboured as part of a gang mending a road in the Centre. They even worked a coconut shy and mucked out animal cages in a travelling carnival.

Rachel missed him. He wrote her a postcard once in a while from pinpricks on the map, now and again from one of the big towns: Whyalla, Coober Pedy, Kalgoorlie, Karratha, Broome. Rachel rolled the words around in her mouth: Kar-rah-thah, Coo-ber-Pee-dee, Why-a-lah. She imagined the spectacle of colour and light, the expanse of the land they travelled through.

Esther phoned. She had seen an ad in a glossy travel magazine.

'They're running a feature on the western deserts this month.'

Rachel asked the newsagent to deliver the journal with the morning paper.

'Each month?' he asked.

'God no, Alb. Just the current issue, thanks.'

When it arrived, she pored over its pages. She wondered if Eli and Angelo had been to this place or that, or might yet get to it. She gazed wistfully at photos of Coober Pedy, Karratha.

In early November the boys returned to Melbourne. Eli began work pulling beers in a bar, biding his time until he started his journalism course, when he expected to find other students to share a house with. To save money, he moved in with Rachel and Jerry.

Eli was uncommunicative and reclusive when he was at home; he went out often. Conversation was polite but distant. It saddened her. When she complained about this state of affairs to Jerry, he became irritated with her.

'For goodness sake, Rachel. He's nineteen, he's travelled around the country, earned his own money for years, even if it was from you. Leave him be. Let them go. Let them get on with their lives. What do you want from them?'

Good question, Jer.

On the phone to Esther, Rachel complained, 'He doesn't want to know about his mother any more.'

'*Ekh*. It's a stage. Everything will be all right. You'll see. Zev and Henry were like that.'

'A stage', Rachel murmured. 'Maybe, but it feels more like smouldering rage.'

So blind was Rachel that she was unable to recognise the graph of Eli's retreat: its curve, had she cared to notice, could be charted in direct response to the rise of Ruby's use of drugs and Rachel's corresponding obsession. As the two women moved closer together in their madness, Eli—not without a measure of gratitude—was left out of their lives.

'I wonder where Ruby—?' Rachel began one day.

'Ruby, Ruby, Ruby!' Eli shouted. 'That's all I ever hear around here. I'm sick to fucking death of it!'

— o —

A photographer friend of Jack's shot some portraits of Eli covering the spectrum of his personality. Smiling, Rachel took the flesh of his cheek between her thumb and forefinger and waggled it.

'Oh, Eli, *du bist ayn mensh*. A prince, you are. So handsome.' He blushed. 'What are they for?' Rachel asked, setting them out in two neat rows on the kitchen table.

'I thought I might have a go at modelling.' His look was at once challenging and shy. 'I've been thinking about it for a while. It's decent money and I think I could do it without losing study time.'

'Modelling', Rachel said, alarmed.

Models use cocaine, speed, pills. Not on your bloody life! Not my son. Not both children.

'Do you think that's a good idea?'

'Why wouldn't it be?'

'Oh, you know.' She tried to sound knowledgeable, nonchalant. 'Erratic hours, lousy pay for beginners. Only a few make it, you know.'

He glared at her.

'So what? Jack said I have a chance. And it would be better money than what I'm earning waiting on drunks.'

'I suppose so. It's . . . well, there are so many superficial people in that industry, Eli.'

'How would you know that, Rachel? Hey? How would you bloody well know?' he yelled. 'You're such a snob.'

'Well, it's up to you of course, but—'

'But what? Damn you, Rachel!'

Eli gathered up his photos and stormed out of the room. It was never discussed again, but Rachel was sure he didn't submit his photos to any agencies.

Many years later, he dropped in to wish her happy birthday.

'I know you always wanted one of these', he'd said. 'Take your pick.'

Surprised—and delighted—Rachel selected her two favourites.

'You know, Eli, I always felt awful about talking you out of trying to be a model.'

'If I'd wanted to do it,' he said bravely, 'I would have done it, Rachel. It wasn't your fault.'

'I always felt it was. I did it because . . .'

She began to cry softly. Eli wrapped his arms around her and held her to his chest.

'I was afraid you'd get into drugs.'

'Drugs.'

They said the word together.

'You knew?'

'Yes.'

Her crying grew louder.

'I couldn't have stood it if both my kids were on dope.'

Eli stroked his mother's hair.

'There was never any chance of that, Rachel. None. You should have trusted me.'

— o —

Ruby came to lunch with Greg. They were stoned. Eli and Rachel cast looks at each other.

'Smack', Eli muttered when the couple went out to the garden. 'Why do you let them come here stoned? I hate seeing her like that.'

'I don't like it either, Eli. But what can I do?'

'What do you mean? It's your house. Ask them to leave. Tell her not to come here like that.'

'I can't', she whimpered.

'Why not?'

'What if she never came back?'

'Don't be pathetic. She would eventually. Aren't you worried about her?'

'You know I am, but what can I do? She's twenty-one. Whenever I try to talk to her about it, we fight.'

'So what?'

'Hush. They'll hear you. We'll talk about this later.'

'I don't give a damn if they hear me! You always say you're going to talk to her but you never do.' He paused to consider. 'I'm leaving.'

'Where are you going? I'm about to serve lunch.'

'Out. I don't want to be here. You should kick them out. They're off their faces!'

'Oh, Eli.'

'Don't "Oh, Eli" me, Rachel. She's got a problem, big time, and you don't want to see it.'

'No. No, she hasn't. They probably had a joint.'

'You have done such a job on yourself, Rachel. Just look at them. They're on more than grass.'

'What are you two squabbling about?' Ruby smiled at them as she came into the kitchen; Greg followed her inside.

'Nothing', Rachel said. 'We're just getting lunch ready.'

Eli glared at her. Turning to Ruby, he said, 'I have to go out. I'll see you later, Ruby, Greg.'

He kissed Ruby affectionately and squeezed her arm, nodded to Rachel and Greg. He rolled his eyes at Jerry, who had drifted into the room. Then he left the house.

'What's wrong with him?' Ruby asked.

Rachel was relieved that neither Ruby nor Greg seemed to have heard their conversation.

'Nothing. He's fine. Let's eat.'

Ruby stared at her, but did not pursue the matter.

Later that night, when Eli returned, Rachel spoke to him.

'Ruby will be fine, Eli. She probably had a joint. I just hope Greg doesn't take her in too deep. I don't like him.'

'He's not such a bad bloke. Anyway, Rachel, you can't blame him. You can't force someone to use it.'

Rachel ignored his commonsense.

'Do you think she'll get into the other stuff?' she asked, as if she'd heard nothing Eli said.

'What are you talking about?'

'You know . . .' she could barely bring herself to say the word, '. . . heroin.'

'Are you mad? Didn't you hear what I said earlier? Can't you see anything? What do you think she's on now? Look,' he tried a different tack, 'I know this must be difficult for you, Rachel, but . . .' He put his hands on her shoulders.

'Not that.' Her voice was whispery desperate, pleading. In slow motion, she shook her head from side to side.

Eli glared at her; he always seemed to be glaring at her.

'Christ, Rachel, how can you deceive yourself this way?'

'Oh God, Eli. I don't want it to be true', she moaned.

He stared at her in disbelief.

'Get real, Rachel. Ruby is on heroin. She's hooked! I know it's sad, but face it. She's a junkie!'

'Do not ever use that word in my presence', she screamed at him.

As it had once been to Esther it was now clear to Eli he would get no further. He turned away from Rachel and went to his room.

Weeks passed and at last, to Rachel's relief, Eli's glaring

ceased. But her relief was tinged with sorrow: the glaring ceased because Eli was no longer there.

— o —

Soon after Eli's journalism course commenced he moved out. It wasn't the sort of departure Rachel had fantasised, not the teenager's leave-taking she'd seen in television commercials or those cheerful American sitcoms that so seduced her into fantasies of what-life-might-have-been-like-if-only . . .

They'd had an argument. Later, she could not recall what it was about, only that it had been fierce and bitter.

Eli loaded his things into the stationwagon and onto the roof-rack; what couldn't be squeezed into his own car, he loaded into Jerry's. Rachel stood at the gate, tears rolling down her cheeks, as he climbed into his car. He leant forward to give her a terse nod and drove off; Jerry drove into line behind him.

'He didn't kiss me', she whispered as she stared at the two sets of tail lights disappearing down the street.

Eli rarely called; he didn't visit. If Rachel missed him when he went bush with Angelo, now his absence left her desolate. She wept often and considered her role as a mother in a grim light; she continued to fret about Ruby. Disturbing dreams left her fearful and exhausted.

'You're grieving', Esther pronounced. 'Phone him. You don't have to sit around waiting.'

'He might think I'm spying on him.'

Esther laughed. 'Don't be pathetic. Is he your son or your husband?'

Rachel's cheeks reddened; she was grateful Esther couldn't see her. That night, when she came in from work, she phoned.

'Hello, Eli. I'm missing you something fierce. Would you like to come to dinner?'

She heard the reserve in his voice.

'Thank you, Rachel. Tuesday after baseball practice. Will Jerry be there?'

'I'll make sure he is.'

Rachel awaited his visit with keen anticipation, rehearsing conversations from which she hoped she could keep Ruby's name. By the appointed night, her nerves were in tatters.

Eli arrived bearing a bunch of tulips; he knew her fondness for them and her frustrating inability to grow them. He kissed Rachel, shook Jerry's hand and hugged him. Twenty minutes into their meal, the phone rang.

'Hello, Ruby. I'm fine, thanks. How are you?'

Rachel dared not look at Eli.

'No, Ruby, I can't.'

Behind her, she heard the thrumming of fingers on the table.

'No, I said. No! Oh damn you, Ruby, how much?'

'Bloody hell!' Eli exploded.

'You will have to come here to get it. Eli's ... he's fine ... he's ...'

Rachel forced herself to turn in the direction where Eli and Jerry sat. Eli glowered, contemptuous; Jerry appeared indifferent.

'... here for dinner.'

'Come on, Rachel,' Eli growled, 'dinner is getting cold.'

'Won't be long', Rachel mouthed at him. Then: 'Can't you get a tax—No, Ruby. I— no, I ca— oh, damn you.'

The thrumming came to an abrupt halt. There was a short silence, followed by the heavy thud of a palm slapped against wood. Eli's chair scraped on the floor then clattered as it fell against the wall. He stood up, red-faced.

'Damn you!' he bellowed. 'Damn *you*, Rachel!' As he strode past the bench, he grabbed the vase of tulips and flung the lot at the wall. Water and blooms flew everywhere, the vase smashed into fragments. 'I'm leaving.'

'No, Eli, stay. Please, Eli. Jerry, get him back.'

Jerry shrugged.

'Just wait there, Ruby. I'll be back in a moment.'

Rachel was frantic. This was not how she had rehearsed it. Damn Ruby for ringing tonight. Damn her for needing money tonight.

'Eli!' she called in the direction of the hallway. Then, back into the phone again, 'Ruby, are you still there? Hold on. I'll be back in a minute.'

There was no sign of him. Not even his tail lights glowing in the night. Rachel ran back to the kitchen where Jerry sat eating his dinner. Resigned and resentful, Rachel picked up the phone and sighed. 'Okay, Ruby. Tell me where you are.'

Eli's housemates were polite and solicitous each time Rachel called. 'I'm sorry, Rachel, Eli is out. Would you like to leave a message?'

'Yes. Tell him . . . tell him I would like to talk to him. Ask him to ring me, please.'

Yes. Tell him I love him. Tell him I am sorry. For everything.

Eli did not return her calls, not for many years.

Ay, Eli. I miss you so.

Synonymy

Synonymy (sino-nimi). 1609. (–late L. synony-
mia—. . . **2.** The use of synonyms or of words
as synonyms; spec. a rhetorical figure by
which synonyms are used for the sake of
amplification 1657.

Shorter Oxford English Dictionary on Historical Principles

Dark as its implications might be, Rachel conceded that the
nomenclature of illegal drug use was not without flair. The parlance had edge, bite.

Language of the netherworld.

This jargon entered Rachel's conversation just as it entered
the conversations of people everywhere. The words became commonplace in books, newspapers and films, on radio and
television. Such was the nature of the times in which she lived.

Usage was employed in sentences that varied in tone according to the context and the speaker: savvy or threatening,
righteous or fearful, glib, anguished. Bravado was not unusual.

On the street Rachel turned her head sharply in the direction
of the words. When she overheard shoppers speaking them, *sotto
voce*, at the supermarket, she would slow her trolley, feign interest in the colourfully packaged products surrounding her and
listen to their conversations.

She strained to hear.

Rachel felt a strong connection to these women—they were usually women—with their sad and worried faces, their angry voices often laced with pain. She wanted to speak to them, suggest they meet. Together they could pour out their bile, their sorrow, and in so doing, rid themselves of it once and for all. Perhaps. 'Hello,' she would like to have said, 'we don't know each other, but I couldn't help overhearing. We seem to have something in common', attempting to make light of it.

She struggled to speak; she kept her mouth shut.

In cafes, too, she eavesdropped, leaning back into her chair, or sitting sideways, affecting nonchalance, eager to imbibe—discreetly, of course—the full context of her neighbours' exchange in the hope she might learn something more about the canvas of Ruby's life, on each occasion terrified she might overhear Ruby's name mentioned in a stranger's conversation.

The language was used in the homes of friends and acquaintances, in the design studio where she continued to work, and by her freelance clients. Even her elderly parents, remote from the world of substance abuse (though not so remote as they imagined), learned to use the language with such alacrity that on hearing either or both of them expressing a opinion on, say, whether or not heroin use should be decriminalised (it should), whether or not addiction was an illness (it was), whether or not one ought feel compassion for addicts (one ought), the listener could be forgiven for thinking this debate had always been a part of their lives.

In Rachel's imagination, the argot took on physical form: language devoid of drug references she saw as the rich yellow batter of a butter cake into which she poured, then folded (with a wooden spoon) lustrous dark chocolate batter, the parlance—and life—of addiction. At first, the two batters retained their individual colours, their sheen, as she wove them, one through the other, in thick, glossy ribbons. But the longer she folded, the more the batters merged. Gone the gloss, gone the clarity; all that remained was a dull, muddy mess.

— o —

One brooding, restless day, for no reason she could think of—unless it was that seeing the words in print might make something more solid of Ruby's life—Rachel came in from the garden and went in search of explanations in the dictionary.

As she removed the dictionary from the bookcase, she remembered another time when, at the age of fourteen, she removed her parents' *Webster's* from the shelf. An American dictionary with a hard, caramel-coloured cover, its pages were made of flimsy paper that rustled like dry leaves when she turned them. Each page was enhanced with a line drawing, pictorial descriptions of one of the words on the page. Black dividers, thumb-pad sized and shaped like half-moons, separated each section where the beginnings of words changed letters. Embossed in gold on each divider was the appropriate letter of the alphabet.

Rachel's teenage reading of the *Webster's* was an expedition to discover the meaning of the sex words. To discover what sex meant. She hoped the *Webster's* would unravel this mystery, shed light on the secrets whispered by older children at school, reveal what they giggled about in groups behind cupped hands.

The American dictionary had let her down. The few words she found in its pages were clinical, restrained; bereft of heat, they lacked excitement. And why would they not? It was, after all, a dictionary, not a handbook on sex.

— o —

In the *Australian Concise Oxford Dictionary* Rachel read the entry for the word **addict** person addicted to a habit, esp. one dependent on a (specific) drug.

Straightforward enough. But the parlance of drug use is more codified, more sectarian: them and us.

Junkie, user, dope fiend, doper, druggie, head, hophead, hammerhead, mainliner and space cadet were some of the names she knew for heroin users.

Snow drifter, snowball, snowflake, flakehead, coke head and tooter were appellations for those who indulged in cocaine (coke, blow, snow, *et al.*).

For amphetamine users, a shorter list: speedster, road runner, speed freak.

Gluehead. Petrolhead. Unimaginative words for a truly desperate lot. And, of course, pillheads. If there were more for these groups, Rachel did not know them.

Head, pothead, dopehead, dope freak, smoker were reserved for those who enjoyed marijuana (dope, grass, green, gunja, reefer, weed) and hash[ish].

Rachel looked up from the dictionary, smiling at a memory.

You were a pothead, Rachel.

Hashish. The smell of it came to her now, as tangible as if she were smoking a joint (a joint, a number, a jay, a log) at that very moment. She breathed the aromatic memory of the thinly curling smoke into her nostrils, drew it into her lungs and held fast. Ah, how she enjoyed it.

There she sat, at the kitchen table, a four-paper joint splayed open, spread from one end to the other with tobacco, ready to receive the hash. The texture of the lump of black, sticky resin skewered on the end of a pearl-knobbed hatpin was almost tangible, the look of pleasurable anticipation on her face as clear as crystal.

Then came the scratchy sound of cheap metal as a cigarette lighter's ratchet spun, or the resounding flick of a Zippo, followed by a strong whiff of lighter fluid. Or the smell might be the sulphuric stink of a struck match.

The flame. Did she move the hash to the flame, or was the movement in the other direction? The precise details of this aspect were a fog. She shrugged: unimportant.

Both elbows resting on the table—she remembered that. She stays her hand, delaying—briefly—the moment of heating the resin and savouring its heady, seductive perfume. Removing the warm, softened lump from the end of the hatpin, delicately, slowly, rolling it first into a ball then pressing it between thumb and forefinger into the shape of a miniature pancake before crumbling it onto the joint that lay in readiness on the tablecloth.

Rolling up the joint, cone-shaped—whippet thin at one end, wide at the other. Sliding the tip of her tongue along the sourish glue of the cigarette papers. Don't forget the filter. Wouldn't want to lose a piece of hash down your throat. Choke on a lump of hash! Ha ha. What a way to go! Curling up a slice of cardboard torn from the packet of cigarette papers and poking it into the thin end of the joint with the hatpin or a match.

Sniff the joint. Savour the fragrance. Fellate the cone,

moistening the paper to impede the burning, prolong the pleasure. Slowly. In and out of her wet lips.

Lighting up. Eyes hooded as she strikes the lighter alive again,
teasing the end of the joint, bringing the flame close, distancing
it, drawing it near again, close enough to singe the papers, burn
off any untidy loose threads of tobacco.

Unable to stay her hand any longer, she secures the narrow
end between her lips and, holding the flame steady, sucks hard,
reels with pleasure as the sweet heaviness of the burning hash
envelops her, fills her up.

— o —

Rachel broke out of her reverie and realised she was clutching
the dictionary hard against her chest. It felt leaden in her arms.
Loosening her grip on the book, she sat down, placed the *Oxford*
square in the middle of the table and continued her reading.

Heroin is a sedative addictive drug prepared from and acting like
morphine, illicitly used to produce intense euphoria.

An equally intense euphoria is produced if the sedative addictive drug is called horse, aitch, shit, scag, junk, hammer, smack,
the hard stuff and monkey.

Même chose.

Spike once offered her a taste. He slipped a tiny plastic bag
from his shirt pocket and caressed it between his fingers.

'Here, Rachel, taste this. See if you like it.'

It might have been her mother offering her a sample of a new
recipe she had just cooked up.

'No. No thanks.' She shook her head, emphatic.

'This one's on me,' he'd offered, thinking he understood her
refusal. 'You'll like it. Give it a burl.'

'Thanks, but no. It's not the money. I'm scared of needles', she
confided, unable to take her eyes off the little packet.

'No worries', he said, feigning casual. 'I'll roll you a smoke.'

'A smoke? I didn't know you could do it like that.' She had
not yet known about Claudine.

'Yeah. Lots of people don't like to jab, so they smoke it, or
snort. Have a go.' His movements were practised.

After a moment's hesitation, she took ... are these called
joints too? ... took it and drew on it as hard as she would a

cigarette. The twin effects of the drug soon took effect: its dream-like, euphoric embrace and nausea battled for ascendancy. Each time the nausea subsided Rachel floated, serene and carefree, shrouded in a welcome weightlessness.

'Oh,' she said to Spike, her voice dreamy, 'heaven must be like this.'

Isn't that what Jennifer Davis said?

'It's cool, eh? I knew you'd like it, Rachel.'

'You did?'

A wave of nausea washed over her.

'Yeah. I could tell. You'll be right', she heard Spike rabbiting on. 'Just takes a couple of goes and you don't get sick any more. You know, like when you had your first cig. Then it's all great after that.' He grinned.

Fucking idiot.

'Shut up, Spike.'

She'd had enough of him, wanted him to leave. It was enough that she felt obliged to have a joint with him from time to time. Socialise with your dealer to make sure he had some decent grass for you next time, assuage your guilt that the only relationship you had with him—wanted with him—was the score, an exchange of grass for dollars. Have a quick smoke (omitting the ritual, the sensuality) and send him, politely but firmly, on his way.

Nausea was overwhelming her. She staggered to the bathroom.

'You okay?' Spike called after her.

'Does it look like I'm okay?' she groaned.

'Yeah, well, I've gotta go, Rachel.' Spike was imperturbable. 'Let me know if you want to try again. I'll come around.'

I'll bet you will, Spike. How many times will you come around before it's not free any more? Next time? Or will it be the time after that? And then? How long will it take, Spike, before I can't live without it? How long before forever?

The slap of the flywire door was followed by the receding sound of Spike's boots crunching along the gravel path. She brushed her teeth, slowly, massaging the peppermint toothpaste around and around, spitting it out and starting again. Three times. When she finished brushing, she stood to a woozy attention and stared at herself in the mirror, concentrating her gaze.

Traces of euphoria lingered and she allowed herself to enjoy it. Over the top of the pleasure the clanging of alarm bells sounded.

'Now you know. You must never, ever touch this stuff again. Not ever. If you do, you will be lost. This is a substance you could fall in love with.'

The idea of a love affair with heroin frightened her. She understood herself well enough to know that's what it would have been. A love affair. At least to start with. And after the initial passion, what then? Once she got started, how would she ever be able to deny herself the bliss, the euphoria? That . . . that . . . mother's milk?

Wrapping herself in the loving comfort of heroin, her life out of control, the possibility of dying. Contemplation of the life disturbed Rachel more than the thought of being dead.

Ironic, isn't it, she mused bitterly, her forefinger still resting on the word 'heroin', the way things turn out?

She never mentioned the experience to anyone. Not to Jerry, not to Esther, nor to Grace. No one.

— o —

With all propriety, the *Oxford* explained that a **syringe** is a tube with nozzle and piston or bulb for drawing in liquid by suction and then ejecting it in fine stream, used in surgery, gardening, etc. Hmm. This seemed remiss, in that it omitted pick, hype, gear, outfit, fit, spike and works, and did not elucidate the many other uses to which the device might be put.

Regarding the word **injection**, the dictionary was circumspect, informing the enquiring reader that an injection is liquid or solution injected. Pointless to expect it would mention a hit, a blast, a shot, a boost, a fix, a pop or a whack. Or mainlining. All of which only serve to explain how a drug is injected into the body. Snorting—sniffing it up the nose (*aka* tooting)—and dropping (eating it) are also avenues of entry.

There exists a cornucopia of possibilities.

'Can you do it by absorption?' Rachel asked Spike that day she tried it.

'What do you mean?' He became attentive.

'You know. Like a smallpox vaccination. Pricking the skin and dropping it onto the site.' She giggled. 'Like an inoculation against life.'

Where there's a will . . .

Whacked, pinned, off one's face, off one's head, off the planet, on the nod, out of it, out to lunch, away with the pixies, dilated, coked, stoked, bent, ripped, flying or smashed were not to be found under the entry for **stoned**. What Rachel found there was this: **8.** Hence **(-)ston**ED[2] (-nd), followed by an entire column of entries of a geological nature.

— o —

Unsatisfied, listless, Rachel returns the *Oxford* to its place on the shelf. It has provided nothing in the way of illumination. As when she was a teenager looking for light to be shed on the meaning of sex, there has been, yet again, no gratification to be had from the exploration of a dictionary.

BOTANICA

Build houses, settle down; plant gardens and eat what they
produce . . .

Jeremiah 29:28

Gardening preoccupied her. At night, in bed, Rachel pored over
books, dog-eared pages bearing items of interest, and from them
made lists of plants she intended to purchase. Resigned to the
hours she was obliged to spend freelancing in design studios and
in her studio at home, Rachel put into the garden as many of
the remaining daylight hours and weekends as possible.

— o —

She began by pulling out everything planted by the previous
owner and paid a local handyman to take it to the tip. This task
completed, she worked on all fours to pick debris from com-
pacted clay soil: rocks of all sizes, rusted offcuts of steel pipe, gobs
of slurry, slices of coloured glass, chunks of crumbled bricks.
Secreted beneath the roots of a polygala (which she grubbed out
and threw away), she found a tobacco tin filled with a collection
of glass marbles; she gave them to Eli, who said he was too old
for that sort of thing now and passed them on to Jake. When she

had finished, she raked over the soil again and picked out more. She dug, hoed, tilled and sweated, turned in chicken manure and mushroom compost, laid down metres of topsoil, fertilised and watered and covered the lot with newspapers and peastraw. She waited. Rachel found herself to have reserves of energy and patience she had never imagined possible. Nurseries near and far were visited to buy the plants on her lists. Once she discovered nurseries that sold by mail order, there was no stopping her.

She began to propagate herbs and planted her first vegetables.

At night in her studio she painted canvases of what she imagined the garden might look like when it was fully grown.

— o —

Gardenias, columbines, blue delphiniums, freckled foxgloves, mock orange, hellebores, yarrows, scabiosa, peonies. The lilies: tigers, lily-of-the-valley, Christmas, ginger. Yellow arums, white callas, orange callas. Jacobean lilies.

Jacobeans. The colour of blood. Can a colour be described as viscous? Technically speaking, I mean. Look, look at them. Don't they appear viscous, like blood? Or is it velvet? Yes, velvet. That's better. Velvet.

Evening primrose, yellow, white and orange ranunculi, red-hot pokers, Solomon's seal and Star of Bethlehem (for that biblical touch), fritillaria, lupins—Rachel began to run out of space.

— o —

There were weeks when, as a result of continuing design commitments, the gardening fell far behind. Some of the labouring, too, was heavy beyond Rachel's strength. Esther put her in touch with Mickey O'Day. Rachel arranged for him to come one day a fortnight, a day she put aside all her design projects to work with him.

Mickey proved to be hard-working. He had an abundance of ideas and was generous with his encyclopaedic knowledge, supplementing Rachel's education by lending her specialist books and extending her garden by bringing cuttings and seedlings from other clients' gardens and his own. His suggestions were made without insistence; he was never offended if she did not accept them.

117

They worked in comfortable silence, now and then breaking into conversation, to lapse once more into quiet. In the quiet moments, Rachel would sneak a look at him.

Mickey O'Day was not handsome exactly, but attractive in a way that made description elusive: impish, that's what it was, and intelligent looking. Dark. His thick black hair showed signs of grey; he grew it long, tied it back in a ponytail, usually with a short piece of magenta or royal-blue ribbon, this latter highlighting his eyes. A diamond stud decorated his left earlobe. Broad-shouldered yet wiry; his chest too was broad and slim. His red mouth was generous and when he laughed his eyes flashed light.

Mickey would remove his T-shirt when the sun grew hot (a sensible man, he always left his straw hat on). Rachel found it difficult not to stare at his white chest with its gathering of dark hair that ran in a stripe from above his breasts and disappeared beneath the waistband of his trousers, or his at raspberry pink nipples and strong arms. Smiling, she would turn away and dig harder in the soil, or remove herself to labour in another part of the garden before he looked up and caught her lustful gaze.

Waking from dreams of him—tactile dreams filled with light and heat, kissing and lubricious sex—Rachel felt radiant with satisfaction. Settling back into her pillow, she would conjure him up again, imagine his succulent nipples or his sensuous mouth before falling back to sleep, hopefully to dream.

Sweet Morpheus.

Mickey was her regular work companion, her teacher. He was her sexual fantasy, in which realm these figments of him were to stay. Congress between Rachel Grinblatt and Mickey O'Day remained that of co-workers in the world of her garden.

— o —

'Learn to call plants by their botanical names', Mickey instructed. 'The botanical name for the Chinese lantern tree is abutilon.'

'Abutilon, abutilon, abutilon.' White, yellow and apricot.

Still she collected. Magenta cosmos and white, bearded iris (yellow, white, mauve), blue sage, echium, nigella. Nigella. The leaves resembled filigree; the blooms—sky blue—were reminiscent of the dress collars worn by the first Queen Elizabeth.

'What's the common name for nigella, Mickey?'

'Love-in-a-mist, or,' he grinned, 'if you want to be really common, fuck-in-a-fog.'

Flanders Field poppies, Queen Anne lace, forget-me-nots and grape hyacinth: a royalist carpet of red, white and blue, they cut a swath along the side of the house.

Plants which did not live up to their promise or for which her original passion had waned were culled without a moment's hesitation, creating space for more plants.

'No point being sentimental', she told Eli. 'If it's no longer pleasing, get rid of it.'

Can one adopt this attitude with a tiresome husband, a wilful child, a bad apple? Green. Red. Golden. Delicious. Golden delicious. **[Adagio]** *'Now there's one bad apple, hanging on the wall/One bad apple hanging on the wall/And if that bad apple should accidentally fall . . .' Muddling your songs there, Rachel. Green bottles, bad apples. Who is this bad apple? Jerry? Ruby? Eli? Maybe it's me. I'm the bad apple. Ever think of that? No thank you.*

Six varieties of poppy flourished: California, Iceland, Shirley, Flanders Field, opium and oriental.

Pretty opium poppies. Papaver somniferum. Pink with burgundy centres. Silvery grey-green foliage that looks as though it's been dusted with a coating of fine white powder. I trembled, Ruby, when you made knowing remarks about the opium poppies. It made me fearful, angry. I thought you would knock them off—all ten of them. What a joke. Ten. Or slice around the pods with a razorblade to bleed their sap. Smoke it. Sniff it. Hit it. What a big thrill that would have been for an old-timer like you. Ten bloody plants. Piddling. I'll bet you didn't know that the only cuts made to them were done by Jerry. He milked the juice, scraped it onto some foil and dried it out. Rolled it into a joint one night, and we smoked it. Best night's sleep I ever had. Did you know that, Ruby? That Jerry and I smoked opium one night? How much we enjoyed it? Bet you didn't. On that night, even with so small an amount of that dreamy narcotic, my comprehension was complete. Yes. I understood that I could love it. And not for the first time, I'll have you know. Love it. What a seduction, eh Rube? What a seduction. Do you love it, Ruby? Not a harsh edge anywhere.

Loving it frightened me. This would be a lover whose embrace I would never want to leave. My understanding of this was instantaneous and profound. Scared me. Scared. Is that any way to start a love affair?

Next, a herb patch; Rachel cleared a space. A damp, sheltered corner was turned over to ferns. After viewing an exhibition of cacti at the Herbarium—crazy shapes, vicious spikes, delicate blooms and bold—she added a selection of them as well.

'You are greedy', Jerry admonished.

'Oh.' She blushed. 'Annalise once accused me of being greedy.'

'Greedy Rachel', Annalise had laughed the night Rachel claimed the last prawn on the dish at a Chinese restaurant.

Greedy, needy. Neediness is the mother of addiction.

'Must be true then. Greedy Rachel', Jerry laughed now.

Hungry's more like it, Jerry. Ravenous. Vo-ray-shuss. Be careful what you say. I might become so hungry—for what? love?—that I will mutate into a Venus flytrap—or, as Mickey would have me say, a Dionaea muscipula. Chew you up, Jerry. Spit you out. Move on to the next feed. Jack for entrée, you for main course. Who's next?

Fences creaked under the weight of creepers and vines. Old-fashioned roses, 'Meg', pale apricot, and 'Mermaid', the creamy pale yellow of well-made lemon butter: each were found a place—Mermaid on the east fence, Meg on the north. Mermaid flowered all year; Meg provided blooms for six months out of every twelve. Their sweet perfumes wafted on the air.

Honeysuckle, clematis, passionfruit and grapes. Outside the livingroom door, where, in all the seasons but winter, the family sat for many a meal, clusters of mauve wisteria dangled from the pergola.

'By the time I've finished with you, my cottage garden,' Rachel murmured, 'you'll be as pretty as any picture in these books.'

Seasons came and went. Flowers bloomed, died back and bloomed once more. Rachel continued to refine her taste. Anything pink (except the Shirley and opium poppies) she extracted, as she did an orange too insipid, a red too murky. The Jacobeans remained safe in the ground. Whites and creams, yellows, blues, mauves and deep purples and, here and there, splashes of clear red ('fire-engine red', Rivka liked to call it), rust and deep orange: these were the hues of her botanical palette. Everywhere the greens.

She turned her attention to fruit trees. Rivka and Nate made her a gift of a Lisbon lemon and a Washington navel, both of which thrived. White peaches and nectarines bore the sweetest, juiciest fruit that Rachel and Jerry had eaten since their childhoods. There were raspberry canes, two blueberry bushes, and an old apple she had a nurseryman graft to miniature stock, the graft coming from Esther's garden. A miniature pomegranate, selected for its scarlet flowers and compact growth, also bore fruit, exquisite to behold, sweet to eat.

Rubious pomegranate seeds. Blood red. Remember the time Gully bought some pomegranates and juiced the seeds together with black muscatels? Liquid refreshment with a bloody mantle. Sweet, aromatic blood. Ruby red blood. Ruby's red blood. What colour is your blood, Ruby? Is it deep red? Rich and syrupy, like pomegranate-and-grape juice? Or has it turned pink, diluted by the sticky sap of Papaver somniferum? Red. Colour of good fortune, the Chinese believe. Lucky red. Pomegranate red. Mars. Passion. Anger. Stop!

— o —

Labourers came to build a potting shed. When their task was completed, Rachel began to move the small plastic herb pots onto its many shelves.

Life as a nurserywoman proceeded in earnest.

— o —

'I have to make space for found garden.'

'What do you mean?' Jerry asked.

Found. Don't you know your verbs, Jerry? I found, you found . . . Allow me to demonstrate. An example, past tense: I found a packet of fits in Ruby's drawer this morning. Permit me another: I found a length of soft plastic hose, just long enough to wrap around an arm and tie off. One of the fits I found was lying loose; there were traces of blood in the syringe. Found. Get it? Here follows an example of present perfect tense: I have found my life to be less troubled when I mind my own business. This is difficult for me to do. Therefore: I find I am perfectly tense at present.

121

'Bits and pieces from other people's gardens', Rachel explained. 'Growing gifts from friends and family pleases me.'

'Christ, Rachel, when will you stop?'

'Not until it's perfect.'

He did not bother to ask when that might be.

Jerry's octogenarian Aunt Mackie favoured Rachel's garden with many gifts. Rachel was thrilled to receive among them a paper bag filled with bulbs of old-fashioned freesias: short-stemmed blooms, cream with yellow throats, and a spicy bouquet Rachel never tired of. She planted the freesias in clumps close to the deep-blue babiana, in sites where they were visible from most parts of the glass-walled living room and kitchen. Annalise gave her rhizomes of blue bearded iris, Rivka *Hydrangea quercifolia* cuttings, Grace cuttings of Italian lavender, and a collection of native grasses was contributed from the Devlins' Eltham property.

Grasses. Weeds. Grass. Weed. Bad seed.

Emboldened by desire, Rachel took to knocking on neighbours' doors—those known to her and strangers alike—to ask for coveted plants; most people were obliging. Into small buff-coloured envelopes, batches of which she kept in her purse and pockets, Rachel shook the seed and sealed the flap; seedlings and cuttings she dropped into plastic shopping bags. If the seed pods weren't dry, she snipped them off at the stem (for which purpose she carried a pair of nail scissors) and took them back to the shed, where Eli laid them on drying racks until they turned brown and crisp.

— o —

The vegetables.

Corn seed, a present from a country friend, was planted in rows.

'These,' said Aunt Mackie in a tone that commanded respect for her family's history, 'were brought to Australia by my great-grandfather.'

She tipped scarlet runner-bean seed from her open palm into Rachel's cupped hand. The bean Rachel rolled between her fingers was almost as long as half a pinky finger, plump, deep purple, with black stripes that resembled brush strokes; it was silky to the touch.

Cucumbers, lettuces, spinach, beetroot, French beans, carrots and peas. Rachel grew them all from seed purchased at an organic shop run by second-generation hippies. Cherry tomatoes, butternut pumpkin, potatoes and zucchini sprouted from the compost and the flower beds where Eli had dug in the mulch and were nurtured there.

The family had watched, expectant, as the first of the sweet corn sprouted. They waited for it to ripen, impatient for the silks to spill from the bright green husks and turn dark. At last the day of ripeness arrived. That night they sliced slabs of butter onto their knives and melted it along the hot, plump corn. On top of the glistening kernels they sprinkled freshly ground pepper. Appreciation was expressed through little moans of pleasure, with slurping and sucking.

'Mmm. This corn is the *best*, Mama.' Ruby.

'Excellent corn, Rachel. Any more?' Eli.

'Good tucker, Rachel. Almost as good as the peaches.' Jerry.

A salad of lettuce, spinach, aruccola and radicchio had been picked from the garden. All the ingredients for the dressing—except the oil—also came from the garden: garlic, basil and lemon juice. While the others ate their salad, Rachel stripped another four ears of corn and eased them into the pot of boiling water. She collected the silks and laid them out on the kitchen bench.

'Cornsilk tea makes a good drink, Eli, particularly for people who have problems with fluid retention.'

Ruby had snickered, 'That's something he really needs to know, Mum.' She laughed at Eli's discomfort.

'I don't have to talk to customers about *that*, do I?' Eli whinged.

Jerry exploded into mirthless laughter.

'No', Rachel sighed. 'I suppose not. I thought you might be interested, that's all.'

I'm interested. Listen to this: 'Heroin use over a protracted period will result in retention of fluid.' Oedema. I read that somewhere. Or was it something Ruby told me? Or Gully? Or someone else, whose name I no longer recall? Who may no longer be alive? Remember when we ate the first corn for dinner that night? Does she retain fluid enough to warrant drinking cornsilk tea? I noticed how swollen her fingers looked the last time she visited, and her ankles. Maybe she ate too much salt the night before. Hah! Would Ruby drink cornsilk tea? Does she remember what I told Eli? Unlikely. Listen to me, Ruby. Listen to your mother. I will make you well with cups of cornsilk tea served in little Chinese cups. See how simple it could be? Simple. Simpleton.

The trees: silver birch, Japanese maple, white magnolia, ceanothus, a small flowering gum, a jacaranda. There was not the space for more.

Textures: soft, coarse, sharp, brittle, smooth, oily, furry, silky, sticky, prickly.

Habit: spiky, serrated, plumose, scalloped, round, ovate.

Habit. See, Rachel? See how words selected to describe that which is most beautiful have their place in the most dread? Do you see how words resemble flowers, or vegetables? In infinite variety they are planted in the fertile soil of the mind. There they grow, singly and in clumps, to form useable clauses, phrases, sentences. Bunches, crops of words, to pick when their time is right. When their season has come. Then, up they pop, out of the mind's rich humus, to roll off the tongue, spill forth from the mouth, be put to use like a bunch of flowers picked to decorate a room, a basket of vegetables selected for a meal. Is that drawing too long a bow? It's my bow; I'll draw as I please. Habit. It is Jerry's habit to withhold. It is Eli's habit to collect paper dreams of men flying high through the air. Does he dream of escaping? And Ruby? Ah, Ruby. Your habit. What is there to say? And me? What of me? My daughter is my habit.

Effect: lush and dishevelled. An intense, shaggy dog of a garden.

— o —

The garden and the nursery became established. Rachel needed less of Mickey's assistance. He came only four or five times a year now, to prune trees and vines and climbers, the heavy work that neither she nor Eli were strong enough or adept enough to do. He weeded and cleared when the work got too much for her. She would phone him—'It's time for us to work together again, Mickey'—and wonder if he heard her smile, as she had heard his.

One afternoon before he left for the tip in his van loaded with rubbish they chatted over a cup of tea.

'You have created something special here, Rachel', he said. 'I've never seen a garden as beautiful as this. It's like a Monet garden.'

Rachel spun around to face him, to see if he was teasing. His face was composed.

'Are you serious? That's pretty high praise.'

'I'm serious. What you've created is a charmed haven of great beauty and tranquillity. There are few other places anywhere I'd rather be.'

She thought she would burst with pride. It was the most thrilling thing anyone had ever said to her; she knew she would never forget it. Mickey offered her a toke on his joint. She declined, shaking her head.

'Thank you, Mickey. That's a lovely thing to say. You know, I sometimes wonder if Gully hadn't fanned my interest all those years ago, whether I'd have gone this far with it.' Rachel had told Mickey about Gully one afternoon in response to his enquiry about how she had become interested in gardening. Occasionally, when Rachel sat alone during a rest from her work, she toasted Gully in tea or coffee and whispered her gratitude to his departed spirit.

'Gully, you old reprobate,' she said the same words each time, 'you weren't a total loss after all.'

'No point trying to fathom that.' Mickey was philosophical. 'You most likely would have. It's connected to your painting, with having gone to art school, I reckon. Gully probably tickled it along at the right time.'

Rachel spoke quietly. 'You've played a part in it too, don't forget.' She paused a moment, then rushed on. 'I miss our work sessions, Mickey.'

'I do too, Rachel. Still …'

His voice trailed off and she heard the shrug of there's-nothing-can-be-done-about-it in his voice.

— o —

Seasons came and went. Jerry withdrew. He conversed little unless it was to criticise, to demean her achievement.

'Look at how this corner has come on', she might say, showing him a site that particularly appealed to her.

'I don't like that blue there', he might reply, pointing with his chin.

'Which one? It's all blue.'

She would turn in time to see the victory in his eyes.

'The peas were a huge success last year. I might plant some along the back fence again. What do you think?'

He would stare in the direction she pointed, long enough mute for Rachel to think he hadn't heard her.

'I've never liked peas.'

'But you always said—'

Before she could complete her sentence he had turned from her and gone inside.

She felt most hurt when he said nothing, wishing he would just once pay her a compliment, a half, a quarter of the magnitude Mickey had.

Jerry baulked.

The hostility between them, germinated in ground grown hard, took root and spread branches gnarled with resentment.

You have become snappy, Rachel, just like a snapdragon. Snapdragon! Remember when Papa picked snapdragons from the garden, tweaking them open and closed, pretending to bite off your nose? You do? You are the snapdragon now, Rachel. The only snapdragon in this entire garden.

— o —

'This is where I hide, Essie.'

'Hide?'

Yes, Essie, haven't you noticed? I hide from life.

'Yes. From my failures. As an artist. A mother. Motherhood, my biggest failure. Being a wife.'

'You are too hard on yourself.'

'No, I'm hopeless.' Rachel flapped away her friend's protest with a wave of her hand. There was, on this occasion, no self-pity in her voice. 'I never seem to get it right. Out here I believe in myself. In this garden I feel creative, confident, I know there is one thing I get right and do well. I would go so far as to say excel at. I can look at it with pride and say, I made this. It is beautiful and it works. But I don't seem to comprehend the rules of the game. What *are* the rules, Esther? You seem to understand them.' She sighed. 'Married to the one man for decades, none of your children on drugs. Is that what the rules are?'

'You romanticise us, Rachel', Esther replied wearily. 'You think everybody else's families are whatever it is you consider to be normal, as if we don't have problems of our own. That is not the case. Do you think Shimon and I don't have our disagreements? Do you think that in all the years we've been married to each other neither of us has threatened to leave, or been attracted to other people? We have, and we do argue, and both of us have come very close to walking out, more than once.'

'But none of your children are on drugs.'

'Rachel, please don't do this.'

Esther's eyes filled with tears as she told Rachel that when he was seventeen, feeling he didn't fit in anywhere, depressed, and bullied by Shimon, Zev had tried to commit suicide.

'I was too ashamed to tell you.'

Ay, Essie.

— o —

I imagine this.

Iron filings. We as iron filings, Esther. You, Grace, me. Drawn by what magnet? Shared joys and passions, certainly; the pleasure of each other's company, unquestionably; a connection of spirit, yes; loyalty and trust. What more?

I wonder this.

An element. Do I act as a magnet to the others, a magnet of sorrow drawing unto myself the iron filings of the others' sorrow? And they in their turn to me? What do you think, my dear Esther, my friend? My magnet, my filings?

— o —

The season had turned to spring. Esther came to visit.

'You have turned this place into a paradise', Esther rhapsodised. The two friends sat beneath the pergola drinking strong tea and smoking cigarettes.

Paradise, Esther. Yes. All the external signs speak of paradise. Why then does this chill settle on me? Why is the shadow's reach so long, its cast so dark? What happened to joy, delight, hope? They have been swamped by waiting, watching, listening, yearning. By spying, and more waiting. Where are you today, Ruby? Beauty all external now. Inside I am as hollow as a bamboo flute. And just as dry. No music emanates from this flute, no mellifluous notes trill forth. Ruby, sweet Ruby, where are you? Are you alive today?

'Mickey said it resembled a Monet.'

'He was right! Well done, Mickey.'

They admired it together: the soft colours peppered with spots and splashes of dazzle, the perfumes intoxicating, the greens and textures manifold, the fruit trees and vegetables fecund and bursting with the promise of another abundant harvest. It was alive with myriad flying and crawling insects: bees hovered and hummed; wasps, ladybirds, dragonflies, mosquitoes, snails and slaters busied themselves in the earth, on the air, on the plants. Honeyeaters hung upside down, pecking seed and pollen from the Chinese lantern tree; swallows and finches swooped and twittered.

They sat peacefully for a while, absorbing different perspectives. Breaking the silence, Rachel remarked, 'At least this part of my life still gives me pleasure, Essie.'

'You don't say', Esther laughed. Then, more serious, 'Tell me the one thing you enjoy most. There must be one thing about this that sustains you, something that's special', Esther prodded.

'Working where I don't have to be beholden to anyone is important. You know, when I arrive or leave, what I wear. I long for the day when I won't have to concern myself with design deadlines, when this is all I do.' She brushed a stray curl from her forehead. 'The physical labour. The pleasant ache in my muscles at the end of the day.' She grinned. 'Sweating. I love the way the sweat runs down my back and from under my breasts and armpits. I like how it settles on my upper lip and the taste of it when I lick it off. How the saltiness makes my eyes smart. The smell of sweat, it's so sexy.'

'Yes, it is.' Unsatisfied, Esther pressed her friend further. 'But, your soul, Rachel. What sustains your soul?'

Rachel drew a deep breath.

'The peace sustains me, Esther. The peace and the solitariness of it. There is solace in this work. Beauty and sensuousness too.

Yes.' She gathered momentum. 'Colour, texture, shape and light. Just like painting. God knows I've done little enough of that in the past few years.' Esther nodded at her sorrowful tone, opened her mouth to speak, but Rachel gave her no opportunity to comment. 'Fragrances, the mud-pie childishness of playing in wet soil, leaves and petals tickling my bare arms and face, the sun on my back when I work.' She laughed. 'These things give me pleasure, particularly when I'm frightened about Ruby or sad about Eli, or ready to kill Jerry.'

Esther waited patiently as Rachel ordered her thoughts.

'The beauty is constant, yet forever changing, depending on the light, the season, my mood. The beauty may be paramount.' Rachel drew another long breath. 'But the inexorability holds me in thrall.'

'What do you mean?'

'Each spring, when I see the first oriental poppy bud, I know exactly what is going to come out. When the calyx bursts open and that deep orange peeks through I swoon with pleasure. Every year when the beans hang off the vines or new irises push their way out of those knotty old rhizomes, when I spot the first of the corn poking through the peastraw or tomatoes thrown from the compost, I'm thrilled.

'It's not about surprises, rather, it's the process that fills me with wonder. The circumstances or forms may differ—fruit or no fruit, big flowers or small, deciduous or evergreen, short, tall, wide, narrow: that's detail.

'Remember the bushfires along the west coast in '83?' Esther raised her eyebrows: how could anyone forget? 'Jerry and I drove down there a few weeks after the devastation. It was heartbreaking. The land was burnt black from Anglesea to Apollo Bay. Locals said the environment would never recover. But it did. We went back again a year later. A lot of the bush was still blackened, but much of it had grown back. We saw exquisite orchids, beautiful, delicate things. The old-timers said they hadn't seen many of them in years. The scarifying had regenerated them.

'You know that section along the Jarosite Road between Bells Beach and Point Addis? Blocks of land there are covered with grass trees. They were in full bloom. Of all the occasions I'd driven down there, the holidays with the kids, I'd never seen a grass tree in flower.' She chuckled. 'They looked very erotic, like giant erect green penises.'

'Shimon and I saw a display like that in Gippsland', Esther beamed. 'It's pretty hot, isn't it? We checked in to a motel for the afternoon.'

Rachel laughed, then continued, serious again. 'Spectacular eucalypt blossoms . . . so many beautiful things. It all seemed to be saying, "Send down your worst—we can take it. We'll always come back." I was deeply moved.'

Rachel looked around. 'Whether it's the seeds I plant, or those carried on the wind, crapped out by birds or brought in on the paws of cats, there is always something here to enjoy, Essie. Always. I tend them, they grow, they die and they come back again, season after season, in all their splendour. Bit of a wonder, don't you think?' As Esther nodded her agreement, Rachel added, 'And none of them give me any bloody lip. If I don't like the way they're behaving, I pull them out and replace them with something new.'

They laughed together. In the background the sound of hammering intruded upon their serenity. Rachel turned her attention to the sound for a moment, listened to the dull thud.

Hammer. Hammer. Hammer. More than one way to skin a cat. Define a word.

She turned back to Esther and continued. 'Except for the gardenias.' Rachel swivelled on her seat to face them.

'What's different about the gardenias?'

'I wanted so much to grow some. They evoked a particularly happy memory.'

'Oh?'

'I always knew when Mama and Papa were going out somewhere special because he bought her a bouquet of two gardenias and maidenhair fern. The stems were held together with fine wire and wrapped in a twist of silverfoil. It came in a clear celluloid box which Papa put in the fridge to keep the flowers fresh. I was very young, yet I understood it was an expensive gift and that it was special. He bought her this bouquet for years and years; still does sometimes.

'Just before he pinned it on her dress, she would hold it close to my nose and say, "Smell them, Rochl. Careful, careful!" she'd say. "If you touch the petals they will turn brown. Gently now." I thought the smell was divine, the white the purest I'd ever seen.'

'What a touching story.'

'Yes, it is. For days after their big event, the bouquet would sit in a bowl of water on the diningroom table. The scent would fill the house. When I started this garden I knew I had to grow some.'

'*Nu*, what was the problem?'

'They are sensitive little buggers. Some people seem to be able to grow them easily. Not me.' Rachel pointed to three plants; all were covered in buds. 'These are numbers five, six and seven. I call them "The Last Chance Gardenias". The four before them died, but I am determined. I bought one after another, fed them, nurtured them, moved them from one part of the garden to another trying to find the perfect spot, to no avail. They just kept dying. Enough was enough, I decided: these three had to make it on their own, without any more fussing and interference from me. No more special attention, no excess of care or worry. Either they made it on their own, or they didn't make it at all.' Satisfied, she settled back in the chair. 'That seemed to work. As you can see, they made it. Aren't they lovely?'

Esther stared at her, dumbfounded, wondering if Rachel saw beyond gardenias in the words she spoke. But Rachel continued, apparently oblivious. Or she chose to ignore them. Esther wasn't sure which.

'The plants bring other life.' Rachel was unable to stop now. 'Ladybirds, dragonflies, bees. Some nights the cicadas are so loud I can hardly hear myself think. Grasshoppers, redbacks and daddy longlegs, worms as thick as my little finger'—she held one up—'slaters and snails and slugs—' She fell silent and gazed into the middle distance, pensive. 'Birds', she muttered. 'Look.' Rachel pointed to a knot of branches in the wisteria. 'A nest. The life of a garden seems so harmonious. And there is peace here. It's the harmony, the peace and the beauty of this garden that sustain my soul, Esther. Its life.'

'A bit like babies.' Esther loved babies, any babies; she would talk about them with the least amount of encouragement. Her face was as bright as sunshine. 'Babies are life.'

'Oh, Essie, you and babies', Rachel laughed.

'You have to admit their arrival is a unique thrill. Oooh, that milk and baby powder smell!' Esther crooned. 'I never tire of it. Their skin is the texture of finest silk. The arrival of a baby is so exciting, isn't it?'

'Yes. Daunting, too, as I recall. Were you scared when you learnt you were pregnant?'

'I was terrified. Such an enormous responsibility. What if I got it wrong?'

'Me too. I was determined to be different, adamant I wouldn't perpetrate any of the crimes I resented my parents for.' Rachel's laughter bore no bitterness. 'I was going to be a better parent. Me? I was going to be the perfect parent. My children would always be happy. They'd never be angry with me. We'd be best friends.' She hooted with laughter. 'Ay Esther, such dreams.' Something in the garden captured her attention and she peered at it for a while. 'How can we know how things will turn out?' Rachel looked down at her hands. 'I sometimes wonder what would have happened if . . .'

Esther remained quiet, waiting for Rachel to complete her sentence, but Rachel shook whatever it was away and resumed talking about the garden.

'Beauty and harmony. They are the sustenance,' she paused, squinted against the sun, saw nothing, 'no matter what else is happening in your life.'

Esther's glance was sharp; Rachel's switch to the second person did not escape her notice.

'More tea?' Rachel deflected enquiry. 'Oh,' she exclaimed, her hand on the teapot, 'it's cold.'

'No thanks, love. I'd better get going. Why don't you and Jerry come to dinner on Sunday?'

'I'll talk to him and let you know.' She paused. 'Just tell me this, Essie, do you think many people have messy lives?'

'Probably more than we care to imagine, but most of us keep the messiness to ourselves. The fictitious ideal family.' Esther snorted. 'Does it exist? On television, or in the pages of magazines, sure. Anywhere else? No one I know.'

They roamed the garden picking Esther a bunch of flowers, then said goodbye at the front gate. After Esther had driven away, Rachel returned to her work in the potting shed where, untended, tears rolled down her cheeks and splashed onto the workbench.

— o —

Despite the frost and damp, Rachel sat outdoors at the table under the pergola. Overhead, denuded of foliage and blossoms, a canopy of entwined wisteria branches snaked through the pergola's beams. Seed pods, hard and black, dangled from the older wood. Steam rose from her cup of tea and mingled with the vapour of her breath, the smoke from her cigarette. Rachel lifted the warm cup from the table and wrapped her hands around it. More than a year had passed since that conversation with Esther, yet she thought about it often. How could she not? Most of her waking hours were spent in the shed and the garden. Life and rebirth, growth and beauty—it was inevitable that she think about them.

About death, too. And emptiness. And the irony that the only beauty she seemed capable of enjoying was that which she created in her garden and in the family life of her imagination.

INTERLUDE II

He'll say . . .
    I'll say . . .
    Then he'll reply . . .
    If he says that, I'll say it was because of . . .
    No, he won't listen. He'll say it was because . . .
    But if I tell him she . . .
    He'll be angry, of course.
    Then the yelling will start.
    Oh God.
    He's bound to say . . . bound to. Unless . . .
    If he does, then I could explain that . . . Then he'll underst . . .
    No. He's going to blame me, no matter how I put it.
    But if I were to say . . .! That might make . . . No.
    Oh, damn! Shit! Shitshitshitshit.
    Perhaps it won't be as bad as . . .
    Yes it will.
    It's bound to be.
    Damn and shit. Damn!

— o —

*It is not the gentle encouragement of her friends, or the ongoing dis-
cussion with Jerry about Jack's right to know that moves Rachel
forward—if indeed forward is the direction she's heading. It is her own
need to quiet the voices, to devolve some of the responsibility, the
worry, or . . . Or what?*

    She refuses to divulge the purpose of her call, saying only that she has something she needs to discuss with him and that she would not have called were it not important. Despite his reluctance, he agrees to meet, nominating the day and the time. A bar in the city.

Neutral territory.

— o —

Waiting for him in a booth at the bar—he is late—she is squeezed by a level of tension previously unsurpassed.

What if he doesn't show up?

Surely he wouldn't not . . .

I hope I don't cry. Let me not cry . . . who?

If he doesn't show up I'll . . .

Jack, I have something . . .

He's not going to . . .

'Good evening, Rachel.' Jack glances as his watch as he sits down at the opposite end of the booth. 'Can we make this brief? The children . . .' He brushes his hair from his eyes. 'What's it all about?'

There seems to be no hostility in his enquiry. Or challenge. Or anything, really. Not even interest. Just a question.

Stammerings and false beginnings.

He waits.

Her wish goes unanswered. She is crying. Maybe it was the wrong wish. Jack passes her a paper serviette. Then, there it all is. A torrent. Quiet, but a torrent all the same.

Ruby. Habit. Heroin. Years. Frightened. Can't handle it on my own any longer, Jack. On and on. On and on.

The torrent subsides. Throughout, he stirs the ice in his glass with a swizzle stick; the ice tinkles. To Rachel, the fairylike tinkling sounds thunderous. Clamouring bells.

This is what Jack says.

'Is this what you wanted to meet about?' His stirring comes to an abrupt halt; he drops the plastic stick on the table. The icecubes continue tinkling for a short while. Then the tinkling stops. The cubes spin, silently, in the vortex of whisky and water. The velocity slows and the ice bobs on the surface, like enormous diamonds, sparkling in the glow of an overhead light fixture. Sparkling diamonds. 'I know about Ruby's habit, Rachel.'

Rachel gasps with disbelief.

'Who told . . .? When did . . .? How long have you . . .? Why didn't you talk . . .?'

She feels betrayed. By which one of them? Why?

She feels as if she's going to faint.

He orders her a whisky. No water, no ice.

It sits on the table, untouched.

She stares at it.

Not one of her rehearsals predicted this.

— o —

Jack has known for twelve months. Eli told him at one of their occasional lunches. Yes, he does still see Eli, though not often, and never at home. He sighs. Eli never got on well with Dorothy. Pity.

Jack doesn't respond to Rachel's wild laughter. How can he? It is tucked away inside her, romping its way through her viscera, her arteries, making her blood sing. Her heart dances. Hah!

He decided to ask her himself. She denied it—at first. Eventually she admitted to him that she was using heroin and that she had a habit. She hadn't wanted him to know.

'But it's not an easy secret to keep, is it?'

He took the information in his stride, he says. Naturally he was upset. What did Rachel think he was? But he did take it in his stride. Nothing he could do. That's what the family doctor told him when he'd asked. Nothing.

Why would he discuss the matter with Rachel? he says now. What transpires between himself and Ruby is their business.

With this statement, any expectation Rachel had that she might get some support from him evaporates.

When Rachel wonders aloud why Ruby didn't tell her, he raise his drink to his mouth and, just before he swallows the last of it, says 'Why don't you ask her?' Then he downs the whisky.

Ruby begged him not to let Rachel know he knew: she didn't want them to fight. She didn't want him to blame Rachel.

Well?

'Who else is there to hold responsible? You were the one who brought them up, Rachel. Let's face it, you made a real bloody mess of it.'

In the first instance, the weight of his accusation bows her head, slumps her shoulders. She stares at the table. Her skin feels slack with shame.

'I still see Ruby from time to time. But I won't allow her to come to the house. I can't have the other children influenced or witness to . . .'

He runs his fingers through his hair then shrugs.

Of course not.

Rachel straightens her spine and faces him. Jack senses that she is about to launch into a conversation he doesn't wish to engage in. He stands and gathers up his briefcase.

'If that's all . . . Dorothy and the children are expecting me. I said I wouldn't be too late.'

On an impulse, Rachel asks, 'Where did you tell Miss Dorothy you were going this evening, Jack?'

He clears his throat. 'I told her I had a late meeting with a client. Not that it's any of your business, Rachel.' A sheepish grin is followed by a defiant toss of the head.

Rachel smiles, the cat who got the cream. His revelation is a small but adequate satisfaction.

'Still lying to your wife, eh Jack?' She smiles 'Thank you for agreeing to meet me.'

Rachel leaves the bar before Jack has finished paying for their drinks. It is to be the last time they see each other.

Girl Talk

'The trouble with Rachel,' Grace pontificated to Esther and Caroline over Saturday morning coffee, 'is that she spends too much time alone worrying about Ruby and criminalising her past. She should get someone new in to help her in the nursery.'

'She won't do it', Caroline predicted. 'She'd prefer to tough it out on her own. I'd like to be around to see the day Rachel Grinblatt asks for help.'

'My, my. You're getting snaky.'

'Rachel finds it impossible to ask for help with anything. You know that as well as I do.'

'She could get a junior,' Esther suggested, 'or a local pensioner. At least then she'd have someone to talk to, someone to boss around a bit.'

The three of them chuckled, then, in unison, they sighed.

'She's a mess. This business with Ruby—'

'Oh, no,' Caroline groaned, 'not this again.'

'Shut up, Caro.'

'According to her, she's fine. Quite frankly, I can't stand being around her any more.'

'Caroline, you know she's not fine', Grace snapped. 'Blind Freddie could see what a bloody mess she is.'

'I know she's a mess,' Caroline replied, unmoved by Grace's outburst, 'but she refuses to acknowledge it. I'm sick and tired of the topic of conversation. On the rare occasion we're together, no matter what we start off talking about, within minutes—bingo! Ruby Ruby Ruby. If—if, mind you—I can drag Rachel along to the studio to look at my work, or we go to an exhibition, she stands there gazing at a picture looking for all the world like she'd been carved from a block of stone herself. Before I know what's hit me, I'm listening to what Ruby did, or what Ruby didn't do, or what she might be doing, or what Rachel wishes she was doing . . . Bugger her. I've had it.'

'When was the last time you saw her?' Esther enquired.

'Months, and that's all right with me. Unless she moves on to another conversation, I don't care if it's never.'

Esther ordered another round of coffees. As the waiter placed their drinks on the table, Grace gave a sudden snort of laughter.

'What?' chorused Esther and Caroline.

'Did she tell you what happened last week?'

'What?' they repeated.

'Ruby told Rachel she was going to have a bath while Rachel was working in the nursery. Apparently, when Rachel came inside an hour later, the bathroom door was still closed and no sign of Ruby. She knocked and banged on the bathroom door, but there was no answer. She went into a panic, convinced Ruby had drowned, or had a hit in the bathroom and died.'

'What did she do?'

'She tried to open the door, but the door was locked, so she bashed it open with her shoulder.'

'Oh, my God', Esther gasped.

'Ruby was sound asleep in the bath', Grace laughed. 'You would have heard, Esther, if anything terrible had happened.'

'True.'

'Rachel scared the shit out of her! Apparently water went sloshing all over the place. They had to get a carpenter in to fix the door!'

Caroline cackled.

'How do you know this? Why did Ruby lock the door?'

'Ruby told me. I saw her at Mario's. We had a coffee together. Later, I dropped in to see Rachel; she told me, too. Her shoulder is killing her. Ruby went home for a few days' break from it, she said. She probably locked the bathroom door because she wanted some peace and quiet from our dear friend, her mother. And no, she wasn't stoned. At least, that's what she said. She said she was thoroughly exhausted and the warm bath put her into a deep sleep. Don't you remember how that girl could always sleep through anything from the time she was a baby?'

Caroline was scathing. 'Bloody pathetic. Can't Rachel leave her alone?'

'She's worried, Caroline.'

'Dear Esther, loyal friend.'

'What's wrong with that?' Esther said indignantly. 'She's my friend and she has every right to be worried.'

'I understand that she's concerned, Esther, but the kind of behaviour she goes on with won't get Ruby off the junk.'

'What will? She's tried everything. Nothing seems to work.'

Here we are again. Is there no escape for any of us?

'She hasn't tried everything. She could try letting go a bit. She could try talking to a counsellor on one of the telephone help lines, or get her own shrink. She could go to one of those bloody meetings they go to.'

'What meetings?'

'Alcoholics Anonymous for relatives. I'm not exactly sure. Al-Anon or something like that.'

'She'd never do that.'

'Why does she torture herself with how awful a parent she's been?' Esther lamented. 'It's not even true. She must know that her kids love and respect her.'

'If she does, you'd never know it.'

'She is unable to accept that everyone has doubts about the sort of parent they are.' Grace was becoming angry. 'Everyone. She berates herself more than anyone else I know.'

'No one blames her for Ruby's condition', said faithful Esther.

'If she's not to blame, who is?' Caroline snapped. 'Of course she's to blame. She smoked joints since her kids were young. What kind of an example is that?'

'Why isn't Linda using heroin then? Or the Merlot kids?' Grace snapped in return.

Caroline sulked, uncertain of her argument in the face of Grace's question.

'Rachel didn't make Ruby take it.' Esther is trying to keep a more generous spirit alive. 'I don't blame her. No one does.'

'Except Caroline', Grace grinned.

'That's right. Except me. I'm sick of smack and sick of seeing what people become when they use it. It's intolerable. Not only users, either. What about the people close to them? After . . .' She stopped.

'After what?' asks Esther.

Grace was more alert. 'The question, Essie, is, "After whom?" isn't it, Caro?' she laughed.

'Never you mind.'

'After Gully! I knew it! I always knew it!'

Grace and Esther were grinning; Caroline scowled.

'Wily old Grace. How did you know?'

'What do you reckon?'

'Oh, no,' Caroline groaned, 'not you too! When?'

'Same time as you, I think. In that student house in Newry Street.'

'Bloody hell. I knew something was going on, but when I asked him, he said, "There is no one but you, sweet. You are the light of my life". Two days later he was gone. Remember the curry banquet he turned on for us?'

Grace nodded, smiling. 'He always called me sweet. It drove me nuts. He made me feel like a boiled lolly.'

'Me too!'

They screamed with laughter.

'He probably called all his lovers sweet. Less troublesome than having to remember all their names.'

Caroline and Grace's thoughts were one: they turned in silent enquiry to Esther.

'Absolutely not!' she swore. 'Not me. No, no, no. I liked him, but not that much. I was already going out with Shimon. Remember?'

'Rachel?' Caroline asked.

'Yes,' Grace confirmed, 'but much later, about a year before she met Jerry, and only for a few weeks. She never let him move in.'

'So, she's not entirely crazy.'

Grace moved the conversation along.

'Are you nearly ready for your show, Caroline?'

'I'll probably work right up to the last minute. I'm pleased with the work. It's looking pretty good.'

'Is that young assistant curator still working there? Esther's hot for him.'

'Grace! Cut it out.'

'Great. I'll let him know. He's in the market for a new lover. An older woman would be right up his alley.'

'He is gorgeous.' Esther smiled. 'If I were fifteen years younger . . .'

'Nah,' Caroline laughed, nudging Esther on the shoulder, 'have a go. He'd love it. Just what you need, Essie, after all these years of stable marriage. We won't tell Shimon, will we, Grace? It'll be a secret, just between the three of us. And him. And whoever he tells.' They were rolling around in their chairs, laughing. 'What do you reckon, Grace?'

Grace was about to reply when Rachel entered the cafe. They observed her as she approached their table: wan, dispirited, worried. She looked as though she no longer cared about her appearance.

'Mind if I join you?'

Two years ago, there would have been no need for the question.

Caroline stood up. 'I was just leaving. See you later.'

'Sit down, Rachel.' Esther pulled out a chair.

'Sit.' Grace slapped the table with the flat of her hand. 'Now, here's the rule, Rachel: no talking about Ruby this morning.'

Rules are made to be broken.

She tried. She did try. They spoke of how well Grace's magazine was doing, Esther's job. By the time they were on to Caroline's forthcoming show at the gallery in Richmond Rachel had withdrawn.

'Ruby called last night.'

'Rachel!' her friends growled a warning.

'She sounded awful. I'm worried about her.'

'Rachel, give yourself a break', Esther pleaded.

'Give us a break. I told you the conditions, Rachel. No Ruby talk this morning.'

Esther glanced at the clock on the wall.

'I must go. Shimon is making lunch.'

All prepared to leave.

'Where's your car?' Grace enquired of Rachel. 'I'll walk you there.'

'I caught the tram. Trying to find a parking space in Brunswick Street on Saturday mornings is a nightmare.'

'Come on, you miserable old bat, I'll drive you home.'

'Thanks, Grace. I'll speak to you tomorrow, Esther.'

Behind Rachel's back, Esther and Grace shrugged helplessly at each other, waved goodbye, and went their separate ways.

— o —

Grace accepted Rachel's offer to stay for lunch. She phoned Pete to tell him she'd be home later in the afternoon. Jerry had left for an afternoon at the football, leaving a note: 'May not be home until late. Eat dinner without me.'

'What has happened to you, Rachel? Where has your life gone?'

Rachel didn't answer.

'You have turned yourself into the Wicked bloody Witch of the West. You romanticise everyone else's family and malign everything about your own, as if you've never done one thing right or had a happy moment with them since Ruby started using. Or before. I know that's not true. *You* know it's not true.

'You act as though everything unpalatable your children do is entirely your responsibility, as if all their behaviour is a reflection on you. You seem to forget they have a father, have a stepfather—if that's what you call Jerry—they have friends.

'More importantly, they have minds and personalities of their own. They are adults, agents of their own lives; they have choices. Ease up on yourself.'

'Ah, Grace,' Rachel sighed, prepared to talk now, 'you have no idea what it's like.'

Rachel had chosen her words badly; Grace exploded.

'Don't you tell me what I don't know, Rachel, as if you are the only person on God's earth who understands suffering! Plenty of people know.'

'Linda? I'm sorry, Grace. I thought she was better.'

'She's struggling with it.'

'Why didn't you tell me?'

'You can't be serious! You are so preoccupied with your own damn misery that you have little perception of anyone else's or any time for it.'

'Do you blame yourself?'

'There are days when I think I'm pathetic. Nothing I do seems

143

to induce my daughter to stop sticking her fingers down her throat for more than a week at a time.' Rachel noticed her friend's hands were shaking, that she was panting as if she had just completed a long run. 'Do I blame myself? Sometimes. But not every waking moment, and not at the complete expense of my own life. Not by flushing my life down the lavatory, the way you have. I have a life and I intend to live it, even if I do make messes. Pete and I have done as much as we can to help Linda. What more can we do now but let her know we love her? The rest is up to her.'

'Courageous Grace.'

'Bullshit, Rachel. Linda has choices just as Ruby has choices. So do you.' She tilted her head to one side, staring at Rachel, considering.

'What?' Rachel braced herself.

'Keep the hell out of Ruby's life and get on with your own. Get on with your painting. Go back to school if you have to. You had something going there, something good. If things are crook between you and Jerry, then tend to that. Leave, don't leave—'

'Grace . . .' Rachel's voice bore a warning.

'No, Rachel. I've started this, I'm going to finish it. Stay with Jerry or don't, but whatever you decide to do, stop using Ruby and her problems to fill the gap. Set some boundaries. Take your own damn life back.' Grace dragged her friend into her arms and hugged her tight. Rachel stiffened. 'We only get one time around, Rachel. Don't throw yours away. Don't let it slip through your fingers until one day you wake up, old and frail, and say, "Where did my life go?" You won't have an answer. I couldn't bear that to happen to you. I care about you too much.'

'I can't stand by and watch her slide into the mire, Grace.'

'It's too late, Rachel. She's in the mire. She's been there for some time. Only she can work her way out of it.'

'I can't.'

Grace gave up.

Rachel persisted. Clarity of vision was beyond her.

ONCE UPON A TIME

Rachel and Jerry were dining out. As had become customary they spoke little during their meal. Jerry made a faint-hearted attempt or two to brighten things up by beginning a conversation, only to be silenced by Rachel's monosyllabic responses or by her uninterested, blank-eyed stare.

'A quickie, eat and run', Rachel had conceded to Jerry's suggestion they dine out, seeing it as the better of two undesirable choices; she preferred even less to cook.

No more than twenty minutes had elapsed from the time she sat down, bossed the waitress around—'We're in a hurry, please bring our meals quickly'—and gobbled down her three-course Japanese meal, the flavours and textures of which escaped her notice. Once she had finished, she placed her chopsticks neatly across the bowl, folded her paper serviette, smoothed its wrinkles, then looked enquiringly at Jerry, who was still eating.

Jerry ignored her.

'Are you ready to leave?'

'No, I'm not. Not yet.' There was no warmth in his smile.

He chewed each morsel with maddening deliberation, took genteel sips of his wine. When he had finished his sushi and drained the last of the wine from his glass, Rachel picked up her purse and beckoned the waitress to come so she could pay for her share of the meal. The waitress arrived and Jerry ordered another glass of chardonnay, which he drank more slowly than the first. Rachel sat in grim, furious silence, hating him.

'Hurry up, Jerry. Ruby said she might come over.' She added, for no apparent reason, 'I left the key in the letterbox for her.'

He waved her remonstrations away.

'Go home if you want to. I'll come when I'm ready.' Before she had a chance to protest, he added, 'It won't do you any good, you know.'

'What do you mean?'

'You know exactly what I mean, Rachel. Either she'll be there or she won't. Either she'll be stoned or she won't. Nothing you can do.' He smirked at her. 'However, you think there is, so, off you go.'

He dismissed her with a wave of his hand.

'I'll wait', she sighed. 'Just hurry.'

Rachel stared, despairing, agitated, as Jerry made a display of enjoying his wine: swirled the green-gold liquid around in the glass, savoured its bouquet, raised the glass to the light to inspect its brilliance before he drank, rested the glass on the table after each sip. Between sips he sat back, languid, first rolling then smoking a cigarette, delicately picking the pieces of dropped tobacco from the front of his shirt between puffs. He rubbed the stray tobacco threads from his fingers into the ashtray. He beckoned the waitress and asked for a clean ashtray.

Cat and mouse.

How had it come to this? This mean-spirited hostility. This grinding emotional war, waged daily, around the clock. This slow demise.

While Jerry savoured the wine, he smoked another cigarette.

'Ruby will wait', he interrupted her thoughts. 'Sit still, Rachel. Relax.'

'She might not. I don't want to miss seeing her. Please hurry, Jerry.'

Pleading now, a hair's breadth from begging.

Rachel wanted to hurry home in case Ruby came home, in case Ruby had already come home, in case Ruby hadn't come home, in case Ruby phoned, in case Ruby had left a message on the answering machine, in case she hadn't.

Incaseanybloodything.

If there was no sign of Ruby, no contact made, Rachel would find a pretext under which to phone her, the third call in the past two days, knowing Ruby would be angry with her for chasing her around Melbourne, clinging to her like a leech.

'Get a life, Mum.'

Get a life, Rachel.

— o —

Grace was not entirely correct. Rachel did remember life before heroin addiction; she thought about it often. There had been light and shade, a full spectrum of colour, not the relentless grey of the present. Not without justification did Rachel recall events from her family's past in a benign light, with a forgiving and philosophical eye. Laughter, trust, and love freely given: these she remembered, moulding the good times into the shape of a fairy story. 'Once upon a time . . .' as if they were times she no longer lived, times she no longer expected to live, no matter how much she longed for their return.

Were there no such times now? No days and nights of love, laughter, generosity? Let us look.

— o —

Just when Rachel was expecting the worst—Rachel had come to always expect the worst—Ruby would arrive, boasting a new hairdo, gift in hand, flowers perhaps, or a packet of Jaffas, or a bundle of red-and-gold labelled Chinese incense wrapped in Cellophane, cappuccinos, a bar of sandalwood soap. She appeared healthy, neatly groomed, smartly dressed. Her speech was lucid, her manner warm, friendly; there was no trace of sullenness, no demands were made. Wicked Witch flew out the window, Fairy Queen came gliding in on gossamer wings.

'Hi Ma! Hi Jerry! New scarf, Mum? Looks lovely! How're the mighty Tiges going, Jer? Lose again last Saturday?' She'd laugh.

'Yeah.' Jerry would make a hangdog expression, then laugh with her and they'd talk football for a while.

'Garden looks lovely, Mama. Mmm, the lavender smells divine. Mind if I pick a bunch to take home?' Not waiting for the answer, she would race on. 'Coffees all 'round?'

Ruby would get the kettle going, prepare the mugs, warm the coffee pot.

'Got any goodies, Mum?'

On a favourite plate she would arrange some of whatever treat Rachel had in a cupboard or in the refrigerator, allocating two equal-sized portions each for whoever was partaking.

Rachel would be swept off her feet by her daughter's charm, her generous spirit, her playfulness. All that pent-up fear and anger, the frustrations and disappointments, would melt like jelly in the sun.

Ruby and Rachel would natter away; Jerry, too, if he was present, laughing, gossiping, exchanging what-have-you-been-up-tos. A pot of coffee would be made and drunk, then another. Ruby and Rachel took turns selecting the music.

'What about some Bonnie, Mum? Yeah, let's have Bonnie', Ruby would say, running her finger down the columns of compact disc spines. 'Which one?'

'You choose.'

Without fail, Ruby chose *Streetlights*, the Bonnie Raitt album she favoured most. Mother and daughter would hum and sing, both a half-tone out of register, a little flat, each oblivious to her own discordance, neither disturbed by the other's. *Streetlights* became the signature album of Ruby's visits, as predictable as the opening bars of music announcing the seven o'clock news.

When *Streetlights* finished, Rachel might suggest:

'I bought a new Leonard Cohen . . .'

Ruby would moan, 'Not that old moocher. Not Leonard', and laugh. 'No way, Mum.'

'Ry Cooder?'

'No, not Ry. John Lee.'

Bonnie. Leonard. Ry. John Lee. Rachel was amused by Ruby's intimate references to musicians.

'Boom, boom, boom, boom.' Twelve-bar beat bounced away in the background.

For a change of pace, Rachel would say, 'I would like to listen to some Miles Davis, Ruby.'

'Miles or Mozart?'

Ruby was not fond of jazz; she addressed the classical composers more formally.

'Mozart will be fine.'

'I like Mozart. Anything classical, so long as it's not Beethoven. I can't stand Beethoven. Ah, here it is.'

'Why? It's beautiful music.'

'No, no, no! His music scares me. He's very angry.'

Takes one to know one.

'You'd be angry, too, if you were a composer and knew you were going deaf.'

'Maybe,' Ruby replied, her stare willing Rachel not to insist, 'but no Beethoven.'

They listened to music and passed the afternoon.

— o —

If she were not in a hurry to leave, Ruby would suggest, 'What about a game of canasta or rummy?'

'Mmm . . . rum—'

'Canasta. I always beat you when we play canasta.'

You usually beat me at gin rummy, too.

'Deal 'em up, Mama.'

'I'll pick a bowl of peaches. You deal.'

Ruby would riffle the cards a few times. Rachel enjoyed the snapping sound of the deck as it flipped through Ruby's thumbs, the slap of one card hitting the next, the rush of air through the cards as they flew through her hands. She would go on for so long that Rachel marvelled she didn't shuffle the pips off them. Finally, the shuffling done, Ruby distributed the cards.

Then they would sit at the big table for a convivial hour or two of canasta or rummy. After three or four rubbers, Ruby would say, 'What about a munchies break, Mum?'

She would prepare a tray on which she laid out an elegant array of serviettes and a pale-green Japanese plate laden with dates, figs, almonds, Italian macaroons, and wedges of Granny Smith apple, the peel a brilliant contrast to the earthy browns of the dried fruit and nuts. In the summer she would prepare golden toast piled high with grilled cheese and slices of homegrown tomato topped with a sprig of basil or parsley picked from the garden. Rachel might peel and slice white peaches from the garden, prepare a mango, or fill a black lacquered-wood bowl with a mound of dark-red cherries. Ice tinkled as they shook up the fruit pulp floating in tall frosty glasses of homemade lemonade.

In the winter there were crumpets oozing butter and honey. Steaming hot mugs of coffee or herb teas were always at hand.

For a change, between rubbers, they would take a break to stroll around the corner to Coffee Lounge—the local coffee bar known affectionately in the neighbourhood by the two words signwritten in red on its plateglass window—to buy coffees and *buondi*, the small, rum-and-vanilla flavoured Italian buttercakes made with currants and dried citrus peel. Munching and chatting, they played and laughed and smoked. The ashtray would fill, the room develop a smoky haze; music played all the while. When one disc ended, Ruby would put on another. On cold-weather days they would make light-hearted battle over who was to put another log on the fire, to stoke the coals; they took it in turns.

— o —

Ruby played cards stone-faced, a thin, hand-rolled cigarette dangling from her lip, her eyes squinted against the rising smoke. She never let on a flicker of what was going on in her hand. Rachel admired her style, attempted to emulate her, but Ruby was savvy to her mother's facial movements, too familiar with how Rachel attempted to hide her responses. Ruby also concentrated better, keeping close watch on the cards Rachel threw off onto the discard pile.

'Canasta!' Her cry was victorious. 'Tote 'em up!' she'd hoot, a grin as wide as Luna Park across her face. She would add up her winning points and write them on the scorepad in the column next to Rachel's losers.

Ruby trounced the pants off her.

In their rummy games, while Rachel pondered her next move, trying to predict what Ruby might do next, searching the table for where she might place her cards, Ruby would whoop, 'Gin! I'm *out*', as she distributed the last of her cards to the

appropriate sets and runs and tossed her last card onto the discard pile, her face a picture of triumphant glee.

These were the occasions when Rachel's heart was full with
pleasure; she could feel the light in the room, the slow, calm beat
of her pulse. The absence of fear was palpable.

Good times. Rachel missed them, missed their frequency. As
Ruby slithered further and further into heroin addiction, as
Rachel followed her down, she wondered if they would ever
return.

Once upon a time . . .

— o —

'Cup of tea?' Jerry asked as they walked through the front gate.

'No', Rachel snapped, still angry over the extra twenty minutes they'd stayed in the restaurant, furious with the snail's pace
at which he, a speedy and incautious driver, had driven home.

Her heart skipped a beat: the key was not in the letterbox, the
light in the front bedroom—'Ruby's room' she continued to call
it—was on. When they entered the house, she saw at once that
the bedroom door was ajar. She's here! But not in her bedroom.

Rachel swept down the hall, looking in all the rooms, switch-
ing off lights as she went. No Ruby.

'Wasteful', Rachel muttered, converting her disappointment
into something more manageable: rage. Her stomach fluttered,
her hands began to tremble.

On the bathroom bench stood an uncapped tube of Ruby's lipstick, the lid upright alongside it. Rachel snapped the lid onto
the lipstick and slammed the tube on the bench. She kicked the
door below the bench.

'Ruby. Yoo hoo', she called. 'Are you home, Rube?'

Eternal hope, what well do you spring from?

The house was silent. Rachel marched back up the hall and
shoved the bedroom door fully open. It cracked against the
wardrobe behind; the sound startled her. Standing in the door
frame, she looked around the room. There were no visible signs.

— o —

Sitting on the bed in Ruby's room, Rachel wondered: What has
happened to my life? The life that wasn't disconsolate, wasn't

clouded with fear, weighed down with guilt and self-pity, seared through with anger, steeped in waiting.

Once upon a time . . .

Once upon a time she had enjoyed the company of her friends, and they hers. She dared not think what many of them thought of her these days, miserable more often than not, her eyes blank, inattentive to the conversation at hand. It amazed her that any of her friends kept in touch; some no longer did. Caroline. How long had it been?

Rachel once had a ready laugh, she enjoyed going to the pictures, listening to jazz in clubs, walking hand-in-hand with Jerry in the Botanic Gardens or on the beach, staying out late with friends, dancing, drinking, smoking joints, sitting around kitchen tables until late into the night solving the problems of the world, philosophising on the meaning of life.

Her work was once pleasurable, her relationship with Jerry loving, affectionate and fun. It had been companionable.

'Jerry,' she might ask, 'do you want to do something tonight?'

'What did you have in mind?'

'Tanya phoned. She asked if we would like to eat with her and Alex.'

'Not tonight. Let's go out just the two of us. We could go and see . . .' He would name a film, or a band.

'Sounds good.'

One summer, Jerry suggested a different kind of outing.

'Let's drive over to Port for the evening.'

They prepared a picnic, wrapped the food in wax paper and packed the parcels with a selection of crockery and cutlery into a wicker basket. While Rachel fetched citronella from the garden to ward off mosquitoes, Jerry wrapped two cold stubbies in newspaper which, together with some books and beach towels, he placed in the basket on top of their meal.

As the sky began to change from daylight's shimmering blue to the fiery red of a summer sunset, they drove off to one of the bayside beaches: Port Melbourne or South Melbourne—'Port' or 'South'—or over the West Gate Bridge to Williamstown, where it was less crowded. There they stayed until past dark, eating, reading, swimming, watching the passing parade of other Melburnians who had escaped the oppressive heat of their homes. The evening picnics became woven into the fabric of their summer lives.

There were nights they didn't go anywhere at all, when they enjoyed making love. Once upon a time there was passion.

'Sam phoned earlier today. She and Jack are having a party on Saturday night. Let's go.'

'Who'll be there?'

'The usual crowd. Do you want to go?'

'Nah.'

'What then?'

'How about we have a little lie down and think about it for a while?'

His mouth would stretch into a lascivious grin, the corners of his eyes crease up with laughter; he would wiggle his eyebrows up and down, Groucho Marx-style. Rachel would return his grin. Kissing and licking and stroking each other, they would wend their way to their bedroom, slowly peel the clothes off each other, then leap onto the bed and make love, their endearments whispered, though no one was there to hear them. They delighted in the pleasure they found in each other.

Jerry's reticence towards her suggestion they make love in the back garden under the stars made her laugh: 'The neighbours might hear!' 'We'll do it quietly.' 'Someone will see us.' 'The fences are too high, the trees too tall; no one can see in.' 'I don't know . . .' 'Come on, Jerry, show a bit of dash.'

Emboldened by Rachel's touch and high spirits, her challenging and talk-dirty words, he permitted her to drag him outdoors. The soft lawn tickled their skin. Making love in the garden excited them beyond anything they had previously known. 'Fooling around in the shrubbery', as Jerry called it, also became part of their summer weave.

Charms of another lifetime.

Nowadays? They rarely made love nowadays, outdoors or in. More pressing matters had claimed too much of Rachel's attention and Jerry had lost interest.

— o —

Rachel remained seated on the bed in Ruby's room for over an hour, lost in thought, smoking cigarettes, shivering with tiredness.

'Where are you, Ruby?' she whispered. 'Are you okay?'

Too exhausted to sit any longer, she rolled over and, fully clothed right down to her shoes, curled up, pulling the eider-down around her. Her fitful sleep was pierced by nightmares.

At around midnight, Jerry stood in the doorway, watching Rachel as she slept. After a time, he shook his head, turned off the light and left the room.

SPY IN THE HOUSE OF LOVE

All day long they carp at my words,
their only thought is to harm me,
they gather together, lie in wait and spy on my movements,
as though determined to take my life.

Psalm 56

Rachel became a spy in her own house. After Ruby used the phone, Rachel waited for an opportunity to sidle up to it and press the Redial button. Hand clamped over the mouthpiece, she listened for the answering voice—'Hello? Hello? Who is this? Who's there? Idiot!'—as if the voice might confirm her suspicions by revealing the speaker to be a dealer, as if dealers had voices distinguishable from the rest of the community.

There was one memorable occasion when the man (Rachel felt sure it was a man) at the other end picked up but did not speak. His calm breathing soothed her. After a minute had passed, she removed her hand from the mouthpiece, but did not hang up. Their breathing fell into syncopated rhythm, even-paced, as each waited . . . for what? More minutes—it seemed like minutes—ticked by. Inhale. Exhale. Inhale. Exhale. Rachel envisaged brushes on a snare drum picking up the beat. More time passed. Were they breathing to the beat of a clock's ticks, its tocks? Rachel, her rage dissipated, hung up first, quietly

155

returning the handset to its cradle. She burst into unbridled laughter.

What satisfied her about this phone call? Why did it induce in her such merriment? So blissful a peace?

She wondered if the stranger laughed too, feeling she had heard it on his breath just before she put the phone down. Their breathing felt harmonious, a coupled meditation on waiting, not caring after the first few breaths to know anything more than the existence, the cadence, of another crazed life.

— o —

When Ruby came to stay, Rachel made regular sorties to her bedroom, there to fossick among her daughter's possessions.

No matter what Rachel was doing, her concentration on the task at hand was never complete. Overdrive, her mind was in overdrive as she schemed to concoct a plausible excuse to enter Ruby's bedroom. She rehearsed ways in which she might conduct a conversation that would appear spontaneous, amiable.

'Excuse me, Ruby,' after a tentative knock on the door, 'I have to put some clothes away', usually worked. At least it got her in the door.

What about:

'Ruby, would you like a cuppa?'

Let's try:

'Ruby, will you be in for dinner tonight?'

Bloody pathetic. But she had to know what Ruby was up to, whether she was stoned or straight.

'Do you know what I used to hate most?'

'What?'

'The sound of your footsteps coming up the hall.'

Rachel, her compulsion leading her by the nose, walked up the hall and knocked on Ruby's bedroom door.

Play it again, Sam.

In Ruby's absence, Rachel needed no excuses, no light-hearted conversation. She entered the bedroom to look around for more evidence—as if she needed more, as if this time she might do something about whatever she found—of Ruby's habit. What if she found one of those little plastic bags of white powder? What then? What would she do upon discovering another slender, plastic hypodermic, a tourniquet, or a teaspoon, its underside blackened by the flame held there to melt the powder into injectable liquid?

Emma at the design studio had known what to do. One of the designers, they suspected, bent or discarded all the teaspoons after using them to have his hits in the toilet.

'Bastard!' Emma shouted one morning when she went to put sugar in her coffee only to find the last of the spoons gone. 'I've had it up to here with this bloke.' She sliced a line across her throat with the edge of her index finger. 'I'll fix him.'

She strode out of the office, straight to the local hardware, where, she reported to the amused staff on her return, she purchased six teaspoons.

'Drill some holes in them, would you?' she demanded of the astonished shop owner. 'Right here.' She pointed to the dead centre of them. 'Small enough to hold the sugar, large enough for any liquid to fall through.'

'What's the point of that?' enquired the hardware man, uncertain as to whether Emma was trying to make a fool of him.

'Got a user in the office. Heroin', Emma replied. 'Melts his junk down in the teaspoons then throws them away. Never any fucking spoons—pardon my French—for us straights to use. Here,' she jabbed a pudgy finger at the spoon again, 'drill.'

The day after the drilled spoons arrived in the office, the designer disappeared, never to be seen again.

— o —

Ruby maintained a tidy room: the bed was neatly made, the *tshatshkes*—ornaments, bits and pieces of decoration, photos—arranged with the greatest care. Soft toys, a collection of many years' standing, sat plumped up and arranged in affectionate companionship against the pillows on the bed. Sticks of pink or brown incense jutted from brass holders on each end of the mantelpiece.

In a hand-painted antique box which stood next to an incense holder she kept her jewellery and smaller memorabilia. Rachel opened the box's hinged lid. Staring at the Cellophane-wrapped hypodermic, she felt nothing. After all, how many times could one look at a syringe and still be shocked? She released the lid from her fingers; it snapped shut. Stepping back, she stared at Ruby's suitcase, which stood in front of the fireplace. Whizzing open the zips she raised the top, lifted the neatly folded clothes and removed the books and art materials so as not to disturb their order, fully aware that Ruby was smarter than that: she knew Rachel had been there all right.

Nothing.

Rachel's face burned with shame.

A different circumstance. In the same vein.

That woman who went to live in London. Margaret, or Mary. Or was it Maureen? Whatever. She had come home to Melbourne for a holiday. Soon after her return to England, letters began to arrive. Jerry accused Rachel of spying on him, of reading the woman's letters.

'You don't trust me!' was her vehement reply.

'Very shifty, Rachel. But you're right, I don't', he replied. 'I know you read them.'

'If you don't want me to read your mail, don't leave it lying around.'

The letters arrived in scented, pastel-pink envelopes. Rachel was contemptuous of their fussy femininity, of the pages filled with pinched handwriting: gushy endearments, declarations of undying love, of the neatly cut-out advertisements for cheap real estate and well-paid jobs, enticements for Jerry to leave Rachel and move to where whatever-her-name-was lived. Jerry kept the letters—which continued to arrive with diminishing frequency for twelve months after their argument— poorly secreted in the wardrobe in an old shoe box. Rachel considered them fair game and read them all.

— o —

The most degrading mission Rachel embarked upon was an examination of the contents of the rubbish bag. Ruby had moved on to her next household in yet another suburb. All that remained in the otherwise tidy room was a large, green plastic bag, filled to the top and bulging.

'What on earth could she have had that would fill such a bag?'

Rachel untied the knot. Without considering that she might be pricked by a syringe, or a thought of how disgusting it was to be sitting on the floor of her daughter's bedroom going through a bag of putrid rubbish that smelled of old bananas and cigarette ash, Rachel rummaged through the contents.

The first items she came upon were clothes, all clean, all neatly folded: a pair of jeans, a T-shirt, two blouses, a jumper, a bra and a silk jacket. A puzzling collection; there seemed to be nothing wrong with any of them.

Was she stoned when she put them in the bag. Did she think she was packing them in her suitcase?

Rachel removed the clothes from the bag and laid them in a pile on the floor next to where she sat. 'I'll wash them and take them to her later.'

Below the clothes, the contents of the bag were covered with a film of grey ash; they were smeared and made sticky with dribblings of a leaked pink liquid. Rachel's exploration turned up makeup tubes and jars, some empty, others half full. There was a bottle (empty) of a mixture used to relieve the skin of itching, empty pill packets (Aspro, codeine, laxatives, Valium) and used tissues (peach and white). There were innumerable cigarette butts, used false fingernails varnished *sang-de-boeuf*, sugarless chewing-gum wrappers (some filled with wads of chewed gum), three party balloons (two red, one yellow), golden chocolate-bar wrappers, a hairbrush (most of its bristles missing), ragged-edged squares of a torn-up photo of Ruby and a former boyfriend, a condom in a gold wrapper, and three shoes (none of which matched).

There were hairpins, syringe wrappers and their used contents, the arm off a pair of sunglasses, shards of a china cup, banana peels and apple cores, junk mail, a buckleless belt, clothes catalogues from department stores, a half-eaten roll filled with rancid chicken salad, a tray of blue-green squares of eyeshadow, envelopes devoid of their contents, empty lipstick tubes and henna packets, plastic shopping bags, torn pantyhose, dead matches and empty matchboxes, a couple of plastic cigarette lighters, Band-aid wrappers, empty tissue boxes, and a plethora of empty cigarette boxes, tobacco pouches and cigarette paper packets.

There was a burnt teaspoon.

At the bottom of the bag were some journals—different sizes, different coloured covers and spines, different shapes and thicknesses.

Rachel pulled them through the rubbish and wiped the ash

and sticky stuff off the covers with the T-shirt she extracted from the pile of clothes on the floor. Riffling through the first of the journals, a smile of fond memory spread across her face. Here was a page with locks of Ruby's hair stuck on it. Written beneath each curl and each straight hank was the date Ruby had worn that style and colour. Rachel removed the page and set it on top of the pile of clothes. She riffled some more but there was no other page like it. Later, she hid it in her bedroom between the pages of a novel.

Every page contained a small drawing, embellishments perhaps to the writing Rachel would not read; she did not permit herself so much as a glance at the writing. Not out of any respect for Ruby's privacy. Not that. Rather, what if there were things written in them about her (and she presumed there were), critical things, spiteful things, things far too humiliating and shaming to read? What if Ruby had written accounts of how she scored her dope that Rachel, even in her wildest, her most deranged fantasies, hadn't thought of?

Looking at Ruby's heroin paraphernalia, searching through her suitcase, her box of treasures, that was one thing; reading her feelings, her deepest, maddest, saddest, craziest, loneliest thoughts was another matter altogether.

Rachel paused in her riffling only at pages that contained artwork. She admired the individual flowers (the oriental poppies were particularly lovely), whole sections of the garden, pencil sketches of Rachel or Eli at work, of Jerry watching television or charcoal drawings of his head, and other pieces that had nothing to do with the garden or the family. When she came to a full-page black-ink drawing of a syringe, she snapped the book closed.

None of the books were fully used. It was as if, at a certain point, Ruby had decided to try again, and thus began another new book.

'Waste of paper.' Even to herself, Rachel's voice sounded prim. 'I'll find a use for them.'

One after the other she opened the books, pulled out wads of used pages, tore each wad in half, then half again, and threw the pieces back into the bag with the other rubbish. When she had finished, she gathered in the corners of the green plastic bag and retied them into a firm knot, at the last minute saving the oriental poppy.

After gathering up the pile of clothes, the stack of journals, the page with the snippets of hair and that with the poppy, Rachel looked around to ensure she had left no trace of her excursion. Then, she picked up the bag of rubbish and tiptoed from the room.

— o —

Inevitably, curiosity overcame reticence: the journals' contents drew her, a siren's call. Rachel retrieved the plastic bag from the rubbish bin. Setting it on the garden table, she carefully removed the torn journal pages, now limp with moisture and grey with ash.

Piece after piece she sorted them, matching tops to tops, bottoms to bottoms, then top halves to bottom halves until, three hours later, she had Sellotaped the lot.

What Rachel read was more heart-breaking than frightening: promises to stop using, pleas to God for relief, commitment to write in the journal every day from now on, desperate wishing to be clean, complimentary, loving or angry words about a friend, an acquaintance or a lover, meditative observations on life, and dates and times for appointments.

Rachel cringed when she read entries about herself.

'Mum is always trying to look at my eyes. Must buy shades.'

'She went through my things again today. Wonder what she'd do if I put a lock on the door? That'd fix her.'

'Poor Mum. Always seems tired.'

'Mum and Jerry arguing again. Will they stay together?'

'Lovely time at Mum and Jerry's tonight. Great meal. She gave me a huge bunch of delphiniums to take home. She's so much nicer to be around when she isn't firing off twenty questions.'

And this, many times:

'Five calls in three days.'

'Three calls today.'

'Four calls in two days. Must get some money together for an answering machine.'

Other entries: how much Ruby hated her at times, arguments they'd had, how Ruby resented Rachel's interference in her life, how humiliating it was for her to come and live with Rachel and

Jerry when she felt she had nowhere else to go. Rachel was grat-
ified to read accounts of good times they'd had together.

So convinced was Rachel that the stuff of Ruby's life revolved
solely around heroin and arguing with her, that when she read
entries describing the fun she'd had at a party, listening to a band
or seeing a film, an account of a friend's visit, a day at work or
a night spent with a lover, it shocked her. Rachel was astonished
to learn that her daughter had any good times at all.

— o —

The written entries, whatever the depth of feeling in them, faded
before the collages. Rachel discovered journals (not particularly
well secreted, she observed) in which Ruby had constructed
exquisite images using pictures cut from glossy magazines as her
starting point, enhancing the cutouts with expensive matte
papers and coloured foils, fabrics and other materials. Each collage—as small as postcards, as large as an accountant's ledger,
depending on the size of the book in which they were made—
was constructed edge to edge over an entire two-page spread.
'Bleeding', designers called it. Ruby's dreams—for so the collages
seemed to Rachel—were bleeding off the pages of her journals.

Rachel made herself comfortable on the bed to examine them.

Three collages were of bedrooms: beds, curtains, lamps, quilts,
pillows and cushions, dressing tables and wardrobes, paintings,
light fittings, rugs.

The first was elegant in its simplicity. A futon on a black lacquered base was covered with a red-and-gold bedspread and
angled, diamond-like, in the middle of the room. Bedside tables,
also black wood, stood at forty-five degree angles from both sides
of the bedhead; on each was pasted a red and white shoji lamp.
The walls of the room were cream, the carpet eucalyptus green.
A brightly coloured kite floated from the ceiling above the bed.
Ruby had constructed the kite a tail, a thread of vermilion silk
to which she'd stuck little butterfly shaped pieces of emerald silk.

At the opposite end of this room stood a rectangular
lacquered wood table, red. In the middle of the table was a
cluster of fat creamy candles of varying heights and thicknesses,
their perfect flames cut from pale golden foil.

'Crikey', whispered Rachel when she saw it. 'This is . . .' she struggled for superlatives, '. . . so . . . beautiful! How is it I've never seen these before?'

The second bedroom, in a book smaller than the first, was rustic, busier. It was decorated with colonial furniture: a chest of drawers, a writing desk, two chairs, a leather-covered couch, on which were arranged two large cushions the same pattern as the Persian rug—matte papers of rich reds and blues and black—that was spread on the floor.

'Look at this!'

Braided tassels of hand-woven wool had been stuck to each end of the rug.

Does she weave the tassels?

Rachel didn't like the third bedroom. It was cold looking, and sparse: greys, royal blue and black, stainless steel and mirrors; the patterns of the fabrics were angular and harsh. It contained no decoration.

Has Ruby been in a room like this?

Bathrooms: black and white, green and white; the fittings, gold. The windows—round, square, rectangular—afforded the occupant a luxuriant botanical view from where they stood in the shower or sat in the bath.

Rachel slid her fingers over the collages, her touch gentle, careful not to damage any of the work.

Livingroom and kitchen combinations outnumbered the other rooms. They seemed to be grouped into styles: modern, Victorian, rustic, professional. Then into colour or texture: wood, stainless steel, Laminex, tiles, slate. Chairs around tables were a feature, as were items on tables or sideboards: a pair of candlesticks, decorative glass bowls, platters of tropical fruit, vases of flowers, a bowl of salad, a roast of meat surrounded by vegetables, a whole fish with what looked like a black olive in its eye socket, an *étagère* arranged with *petit fours*.

Look! Here are collages of her favourite musicians. Bonnie, Ry, John Lee, rock'n'rollers Rachel did not know. She smiled with satisfaction at the inclusion of Miles Davis in two of the music collages, assuming it to mean that Ruby had come to enjoy his music.

— o —

The garden collages took Rachel's breath away.

Trees had been neatly cut around their outlines: leaves, blossoms and fruit. Similarly with flowers. Mauve bearded irises—buds and full blooms—cut around the delicate tracery of their shapes, appeared in clumps, as did creamy California poppies, deep blue ixia and yellow ranunculi. Ruby had pasted them into garden beds, others into a broad sweep across whole patches of garden, still more grouped in the middle or on the edges of lawns. At the base of one tree stood a Japanese lantern made of stone. From its slots shone slices of gold-foil candlelight.

Overhead, in the blue of the sky, flew exotic and vibrant-coloured birds of all sizes from continents far away, their feathers made from foil. There were others, brown or black local birds (matte papers). Some flew in small flocks, others alone. A few pecked in the grass.

There was even a vegetable garden collage, in which no heed had been paid to the seasons for growth.

Two of the garden collages had fish ponds. In one, shaped like the curved blade of a Chinese chopping knife, six pockets had been cut. Each slit was filled with foil and gloss-paper fish: gold, black, orange, white, speckled, and one, made from foil, a brilliant turquoise. Each fish had an eye fashioned from a miniature black sequin.

The night-sky collage, that was the most exquisite of all.

A gold-foil architrave glowed around the edges of a double-page spread. To the left was a large tree (matte paper), on the right a mass of flowering shrubs (matte paper again); a path of terracotta bricks (and again) ran through green foil grass.

The sky, hand-painted, ranged from phthalo blue at the top, through ultramarine to pale cobalt at the horizon. This rich and sensual firmament was ablaze with tiny gold stars which had been stuck into place to create a sparkling Milky Way. Here and there, a few larger stars—iridescent pale blues, rich mauves, glittering golds. See here! A red star. Mars?

High in the sky was a silver sliver of moon. At the intersection of sky and land lay a strand of reddish-orange silk thread.

In the evenin' when the sun goes down . . .

When Rachel saw the garden collages she gasped, enthralled; the radiance of the night-sky collage made her weep.

Rachel marvelled at the amount of work, the finesse, that had gone into creating the collages; she was captivated by their beauty, awed by the patience, love and care that was required to make the gardens and the night sky. She shook her head in wonder. How long did it take Ruby to do each one? Did she work without pause? Did she construct pieces concurrently or one at a time? Who did she show them to? Were they made here, in her bedroom?

Search as she might, Rachel turned up not one scrap of evidence: no magazines, no scissors, no blades or glue, not so much as the thinnest slice of paper. Not a single, tiny, fallen star.

Two days after Rachel's discovery of the collages, Ruby came to dinner. No mention was made of her artwork during their amicable meal, nor later, when Rachel, Ruby and Jerry strolled around the corner for coffee. As Ruby ran for the tram, her backpack swinging from her shoulder, she promised to phone soon. When Jerry and Rachel arrived home, the books had gone.

Interlude III—Odium

A belt. Any kind of belt. Brown, black, sometimes red; the leather new, old, shiny, dull; its texture smooth, braided, tooled. The buckle brass or silver, plain or ornate.

The belt lies on the bed, the bedroom floor, in an armchair or on the bench in the bathroom, coiled up, partly coiled, or stretched out, like a viper. The buckle is always at the outer end, a metal Cyclops staring up at her.

Seeing a belt lying about the house pulls Rachel up short. Does the belt belong to Ruby or Jerry? She wonders what it might have been used for. Standing in Ruby's bedroom (the livingroom, the bathroom), immobilised, she stares at it, stark against the pale cover of the feather quilt (a fine contrast to the gumleaf green of the couch, a natural blend with the timber grain of the bathroom bench).

A belt has become a tourniquet to bring up a vein in readiness for the needle, paraphernalia for a shot of heroin. Has Ruby used it to get some heroin into her arm, to have a hit? (Is this where that slang comes from: a belt, a hit?) Impossible to see a belt and believe it's nothing more than that—a belt, a fashionable convenience to hold up a pair of trousers, to pull a blouse in at the waist.

One evening Rachel goes to fetch a jumper from her wardrobe in Ruby's bedroom. On the bed is a soft black-leather belt with an elegant silver buckle. She picks it up. Wraps the unbuckled end around the fingers of her left hand. Hears the crack of her elbow joint as she juts her right arm out in front of her. White underside up. Winds the belt around her arm, just above the elbow. Slides the leather first through the metal, then back over the top. Pulls as tight as she can.

The belt secured, she makes a fist. Opens and closes her fingers with an even pumping, as she tries to bring up a vein. Open close, open close, open close.

Is this how they do it?

Her breathing is rapid. Shallow gasps for air, the same metre as the pumping. In out, in out, in out.

Beneath the soft flesh of her arm the veins remain obstinately hidden, refuse to surface. Her eyes smart from the sweat that pours down her face. She licks away the drops gathered along her upper lip.

The leather, though soft, begins to chafe her skin. It pinches her flesh. Rachel does not care; she wants to hurt herself. She persists. Her fingers begin to ache from the pumping, the muscles in her forearm become tired. She slackens her grip on the belt, allows it to slip down her arm. As the belt drops to her wrist, she observes red welts and a ring of subcutaneous bleeding just above the inside of her elbow.

Pulling the leather back through the buckle, she wrenches it off her wrist. Grabbing the belt at both ends, she stretches it as hard as she can, tries to break it in two. Her knuckles crack.

With all her strength she tugs, twists.

'You fuck!' Sprays saliva.

Unable to break the belt, she uncoils the buckled end from around her hand and lashes it around. Whips the air with it. The room is small. The buckle thwacks against the mantelpiece, the cupboard doors; it knocks against the wall. Plaster dust, coarse and grey, rains onto the carpet.

'Fuck you! Fuck you! I hate you!' she shrieks as she flails the air.

The buckle hits the naked light globe at the end of the flex dangling from the ceiling. Thin glass shatters around the room, into her hair. Abruptly she stops. Becomes aware of what she has done. Sees the chipped plaster, the scratched paint. Feels the prickle of glass in her scalp. Reaches up her hand and tries to flick it away. Scratches at it.

She attempts to regain her composure, forces herself to breathe deeply. An effort of will.

Dropping the belt onto the bed, she wipes the sweat from her forehead and face with one long sleeve of her T-shirt. She wipes the mucus running from her nose with the other. Gingerly now, she picks at the splinters in her head, wincing as she feels them sink deeper into her flesh. Her scalp is bleeding where glass has pierced her skin. Fingers, too, are nicked by glass; they drip blood.

'Tweezers', she mutters.

She turns to leave the room and sees it there, the belt: it lies once more on the quilt cover, stretched out, like a snake sunning itself, its dispassionate, silver-buckle eye staring up at her.

'Help me,' she whispers, 'I'm so frightened.'

She has no idea to whom she pleads. There is only the empty room.

— o —

Band-aids. What could be more innocuous than a Band-aid? Comfort for a child's playground wound, an adult's finger cut while chopping food, a blister on a heel rubbed raw by a new shoe.

Rachel sees crumpled Band-aids on the bathroom bench, their padding stained the dirty brown of dried blood. Are they from wounds where Ruby sticks needles into her arm? Or are they, more innocently, from her fingers, which bleed where she mercilessly chews away at herself, biting her nails to the quick?

What on earth does Ruby do with so many Band-aids?

'Mum, do you have any Band-aids?'

'I think so, Ruby. Look in the bathroom cupboard. Cut yourself?'

'Nah', Ruby replies. 'Just need a Band-aid or two. I'll be right.'

Ruby disappears into the bathroom, closing the door behind her. When she ventures out, Rachel casts a surreptitious look to see where she might have pasted the Band-aids. There are times when Ruby emerges from the bathroom, her eyelids heavy, her head lolling; other times she is bright-eyed, quite capable—were she to be asked—of walking a straight line. Sometimes Rachel sees the Band-aids wrapped around a finger or two; other times, no sign.

'What are you looking at?' Ruby snaps at her.

'Eh? Oh, nothing. All fixed?'

'Fixed?'

'The Band-aids.'

'Oh, the Band-aids. Yes, I'm okay, thanks.'

One morning, Rachel selects a pair of white socks from her wardrobe. She notices, upon unrolling them, at the toe of one sock is a stain that looks like a tiny circle of dried blood.

'Hmm,' she says, 'rust.'

Still, she looks at her bare feet to see if there is a scab in the corresponding site on either foot. Of course there is not. Ruby must have borrowed the socks; Jerry would never wear white socks.

Does she inject into a vein between her toes?

Was she unable to find a Band-aid to stanch the bleeding?

Did she bleed so much that the blood seeped through the Band-aid?

Was one of the used Band-aids I saw on the bathroom bench used on her foot? Some other part of her body?

Heroin users, Rachel knows, inject in bizarre parts of their bodies: the stomach (she read somewhere), even (she overhead someone say)—if they become truly desperate after the collapse of all other useable veins—into their eyeballs.

Rachel wants to stop Ruby using the Band-aids, as if, by osmosis, this will stop her using heroin. In the meantime, she continues to wonder and watch.

— o —

The siren doesn't need to be blaring. Nor the red and blue lights be flashing on the white roof. It is enough to see a police car driving past or parked in the vicinity for fear to immobilise her.

It is because she always expects the worst. It is because, when all is said and done, she knows so little about the life of a heroin addict. A sprinkling of facts, a pinch of popular wisdom (and culture), and lashings of the dramas of her own imagination. It is because she anticipates tidings of her daughter's death or incarceration, which, she expects, will come to her in the form of a pair of uniformed police officers.

Picture this.

Rachel is working in the front garden when a patrol car

cruises by. The officer on the passenger's side peers out the window, apparently looking at the house numbers. Rachel wishes her neighbours no ill, but hopes it is they who will be the recipients of the officers' call. Down the street a house or two, perhaps three, the car pulls into the kerb. The two officers get out, tuck in their shirts. She stares, transfixed, at the guns, handcuffs, batons hanging from the belts around their waists. Regardless of their distance from her, she believes she hears them speak her name into their walkie-talkies.

'This is it.' She holds her breath. Even on the hottest days of summer her skin puckers with goosepimples as she watches them amble along the street. Amble? Why should they hurry? The young woman in question is in a holding cell. Or dead.

Waiting. Time without end.

Each man mumbles a perfunctory greeting as they stroll past her house to the main road a few metres away. She inches her way to the fence, leans over just far enough so as, should they turn, she can step back without them seeing her. Ten minutes elapse and she begins to think they might not be coming to see her after all. Ah, no! First they will buy their lunches, *then* they will come.

They return, laughing, leisurely. Each carries a can of Coke; in the other hand, a brown paper bag out of which pokes a bread roll bulging with salame and lettuce. The men climb into their patrol car and drive away.

— o —

She comes to dread the ringing of the phone. Also its silence.

Which is worse? The silence. The silence is unbearable.

Whenever she goes out, she won't stay away too long in case Ruby phones. When she is at home, she won't move too far from the phones (three are installed). She sneaks looks at the answering machine; perhaps Ruby called and she didn't hear the phones ring over the radio, over the water running in the kitchen sink. Over the raucous racing of her mind.

What if the phone is broken? Oh dear. Her brow is knotted

with anxiety. She lifts the handset and listens: the phone is in working order.

There it goes! Ruby! She hastens her step so as to reach the phone before the answering machine kicks in, but when she plucks the receiver from its cradle, all she hears is the gentle purring of the dial tone. Disappointment overwhelms her.

Rachel wishes Jerry was not there to witness her peeping at the answering machine, picking up a phone that hasn't rung to listen for a voice that isn't there.

She waits for Ruby's calls with a mixture of longing and dread.

She hopes, too, that the caller will not be Ruby asking her for assistance, or money, or if she may come to stay for the night. Rachel hates these calls. Unable to deny Ruby's requests, she becomes angry with herself for succumbing (though she always blames Ruby for asking).

Acquiescence and sinking of the heart.

There are nights when Ruby phones late. In the midnight hour, she is ready to hunker down and chat, full of enthusiasm and good cheer, full of plans Rachel knows won't come to fruition. Full of dope.

One midnight Rachel gathers her courage.

'Ruby, I would prefer it if you didn't phone after eleven, please.'

'Sure. What's the time?'

'Five to twelve.'

'Oh, sorry. I didn't realise. Sorry, Mama. I'll call you tomorrow. See ya.'

Ruby rarely calls back on those tomorrows and Rachel's guilt flourishes anew.

'What would it have cost me? I could have chatted for a few minutes.'

'She shouldn't be phoning at that hour', Jerry replies.

'I feel so mean.'

Rachel waits for Ruby's calls with a mixture of longing and dread.

Relief is Rachel's first response when she hears Ruby's voice. Ruby, you're alive! Then comes wariness. What will be the purpose of this call?

When Ruby is straight and cheerful Rachel's spirit soars. She is filled with excitement and the faith of the devout that at last her daughter must be clean, or getting clean, that Ruby is ready to lead a life away from the torpor of heroin. In these conversations Rachel's expectations for her daughter's life reach their zenith. She feels free to invite Ruby to come for a meal or to suggest they meet for coffee. Ruby seems pleased to accept her invitation, though she does not always show up on the appointed day.

Rachel waits for Ruby's calls with a mixture of longing and dread. If Ruby is unhappy, the conversation might take this shape.

'Hi, Mama. It's me.' A whisper of a voice.

'Hello, Ruby. How are you?'

Rachel's heart is sinking.

'I'm so depressed.'

'I'm sorry to hear that, sweetheart.'

Silence.

'Can I come over?'

Sinking further and further.

'If you like.'

Silence.

'Can I stay the night?'

'I suppose so. All right. Yes.'

Silence.

'Will you come and get me? I haven't got any money.'

Rachel's heart has dropped into a deep, cold well.

'Oh, Ruby, don't you even have train fare?'

'No. Not a cracker. I'm flat broke, Mama, completely broke.' Silence. 'I haven't eaten since yesterday.'

The hook!

When Rachel doesn't reply:

'Oh well, don't worry. I'll be all right. I'll come another day.'

Clinched.

'No, no. It's okay. I'll come and get you. I'll be there in an hour or so.'

Rachel heaves her martyr's sigh.

'Thanks, Mum. See you soon. I love you.'

'I love you too, Ruby. See you soon.'

Brava. Bravissima!

Each has played her part to perfection.

— o —

'I love you, Mama.'

Rachel grows to hate 'I love you, Mama' and wishes Ruby wouldn't say it, wishes she didn't feel compelled to respond in kind. But they carry on with it, each seeking absolution, each believing there is something to forgive, that love is conditional upon their respective good behaviour.

'I love you, Mama.'

'I love you too, Ruby.'

They used to play a game with 'I love you', a race to see who could say it first at the completion of the bedtime story or, later, at the end of a phone conversation.

'Love you! Hah,' Ruby would chortle, 'I said it first!'

'Love you too, Rube', Rachel would laugh in return.

'See you soon, Mum.'

Leave 'em smiling.

Before heroin, the sentiment is as it is spoken: no exchange of approval or forgiveness is asked for or required. Ensnared in heroin's grasp, conditions apply. As Ruby's habit becomes worse, the frequency of the game increases, its intent shifts ground. These days, when Ruby says, 'I love you, Mama', her voice is tinged with sadness, with hopelessness. She says it most, Rachel believes, in times of heavy using.

Rachel comes to understand this phrase, when uttered by Ruby, to mean 'I'm sorry, Mama', and, 'Do you love me, Mama, even though I'm an addict? Despite the life I lead?'

'I love you, Mama.'

'Yes, Ruby. I love you, too.'

— o —

Odious, too, the word 'junkie'; young men and women attired in black leather and silver; tattoos; the blue mark—fine as a needle— between Ruby's toes which Rachel can't take her eyes off whenever she sees Ruby's bare feet; any mention of hypodermic needles; films, television programs and books that discuss, show scenes of, or in any way allude to drug use (even if the approach is medical, sociological or scientific); dealers; petty thieves; secrets; and lies.

And dreams of addiction and death, because even in unwitting sleep there is no relief.

WAITING

Rachel stands in the upstairs verandah kitchen stirring a large pot of soup. The louvred windows facing onto the garden below are open, letting in a pleasant breeze, which causes the white muslin curtains at the sides of the windows to flutter. As Rachel stirs, two officers of the Gestapo come pounding up the outside wood-slat stairs to the kitchen. They kick in the door.

'Where is she?' one of them yells, looking around the room.

'Don't lie to us. We know she's here', screams the other, his face close to Rachel's.

Rachel is unperturbed by these men and their yelling. She continues to stir the soup.

The men catch sight of Ruby sitting at the table. Rachel watches, detached, as they grab her roughly, one by the hair, the other by the feet, and throw her down the stairs. She watches her daughter's body bounce, tumbling down step by step, until it reaches the bottom. At the foot of the steep staircase, Ruby is picked up by two more Gestapo—so gaunt-faced and thin they look like emissaries of death— who hold her aloft by her feet and dunk her, head first, into an eighteen-gallon wooden beer barrel filled with icy water. Rather than revive her, the water serves to make Ruby splutter and gasp, its iciness closing down her lungs until, finally, she hangs upside down from the hands of the Gestapo, blue, dead, water running from her long dark hair and the silver-zipped pockets of her black leather jacket.

— o —

Of the many fears Rachel carried in her soul the greatest was that Ruby would die. Sad, lonely, alone, in a squalid room, her cold body the pasty bluish-grey of death, drool dribbling from a corner of her mouth, a needle hanging out of her arm. Or that she would be beaten up—her body broken and bleeding, her face pinched with fear—by a dealer, a deathly piper to whom she had been unable to pay the price of the tune.

Pounce!

The grisly images intruded, usually when she least expected them.

Dear God, she would pray then to a deity in whom she did not believe, relieve me of this.

— o —

There were moments, too, when Rachel did indeed wish her daughter would die, though it was a wish entirely without malice and its cast of a most tender nature. Born of frustration and an inability to envisage a solution to their ongoing miseries, this desire was induced by a longing for mutual peace. In her fantasy, Rachel imagined that Ruby would, in dying, at last be at rest, relieved of the torment of those of her demons that Rachel assumed goaded her addiction. For her own part, Rachel under-stood that the loss of her daughter would be grievous and incalculable. Eventually, however, in the fullness of time—so the fantasy went—Rachel too would find a much-longed-for serenity.

— o —

In the madness that had become their lives, five days without a call from Ruby was a long time. It was Rachel's belief that of the many reasons Ruby might have for phoning her, one was to let Rachel know she was still alive.

Rachel paced the livingroom, frowning, chewing the quicks of her fingernails. Jerry sat on the couch, reading.

'I should contact her. What do you think, Jerry?'

He looked up from the newspaper.

'You don't even know where she's living.'

'I could ask around.'

'Leave her alone.'

'Something's wrong, I can feel it.'

'Feel it', he snickered. 'Just like all the other times?'

'You're so damned complacent.'

'And you're always dramatising.'

'That's not fair!'

'Fair', he scoffed. 'Well, she usually is all right, isn't she?'

'If you think being stoned, and whatever else her life is, is all right.'

'I don't, but I'm sick of her being stoned impinging on my life.'

'Why don't you piss off?'

Good question, Rach.

Jerry doesn't reply; he's not sure he knows the answer. Instead, he says:

'Leave her alone.'

'I'm her mother.'

'So what?'

'She needs me.'

'Really?' Sarcastic. 'I wonder who really needs whom, Rachel? You are forever at her beck and call. What she needs is somewhere to crash from time to time, a meal. What you need is to get on with your own life. You cannot continue this way, living every moment as if she's about to come home to be your baby again. That part of your life is over, Rachel. Long gone.'

Rachel continued as if he hadn't spoken.

'She never lets this many days go by without ringing. Never.'

'Oh, for Christ's sake. I've had enough of this.' Jerry stood up from the couch.

'I know I'm right, Jerry.'

'Good. So, you're right. Go ahead and do whatever you have to do.'

Mellowing, Rachel pleaded with him. 'Jerry, please. She's in trouble. Sitting around doing nothing is driving me crazy.'

'How many times have we been through this, Rachel?' The battle lines were so familiar now, so wearing. 'No matter what I say, you'll do as you please. I am nothing than a bystander. This has been something between the two of you for . . .' He shrugged, as if the amount of time was too long to utter. 'Phone who you have to. It won't get you anywhere.' He folded the newspaper.

'I'll phone from the bedroom.'

Rachel turned back the quilt and settled cross-legged on the bed, her back against a collection of large feather pillows. The comfort of the bedding made her drowsy; she would like to have gone to sleep—months and months of sleep—but the fear persisted and grew, and with it her need to search for Ruby.

Rachel shook a cigarette from the packet and lit up, inhaling deeply. Jerry brought her a cup of tea; he stroked her hair, the single mechanical stroke a gesture more resigned than affectionate. In her diary she located the phone number (copied from Ruby's address book) of a woman Ruby had once introduced her to. Annie. Ruby met Annie during a brief stay in a rehabilitation centre. Rachel knew they kept in touch.

Sipping the scalding tea, Rachel pressed out Annie's phone number.

'Annie', a cheerful voice announced.

'Hello, Annie. This is Rachel Grinblatt. Ruby's mother. We met—'

'Hi!' Her greeting was warm. 'How are you, Rachel?'

'I'm fine, Annie. How about you?'

'Well, thanks. What can I do for you, Rachel? How's that Ruby going?'

'I don't know. I haven't heard from her . . .' Rachel felt her cheeks flush. She spat out the words, as if they were sour milk. 'I haven't heard from her for five days.'

Was that a long-suffering sigh she heard?

'Rachel, Ruby is an adult. What is she now? Twenty-four? Five? Five days not speaking to your mum isn't such a big deal.'

It is where I come from.

She heard the smile in Annie's voice, the tone of an adult who, with eternal patience, explains and explains something to a child who is unable—or unwilling—to comprehend.

'It might sound pathetic to you, Annie, but I'm scared.'

'Rachel, if you get frightened every time you don't hear from Ruby for more than a few days,' Annie chuckled, 'you'll drive yourself mad.'

'I don't feel like this every time', Rachel snapped. 'I feel it this time. It's rare that more than three days go by without her contacting me, even if it's just to say hello or to tell me she feels lousy.'

'Ruby's pretty tough. She'll be okay.'

'Pretty tough? I'm tired of being told she'll be okay. How do you know that, Annie? Do you have a direct line to God?'

'Stop shouting. Nobody knows anything for sure, but I happen to think Ruby's a survivor.'

'Even survivors struggle, Annie.'

'Calm down, will you. Tell me what you think is wrong.'

'I . . . I . . . don't know . . . exactly.'

Rachel could not bring herself to say the words.

'Come on', Annie enticed. 'Tell me what it is. What is the problem?'

Rachel exploded.

'I have dreams, Annie. Dreams about Ruby and heroin and violence and death. Death', she repeated the word softly. 'Whenever I dream of terrible things happening to her, the worst things, I know something is wrong. And I'm always right. Every time!' There was nothing smug in the claim, only terror and grief and pain. 'I'll tell you this, too, Annie. I hate knowing. Hate it!'

Rachel moaned like a wounded animal, then burst into heaving sobs. Annie intruded on her keening.

'Say what you think it is.'

'I'm afraid she's dead.'

'Hmm.' There was a short silence. 'Listen to me now. You know I don't usually go chasing up people I've had dealings with in rehab. If they need help, they have to ask for it.'

'Oh, for Chrissake, Annie, I am not interested in the party line.'

'Cut that out, Rachel. Listen to what I have to say before you go flying off the handle. I am going to make an exception this time.'

Rachel snuffled.

'I'll phone a couple of people and ask if anyone's seen her around, put the word out that I'm looking for her. See if that nets anything. If I hear something I'll call you.'

'Thank you, Annie. Annie? I know I'm right about this.'

'We'll see. In the meantime, you look after yourself. Okay? Goodbye, Rachel. Take it easy.'

'Goodbye, Annie. Thanks again.'

'Well?' Jerry was sitting on the edge of the bed.

'Annie hasn't heard from her in weeks. She's going to ring people to see if anyone knows where she is.'

Rachel wiped her nose on the handkerchief he proffered. Rachel enjoyed using his handkerchiefs; they were infused with the light, sweaty smell of his body.

'I'll try the people she used to live with in Moonee Ponds. Maybe they know where she is.'

If they knew, they weren't telling Rachel.

Adam was icy, his responses punctuated by sniffing, a sound Rachel had grown to detest, even in young children.

'I'm looking for Ruby, Adam. Do you know where she is?'

'Nope.'

'This is important, Adam.'

His muttered reply was inaudible.

'I beg your pardon?'

'Nothing. Didn't say a thing.'

Except for the sound of his rattling mucus, there was silence. She wanted to yell: Get a goddamned hankie. Blow. Your. Fucking. Nose!

'Is that all?'

'I suppose so. If you see her—'

'Yeah, yeah. I know. Tell her to call you.'

He didn't bother to say goodbye.

Rachel's fortunes did not improve with the next call. Rhyll was more than distant; she was angry.

'What the hell are you ringing here for? What if she was here? You're always ringing here looking for her. Why don't you bloody well leave her alone? Leave me alone, too. Piss off, Rachel. Live your own damn life.'

Rhyll and Rachel slammed their phones down at the same time.

At Warwick's, over a background cacophony of heavy rock'n'roll music, the voice of the answering machine imparted a message—for the fourth time that hour—that no one was available to take her call and suggested the caller leave a message after the tone, man. Once again, Rachel slammed down the phone.

'Going great guns, I see. Give it a rest, Rachel.'

'I'll have to give it a rest whether I want to or not. I don't know who else to call.'

'Let's go to Coffee Lounge.'

'What if she phones? What if Annie phones?'

'We have an answering machine', he replied. 'Come on, we'll take the long way around. The walk will do you good.'

As they stepped through the gate onto the street, Jerry put his arm through Rachel's, but she shook him away. He shrugged.

They walked to Coffee Lounge, twin pictures of misery and defeat.

— o —

Jerry was right: the walk did improve her disposition. By the time they'd had coffee and *buondi*, Rachel had softened enough to accommodate Jerry's affection; they walked home arm in arm. He opened the front door and Rachel ran down the hall. The red digital dot on the answering machine was flashing. She hit the playback button, lit a cigarette and waited, impatient for the voice.

'Hi Rachel, it's Annie. I spoke to someone who saw Ruby four days ago. They said she was stoned but okay. If you want to talk, phone me, but no later than eleven please.'

Ten to. Rachel dialled.

'Hello, Rachel. Since I left the message, I've spoken to someone else who saw her last week.'

Rachel did not feel reassured, and said so.

'Rachel, it's late. I'm not going to do any more now. I'll have another go tomorrow. Try to get some sleep now.'

'Sleep! You can't be serious?'

'I'm serious. I'll admit it is a bit unusual that no one in the scene seems to have sighted her in at least four days, even if it's just to score. But it doesn't mean she's dead. Still,' Rachel heard her shrug, 'I've been wrong before.'

'You callous bitch, Annie!'

'Rachel, I deal with people like Ruby all day, every day. I care for them, but if my heart bled the way you seem to think it should, I'd be no use to anyone, least of all to myself.' Her tone was firm, though not unkind. Annie paused for a moment, considering. 'I probably shouldn't tell you this, but Ruby does disappear from the scene from time to time to do cold turkey.'

'Does she?'

'Yes. But she usually busts. It's very difficult, virtually impossible for most people, to break a heavy habit on their own, without some kind of help.'

'I had no idea! She never said anything about it to me.'

'Why should she? I know how much you want her to get clean, but it's not your business, Rachel. Heroin addiction makes a mess of families. Relationships often disintegrate, everyone is embroiled in everyone else's business, people hurt, everyone blaming, everyone guilty. I've met addicts who've been banished by their families, others whose families want to do everything for them in order to make up for behaviours they believe caused the addiction. Believe me, parents are often the last ones who can help. Not directly, anyway. Getting clean is something Ruby has to do without your intervention, in a rehab, preferably in a program with people who will be tough with her, as well as caring. When she's ready, really ready, she'll do it herself, without you hovering in the wings worrying how she's going all the time.'

'Is that what she says I do?'

'What difference does it make?'

'Do you think she'll ever get clean?'

'I don't read futures, Rachel. She may, she may not. If she does, it's unlikely to be at the pace you'd like. Getting clean is hard work. It takes a long time and eternal vigilance. It took me years. You name it, I tried it. I swapped smack for grog. After a month I realised I was drunk all the time. I went in and out of detoxes, rehabs and Narcotics Anonymous meetings. Odyssey House. I only managed a couple of months there. Ran away. Then there were the years on and off methadone. Still,' Annie sighed, 'at least it enabled me to put some order in my life. Hell, I even ran off to live in the country once, a big-city girl like me! Can you imagine?'

Annie laughed at what her life had been. Rachel grabbed the fragment she offered and held it fast.

'Now, listen to me,' Annie said. 'Have yourself a steaming hot bath. Have a good long soak then get some sleep. Do you have any lavender oil? Buy some tomorrow. If you hear anything, you phone me. Day or night.'

'Day or night? You don't mind?'

'No, I don't mind.'

'I'm sorry I yelled at you, Annie. I was at my wits' end. Thank you for all you've done.'

'No need to apologise. The madness has a particularly sharp edge when it's your own kid.'

'How do you know that?'

'Do you think you're the only parent who goes through this?' She paused. 'You might consider getting some help for yourself, Rachel. Learn to let go of her.'

Rachel didn't reply. Oh, Rachel, Annie thought, you're not ready, are you? It's going to be a while yet.

'Take it easy, Rachel', she said kindly. 'Goodnight.'

'Goodnight, Annie. Will you . . .?'

'Yes, Rachel. If I hear anything I'll call you. Goodnight.'

— o —

The last time Rachel looked at the clock it was a quarter past four; after that she slept fitfully until eight. As soon as Rachel woke the fear was with her again. A film of sweat, different from the sweat of gardening, covered her body. Her armpits felt sticky; no matter how many times she wiped her hands, they remained clammy.

She dressed and wandered around the house, out into the garden, back into the house, out into the garden again. She poked a spoon around in the breakfast Jerry made, guzzled a cup of coffee, made a fresh pot and poured them both a second cup. Butts piled up in the ashtray; the newspaper lay folded, unread, on the table.

At ten-thirty the phone rang. Rachel grabbed it.

'Mama?'

'Ruby? Is that you?'

'Yes. It's me'

She spoke in a rasp, a grating monotone.

'Ruby? I can hardly hear you.'

'I want to talk to Annie. Only Annie. I don't want to talk to you now.'

'Then why did you ring?'

A brief pause followed.

'I haven't got my phone book with me and I only had enough money to make one call. I know you have her number. Phone her for me and ask her to ring me at Safehaven.'

Ruby rasped out the detoxification centre's phone number.

'What are you doing at Safehaven? Are you all right?'

'I'm shithouse, but I'll be all right.'

'What happened?'

Don'ttellmedon'ttellmedon'ttellmedon'ttellmedon'ttellmedon't tellmedon'ttellmedon'ttellmedon'ttellmedon'ttellmedon'ttellmedon't tellmedon'ttellmedon'ttellmedon'ttellmedon'ttellmedon'ttellmedon't

'I don't want to talk about it. Just phone Annie.'

There was deep weariness in Ruby's voice.

'Ruby?' Rachel couldn't help herself.

Silence. Rachel heard indecision in the quiet. 'I tried to kill myself last night.'

'Oh my God', Rachel whispered. 'Are you all right? What did you . . .?'

Ruby did not respond.

'Tell me', Rachel insisted. 'I want to know.'

'Heroin, pills, a bottle of Jack.'

Rachel gasped, bit hard on the inside of her cheeks. Jagged teeth cut soft flesh. The blood was thick; it tasted salty.

'I got scared and changed my mind. I managed to get to a phone and call an ambulance. They took me to the hospital. The doctor gave me the charcoal treatment then they packed me off to Safehaven.'

How did she manage? Did she crawl to the phone? Walk on twisted, rubbery legs? Slither?

'What's the charcoal treatment? Why didn't they let you stay in the hospital?' Tears streamed down Rachel's face.

'They don't pump your stomach any more . . .'

Any more? Was this user gossip or did it mean Ruby had tried to commit suicide on other occasions, in the days when doctors still pumped stomachs?

'. . . they give you a charcoal compound. It absorbs the drugs. Then they turf you out to a detox.' She coughed. 'No more, Mama. I don't want to talk to you any more.'

'Can I do anything?'

'Phone Annie.'

'Yes, yes. Right away.'

'I'll talk to you later. Don't try to ring me here. Do not ring me. Promise.'

A command.

'Promise, Mum.'

'All right. Yes. I promise. Oh, Ruby, I'm so—'

'Goodbye, Mama. I'll talk to you later.'

Gone.

Rachel wasted no time.

'Annie? This is Rachel. Ruby just phoned.' She recounted all Ruby had said. 'She wants you to call her.'

'Well,' Annie said, 'looks like you were right. Poor chook. I'll get in touch with her. Now listen carefully, Rachel: consider what she said and think about what we spoke of last night. This may be painful for you to accept, but you are not the one who is going to help her with this. And I am not referring only to this incident. Do you understand?'

'Yes, I do. Really. Yes. And that's all right. Just so as there's someone. I mean that, Annie.'

Do I? Do I understand? Do I mean it? Is it all right? Is it a pre-requisite that comprehension be unpalatable?

Rachel was consumed by a longing to put her arms around Ruby, to comfort her. She wanted to coo tender phrases, 'My child . . .', 'My baby . . .', '*Mayn tokhter*', to stroke Ruby's cheek as she held her head against her breasts.

The time for these phrases had long passed.

Annie said she would keep in touch.

Sad as Rachel felt, she was no longer afraid. Beckoning Jerry with her head, Rachel returned to the garden; she needed to be where the light was brightest, where the sun was warm on her skin. As they sat facing each other astride the garden bench, tears commenced anew and continued unchecked. Jerry put his arms around her and drew her to him. He rubbed her back as he might a baby's, around and around with the flat of his hand until, twenty minutes later, she grew quiet.

'She tried to kill herself.'

'Yes, I heard. Poor chook.'

Rachel's smile was melancholy.

'That's what Annie said. "Poor chook".'

'How is she?'

'She sounded terrible, but all right, I think. For this round at least.'

Waiting for Ruby to die by her own hand, accidentally or with intent, had become an integral part of Rachel's life, in her waking hours and in her sleep.

What could be more frightening than living with that?

In that moment, sitting with Jerry on the garden bench in the late morning sun, Rachel could not think of a single thing.

BUSTED

There's a night of judgement coming
But I might be wrong

Leonard Cohen, 'The Tower of Song'

'I've been busted.'

This is it. Jail.

Bitter resentment, crackling, more fleet than the spark of an electric current—*Why in hell did you come and tell me?*—was replaced in an instant by terror. A nightmare is given life.

'What do you mean, busted?'

'What do you think I mean? *I* was carrying dope. The *cops* picked me up. *They* arrested me. *Busted.* Get it?' Face ashen, lips drawn into a tight, thin line.

'Picked you up where?'

'That bastard', Ruby snarled.

'What bastard?'

'He said there would only be grass.'

'Who said?'

My wits have deserted me. Listen to these foolish questions. But what is a correct question? No precedent, no form to guide me.

'What difference does it make who?' she hissed. 'I went to get

186

some grass from this bloke. I was going to sell enough deals so I could keep one for myself. When I left his house the coppers were outside, waiting. Bastards. Bastard.'

Waiting. Everybody's waiting for something. Waiting for Ruby.

'What happened?' Rachel's breath was laboured.

Ruby pondered. 'It was almost as if they knew.'

'Knew what?'

'They took me to the station and when they opened the packet there two caps of smack as well as the grass. So I'm busted for grass and for heroin.' Her voice was bitter. 'I had no idea he was going to do that.'

Liar! Liar!

Did I say that out loud?

Ruby's face told her the accusation had gone unspoken.

'I knew I shouldn't have trusted him. I just knew it.'

'Why in hell did you agree to deal at all?'

Livid. Both of them.

'What do you care?' Voice rising. She let out a long, hard breath. Voice dropping. 'I don't need this, Mum. Really I don't.'

'Where did you meet him? Who is he?'

'Just someone, okay? It's not as if I were going to marry him.' Her shoulders sagged, her voice dropped. 'Just someone. All I wanted was some weed. The bastard never said anything about any hard stuff. Anyway,' her smile was malevolent, 'they picked him up, too. I hope he goes for a fucking ton', she hissed.

Ruby marched over to the stove and turned on the kettle. She slammed the cups onto the kitchen bench.

I'll kill you if you break my cups.

'Calm down, Ruby. What are you going to do?'

'Do? I'm going to find a lawyer, that's what I'm going to do, and try to get off this bloody thing.'

Distracted, she put too much coffee into the pot. Or perhaps it was her intention, the caffeine being the only hit available to her since she had been arrested.

'What did they do to you?'

'Do? What do you mean "do to me"?'

'Did they . . .? The police? You know . . . did they . . . did they hurt you or anything?'

'Hurt me? Of course they didn't hurt me. They took the

187

parcel, then they left me there to sit and stew. Look,' she said, holding out her hands, 'not a fingernail left. Have you got any Band-aids?' Her eyes filled with disgust as she appraised the remains of her gnawed fingernails and the skin around them. 'They asked me all this stuff like where I met him, how long I'd known him. Things like that. Over and over again. Then they let me go. As a matter of fact,' she considered for a moment, 'they were quite polite.'

'What did you tell them?'

'There was nothing to tell. I met him at a nightclub. I gave him some money, we arranged where I was to come to collect it and give him the rest of the money. End of story. What's to tell?'

'You gave money to a stranger in a nightclub? Then you went to his *house?*'

Was she really so stupid? So desperate? Even I know you don't do that.

'I didn't say I went to his house. Can we drop this, please?'

'What's going to happen?'

I'll die if she goes to jail. Her habit will get worse in jail. How will I tell Mama and Papa? They'll say it's my fault. Confirm, once and for all, their belief that I am a failure as a mother. She'll be . . .

Fantasies about life in women's prison—about which Rachel knew nothing other than what she had seen on worse-than-B-grade television shows—swam before her eyes: a Pandora's box of beating, rape, drug-taking.

'I'll go to court and a magistrate will decide. That bastard. I'd like to give him a serve.'

'Forget him', Rachel snapped. 'Find yourself a lawyer and get on with it. Bloody stupid. Stupid! Dealing drugs, and with strangers to boot.'

'I told you, I don't need your lectures. Here.' She handed Rachel her coffee. 'I never would have done it if I'd known there was going to be hard stuff.'

'Why would he put it in there?' Rachel ventured.

'You don't believe me?' Ruby squinted, pursed her lips. Her eyes darkened.

'I . . . well, I suppose if you say . . .' Rachel groaned.

The sentence hung in the room.

'I don't need you freaking out about this, Mum. Okay?'

'Damn you, Ruby. I am freaked out. I'm angry and I'm frightened.'

'Okay, okay. I'm sorry. I'll find a lawyer tomorrow and see where I stand. It'll be all right.'

'How do you know it will be all right?'

Ruby's expression became rueful. 'I suppose I don't, but I sure as hell hope it is.'

— o —

Rhea and Josh met at the Punters Club Hotel in Brunswick Street.

'If she gets off this, I'm going to try to get her to go to a rehab again', Rhea said. 'Really try this time.'

'She never stays.'

'Yeah. She's pretty stubborn, our Rube.'

'I know. She thinks if she doesn't do it on her own, it's not done right.'

'Yeah, well, she'll end up dead if she keeps that up.' Rhea looked pleadingly at Josh. 'I don't want her to die, Josh.'

'Me either. Look, even if she doesn't stay, she does keep trying. Isn't that something?'

'I think it is.' Rhea was glum. 'She thinks it's pathetic.'

Josh nodded. He and Rhea remained faithful to Ruby, though, loyal friends that they were, even they had moments of wavering.

'She used to be so different, Josh.'

'There are still flashes of the old Ruby', he said with little conviction.

'Flashes! Flashes aren't enough, Josh, and besides, they're becoming rarer. I really miss who she was.'

'Me too. Hey, Rhea, don't cry.' Josh squeezed her hand. 'Let's wait and see what happens in court. Maybe this'll give her enough of a fright to stop using.'

'I bloody well hope it does', Rhea replied fiercely. 'I hope she shits herself.'

Josh grinned. 'Let's get out of here. What about a bowl of spag at Mario's?'

Rhea collected her backpack and together they walked up Brunswick Street, each reminiscing about the friend they'd known since their first year at high school: who she was, what she'd become.

— o —

Ruby rang to say she'd found herself a lawyer, Patrick Someone in Brunswick.

'Will you come on the day? Patrick said it gives a better impression if family members are there. Supportive, you know.'

'You know I will', Rachel replied, shocked that Ruby felt the need to ask.

'He said he won't call you to the stand.'

'Why not?'

Ruby laughed heartily. 'You're my *mother*.'

'I'll be there.'

'Do you think Annalise would be a character witness?'

Regarding Ruby's addiction, Annalise was sympathetic and concerned; she was never judgemental.

'She might. Give her a call.'

'Would you do it? I feel embarrassed.'

'It would be more appropriate if you did, don't you think?'

'I'd rather you did. Please.'

'All right, *all right*, Ruby. I'll do it.'

— o —

The two friends met for lunch. Annalise was distressed to hear the news.

'Dear, oh dear. Bloody idiot.' Annalise murmured consoling words. 'She'll probably get a fine and a good-behaviour bond.'

'Do you think so?'

'Don't get too excited, Rachel. However, it is her first offence and it's pretty minor.' Then, without further ado: 'Do you believe her about the heroin?'

'I want to. It sounds improbable, doesn't it? Still, to be perfectly frank, Annalise,' Rachel swallowed a mouthful of food, 'I don't care. She said her lawyer won't be calling me to the stand, but if he did, I'd say whatever was necessary to prevent her from going to jail. Anything. It's as simple as that.' She placed her fork on the plate, no longer interested in eating.

'It doesn't sound too plausible, does it? But who knows,

Rachel? Maybe it is true.' She shrugged. 'Whatever the truth of it, I will be her character witness. It would be terrible if she were to go to jail. And pointless. What good would it serve?'

'You are always so kind to her, Anna', Rachel said. 'You never seem to pass judgement.'

'Kind? This has nothing to do with kindness. You are my dear friend and Ruby is your daughter. I love you both. It would be upsetting for me too if she were to go to jail.'

'And?'

'And', Annalise repeated. She hesitated. 'You're right, of course, there is something else.'

Rachel waited.

'Ruby's life could just as easily have been Jean-Luc or Paul's lives.' She shivered.

'I wonder if they have ever tried it?'

'They say not.'

'Do you believe them?'

'Yes. I see no signs that they have.'

'They're hardly going to try it with you watching, Annalise, or tell you about it.'

'Perhaps. I like to think we have an open enough relationship that they would. Then again, they may not. They have tried marijuana.'

'How do you know?'

'I was putting some clothes away in Jean-Luc's cupboard and I found some under his T-shirts in a plastic pouch.'

'Anna! You went looking!'

Annalise blushed. 'I will deny it until my dying day to anyone else, Rachel, but yes, I did.'

Well, well. So I'm not the only ferreting mother.

'What did you do?'

'I manipulated a dinner-table conversation to a talk about drugs, the dangers of excess.'

'How on earth did you define excess? My guess is that by the time you've reached a certain point, there can never be an excess, only never enough. Then it's too late.'

'True.'

'When you asked them if they'd used heroin, weren't you

afraid they'd accuse you of interfering in their lives, of not trusting them?'

Annalise's reply was spoken very gently.

'No, dear Rachel, never afraid of that. They'd get over their anger. I was far more fearful of them becoming addicted to heroin. I'm sure the boys know as well as anyone that all drugs have their pleasant side.' She held her wine glass to the light. 'Very pleasant. Our strategy with Jean-Luc and Paul is not foolproof, but we would be remiss not to raise the issues with them.' She looked directly at Rachel. 'We told them about Ruby.'

'Annalise!'

'We intended no harm, Rachel. Our explanation was put in terms of her having a sickness, of living a life that was, in all probability, not particularly pleasant. We hoped it would engender some compassion in them and, I concede, some fear. I think we were successful, on both counts.'

'What did they say?' It was barely a whisper.

'They already guessed and were upset for her. They like Ruby. Don't think she is the only person they know. Paul told us about a lad in his course, and another, a girl, who dropped out of university because of drugs.' Annalise fiddled with breadcrumbs on the tablecloth. 'Why your child and not mine, Rachel? Why Ruby and not Eli? Gully and not Jerry or Marcel? What of Claudine? Addiction could have happened to any of us, to any of our kids. What is the answer?'

'Annalise, it didn't happen to *any* of our kids. It happened to one of mine!'

Annalise reached across the table for Rachel's hand.

'Yes, it did, and I will be the first to admit, Rachel,' again she looked directly into her friend's eyes, 'Marcel and I are immeasurably grateful it didn't happen to ours. It saddens me to see what has become of Ruby. You too, if it comes to that.'

Rachel flinched but said nothing. Annalise wiped the corners of her mouth with her serviette. When she had finished she set the white linen on the table.

'Whether she knew about the heroin or not is of no interest to me. She has a habit. You know better than I, Rachel, that she will do whatever is required to obtain what she needs. Jail won't do anything to improve Ruby's condition, so, if there is something I can do to keep her out of jail, I shall do it.' Annalise raised her hand and pushed her thick, straight hair off her face. Rachel watched it spring forward again, bright and golden, over her forehead.

'Who's the barrister?' Annalise said after a while.

'David Goldberg. Remember him?'

'From high school. Yes. Father mentions him from time to time.' Annalise's father was also a barrister. 'Once in a blue moon I see him at fundraisers. He's reputed to be good.'

'Patrick Kinsella says he's the best drugs barrister around.'

'Let's hope he is.'

'Time to get back to the garden', Rachel said, looking at her watch.

They drained their coffee cups. Annalise said she would keep in touch.

— o —

Annalise and Marcel were seated on armchairs opposite each other.

'How was she?'

'Frightened. She will do anything to keep Ruby from going to jail. Not that it will be up to her. David's skill will carry most of it. The rest is up to Ruby, then me, and the temperament and views of the magistrate. David won't call Rachel to the stand. A loyal, loving mother? What magistrate is going to listen to a mother?'

'You have no qualms about it?'

'None, Marcel. You know my feelings.' Annalise sipped the last of her cognac. 'What is it that is so despised about heroin use? The using, or the inevitable crime? As a community, we handle this problem appallingly', she hectored. 'Mark my words, Marcel, this is a problem that can only get worse. For as long as we continue to regard heroin use as a criminal issue, the effects of its use will continue to grow to dimensions we can now only guess at.'

Marcel grinned as he poured her another cognac.

'You are not arguing before His Worship now, counsellor. You know I agree with you.'

They laughed.

'I apologise, Marcel', she said. 'You know how agitated this subject makes me. Being Rachel's friend highlights it. No one in that family has remained unscathed.'

'I have to admit, Anna, that I never completely understood why Rachel took so much blame upon herself. Her life seems to have disintegrated.'

'Ah, Marcel,' Annalise sighed, 'mothers and their daughters. Who can fully explain the knots and splices of that most complex relationship? I've often thought that a version of the marriage vows should be recited when women give birth to daughters: in sickness and health, in good times and bad, in needing and in not, I promise to love and hate, respect and despise you. To involve you in my life, be irritated with your interference, want and not want you near me, forever. Daughter, you may now kiss your mother. Mother, kiss your daughter. We wish you a long and interesting life.'

'What of sons?'

'There's not the competition between mothers and son.' She grinned. 'And not the same fear for sons out in the world as there is for daughters.' Annalise looked lovingly at the gold-framed photographs of Jean-Luc and Paul which stood alongside each other on top of the television. 'Rachel has said herself that she doesn't worry about Eli the same way she worries about Ruby.'

'Just as well!'

'Now, now, Marcel. Don't be unkind.'

'I'm not', he protested. 'But just as well, all the same.' Smiling, he rose from his chair. 'The students' essays await my marking, Anna. I must leave you to your own company for a while.'

Marcel retired to his study.

Thank God it isn't Jean-Luc or Paul.

— o —

The slightest sound made Rachel jump. Try as she might, she could not stop running the women's prison films in her head, or hearing the conversation she hoped she wouldn't have to have with her parents. How would she break the news to them?

She saw their distress, their fear, their shame. Worse: their disapproving faces.

Ruby was living with Biff (another 'hit' word, Rachel observed when Ruby had introduced them). Whenever she phoned or came to visit, Rachel's first question was always, 'Nu, what's happening with the court case?'

'There's nothing more to happen now, Mum. Not until the day. I just have to wait.'

'The waiting is intolerable. I imagine you in jail . . .'

Ruby interrupted. 'Patrick said it's pretty unlikely.'

Rachel decided she didn't believe her. Neither the heroin story, nor that Ruby would get off the charge. She burst into tears.

'Mama, don't cry!'

Ruby put her arms around her and rubbed her back. Taking a tissue from her jacket pocket she wiped the corners of Rachel's eyes then handed her the soggy tissue.

'I'm frightened, Ruby. I have nightmares', Rachel wept. 'Aren't you scared?'

If Ruby felt apprehensive, she did not confide it. 'Why don't you ring Patrick and talk to him?'

'Do you think he'd mind?'

'Here, I'll do it.'

Ruby dialled her solicitor. She explained why she was calling then handed the phone to Rachel.

'Hello, Rachel. How are you?'

'I'm extremely tense. Ruby's reassurances are wasted on me. She suggested yours might be more effective.'

Patrick Kinsella chuckled.

'I can't give you any guarantees. Naturally we can't be sure until it's over, but it is unlikely Ruby will go to jail. I can tell you that they rarely put someone away for a first offence, particularly someone holding so small an amount. She'll more likely get a warning and a good-behaviour bond. Try not to worry. If you have any further questions, don't hesitate to phone me.'

The confidence in the solicitor's voice had the desired effect.

'Thank you, Patrick. I appreciate you taking the time to talk with me.'

'My pleasure. By the way, David Goldberg is one of the best in this field. You can depend on him to do a good job.'

Her fear assuaged, Rachel put the phone down and looked at Ruby.

'Feel better?'

Rachel nodded. An affectionate look passed from one to the other. Ruby suggested they go for coffee. Holding Rachel's hand, Ruby led her around the corner to Coffee Lounge.

— o —

The ease at which Patrick put her was short-lived. As the court date approached—alternately at snail's pace and with alarming speed—Rachel grew more agitated. No matter what reassurances Ruby gave or how often she phoned Patrick, her apprehension grew.

The few design projects she maintained were lacklustre and amateurish. Desultory was the only way to describe her performance of gardening tasks. Weeds overtook flowers; flowers drooped and died. The downward spiral of her life with Jerry gathered momentum.

— o —

Pete and Jerry met for a drink after work.

'I hear life is pretty tense at your place', Pete said. 'How long before the court case?'

'Couple of weeks.'

'Are you going?'

'Nope.'

'Why not?'

'I don't want to go. Look, Pete,' he did not lower his eyes in the face of Pete's shock, 'if you use heroin, you have to be prepared to suffer the consequences of your actions, just as you do with anything else in life. Ruby got herself into this mess, she can get herself out of it.'

'You've become a bit hard-line, haven't you, Jerry? A bit moralistic.'

'Have I, Pete?'

'I reckon you have.'

'You try living with it.'

'Jerry, even if you don't go for Ruby's sake, at least go to give Rachel some support. She's terrified.'

'Rachel and I don't see eye to eye on this, Pete. I've told her she should let Ruby face what's coming to her, then she might learn the lesson she needs to learn and give it up. My suggestion is met with another of our inexhaustible supply of arguments. I'm tired of it.' He sighed. 'There's no point in my going to court. Annalise will look after her.'

Pete thought Jerry had missed the point and said so. Jerry said: 'Another drink, Pete?'

Pete declined, saying it was time he went home. He left a tight-lipped Jerry standing at the bar, ordering himself another whisky.

— o —

'I have to buy some clothes to wear to court', Ruby announced on the phone a week before the hearing. 'Will you come shopping with me? Patrick said feminine looks more respectable.'

They did the rounds of the Bourke Street shops. More decisive than usual, Ruby settled on a long-sleeved cream cotton blouse, a dark-green skirt which stopped above her ankles, a pair of tan suede court shoes and a matching belt. In a hippie shop, she found a deep-purple scarf threaded with silver to drape across her shoulders. Pantyhose and a lipstick from a discount shop. At Rachel and Jerry's, Ruby tried on the entire outfit, including the lipstick. She twirled around in front of Rachel. Ruby's appearance delighted her.

'What do you think?'

I think this modelling makes me uneasy. Pretending nothing untoward is happening. Companionable shopping for clothes a few days before a trial that could land you in jail. It is as if we are outfitting you for a party, not for court.

'You look pretty. The colours suit you. It looks soft', Rachel murmured.

Together they admired Ruby's image, reflected in the large oval mirror affixed to the wall.

'It's not bad, is it? I quite like it myself.'

Ten minutes later she had changed into her customary

uniform of silver-zippered black leather jacket, black blouse, jeans and riding boots.

'Have to go. Biff's waiting for me at work. Don't forget, Wednesday, ten o'clock. See you there, Mum.'

'Forget? I could hardly forget, Ruby. I'll be there at quarter to. See you then.'

They kissed goodbye.

— o —

Tuesday evening's dinner was eaten in silence. Rachel longed for sleep. She phoned Rivka to ask for two sleeping pills, claiming to be exhausted from the broken, nightmarish sleep she'd been having for the past two weeks. 'That, at least, was not a lie', she later told Annalise. Rivka drove over with Nate, making a visit of it. Rachel washed the pills down with her after-dinner coffee. By ten o'clock she was lolling in the bath, enjoying the effect of the barbiturate.

She dozed, head resting on the bath's rim. Startled into wakefulness by vivid little dreams, she ran more hot water, dozed and dreamt again. An hour passed in this way, after which she climbed out of the tepid water, dried off and put on her nightgown. By eleven o'clock Rachel was sound asleep and didn't wake until eight.

'See you tonight', Jerry said as he left for work. As an afterthought, he added, 'Good luck.'

Rachel drank two cups of coffee, dressed and left for the city, there to meet Ruby for her day in court.

— o —

Most of the verdigris on the short, squat spire above the arched portal of the Melbourne Magistrate's Court was discoloured by a brownish soot, years of accumulated deposits from the exhausts of thousands of passing cars and buses. The court was a solid, nineteenth-century bluestone building at the north-east end of the city. Though the foyer was lit with fluorescent lights, it felt bleak, a presentiment perhaps that some might be unsuccessful in their mission here. Inside its walls, Rachel felt cold, small, overwhelmed by the weight of the building and her awareness of its long history as a site where penal servitude and hangings were administered to the wayward.

Smartly dressed barristers arrived in groups or alone, greeting and talking to colleagues, their eyes darting as they searched out their constituents from among the crowd.

As defendants and plaintiffs arrived, one or another barrister peeled off from their colleagues to huddle with clients. Family members hovered, uncertain whether they were to be included in these conferences. The more daring moved into hearing range. Some barristers—respectful but firm—requested relatives to please wait over there; my client will join you shortly. Others drew relatives or friends in close with a reassuring nod, a hand placed lightly on a shoulder, an elbow, to partake in the discussion on procedure or last-minute details.

Neither Annalise nor Ruby were anywhere to be seen. Rachel wandered outside. Standing on the stone steps in the sun, she smoked a cigarette.

'Rachel', called Annalise, waving. Annalise had a way of saying hello with a question on her face: How are you?

'Hello, Annalise. Thanks for coming.'

'How is she?'

'I don't know. I haven't seen her yet.'

'What about you?'

'My nerves are shot to pieces. I desperately need to pee but I don't dare move from here. I'm so scared, Annalise.'

'Ruby must be frightened, too. Poor darling.'

'You know how she is. She puts on her usual bravado; she's been like that since she told me she'd been arrested.'

Rachel lit another cigarette, cupping her hands against the breeze to keep the match alight. Both women saw Ruby at the same time, observed her chewing the inside of her mouth as she approached.

'Thank God, she's here.'

'Good morning, Annalise. Thanks for coming. Hello, Mama. You okay?' First she kissed Rachel, then Annalise, then she returned to chewing her mouth. Annalise hugged her firmly.

'I'm nervous. How about you?'

'Pretty scared, but I don't want to talk about that. How do I look?'

'Lovely', the older women chorused.

'Here comes David', Ruby pointed. 'He remembers you, Mum. You too, Annalise.'

David Goldberg bounded up the steps of the Magistrate's Court, a bundle of legal briefs under his left arm, a tasteful and very expensive burgundy leather briefcase in his right hand. He greeted Ruby, enquiring as to the state of her nerves, nodded a brisk acknowledgement to Annalise and bussed Rachel on both cheeks.

'Rachel. Nice to see you!'

'It's nice to see you too, David, circumstances notwithstanding.'

Pink ribbons dangled from the bundle of briefs, gaudy against his elegant navy pinstriped suit—silk, three-piece.

'Drongo', he said, pointing his chin in Ruby's direction. Rachel nodded. Ruby had the good grace to look contrite while they looked at her indulgently. David turned to Annalise.

'Aha, the character witness', he remarked, as if he had not already seen her. 'Thanks for being here, Annalise. How's your father?'

They shook hands.

'Hello, David. He's well, thank you.'

'My regards when next you see him.' He turned to Rachel. 'What are you up to these days? I hear you are a nurserywoman.'

'Are you trying to pacify me?' Rachel frowned.

'If what Ruby tells me is true, any attempt to pacify you would be a waste of time.'

Ruby took hold of Rachel's hand.

'That's true.'

Rachel played the game of sociability, keeping up the small talk, cracking an occasional joke. It passed the time, made time manageable. Pretend nothing's going on here other than a convivial meeting of old friends. David reciprocated, providing news of his wife and four children, then turned his attention to the matter at hand.

'I'll go and see where we are on the list. Won't be long. Ruby, come with me, please. There are one or two matters I need to discuss with you.'

David and Ruby vanished into the inner sanctum of the courthouse.

'What matters? I thought we'd discussed everything.'

'You looked as if you needed a few minutes' reprieve.'

'Thanks, David. Mum's tension makes me feel worse.'

Rachel was relieved to see them go; now she could go to the lavatory. Returning from that chilly room down the corridor, she stood quietly with Annalise. They lit fresh cigarettes, smoked in silence.

Five minutes had elapsed when David came rushing out.

'Quick, this way. We were booked in at Court Six at ten-thirty. Demon of a magistrate. Hates druggies, anything to do with drugs. He's the type of bloke who'd slug you for carrying one headache pill in your handbag. There's a vacant spot in another court at eleven. The magistrate there is more liberal, especially with first offenders. Come on! Hurry! *Hurry!* I'll try to get that spot; you have to be there. Especially you, Annalise. Let's go!'

David rounded them up, a flock of sheep to his kelpie, gathered in Ruby on the way, and shepherded them through the maze of corridors with dizzying speed.

'Wait here', David commanded.

The women stopped in their tracks. David disappeared and returned soon after, a triumphant gleam in his eyes; he gave them the thumbs up.

'Got it! Court Three at eleven. Stay there', he pointed. 'Don't move, any of you.'

He directed them to a bench in the sunny courtyard, where they made small talk for a while, then fell silent, pensive. Ruby and Rachel looked at their watches every few minutes. Each of them lit one cigarette after another.

Ten twenty-four.

'I'm going to get a coffee', Ruby announced.

'Come here', Rachel hissed. 'David said not to leave.'

'Cut it out, will you, Mum. The machine's right there. Do you two want anything?'

They shook their heads. Annalise placed a calming hand on Rachel's arm.

Ten-thirty.

Ruby returned with her coffee. Where was David? Rachel wanted to be sick.

Ten forty-two.

Come on, David. Come on. Where in hell are you? Rachel stood up and began to wander around, ostensibly to stretch her legs, searching for him among the bustle of lawyers and litigants.

Rachel lit her fifth cigarette—her sixth? seventh?—since arriving at court. She noticed Annalise and Ruby were holding hands.

Ten fifty-three.

David startled her by coming up behind and whispering, 'We're on', as he swept past on his way to Ruby.

He gripped Ruby's elbow and steered her towards Court Three, waving Annalise and Rachel to join them, murmuring to Ruby as they went, 'Deep breath, kiddo. This is it.'

'Good luck, darling', Rachel said, moving towards Ruby.

Ruby put up her hand.

'No. No mush. I'll fall apart. I can't afford that. I'll be all right. I'm fine.'

Ruby allowed Annalise to hug her. David Goldberg placed a hand on Ruby's shoulder and ushered her through the doorway of Court Three.

— o —

Magistrate Collings was in his early forties. He wore sports pants and a white shirt; his tie, slightly askew, was not fully closed around his collar. A button of his shirt was missing, or undone, at his midriff. His black-framed spectacles sat perched halfway down his sharp nose.

A police officer, who had walked in behind their entourage, seated himself in the front row of the courtroom and rested his cap neatly on the seat alongside him.

'And what do we have here, gentlemen?' was Magistrate Collings' amiable enquiry.

Reading in a monotone from notes clipped to a blue plastic clipboard, the officer delivered the case for the prosecution.

'Mr Goldberg. What do you have to say in this matter?'

David rose, bowed to the court from the waist. He commenced a quiet monologue liberally punctuated with Your Worship's: Ruby Brigg is a young woman of good character, Your Worship, who made this one slip, Your Worship. The cannabis,

Your Worship, had been for her own use. She'd been duped by a second party. She had not known about the heroin, Your Worship.

And so on. It seemed he would go on forever. Then:

'If it pleases the Court, I call Mrs Annalise Merlot to the stand.'

The magistrate nodded, peered at Annalise over the top of his spectacles as she was sworn in. Annalise waxed eloquent. She had known Ruby since birth, how Ruby had worked in a manner nothing short of commendable in an afterschool job and during the school holidays as a teenager, had been an excellent student, and had become an artist who displayed considerable promise. She had grown into a fine young woman. I, Mrs Annalise Merlot, feel quite sure that this matter is an aberration Ruby will put behind her the minute she is permitted to walk out of the courtroom and get on with her life.

'Thank you, Mrs Merlot.' David nodded, indicating Annalise could step down and return to her seat. Out of the magistrate's line of vision, thumbs up again: Well done, Annalise.

Then it was Ruby's turn.

On the stand she appeared composed, demure. Her voice remained even and she didn't whine about being diddled by The Bastard, as he had become known to them (she had never once mentioned him by name). Looking David in the eye, she spoke clearly and didn't fidget or chew the inside of her mouth.

'Thank you, Ruby,' Rachel heard David say over the thumping of her heart, 'you may step down now.'

After David's summation, the magistrate peered over the top of his spectacles again and addressed them. Magistrate Collings suggested Ruby's actions had been ill-considered and, contrary to any expectation, told Mr Goldberg that this case was so damned paltry it should never have come before him.

'Waste of the court's time . . . money . . .' he muttered. 'However,' he continued, brightening, 'as it has come before me, I am obliged to do something about it. You will place three hundred dollars in the Poor Box by the end of the week, young lady, and I will put you on a good behaviour bond. Twelve months. Don't let me see you in here again.

'Thank you, Senior Constable Patterson, and you, Mr Goldberg. Good day, ladies.'

He encompassed them all in his nod and sauntered from the room.

'There you go', David grinned.

Colour returned to Ruby's cheeks. 'Whew', she said, as she stood up. 'Let's get out of here.'

Annalise hugged Ruby then Rachel; Rachel broke free from her embrace.

'Mama?' Ruby called as Rachel ran off.

Holding her hand firmly over her mouth, breathing hard and fast through her nose, Rachel ran from the courtroom, down the stone corridors to the lavatories. Inside the cubicle she flung the lavatory seat up, dropped to a kneel on the cold tiles and, head down over the bowl, began to vomit. Bitter, lumpy slime poured from her mouth in an endless stream. When the vomiting was finished, she cupped her hands under the washbasin tap. After she had rinsed out her mouth, she drank handful after handful of the icy water. In her haste, water dribbled down her chin, into the collar of her blouse and down her chest, making her shiver. She splashed her face, dried off with a paper towel. Ruby and Annalise were standing with David in the foyer.

'Are you all right?' Annalise enquired.

'What happened?' Ruby asked.

'I had some tension to get rid of. I'm fine now. You okay, Ruby?'

'Yes thanks, Mum. Pretty relieved.'

'So you should be', Rachel grumbled.

'Don't start, all right?'

They glared at each other for a moment; simultaneously their bodies relaxed. Ruby permitted Rachel to give her a hug.

'Well,' David smiled, rubbing his hands together, 'that's that. Lunch everyone? What about yum cha at the Dragon Boat? My shout.'

Just another hour in court for you, isn't it? Ah, what the hell. Why shouldn't it be?

Rachel was grateful for his success today, but it wouldn't bother her if she didn't see David Goldberg for another twenty-five years.

On the street, they fell into pairs for the stroll down the Russell Street hill, Ruby and Annalise arm-in-arm in front, Rachel and David bringing up the rear.

What purpose had the events of the past two months served? Has anything changed in the larger world or our own small world?

Money would be paid to the Poor Box (who would be the recipient?), the principals would go about the business of their daily lives. By two o'clock, David Goldberg will be bowing before another magistrate, possibly the same magistrate. Annalise will have returned to her office, Rachel her garden. Will Ruby's habit be broken? Unlikely. Will Rachel's madness flourish anew? Probably.

By the time they had left the Magistrate's Court, Ruby was chewing the inside of her mouth, picking the silver threads from the fringe of her scarf, rolling the pulled threads around and around between her thumb and forefinger, leaving a trail of barely visible, tiny silver balls on the path behind her. Rachel assumed that as soon as lunch was over, Ruby would bid hasty farewells and be off, skimming the zone to secure a hit.

Who, other than themselves, would be touched by today's events? Did anyone care?

The heroin trade. A juggernaut of corruption and high finance, trailing misery and hopelessness in its wake. Lives ruined. Lives lost, and not only losses incurred by death.

Anger, sudden, hot as a furnace, engulfed her; its force made her dizzy. Nausea rose from her stomach again, sweat beaded her brow. Rachel stopped to pat the moisture away with her handkerchief.

Fuck our lies and duplicity. Fuck the law. Fuck the drugs and fuck this fucking life.

'Are you okay, Mama?' Ruby's voice broke in.

Composing herself, Rachel dropped her damp handkerchief into her handbag. Then she trotted down the hill to join the others for what she felt sure would be a perfectly delicious Chinese lunch.

INTERLUDE IV

'I cannot imagine, Rachel,' Nate remarks, all disingenuousness and longing to know, 'how awful it would be to have a child who is a drug addict.' They are having coffee at Pellegrini's.

Here we go again. Again.

'Yes, Papa, awful', Rachel replies. She glances at herself in the mirrored wall in front of her to ensure her expression is as noncommittal as she has worked so hard to make it.

Nate draws his lips into taut, thin lines; he makes soft but distinguishable Hurricane bursts. Three. Through the mirror, Rachel sees the man sitting on the other side of him smile his appreciation of Nate's skill.

Ask me outright. I dare you. Is Ruby on drugs? Then I would confirm your suspicions, Papa. Perhaps.

What would be my reply? How would I phrase it? Sure, Papa. Isn't that something? How'd you guess?

Ah, Papa, I don't mean to sound bitter (she says to herself). Here's my dilemma. I'm too proud and too ashamed. Too proud to ask for help (Mama's family's pig-headedness, you'd be more likely to call it, eh?), too ashamed of revealing to you my pervasive sense of failure. You are, after all, inclined to perfection. And didn't you always say, 'The apple never falls far from the tree, Rachel'? There you have it.

Or, as Eli would say, I rest my case.

They sit in silence now, finishing their coffee, careful to avoid looking into the mirrors, careful to avert their eyes, each from the other.

Nate's concern—she knows it is concern, not idle curiosity—doesn't surprise her; it never comes as a bolt out of the blue. Rachel anticipates it, always. He never disappoints. His seemingly innocent enquiry is a drop of water—another drop of water—dripping away at the stone that is Rachel. Rachel the stone knows she will not be able to stave off the dripping much longer.

She feels the build-up of pressure at the floodgate.

They have finished their coffee. Out on the street, Nate hugs her.

'Bye bye, Papa.' She kisses him. 'Lovely to see you.'

Small DC3.

— o —

Jerry and Rachel are at the Grinblatts' for dinner. Here, in his own home (no strangers to eavesdrop, to see their pain), Nate tries a different approach.

'All this drugs business is a terrible thing, don't you think, Rachel? Damn fool government, not decriminalising.'

Nate shakes a newspaper in the air.

Jerry removes himself to the study to read, watch television, anything but this again. Again.

'Yes, Papa. Terrible.'

'It seems to be everywhere these days.'

This time his gaze is direct.

'Yes, it does, everywhere', Rachel replies, her tone of voice cluck-clucky. Nate waits. Rivka busies herself at the kitchen bench; she too waits.

'Especially among young people.'

He fusses with some cutlery, other items on the dining table, a habit Rachel recollects as one of his mother's: repositions a knife a centimetre or two from its setting, returns it to its original place, lines it up with the soupspoon, straightens imaginary wrinkles in the table-cloth, brushes non-existent crumbs from the cloth into his hand (they haven't eaten yet; how can there be crumbs?), perfects the location of the vase of flowers to dead centre, places the basket of bread just so.

'Yes. Especially among young people.'

Rivka chimes in. 'You look tense, dear. Is everything all right?'

'I'm tired, Mama. Just tired. I've been working too hard.'

The sounds of the television can be heard from the study.

'*You always seem to be tired these days. Are you sure it's only work?*'

'*Yes, only work. I'm fine.*'

I hate this.

'*How are the kids?*'

We Grinblatts are so good at this. Beating around the bush. Hinting. Intimating. Probing. Subterfuge.

Family motto: Never ask the straightforward question. Might hurt someone's feelings. Be accused of interfering. Of not wanting to hear—of being afraid to hear—the answers.

Translation of Grinblatt: 'Walking on Eggshells'. Mr and Mrs Walking on Eggshells and their brittle daughter, Ms Rachel Walking on Eggshells. That's us.

'*They're fine. They're fine and I'm fine. Honest.*'

'*What about Ruby?*' *The floodgate is groaning under the pressure.* '*Ruby's fine?*'

You can tell me, Rivka's eyes say.

I can't, Rachel's respond.

'*She's great.*'

When Nate or Rivka start with the questions Rachel adjusts her mouth and eyes into a hideous smile; at least, in her mind's eye it's hideous (or is it in her mind's eye a smile?). What does her face look like to her parents in these moments? She imagines she looks like a liar.

'*You look so pale*', *Rivka persists.* '*Is it Jerry?*' *She feels safe to ask under cover of the television.* '*How are things with you and Jerry?*'

'*Stop it, Mama. Please stop! Jerry's fine.*' *The smile collapses.* '*Please stop.*'

Rachel wants to scream. She struggles to repress the anger in her voice. Rivka stares at her, disbelieving.

Miffed, Rivka returns to preparing the salad. '*Something's going on*', *she snaps.*

This might help, Mama. You too, Papa.

Fact: I am a woman obsessed.

Fact: Obsession is a sickness of body, mind and spirit.

Fact: Lying is one of its many side effects, delusion another.

Fact: Candour, energy and joy are losses on the road.

Fact: Obsession creeps stealthily into your life. Once you're hooked, you are unaware that you have arrived in this dark and hopeless place.

Fact: When—and if—you finally realise you have arrived, you have no idea how you got there. You have no desire to leave. Nor are you able.

You know how you like to suck the marrow out of chicken bones, Mama? The sweet, juicy centre of the veal bones? Obsession is like that. Obsession sucks the life out of you. By the time the sucking is finished, nothing's left. No juice. No sweetness. There is little that, within any amount of reason, could be called a life.

The dry remains are exhaustion, anxiety, distrust, preoccupation, deceit.

Love? Love between the obsessed and the object of their attention is skewed. All that remains is unrequited yearning.

Maybe, Mama, that is why I'm always tired. Not from work. No. From yearning. Your daughter is exhausted from yearning.

— o —

In not wanting to give up her secret, Rachel remains—as she sees it— loyal to Ruby. She hears her parents' reproach. She cringes from their accusation: you have made such an appalling mess of being a parent.

She sees the way they look at Ruby. How could she bear Nate and Rivka looking at Ruby that way? The way she knows people look at addicts—with suspicion and fear, contempt, disgust.

She doesn't want that for her daughter.

She doesn't want that for them.

She does not want it for herself.

Rachel is blind; she sees nothing.

— o —

'Tell them', Jerry says. 'They want you to tell them.'

'Jerry, you are mad. You have no idea what you are talking about.'

If Rachel were to tell, would her mother cradle her in her arms, allow her to weep on her bosom? Would she croon, 'Hush, Rachel, hush mayn tokhter, *everything will be all right', as she did when Rachel was a child? Hum to her a Yiddish lullaby in a melancholy minor key?*

Rachel longs to reveal her dark secret, yearns for Rivka's comfort.

Thought of her mother's comfort moves her forward. Oh, this secret, this lie. I am so sick and so tired of living them. Maybe I'll phone.

Not yet. Almost. Nearly. Rachel nearly phones. She lifts the handset from its cradle. Puts it down again.

Almost. Nearly.

But not just yet.

SWEET LIGHT

Truly the light is sweet
and a pleasant thing it is for the eyes to behold the sun!

Ecclesiastes 11:8

'Mrs Bradman? Mrs Rachel Bradman? . . . Sister . . . hospital . . . an accident.'

I am coming, Ruby. Coming. See how I swim upwards, surging, slicing through dark waters to reach you? I am hurtling to the surface. Wait, Ruby. Don't die. No! Wait! Wait! I'm almost there!

'Who? What did you say?'

A dolphin, I have broken free. Green salt water sprays myriad rainbow arcs around my glistening form, sparkling in the sunlight.

The caller spoke again—'Is that Mrs Bradman? This is Sister Macklin from the Royal Melbourne Hospital'—and waited.

Hospital. She said hospital. Which hospital?

Rachel became fully awake.

No, oh God no. She's dead. Please God, no. Ruby? Please, Ruby, please. Please don't die, Rube. Please. **Do. Not Die.** *What will I do? How will I bear life without you? Don't let her die.*

Every hair on Rachel's body stood up. It was eleven forty-seven; from the bedside table the numbers on the digital clock glowed red in the night.

'Jerry', she whispered—*did I whisper? scream?*—afraid to speak loudly, as if the full resonance of her voice might cause her to shatter into thousands of tiny pieces, flecks of self, spattered, bloodied pulp.

'Who is it? What's going on?'

Rachel gripped Jerry's hand so tightly that he grimaced with pain. Finally she spoke, the timbre of her voice strangely imperious as she marked time, struggling to comprehend.

'It's Grinblatt. Ms Rachel Grinblatt', Rachel babbled. 'Who told you to call me Bradman? Did Ruby tell you to call me Mrs Bradman? Of course she didn't. Ruby would *never* have told you to call me Mrs Bradman. Never. I use my maiden name. She knows that. Eli too. Both my children know that. Only my maiden name. Jerry doesn't mind. He said so. He said it was fine with him if I wanted to keep my maiden name. It was the only thing Jewish about me that was left. Don't you see? I had to keep *something*. I needed—'

Time to put an end to this. Sister Macklin interrupted, brisk though not unkind, sailing straight through Rachel's ravings.

'Ms Grinblatt', she corrected herself. 'I beg your pardon. Ms Grinblatt, your parents have been in a car accident. We have them here, at the hospital. Your mother has a minor concussion and one of her fingers is fractured. There's also some heavy bruising. She'll be all right in a few days, but your father wasn't so fortunate. He—'

'Mum? Papa? What are you talking about? What accident? What about Ruby? Is she de— is she badly hurt?'

'There was no Ruby with them', the nurse replied. 'Ms Grinblatt, are you all right? I know this is a shock, especially being called so late at night. Your mother gave us your phone number. We thought you would want to be informed. I thought you'd want to come in and see them.'

No Ruby? No Ruby!

Sister Macklin waited.

'See them. Yes, yes, of course I want to see them.' Hearing the snippy tone in her voice, Rachel retreated. 'I'm sorry, Sister.

Thank you for phoning.' Giving no thought to whether Rivka might be conscious, she added, 'Tell Mama I'll be there in half an hour.'

Rachel replaced the handset in its cradle. Jerry freed his hand and rubbed the circulation back into his fingers.

She turned and stared at him, blind-eyed.

Turned away.

Buried her face in her pillow.

And into the pillow's heedless feathers, she screamed and screamed and screamed.

Five minutes later, she was dressed and driving across town at breakneck speed to the Royal Melbourne Hospital.

Jerry came out of the bathroom to find her gone.

— o —

The receptionist directed Rachel to the fourth floor. Rachel tiptoed across the ward and stood beside her mother's bed. Rivka was sleeping. Perhaps sensing Rachel's presence, her eyelids fluttered to half open. She managed a wan smile and gave a single, scratchy tap of her plump fingers on the white, thermal-cotton blanket, a movement Rachel recognised as beckoning. As Rachel approached, Rivka muttered, 'Nate . . . your father . . .' and began to weep; a deep frown creased her forehead. Pain? Worry? Rachel had no way of knowing. In shock and medicated, Rivka soon succumbed once more to sleep.

'It'll be okay, Mama. He'll live', Rachel whispered.

It was simply something to say.

Say something simple to me, Mama. Tell me everything's going to be okay.

Rachel drew up a chair and sat beside the bed. She brought Rivka's right hand to her lips, kissed the palm of it, held it against her cheek; she turned the hand over and stroked the soft wrinkled skin on the back. 'Lustrous Rose', the frosted-carmine nail polish Rivka had favoured for decades, gleamed on her long, manicured fingernails. Two nails were broken; on another the varnish was chipped. Running her finger slowly back and forth against the fine ridge made by the chip, Rachel inspected the splint. Without her wedding and engagement rings, which had been removed, Rivka's hand looked naked, younger in some inexplicable way.

'You are still more beautiful than the film stars, Mama', Rachel whispered, gazing at her mother's face, framed in a circle of soft, curly grey hair. She leaned forward and hooked a wayward strand into place behind Rivka's ear. 'How did this happen, Mama? Was he daydreaming at the wheel again? Flying his damn aeroplanes?'

Rachel heard the rustle of fabric, the rub of nylon-clad legs.

'Ms Grinblatt? I'm Wendy Macklin. I'm the charge sister on this ward tonight. I phoned you.'

Each nodded her greeting.

'Hello Sister. How bad is she?'

'She's had a nasty shock. The concussion and bruising I mentioned. And the factured finger.' Seeing the puzzled look come over Rachel's face, Wendy Macklin said, 'I told you on the phone. There's a graze or two. Nothing too serious.'

Rachel sighed.

'We removed your mother's rings in case any swelling occurs from the fracture.'

Wendy Macklin unlocked the drugs drawer of the bedside cabinet and removed an envelope, which she handed to Rachel. Rachel slipped the rings onto her finger. 'Let's leave her to rest.' They adjourned to the visitors' lounge. 'Your mother will be fine. She should be ready to go home in twenty-four hours, two days at most.'

'Papa?'

'Your father is pretty knocked about.'

Rachel braced herself.

'Tell me. All of it.'

In a calm voice the charge sister recited the damage inflicted upon Nate's body as if she were reading off a list. Each wound a new line. Starting with her index finger, she marked off each item; when she ran out of fingers, she returned to her index finger.

'Compound fracture of the femur. Flailed segment—multiple rib fractures is the simple way to put that. Compromised breathing. Severe lacerations to the cheek and head (a finger each). Black eye.' She dipped her head for emphasis. 'Very black eye.

But, as awful as it sounds, none of it is life threatening.' Sister Macklin spoke softly, placed a hand on Rachel's arm. 'You might get a shock when you see him.'

'I'll be all right.'

'He's comfortable, Ms Grinblatt, and he'll be able to hear you if you speak to him.'

Rachel stared at her.

'Please, call me Rachel', was all she could think of to say.

'Thanks. I'm Wendy. Would you like to see him?'

Rachel nodded.

'Yes, please, I would.'

'You will probably find the sight of him shocking. Would you like me to come with you?'

'Thank you. I appreciate the . . . some . . . I'd . . . some support. I'm afraid of seeing him damaged.'

Wendy turned and led the way.

— o —

The corridors were eerily quiet, devoid as they were of shuffling patients and their visitors, free of the whirr of vacuum cleaners and waxing machines dragged through wards and corridors by chattering domestic staff, of the rattle of meal trolleys bearing columns of plastic trays. Little of the purposeful bustle of hospital life was in evidence, most activity being on hold for another four hours. Few other sounds could be heard: the lowered voices of the night staff, a patient's occasional cough, a snore, or a moan. A cry from the depths of a dream.

Rachel and Wendy strode comfortably together through the quiet, their footfalls a soft, rhythmic patter on the high-gloss Vinyl tiles.

'Who's Ruby?' Wendy Macklin asked as they approached Nate's ward.

'I beg your pardon?'

Why is she asking me about Ruby? How does she know? Who told her? Has she met Ruby somewhere? Done a deal with her? Is she an addict? It's rife in the medical profession. Everyone knows that. Doctors, nurses. They get the best drugs. Who told her about Ruby? What does—?

'When I phoned, you seemed to think someone called Ruby

had been in the accident. I wondered who she was. You sounded as if you were expecting bad news.'

Ay, Wendy, if only you knew.

'Did I mention Ruby? She's my daughter. I must have been dreaming.'

— o —

Wendy Macklin had anticipated correctly: on entering the ward, Rachel gasped. She wanted—and did not want—to retreat, wished to be protected from the sight of her battered father. Wendy placed an encouraging hand on Rachel's elbow and led her through the doorway.

Two thoughts, uncontrollable, demented, flashed through Rachel's mind.

The first.

How considerate these nurses are. They've decked Papa out in the colours of his football team, St Kilda.

Nate's face and head were covered in sutures, ladders of fine thread (black) that held his damaged flesh together. Each suture had been daubed with Mercurochrome (red). Pieces of white SteriStrip had been stuck on some of the more damaged sites. Red, white and black. His nose looked large and sore; it too was red. One leg was in plaster.

Are there other accident victims, surgery patients in other wards, dressed in their team colours? Hawthorn patients, with brown sutures and yellow bandages? Sky blue and white for Geelong supporters? Red, yellow and blue? That's what they'd dress Eli in. Fitzroy. The mighty Lions. I wonder if there is a question on the admission form?

4	Football Team
	_____

Boris Karloff, that was the second thought. Papa looks like Frankenstein's monster.

Wild giggling welled up in Rachel's throat, but when she noticed a sprout of his thick white hair poking through a bandage at the top of his head, the threatening laughter choked in her gullet and a rush of tenderness swept over her.

'Some of you managed to escape, Papa.'

Oozing through the dressing over his right eyebrow was a spot of dark-red blood.

'Oh, Papa,' Rachel wept softly now, 'you look so helpless.'

Set into the wall above the head of Nate's bed was a bewildering assortment of electronic monitoring equipment; two drips stood alongside, centurions of the bedhead.

'Dextrose and fluids in that one, pethidine in the other', Wendy explained, pointing to the infusions in turn. 'The equipment at the back monitors his vitals—heart, and blood pressure. His condition is stable, Rachel.'

'Pethidine', Rachel murmured.

'It's the best painkiller there is.'

Rachel shook her head. How ironic. 'How long will he be on that?'

Perhaps it was something in her voice, though she had tried to keep it bland. Wendy's gaze become curious. Before turning back to look at Nate, Rachel thought she saw the nurse cock an eyebrow.

Filial concern, Wendy. Nothing more. A concerned daughter. A dutiful daughter. Shouldn't a daughter keep herself informed? Just asking, Wendy. Just asking.

'It depends on his rate of recovery, but it's likely to be around a week. Then he'll go on a three- or four-hourly injection. Don't worry,' Wendy assured her, 'it is strictly controlled.'

Did she emphasise strictly?

In the subdued light of the ward, Rachel turned away from her to peer at Nate, who, despite his large girth, looked small, enfeebled. One giggle escaped, a whinnying sound.

'Are you all right?' Wendy Macklin asked. 'Can I get you something? Tea?'

'Oh dear. I'm sorry. I shouldn't laugh.' She giggled again.

'No need to apologise. People respond to trauma in many ways.' The nurse smiled. 'Giggling is not unusual.'

Rachel began weeping again, soft, sad weeping.

Wendy said gently, 'Come on, Rachel. You can come and sit with him later. He'll be asleep for a while. Let's get you a cup of tea.'

— o —

Twenty-four hours after being admitted, Rivka was released from hospital; Nate's stay was to be much longer.

The contusions on Rivka's arms faded from blue-black to puce, then yellow; eventually they disappeared. The swelling in her hand subsided enough for her to wear her rings again. Despite joints which ached from the knocks she received in the accident, Rivka drove to the hospital every day to visit Nate. There she would sit, for hours on end, reading books, solving crossword puzzles, knitting, dozing, and tending to those of her husband's needs that didn't require the attention of a nurse: she poured him glasses of water, straightened his blankets, fluffed his pillows, washed his pyjamas in the bathroom basin, and passed him anything he asked for so he might be as comfortable as possible.

Daily, at lunchtime, Rivka filled a warmed teacup with chicken soup poured from the Thermos flask she brought from home. At first Nate was grateful to receive her broth; before long it held no interest for him.

Rivka and Rachel noticed the crescendo of Nate's complaining. The nurses had become slack, he said; stabbing at his watch, he berated them for the time they took to respond to his buzzer, to bring his medication, to provide him with a pan. The hospital food was inedible—'As plastic as the plate they serve it on', he grumped. Noise bedevilled the ward, which was too bright or too dark, its temperature inappropriate. His doctor didn't visit often enough; when she finally arrived (too late, too early), her consultation was brief, he said, the information she imparted insufficient or incomprehensible.

'Nobody explains anything to me properly', he *kwetched*.

He was afraid of the pain in his leg, his chest hurt. With the pethidine infusion removed, he asked often for an injection.

'Nurse,' he whimpered, 'the medication's wearing off. Do you think I could have another injection?'

'In about an hour, Mr Grinblatt.'

His nightly dreams—nightmares, more accurately—frightened him.

'I don't like the dreams, Rachel', he said, tears filling his eyes. He waved a commanding hand in the direction of the tissues: bring me one. 'I don't know what's going on. The dreams, they frighten me.'

Nate would prefer not to experience the nightmares, but here was an aspect of his life he was unable to control, which fact both frustrated and disturbed him.

Messerschmitts, low and menacing, punctuated his litany of complaint.

— o —

By the end of the second week of his hospitalisation, Nate was sleeping through many of Rachel's and Rivka's visits. When he awoke, he sometimes mumbled a few slurred words, or reprimanded whoever was present for waking him. Time distorted. Morning became confused with afternoon, entire days seemed to conflate into each other. For three consecutive days, having quizzed Rivka, he then asked Rachel if it was Tuesday and said, much to Rachel and Rivka's astonishment, 'Fucking hell', when they informed him today was Wednesday, Thursday. He continued to variously extol the virtues of or complain bitterly about the quality of the food and the nursing, then, losing track of what he was saying, would complain about something else or nod off to sleep again. If Rachel was present during mealtimes, she watched as he pecked at his food; most of it he left for the catering staff to remove. The only dishes he approached with gusto were the desserts.

A scenario. The day of the week is unimportant.

'Where's Rivka? Why didn't Rivka bring the chicken soup for my lunch?'

'Mum's gone to stretch her legs, Papa. She brought the soup. You told her you didn't want it. Don't you remember?' Rachel moved to the bed and held his hand.

He shook himself free of her.

'I did not!'

Rachel said nothing more.

Do you know what's happening to you, Papa? I know. I know what is happening to you. Do you think about Ruby in your lucid moments? Do you recognise my daughter's antics in your own? I'll bet you do. How long will it be before you ask me one of your questions, eh? Put me on the spot? Confirm your suspicions? Make me tell you, once and for all? Or are you, like all addicts, concerned only with the satisfaction of your own desire?

— o —

Another day.

Arising from her post beside Nate's bed, Rivka greeted Rachel with a quiet kiss. Rivka grimaced, jerking her head in the direction of her dozing spouse.

'Is he giving you a hard time?' Rachel whispered.

'Quiet, Rachel', Nate growled, not opening his eyes. 'How many times do I have to ask you?'

Rivka coughed lightly to attract Rachel's attention—'Stop that coughing, Rivka. If you're sick, see the doctor!'—and beckoned her into the corridor: a confidence was coming.

'I don't know what's the matter with him', Rivka remarked crossly. 'They look after him beautifully here. What's he got to complain about? All the time irritable. Do you know what he said yesterday? He said I make him angry. If I don't stop, he would leave me! *Shlemiel!* Idiot. He thinks he could live alone? And if not? Who would have him at his age, cranky old man? I sit here, day after day. I bring anything he wants. Does he ever once say thanks? No. *Er iz ayn emesdiker chazer.* Ingrate. All he does is *kwetch* about pain. Let him have a baby, then he'd know what pain is!'

Rachel could not contain her smile. The pain and near death Rivka had suffered in giving birth to her had become the stuff of family legend; her mother's endurance in childbirth was her benchmark for how much physical pain anyone else should be able to tolerate in this life.

'He has been rather cranky. Why don't you go home a bit earlier? Leave him to the nurses.'

'You know I can't do that. *He* feels deserted, *I* worry. It's enough I go home at night. I don't mind staying. I'll be all right.'

'Mama, you look exhausted. Go home. Come in a bit later some days. He sleeps so much of the time anyway.'

'No, Rachel. No, I couldn't do it. He doesn't like being here alone.' Seeing Rachel about to protest, she ran right on, her voice rising. 'I'll be fine, really. Fine. I just wish he wasn't so bloody bad-tempered. I'm sick of him criticising me all the time. I don't understand it, and I don't need it.'

Hurt and indignation jockeyed for position in her eyes. The

sound of Nate's groan reached them. Rachel tiptoed into the ward in time to see him raise his eyelids; his eyes rolled back into his head. 'Quiet', he yelled, then went back to sleep. Rachel stepped into the corridor again.

'You know how he hates being cooped up', she suggested. 'Maybe that's what's making him so bad-tempered.'

Now, Mama, you don't believe that, do you? Any more than you believe my other lies. Have you worked it out yet, Mama? Of course you have. You know, don't you, that Papa is hooked on pethidine?

'Maybe', said Rivka, doubt in her voice. 'Even so, that's no reason to take it out on me.' Hurt won. 'I'm going to the canteen. What do you want?'

'Coffee. Don't rush back. I'll sit for a while.'

'Something to eat?'

'No, thanks. I'm not hungry.'

'I'll bring you a sandwich. What would you like in it?'

'Nothing, thanks.'

'Fruit? Maybe a muffin, or a piece of cake?'

Rachel sighed. 'Nothing, thanks Mum.'

Shaking her head, Rivka picked up her handbag and marched to the lift. In the canteen, she sat for a peaceful half an hour, safe from the demands and insults of her cantankerous husband.

— o —

Rachel occupied the chair her mother had vacated. She had been seated a few minutes when Nate awoke. Flouncing around in the blankets, he demanded to know, 'Where in hell is the nurse? Where's that damned buzzer? Rachel, find me the buzzer.'

'Hello, Papa. Let me fix your blankets. You look uncomfortable.'

I am always so formal with him. In four weeks the lily of the valley will be in bloom. Why don't I ever call him Dad? Two weeks after that, the gardenias. Where are you, Ruby?

'Where's your mother?'

'Hello, Papa', she repeated, hoping he heard the nasty edge to her voice. 'Mum's gone for a coffee. She'll be back soon. How are you feeling?'

'Not bad today, thanks', he conceded.

Ranunculi and grape hyacinth and my darling freesias. All the bulbs.

'Where's that buzzer?'

Nate found the cord without assistance; he placed his thumb firmly on the plastic nipple and pressed hard.

Then the . . . what comes next? The wisteria. Passionfruit blossoms. Yes, passiflora.

'You bastard.' A lightning bolt of recognition shot through her. 'I know what you're after.'

'What? What's that you said? How many times have I told you not to mutter, Rachel? Where is that . . .?'

Sylvia entered the room.

'About time', Nate snapped at her. 'What kept you so long?'

'What's the problem, Mr Grinblatt?' Sylvia remained professionally pleasant. 'Goodness me, you can't be too comfortable in that mess', she exclaimed, seeing the bedraggled state of his bedding. 'Come on, let's straighten you up.'

From the foot of the bed, Sylvia cranked the top half of the bed to semi-sitting position.

The Morris! The Morris had a crank handle! The little blue Morris, with the canvas roof that Papa rolled back when we went on summer picnics. Sunday drives to the Dandenongs, Mama and me dressed in printed cotton frocks and open-toed sandals, Papa in shorts, his legs brown-skinned and hairy. He let me wear his leather flyer's helmet. How I loved riding in the Morris's dicky seat, gripping the sides. I pretended I was flying. My stomach was left behind whenever we drove over a hill. Waiting for it to catch up with the Morris. The crank handle. Whenever the Morris conked out, Papa would pull over, get out and crank it up to get it started again.

As Sylvia began to reorganise his pillows, Nate snapped at her, 'Not like that! You're too rough!'

Rachel cringed.

The peaches. The peas and beans. Ah, the pomegranates.

'Come on now, Mr Grinblatt.' Sylvia remained calm. 'Be nice. Let me straighten up this bedding. You'll feel much better.' She consulted her watch. 'The physiotherapist will be along soon. Nearly time for your session.'

'What are you talking about? You know I'm in pain. How can I have a session with the physiotherapist if I'm in so much pain?' he snapped at her. 'I'll report you.'

Rachel could tolerate it no longer.

'Cut it out, Papa. Sylvia is just trying to make you comfortable.'

'Mind your own bloody business, Rachel. Who asked you?'

Tears of anger and humiliation smarted in Rachel's eyes. She glanced at Sylvia, who returned her a look: Don't worry about me.

'Nearly finished, Mr Grinblatt.'

At last the blankets were arranged and the ends tucked in: impeccable, neatly executed envelope corners.

'My leg', Nate whined. Fascinated, Rachel watched as Nate the Intractable metamorphosed into Nate the Supplicant. A sly look came over his face; he tempered his bullying. 'Anna, how can I do my physio if I'm in pain, hmm? Do you think you could get me something? There's a good girl.'

Good girl? Good grief!

What colour pansies shall I put in this year? Does she know what's going on? Surely . . . How long are they going to let this go on? I wonder if there's enough space for a cherry tree? Aren't two required for pollination? Not enough space for two cherries. Apricots? This is some madness. Ruby goes to rehab to get clean and Papa lies here getting it whenever he wants it. Did I plant scabiosa for this season? No matter, the babiana are there. I wonder if Eli will phone this week? Blue scabiosa. Of course I did.

'Ooh, the pain is killing me. Help me Anna.' He remembered: 'Please.'

Sylvia cranked the bed into full sitting position. 'I'm Sylvia, Mr Grinblatt. Remember? I'm your ward sister today. Let me have a look.'

She removed the plastic folder containing Nate's charts from the slot at the end of the bed and ran her eyes down the narrow, ruled columns. 'Hold tight, Mr Grinblatt. I'll be back in a tick.'

Nate moaned, holding his hand above his eyes as Sylvia turned and left the ward.

Rachel stared in disbelief.

He's begging her, begging for a hit!

'Why are you staring at me like that, Rachel?' He glared. 'Where's Rivka?'

Apples will herald the autumn.

Rachel wanted to leave the room yet she was mesmerised, transfixed.

At the nurses' station, Sylvia consulted Wendy.

'What will I do? His last shot was little more than three hours ago.'

'Let me see that.' Wendy studied the chart. 'Hmm. Tell him he can have this one, but we're going to have to look at this.'

Sylvia returned to the ward.

'Rachel, I'm going to give your father something to ease the pain. If you wouldn't mind stepping outside for a few minutes . . .'

Rachel was about to protest when Rivka entered the room.

'You're giving him more of that stuff?'

'Yes, Mrs Grinblatt. We want Mr Grinblatt to be comfortable for his session with the physio.' She beamed at Rivka. 'We don't want him getting pneumonia, do we?'

'Pneumonia?'

'He must get moving, Mrs Grinblatt, otherwise he runs the risk of pneumonia. This injection will enable him to do his physiotherapy in comfort.' Sylvia checked her watch again. 'If you wouldn't mind waiting outside . . .' She drew the curtain around Nate's bed.

'That's what's making him so bad-tempered and mean, isn't it?' Rivka insisted, pointing an accusing finger. 'It's the pethidine.'

A diatribe of angry words and curses in Yiddish.

'Rivka,' Nate snarled from behind the curtain, 'that's enough. Go out—'

'Isn't it?' Rivka demanded to know.

'If you have concerns, Mrs Grinblatt, you should speak to his doctor.'

'You just bet I will, Sister.'

Sylvia vanished behind the curtain.

Rivka refused to leave the room. Rachel waited in the visitors' lounge.

Five minutes later, Sylvia came to tell her she could return to the ward.

'Papa has a problem with the pethidine, doesn't he, Sylvia?'

A door closed on the light in Sylvia's eyes.

'If you think there's something amiss, Rachel, it would be best if you had a talk to his doctor', was Sylvia's circumspect reply.

'Listen to me, Sylvia. I am not an innocent. I know what I'm looking at. My father has developed . . . how discreet would you like me to be? . . . Papa's addicted to pethidine.'

Sweet corn, pump—

'Discuss it with Doctor Gresham, Rachel.' She was firmer now.

'How did this happen?'

Sylvia had nothing more to say.

— o —

'Rachel thinks her father is dependent on the pethidine', Sylvia reported to Wendy and Anna on her return to the nurses' station.

'Is that what she said?'

'She said it like someone who knows what they're talking about.'

'Mrs Grinblatt is acting up, too', Anna said.

'Have you noticed Rachel reading his chart?' Sylvia asked the others. 'You've said from the start there seemed to be something about her and drugs, Wendy. '

'Yes. I've noticed. Damn.' Wendy paused. 'I'll talk to doctor when she comes in. We're going to have to start reducing him.'

Wendy, Sylvia and Anna stood close together, staring at the doorway of Mr Grinblatt's ward from whence came the patient, cooing voice of the woman who was the subject of their speculation.

— o —

Weary to her bonemarrow, Rachel murmured soothing words to her father. Nate nodded off, a grateful receptor of the hit, exhausted, too, from the effort required to make his score. A thin line of drool ran from a corner of his slack mouth. Rachel stood close to the bed, holding his limp hand in her own. Leaning forward to kiss him on the forehead, she was repelled by the texture of his clammy skin.

Look at you, Papa, you poor old bugger. Stoned as any street addict and just as hooked.

Seated once more at her watch by the bed, Rivka looked at her husband, then at her daughter. She hesitated a moment before she spoke. Her mind made up, she said:

'*Es iz genug.* Enough is enough, Rachel. They give him too much of that stuff, don't you think?'

'Yes, Mama, I do.'

'That's why he's so irritable, isn't it?'

'I think so.'

'I think so too. I know he's hopeless about pain, but this . . . I don't like this; it's been going on too long. He should be much better by now. He was crying the other day, Rochl. Crying! He said he thought he might be hooked on that stuff. Your father!'

'He said that to you?'

'That's what he said. Has he told you about the nightmares, those hallucinations?' Yes, Rachel nodded. 'He told me too. Every night he has them. Now he's afraid to go to sleep. That's why he was crying. Oy, those dreams. They sound terrible.'

'Why didn't you talk to me about this?'

'What for? You've got enough to worry about.'

'What are you talking about?'

Here it comes. Here it comes. Here it comes. This is it.

Rivka rose from the chair. She stood erect, took a deep breath and looked directly into her daughter's eyes. 'You think we don't know about Ruby? We know.'

'What are you talking about?'

I sound like a parrot.

Rivka's expression was sad. 'Rachel, dear Rachel, you know what I'm talking about.' She touched Rachel tenderly on the cheek. 'Let's stop pretending now.'

Later, Rachel would marvel at how willing she had been to concede, at how generous her mother had been; Papa, too, once he'd recovered.

'Who told you?'

'Who needs to tell us? We have known for . . . how long? . . . a long time something's been wrong. Jerry, yes. We know you're not happy with Jerry.' Rivka sighed. 'We don't know why. He's not such a bad husband. Whatever you do, your father and me, we just want you to be happy. If you're happy, we're happy.' She sighed again and accompanied it with a philosophical shrug. 'You'll stay, you'll leave.'

Grace! You bitch! You talked to my parents about me. About Ruby.

'At least you talk to us about your life with Jerry. The same as with Jack. About husbands you talk. About Ruby you say nothing but she's more important to us than any of your husbands. Everything's fine, that's all you say. Fine! Look at you. You don't look fine, Rochl. You haven't looked fine for too long. Years. Always pain in your eyes, sadness in your voice. And tense! Your father and me, we hardly dare say anything but small talk in case you bite our heads off. Do you think we are so insensitive that we don't know when something's the matter with our own daughter? Our granddaughter?'

'How did you know?'

'How did we know? She comes to visit. Unusual behaviour, not looking well, too thin, borrowing money, nodding off to sleep at dinner, talking strange. After a long time, your father says maybe it's drugs. Drugs? What do I know? What does he know? I told him he was talking rubbish. I didn't want to believe it. He didn't want to believe it either. We love her. We weren't sure, but we thought maybe.

'One day, a Sunday, Abe and Minna Steingeld came to lunch. I made chicken, the way you like. They told us about their son. You remember him? Asher? He's younger than you, older than Ruby. *Ekh*, don't worry,' Rivka said, seeing the look of horror spread over Rachel's face, 'we didn't say anything. We just listened. Then we knew for sure.'

Sorry, Grace. . . . pumpkin. Peas. Beans . . . broadbeans! This year, I'll plant broadbeans.

'But Rachel, this is not the time or the place. It's your father I'm worried about here. Later we can talk about Ruby,' adding hastily as Rachel withdrew, 'if you want to. Come home with me. We'll have some dinner together. Play a little rummy.'

Rachel told her what Sylvia had said. Rivka shook her worried self out and remoulded into battle lines.

'I'm going to have a word to Wendy Macklin and to that Doctor Grisham. How are they going to get him off it? Tell me that.'

Send him to dry out in some picturesque north-coast town, Mama. Check him in at a rehab. He'd love that. St Kilda? Or perhaps he'd prefer Brunswick. What do you think? Papa could go to group therapy with addicts of all ages and sexes and speak there his bitterness, his unhappiness, his pain. Just as they do. Or what about a meeting? Do you think Papa would enjoy Narcotics Anonymous, Mama?

'I don't know', she replied.

How would they do it? Cold turkey? Slow decrease of his dosage? Methadone? Therapy? A combination? Rachel had no idea.

'*Ikh vayt gurnisht* about these matters. What I do know is that I've had enough. He shouldn't be needing that stuff any more. A pill maybe, when he needs to sleep. But not all that pethidine.'

There would be no turning her back. Rachel knew her mother would keep on at the doctor, the nurses—whoever of the medical staff were responsible, whatever and however long it took—until Nate was clean. 'Wait here with him in case he wakes up. I'm going to find Wendy Macklin. I'll start with her. I'm not putting up with this *drek* any longer! Nor is your father, whether he likes it or not.'

Rivka Grinblatt, determination set on her face and in her bearing, left the room to commence the process of putting an end to her husband's distressing behaviour.

Ay, Mama, if only I had your courage.

'And you,' Rachel was startled out of her reverie by Rivka's momentary return and her waggling finger, 'it's time you should do something about your daughter.'

Almost out the door, she thought of something else. Her parting shot to Rachel was this:

'And if there's nothing you can do for her, do for yourself.' She moved close to Rachel, cradled her face in her hands. 'Look after yourself, *mayn tokhter*. Look after yourself. You only have one life and you are not getting any younger.'

Rivka kissed Rachel on both cheeks and left the room.

Ah, sweet light.

RIDING THE DOG

Rachel enters a waiting room in a hospital where Ruby is sitting. At first she is glad to see her daughter, but soon she notices some large spots on Ruby's face, then on her neck and chest.

'Oh, you've got—'

She is about to say chicken pox but stops because she sees it's not chicken pox at all. As Rachel looks more closely she realises the large, flat spots are dark red, similar to the angry blotches formed when large numbers of blood vessels have popped below the skin. She becomes frightened.

Ruby, seeing Rachel looking at her, touches her neck self-consciously and says, 'Don't worry, Mama, it's just from dieting too heavily.'

'My God! Look at your lips. They're blue. All around your lips is blue! What's going on?' *She starts to cry, softly.*

'It's okay. Don't cry, Mama. I'm all right.'

'No. No. You're not all right. You are going to die.'

'It's just the dieting, really.'

Though Rachel stops crying, her fear does not subside. She looks around at her surroundings, and becomes aware that she is in the long corridor of a hospital. She and Ruby are near the nurses' station. Brian, a man known to Rachel, comes into the reception area and says, 'Rachel, you may come in now.'

He notices Ruby, who is now curled up in a ball on the floor, thoroughly exhausted. Large areas of her skin, which is greyish-white, are covered with the angry red blotches. Rachel watches Brian looking at

Ruby, a stranger to him, wondering who she is, considering what to do about her lying there.

'It's okay,' Rachel tells him, 'she's my daughter.'

She speaks to Brian in a soothing tone to reassure him that the woman on the floor poses no threat. He nods, a curt movement, then indicates the way down the corridor Rachel should go to get to his room.

Rachel looks down at Ruby. The two women smile wistfully at each other, both smiles acknowledging that mother and daughter may never see each other again. Neither woman speaks.

There is no fear in Rachel's heart now; it has been replaced by a feeling of deep peace. She feels sad for her daughter but content for herself. She walks down the corridor after Brian, following him to his room.

— o —

On a day in early summer Ruby phoned Rachel to see if she would like to meet for coffee. They met in the city, at Pellegrini's. Seated on barstools facing tinted-mirror walls, they conducted a desultory conversation, both of them secretly wishing they had not come.

Ruby had grown distrubingly thin. Her face was pale, her skin dry. There were spots around her chin. Her eyebrows, plucked Mae West style, were, in Rachel's opinion, too severe.

'You look good', said Rachel.

'Thanks', replied Ruby, unmoved. She leaned towards the copper-coloured mirror, jutted her chin forward, and ran her index finger over her chin.

'What have you been up to?' Rachel tried again, watching Ruby as she traced the line of pimples.

'Nothing much.'

In their silences Rachel listened to the coffee machine hiss. Cups and plates clattered as they were dropped onto the steel counter; running water gurgled into the sink. Waiters shouted orders through the old intercom hanging on the wall in the bar to the kitchen out the back.

'Due marinara, due.'

'Un pollo e pizzelli, uno.'

'Let's go shopping', Ruby suggested, seizing the opportunity provided by Rachel's obvious irritation. To her mother's dejected response, she added, 'We'll just look. Okay?'

'I suppose so.'

'Come on. It'll be fun.'

Rachel paid for the coffees and they set off for the clothes shops and emporia of Bourke Street. Rarely an enthusiastic shopper, Rachel particularly disliked such expeditions in the city, preferring to proceed, purchase and depart. Ruby, on the other hand, enjoyed a leisurely browse in a number of shops before making her decision.

A typical scenario.

Ruby would select clothes from the racks, take them into the change-room, then come out to ask Rachel's opinion.

'Do you like this, Mama?'

She would strike the pose: hands resting on hips thrust forward, feet pointed out. Her hair gleamed under the shop's bright lights.

'Yes, I do. It's very nice.'

'You do?'

'The style of the top suits you. The colour is lovely.'

'I don't like it. Hang on, I'll try the other one.'

Out she would come again, twirling around.

'What do you think?'

'I prefer the one you tried first.'

'I really like this.'

Exasperated, Rachel would reply, 'Very well, get that one.'

'No, I don't think so. Wait another minute while I see what else is here.'

Browsing through the racks while she waited for Ruby, Rachel might select a garment and bring it to the change-room.

'What about this?'

Rachel would hold it up by its hanger, her fingers squeezed through the cubicle door which Ruby opened only slightly for her.

'*God* no, that's awful! I would never wear anything like that!'

Out again, dressed once more in the first outfit.

'What do you think?'

'I like it. Really I do.'

'I don't. There's nothing I like here. Let's go.'

No matter how flattering Rachel said this or that colour was, how attractive a style, or what she brought from the rack to the change-room, Ruby disagreed, declaring the item ghastly. Rachel wondered whether Ruby did it perversely, deliberately, rejecting garments to prove to Rachel that their opinions, their tastes, indeed, everything about them, was worlds apart. Shopping for clothes with Ruby became a metaphor for all the matter of their lives.

On this afternoon, as they walked along Bourke Street, they peered into windows, entering only one shop. Here, Ruby flicked two or three dresses out by their hems from the circular steel rack to examine the fabric. Uninterested, she let each dress drop in turn. After the fourth window, mother and daughter walked aimlessly and without talking through Myer into Little Bourke Street.

Ruby scuffed her feet. Rachel want to scream.

'Mama,' Ruby finally spoke, 'I'm so miserable.' She linked her arm through Rachel's and began to cry.

'I've been thinking about going up north. I've got to get out of the scene. Maybe that's what I'll do. Leave here. Go up north. Get out of the scene.' She began to cry in earnest, repeating, 'Out of Melbourne, quit this scene.' She leaned her forehead into Rachel's chest from where she continued to mutter about leaving the scene. Rachel held her in her arms, oblivious to the people skirting around them.

'Okay, that's it. I've decided. I'm going.'

Abrupt, tough again. Crying ceased.

'Well, it could work', said Rachel doubtfully.

Rachel thought about people she had known who had left the network of drugs and crime to get clean in the countryside, on the coast, in another state.

'I'll leave on Friday. Get the bus to Maroochydore. Stay with Pete. Did you ever meet Pete? He got clean up there. If he can, I can. I told him I might come up. I'll ring him tonight. See if I can stay with him. Can I phone from your place? Friday. Yes, Friday morning, that's when I'll go. Will you mind my cat while I'm gone? Would you lend me some money for the fare? I'll pay you back. Promise.'

Ruby smiled for the first time that afternoon. She kissed Rachel on the cheek.

'I'm off. Have to get organised. I'll phone you before I go. Bye, Mum. Oh,' she turned back to flash Rachel a winning smile, 'thanks for the coffee.'

Then she left, purposeful, brisk-paced, no scuffing, leaving Rachel standing in Little Bourke Street breathless from the speed of events, anxious, bewildered. Hope was a pinhead of light.

Maybe it would work. It had worked for others. Why not for Ruby?

Hello. What's this? Here's a feeling almost forgotten!

A quiver of excitement. Ruby would be out of her hair for a while.

Ah, but wait!

Hot on the heels of excitement, a familiar old acquaintance: with the thrill of anticipation came the admonishing wet blanket of guilt.

'Ah dear,' Rachel sighed aloud as she stood in Little Bourke Street, 'is there a woman in this world more guilt-ridden than me?'

— o —

Will she actually leave?
   Will she stay away long?
   Will she get clean?
   Stay clean?
   Get a job?
   Find a decent boyfriend?
   Get a life?

To each of these questions, the same response: I hope so. Oh God, how I hope so.

— o —

How many songs have I listened to in my life about leaving town on the Greyhound? Rachel mused.

Riding the dog, bus travellers called it. Rachel rode the dog once. She had been three months pregnant with Ruby. Two days before their long-awaited summer holiday, Jack had phoned from work to say that on his way to work something calamitous had happened to their car, something technical Rachel did not understand. Mario, the garage man, would not be able to repair it in time. With no plane or rail reservations available at such short notice, and no hire car to be had anywhere, Jack booked two seats on a Greyhound bus. A few miles south of Holbrook, the air-conditioning broke down. In the strangling heat of the New South Wales summer, they sweated and sweltered and cursed for the remainder of their journey to Sydney.

'I shall never travel by bus again', Rachel had declared to Jack. And nor she did.

— o —

Friday came.

Maternal goodwill had little to do with Rachel's offer to drive Ruby to the bus depot. More significantly, she wanted to be certain that Ruby left Melbourne as she had said three days ago she would.

The cafeteria at the depot was neon-bright. Seated on blue Vinyl barstools by seven-thirty—half an hour before the bus was due to depart—Rachel and Ruby sipped cups of bitter brewed coffee, which, even at that early hour, already tasted stale. Ruby's disposition was sullen. Her eyes never met Rachel's. She lit one cigarette after another, glancing up whenever someone entered the cafeteria.

'I wonder if the bus will leave on time?' Rachel said, looking at her watch.

'You didn't have to come, you know. Leave if you want to', was Ruby's reply.

Rachel wished now she hadn't come, that she'd had the courage to say goodbye on the phone, that she'd left her daughter to go off alone on her journey.

'Time to go', Ruby announced as she leapt off the barstool.

'Paradox' was the word turning over and over in Rachel's mind as she stepped away from the bar, for, despite all the unhappiness that had led to Ruby's departure for the Queensland coast, she felt miserable. It might be some time before they met again.

It was in this wistful frame of mind that Rachel rode with Ruby down the escalator to the waiting bus. Middle-aged couples in their casual best, foreign backpackers wearing shorts and T-shirts, their hair blonded and their skin browned by the sun, freckle-faced young men in tight jeans, cowboy shirts and riding boots (Cuban heels, all), elderly women in floral-print dresses carrying cream or white imitation-leather handbags, their hair tidy, their sandals new, their lipstick rosy, single mothers with babes in arms and toddlers in tow: all were boarding. Bound for glory? Rachel doubted there was much glory to be found at the end of a Greyhound ride. Maybe—just maybe—there was clean.

Struggling to hold back her tears, Rachel leaned towards Ruby and kissed her.

'Goodbye, Rube. I do hope—'

'See ya', said Ruby, cutting Rachel off. 'Don't wait. Go home.'

'I don't mind waiting.'

Shrug. 'Suit yourself.'

Ruby sucked heavily on the last of her cigarette, flicked the butt into the gutter of the bus bay then, without turning back, stepped aboard.

It was difficult for Rachel to see anything more than shadowy outlines of seats, the ghost-like movements of human shapes, through the black-tinted windows.

I hope Ruby isn't sitting next to one of those young men in jeans and cowboy shirts. What if they're carrying drugs?

Straining to see Ruby's familiar shape, Rachel saw her lean across a window-seat passenger—an elderly woman, next to whom she was preparing to sit—and wave goodbye. She was grinning. It shocked Rachel to recognise the message in that grin: 'Hah, I'm escaping!'

Resentment exploded through Rachel's sorrow.

The driver rounded up the stragglers. Rachel's face ached from the fixed smile she had held for the past ten minutes. Though she knew Ruby wouldn't come to the window again, she stood rooted to the spot, staring at the window behind which Ruby sat. At last, everyone was on board. The driver slammed the door, started the engine and began to back out of the bus bay in a cloud of foul-smelling diesel fumes.

'Goodbye, Ruby', she whispered to the black window. 'I hope you make it.'

The gruesome smile slipped from her face.

Tears fell, large and warm. Rachel thought they might never stop flowing. How could eyes gush so much water? Her blouse grew wet. Tears sluiced down from her jaw and tickled her neck;

she brushed the tears away. A warm, thin slime, almost as copious as her tears, dribbled from her nose. She snuffled loudly and wiped her nose with an old tissue she found in her pocket. When the tissue became sodden, she used the back of her hand. Mascara and eyeliner ran in black rivulets, smudging her eyes, staining her cheeks. Rachel didn't care; she was beyond vanity.

With heavy, dragging steps, Rachel walked slowly from the bus bay to the street. Wearily she climbed into her car and drove up Franklin Street, away from the bus depot, eastward into the morning sun, toward the work that was awaiting her in the nursery.

I hope you make it, Rube. I hope this is the one.

— o —

'Would you like a piece of chocolate, dear?' the elderly woman seated beside Ruby offered as Ruby woke from a light sleep. They were passing through Euroa.

'Thank you.'

'Where are you off to?'

'Queensland.'

'That's nice, dear. Holiday, is it?'

'Yes.' Ruby's laughter was rich with pleasure. 'A holiday. A hard-earned rest. Where are you off to?'

'I'm going to Newcastle to see my grandchildren.'

'That's nice, too. What's your name?'

'Gertrude, but most people call me Gert. You can call me Gert. What's yours?'

'Ruby.'

'What a beautiful name. Pleased to meet you, Ruby.'

'Pleased to meet you, too, Gert.'

'You'll miss your family, will you, Ruby?'

Ruby's reply was thoughtful. 'I probably will.'

They rode through the landscape, chatting, dozing. When they reached Benalla, Ruby enquired, 'Do you play cards, Gertrude?'

'Gert. Yes, I do, I've always enjoyed a game of rummy. Why do you ask?'

'Rummy, eh? I brought a deck of travelling cards with me. I was going to play patience to pass the time, but I love rummy, too. I play with my mum. That was her waving goodbye. Did you notice?'

'Yes, I did. A fine-looking woman.'

'Thanks. Would you like a couple of rounds, Gert?' Realising the implication of Gertrude's reticence, Ruby hurriedly added: 'Not for money. Just for fun.'

Gertrude relaxed. What a friendly young woman. 'Yes, dear. Thank you. A game or two of rummy. I'd enjoy that.'

Ruby released the tray from the seat in front of her travelling companion. As she dealt the cards, she smiled happily at the appearance of a vision of freshly picked peaches and plates of toast piled high with tomatoes and basil.

Conversation ceased. The two women played cards until, a few miles the other side of Wangaratta, Gertrude said she was feeling drowsy and needed to have a little snooze. They could resume play when she woke, if Ruby would like to. Would Ruby like the window seat while she was sleeping? They changed places. Ruby assisted the older woman to settle, adjusting her travel rug and pillow.

For the next hundred miles, Ruby watched the muted colours of the Australian landscape slip by. She was imbued with a tranquillity the like of which she had not known for many years. At the comfort stop in Albury, she opened her backpack and removed from it a set of coloured pencils and a sketch pad.

I hope I make it. I hope this is the one.

SLIP SLIDIN' AWAY

Slip slidin' away
Slip slidin' away
You know the nearer your destination
The more you're slip slidin' away

'Slip Slidin' Away', Paul Simon

Dear Mum and Jerry

Maroochydore is beautiful. Feels great to be out the scene. Made new friends. No addicts. Pete helping me keep straight. Other house-mate—Lucy. Settling into house well. More soon. Send Eli's address. Might write.

Love you both, Ruby xxx

— o —

Four weeks and five days had elapsed since Ruby left Melbourne to go north—'Maybe forever, Mum', she'd said to Rachel at the bus depot, unaware of the sceptical look on Rachel's face—to get clean, kick the habit. As the days of Ruby's absence accrued and became the past, Rachel became cautiously optimistic.

For the first two weeks small shards of fear lingered. Each day when the postman delivered mail, each time the phone rang, Rachel expected to be informed that Ruby had busted and was

238

coming home. She didn't want Ruby to come home. She wanted Ruby to stay away and get well.

On Sundays, around evening, Ruby phoned. Rachel grew accustomed to the regularity of her calls and came to look forward to them. Ruby was always cheerful, the calls were affectionate and brief. It was a small but satisfying contact.

— o —

Dear Mama
Five weeks clean. Feeling good. Should have done this years ago.
What's happening in the garden? Are you painting?
  Love to Jerry, Rube xxx

— o —

Rachel didn't miss Ruby as much as she thought she would. Truth was, she rarely thought about her, and when she did, it was in the most loving and hopeful terms. In fact, hopeful was an inadequate description of her feelings: Ruby was getting along fine up there on the coast, working away at a job, enjoying life. Everything was going to be all right. All Ruby had needed to get clean was to leave the scene. It had, after all, been as simple as that.

— o —

'Lighten up, Mum!' had been Ruby's constant admonition. Rachel began to lighten up. Her work in the nursery and the garden was performed with renewed vigour and enthusiasm.

Jerry, tentative at first, began to relax. He ventured suggestions. 'Would you like go out to dinner tonight?', 'Do you want to see the film at the Kino?', 'How about a drive to the coast on Sunday?' Encouraged by her responses, he proposed they check into the Regency for the night and run up some room service.

'It will cost a fortune!'

'Good. Let's do it.'

It had been months since Rachel had seen Eli. She painted a card. On the back she wrote him an invitation to dinner. Eli accepted with good grace. On the designated night, he arrived carrying a bunch of tulips. In a mood as buoyant as her own, he spent the evening talking about his job as a journalist with a local newspaper, his new girlfriend, and other events in his life. It was midnight when he left.

'It was lovely to see you, Eli. Next time bring your girlfriend. Let us meet her.'

'Don't let's overdo it, Rachel.'

They both smiled. Eli kissed her goodbye, almost squeezing the breath out of her with his hug. Jerry walked him to his car.

'She's in good nick', Eli smiled.

'Let's hope she stays that way', was Jerry's wry reply.

'Have you heard from Ruby lately?'

Jerry told Eli that they heard regularly; he gave Eli a rundown on Ruby's news.

'Good on her. I hope that shit's over for her.'

'And so say all of us. It was pleasure to see you, Eli.'

'You, too, Jerry. What about footy next time Richmond plays Fitzroy?'

'You're on. Give me a call.'

— o —

Dear Eli

What a relief, to be clean and out of the scummy life. It feels like peace. I like it up here, though I do miss some aspects of Melbourne— I think I'm the only person in Maroochy who knows how to make a decent coffee! Everyone's lining up for lessons. I'm doing a bit of painting, though not much. Don't know if that's what I want to do with the rest of my life. Don't tell Mum I said that! Being away from Mum and Jerry is a relief. Mum especially was driving me around the bend. An excess of concern. Do you see much of them? Are they still in stand-off mode with each other? Hope you're fit and ferreting out prize-winning stories for your newspaper. If you get a minute, drop me a line. Would love to hear from you.

Your ever-lovin' sister, Ruby xxx

— o —

Friends were invited to dinner; films and jazz clubs were back on the agenda. Jerry and Rachel passed an occasional weeknight in a city hotel, and drove to the country for weekends. On Sunday mornings, they lay in the bed reading the weekend newspapers.

They kissed often and made love at night. They made love

again in the morning, their caresses sometimes slow and gentle, other times strong and urgent as they rediscovered the passion they had once enjoyed. Rachel's eyes sparkled, her skin glowed.

'I hope this works for her', she said to Jerry one night as they cleared away the dinner dishes.

'She'll do the best she can', he said, as ever, more realistic. 'Have you given any thought to what you'll do if it doesn't work?'

'Doesn't work?'

'What do you want for yourself, independent of what happens to Ruby? Are you going to get back to your painting? What about our life together? They're the things I'm talking about. You can't spend your entire life feeling as if everything that goes wrong in your kids' lives is your fault, or that you have to protect them from their own lives.'

'I wish I didn't find that so difficult to accept.'

'Yes,' he grinned, 'you enjoy beating yourself up, don't you?'

'Jerry Bradman, the master of understatement.'

Jerry had never felt any compunction in letting Ruby know when he found her behaviour unacceptable.

'That was a dickhead thing to do', he might say.

Or:

'There's no need to behave like that. Who do you think you are?'

Or:

'All hate is self-hate.' This slogan from his hippie days was recited with all the smugness of one delivering an irrefutable truth.

If he shouted at her—though it was a rare occasion that Jerry Bradman shouted at anyone—Ruby's most frequent response was to storm off to her bedroom and slam the door behind her. At worst, she stamped her way around the block, returning fifteen minutes later, her anger dissipated, apologetic, and in a matey mood with Jerry. Ruby respected his directness. The lessons of these exchanges were beyond Rachel's ability to grasp.

Years later, Jerry was to tell Rachel that though he had always liked Ruby, he knew there was nothing he could do about her habit and its attendant behaviour other than wait it out. Either she would grow sick of the life and seek help, or she would die.

'It was you I never knew how to deal with.'

— o —

Hi Mum Hi Jerry
Still off dope. Good on me! Part-time job still happening. I still like
cafe life. Come for a visit. I'll make you best coffee you've ever had.
Sunny, sunny, sunny, warm, warm, warm. How are you? How's
Eli? How's cat? Still no win for the Tigers, Jerry? Hah! Gone blonde.
Like it?'

Lotsa luv Ruby **xxx**

Ruby's note was written on the back of a small oil painting of
their house. It was the first piece of Ruby's artwork Rachel had
been shown in many a year.

A wad of photos was enclosed: the main street of Maroochydore (a pleasant-looking town), Ruby and Pete sitting next to
each other on the verandah step, Ruby and Pete separately in
front of a pink hibiscus bush, and groups of people Rachel assumed
to be some of the new friends. Then came half a dozen of two
healthy looking young women: Ruby and Lucy. Tanned limbs, and
yes, Rachel did like the streaked blonde hair that surrounded their
tanned and freckled faces, highlighting the whiteness of their
teeth. In another, the three housemates leaned into each other as
they ginned goofily at the camera. Scrambled sets of crooked fingers were raised above heads in imitation of rabbit's ears. Rachel
gawped; she hardly recognised her own daughter.

'Looks like she's put on a bit of weight at last', Jerry observed,
grinning. 'She must be being a good girl.'

The letter and the photos—especially the photos—made
Rachel's heart sing. The eggshells beneath her feet transmuted
into soft, fluffy clouds.

— o —

Good idea, Ruby, Rachel said to herself as she dragged her art
materials from the back of a cupboard. Thrilled by her renewed
acquaintance with the smell of the paint, its glutinous texture
and glorious colours, she set to work.

'About bloody time', Jerry remarked, pleased. 'I was afraid you
had given up forever.'

'Your mother's painting again', he informed Eli.

'About bloody time,' Eli said, 'I was afraid she'd never pick up a brush again.'

Jerry laughed. 'Football on Saturday? Want to see the mighty Tigers thrash the Lions?'

'Dream on, Jerry. One-thirty at the ground.'

'See you there.'

— o —

Rachel stopped worrying and got on with her life.

Go, Ruby, you can do it. Go.

— o —

Dear Mama and Jerry

We drove to Noosa for long weekend. Pete taught me how to body-surf. Board surfing next. Great time had by all. Saw some dolphins!!! Got really pissed at a party. Aching head Sunday—yow! Our garden. Like it?

Much love, R xxx

A gouache garden of subtropical flowers.

— o —

The weekly calls increased to twice weekly, then thrice. With growing frequency, Ruby spoke of how drunk she'd been the night before, or was planning to be at this or that celebration.

Mention of the blackouts came next. An hour lost here or there, she giggled nervously. But as the number of hours increased— two, three, eventually whole nights—her giggling ceased.

'Try drinking less.'

'I mean to. It seems to get away from me.'

Rachel felt the chill rising with every phone call. From the soles of her feet, it crawled its way up her body, slithered into every pore and crevice. Her heart began to constrict, tightening into a hard lump of fear.

Twelve weeks after she'd left Melbourne, Ruby phoned to say she'd be back in two days. Sunday. Could she move in with Rachel and Jerry? Just until she found somewhere else to live.

Slip slidin' away . . .

— o —

Rachel was delighted to see her.

'Ruby, you look fabulous. You haven't looked this good in years.'

'Nah, too fat.' Ruby grinned, hugging her mother. They kissed.

'Rubbish. You look beautiful! Doesn't she, Jerry? How are you?'

'Good, but fat.'

They laughed.

'How're things, Jer?' Ruby planted a kiss on his cheek. 'Tiges won one yet?'

'I'm well, Ruby.' He nodded approvingly at her. 'You do look good. Very healthy.'

'You're looking fit yourself, Jerry', she said, patting the small roundness of his newly forming pot belly. 'Better keep an eye on that, though.'

Sitting around the table, Ruby entertained Rachel and Jerry with tales of her sojourn to the coast. An ebullient threesome, they laughed and talked and ate and drank and listened to music late into the afternoon. Rachel beamed with pleasure.

This feels like family. This is how it should be.

At six o'clock, Rhea arrived. She and Ruby sat at the kitchen table making plans for the evening. Half an hour later, Eli dropped in.

'You made it!' Ruby shrieked. Turning to Rachel and Jerry, she explained, 'I rang him to say I was going to be here.'

Who was more pleased to see him? Rachel? Ruby? Moot point.

'Oops,' he said at seven, 'I have to go, otherwise I'll be late for the movies.'

'Can't keep the girlfriend waiting', Ruby teased. All four turned to Rachel, already laughing before she had begun to say, 'Who is she?'

'Her name's Angelo', Eli chuckled, and waved them goodbye.

The girls—*will they ever be old enough for me to not think of them as girls?*—decided to catch up with friends at the Cornish Castle Hotel, where a band was playing. They would have a drink or two and see how the night panned out. Laughing and gossiping, they said their farewells and headed off into the balmy evening.

Rachel and Jerry turned to each other and grinned.

— o —

Four past four. Rachel awoke, alert to a danger. Was it the rapidly fading images of a dream? Something else? She rose from the bed.

An icy shiver ran down her spine. She stood in the middle of the room, sniffing the air like an animal alert to impending danger.

Smoke!

In the hallway the smell was stronger: it mingled with the sour, heavy tang of whisky. Rachel wrinkled her nose as she tracked the odour to the front room. There, face down on the bed, lay Ruby. Less than three inches from her face, a patch of mattress the size of a dinner plate was burning. Bright orange-red flames and sparks were smouldering in the centre of an outer ring of ash, determinedly burrowing their way deeper and wider into the wadding of the futon.

'Ruby! Ruby!' Rachel's cry was shrill. She shook her daughter's shoulder, her grip vice-like. 'Wake up! Wake up, Ruby. Jerry!' she cried out. 'Jerry!'

Ruby lay motionless, a moulded slab of flesh. Acrid smoke curled over her face and up her nostrils; it drifted through her hair. Rachel was momentarily transfixed.

So, this is how it happens.

She turned on her heel and raced down the hallway.

In the kitchen she filled a saucepan. Returning to the front room, she poured the water into the fire, jiggling the mattress around to make sure all the flames were drenched. The fire hissed and went out, sending up clouds of rank-smelling smoke. The stink filled the room, billowed out the door and through to the rest of the house.

Ruby had not moved so much as an eyelash. If Rachel hadn't observed her back moving up and down with the rhythm of her breathing, she might have thought Ruby was dead. Rachel had never felt so cold or so frightened in her life. She had never felt so alone.

Leaning down, Rachel stroked Ruby's back.

'You poor baby', she whispered. 'What's to become of you?'

She kissed Ruby's face, smoothed her damp hair. After covering her with a blanket, Rachel opened a window to let some fresh air into the room and returned to the livingroom.

Inky night gave way to the pallid blue of early morning. The sky was streaked from the north to the east with a wide arc of livid, orange-red stripes and dark, flocculent cloud.

'Sailor's warning', said Rachel quietly.

From the back garden, where she now stood, she heard a tram roll by, rattling along the steel tracks on its way to collect its first passengers of the day.

Must be five o'clock.

The hot tea she'd made warmed her.

'Sugar.'

She loaded a teaspoon with brown crystals. Poured them slowly off the tip of the spoon into the steaming liquid. Dissolved them in the tea. Finished drinking. Heaved a forlorn sigh. Surveyed the garden.

Hello, you are back. My old companions. Anxiety, sorrow. I feel your presence. Obsession—the overarching member of the trinity— will follow close on your heels.

Returned to bed.

Slip slidin' away . . .

— o —

'What's that stink?' Jerry asked, wrinkling up his nose as he joined Rachel at the table. She told him about the fire he had slept through.

'Why didn't you wake me?' He was indignant.

'I tried, Jerry. You didn't hear me.' She, weary.

Rachel swallowed the last of her tea, extinguished her cigarette. 'I must talk to her.'

'Leave her sleep. You can talk later.'

'I'll see if she's awake.'

He heard the misery in her voice.

'I'll come with you', he offered, placing a hand on her sagging shoulders. Hopelessness had returned to her eyes, a look he hadn't seen for three months. The halcyon days were over.

You know the nearer your destination . . .

— o —

Ruby was sitting up in bed picking at the edges of the burnt portion of the mattress. Her face was pale. A pall of smoke and whisky hung in the air.

'Good morning, Ruby.'

Rachel followed Jerry into the bedroom. She kissed her daughter on the cheek then seated herself on the end of the bed. Jerry, perched on the other side and lit a cigarette. Ruby put out her hand to him, index and middle fingers open in a stiff V. He placed the cigarette between her fingers and rolled himself another, staring at the floor while he smoked it.

'Hello, Mama. Hi Jerry.' A pause, a quick glance at the burnt mattress. 'Did I do this?'

'Yes, Ruby, you did.'

'What happened?'

'You must have come home drunk and fallen asleep with a cigarette still burning.' Every ounce of effort was engaged to maintain a low and even voice. Ruby snuggled up to her. Rachel rocked her gently, backwards and forwards, as she recounted the events. Had a stranger looked into the room, they could have been forgiven for believing Rachel was telling Ruby a bedtime story, or comforting her after a bad dream.

I am comforting her after a bad dream.

'The smell of smoke woke me. I put out the fire. You didn't stir the whole time.'

'Not at all?'

Ruby ran her fingertips across her cheek. 'Did the fire come close to my face?'

'Yes, very.' Rachel indicated the distance with thumb and forefinger.

Ruby disentangled herself from Rachel's arms and sat back. A look—sheepishness tinged with a faint air of bravado—flitted across her face. Rachel felt a sudden surge of anger. She wanted to knock that look off Ruby's face with a sharp slap.

'Is there something amusing about this, Ruby?' she snapped. 'Something I'm missing?'

'No, no, nothing. I'm embarrassed. I don't know what to say.'

Jerry stood up.

'If I don't leave now, I'll be late for work. See you tonight. Take it easy, Rube.'

'Yeah. Thanks. Bye, Jerry.'

He kissed Rachel, hugged Ruby, said goodbye to them and left. Both women sat there, lost in contemplation, unnerved by what more could have occurred.

'What am I going to do, Mama?' Ruby said, leaning her face into Rachel's chest. 'This is serious.'

Rachel felt the drip of Ruby's tears through her blouse, like leakage; there was no sobbing, no heaving. Ruby's body was completely still.

'Do you think you have a problem, Ruby? If you don't, there's nothing can be done, nothing to talk about.'

'I suppose I have.'

'Aren't you frightened, Ruby? I'm frightened. I am so scared. Where is this going to end?' Rachel wept. 'What if Jerry and I had been out? What if you'd been somewhere alone or with someone as smashed as you were?' She pulled a tissue from her sleeve and blew her nose. 'How long do you think this guardian angel of yours will continue watching over you?'

'It's all right, Mama. Don't worry. It's all right.'

'No, Ruby. No. It's not all right. I cannot bear to see what has become of you. I keep expecting you to die. I don't want you to die, Ruby. Children aren't supposed to die before their parents.'

Ruby stroked her hair.

'Hush Mama. I'm not going to die, not yet anyway.' She paused, ruminating on something. 'Maybe I'll go to an Alcoholics Anonymous meeting, or get myself into a rehab again. God,' her laugh was ironic, 'no drugs, no grog. What will I do?'

'You'll think of something', Rachel retorted.

'I'm frightened, too, Mum. Frightened of being clean and sober. I don't know who I am without it any more. Just thinking about it makes me want a drink, or a hit.'

They sat quietly.

'Pete and Lucy tried to get me to go to meetings.'

'They did?'

'Yes, Mama, they did. That seems to surprise you.'

'Did you go?'

'No, I refused. I'm not an alcoholic, I said. I told them AA was for down and outers, gutter drunks, punch-up merchants, scungy men, not for the likes of a middle-class girl like me. I'd handle it without those meetings, I said. Hah! Snotty old me. Too proud.' She sighed. Already, her suntan seemed to have paled. 'So I'd better get myself to a meeting, eh?'

There, on the horizon! See? Rising with the morning sun. Elusive, feeble, flickering ray of hope. Eternal blind faith. Alcoholics Anonymous!

'Alcoholics Anonymous. Well, it's a starting point', Rachel agreed, dubious, relieved nonetheless to hear of any attempt at progress. She thought about drunks on the street, men sleeping it off in parks and smelling of piss: uncontrollable, shabby, violent, loud. It embarrassed her to think that her daughter would join their throng. But Ruby was right. She had become one of them, even if she didn't sleep in parks.

And what would I know about that?

As if reading her thoughts, Ruby said, 'Alcoholics and junkies come from across the entire spectrum, Mum. You'd be surprised.'

I don't want to be surprised.

'So, how do you get in touch with Alcoholics Anonymous? Are they in the phone book? Why don't you give them a call.'

Ruby paused before answering. When she replied, her words were as measured as Rachel's had been when she first entered the room. She reached for Rachel's hand and held it.

'Don't tell me what to do, Mama, or how to do it. This is for me to take care of.'

It was nine-thirty, yet the morning was already hot; a strong northerly was howling.

Rachel extricated herself. 'Very well. I'm sorry.' She stood up. 'I have to get some work done. This wind will wreak havoc on the garden. Will you be all right?'

In the bathroom Rachel wiped her face and neck with a cool face-washer, repaired her eye makeup, brushed her hair and slipped her tortoiseshell combs into place.

As she stepped into the garden she looked up. The fire had gone from the sky as it had from the mattress and, like the mattress, it was blackened, dirty looking. Billowing purple cloud continued to build, dark and ominous. The northerly blew hard, flipping Rachel's hair around her face, flapping her clothes.

Flowers were bent flat, leaves fluttered wildly; dust and peastraw swirled up from the garden beds.

A storm was coming. By afternoon it would be raining.

INTERLUDE V

Temptations are many and seductive. Thus, the days of Ruby's detoxification and subsequent rehabilitation are short-lived.

Faster, faster, through the loops of the slide.

Rachel's attendant fears and worries, her obsession, return. Naturally.

Jerry's retreat, his frustration and anger, return. Of course. He remembers with fondness the sweet little cottage in Clifton Hill. His fulsome adjectives embellish what was, in reality, a falling-down Edwardian timber shack, with a back yard covered in concrete.

Only Eli remains safe. He ensures his absence from the carnival by vigilant disengagement.

— o —

What is to be deduced from this Sisyphean existence? What is to be deduced?

It is time for change. Time to take command of the rock.

— o —

Without informing Jerry, Rachel investigates counselling. She consults the family doctor to seek his advice. The doctor gives her the name of a therapist.

Weeks of procrastination ensue before she makes an appointment. Settling into the therapist's exquisitely comfortable leather chair, she begins to cry.

'What brings you here?' the therapist asks in a quiet voice.

'My daughter is on drugs. I'm so frightened', she sobs.

'What drugs does she use?'

'Heroin.'

'That would be very frightening', he sympathises.

Following this remark he says little, a behaviour Rachel finds disconcerting. She imagines him to be a large ear, listening to words and phrases as they spill from her mouth, often incoherent through the weeping. A bodiless, headless ear, the size of a man.

Fifty minutes after it commences, the session draws to an end. The therapist mentions how busy he is this year: clients, committees. Of his softly spoken remarks, Rachel hears only 'I am busy'. She thinks he is telling her he shall not have time to see her again.

Hurt, embarrassed, angry. Why has he bothered with this session if he has not the time to see her again? Perhaps he has the time but found her dull, a weepy, tedious matron. Perhaps he doesn't want a client like her.

Three weeks pass. Desperate, bleeding from wounds where she scratched herself with the pointed end of a steel nail file, she phones to beg.

'Please, please, find some time for me', Rachel weeps.

'I offered you my last appointment', the therapist says. 'When you didn't call I presumed you had made other arrangements. The appointment is no longer available.'

'No!' she screams. 'No. You said you were too busy to see me!'

'I mentioned that my year was busy but I had one regular appointment remaining in my schedule. If you wished to see me and if the time suited you, you could have it. You were to let me know, promptly.'

'Please.'

'I am very sorry, it is no longer possible.'

A month later she returns to the family doctor.

'What a shame. He's a good man. Sounds like you were running away, Rachel.'

His smile is kind.

'Running away?'

'From help. From change.'

'He said he didn't have time to see me', she protests.

'So you say. Would you like to try someone else?'

Rachel tries again; this time the recommendation is a woman, a counsellor, she calls herself. At the appointed time, Rachel sits in the counsellor's waiting room flipping through tattered copies of New Idea, which magazine's presence, she feels, does not augur well. She waits. And waits. Twenty minutes becomes the shortest wait; half an hour is not uncommon. During the sessions, the counsellor sits so close to her on the couch that Rachel feels tense. The woman's proximity feels invasive.

Positive thinking seems to be the counsellor's approach: 'How lovely that colour looks on you, Rachel', 'Your hair is so pretty today', 'You seem to have lost some weight in the past week' (this remark arousing particular indignation), 'What have you done to have a fun week?' During the sessions the counsellor takes calls from other patients and from members of her family. Rachel knows little of the practice of psychotherapy, but she understands enough to know that this is not the place for her. At the fifth session (twenty-five minutes late starting), Rachel tells the counsellor she wants to sit alone on the couch, reprimands her for her tardiness, expresses her disapproval of the phone calls taken during her sessions, and announces that she is leaving.

By which time the session is almost over.

'Oh, Rachel,' the counsellor croons, 'isn't it exciting? You are expressing your anger at last.' She lays a hand on Rachel's arm. 'Same time next week?'

'Not fucking likely', Rachel fumes. She pays her session fee and marches out of the room.

She never asks the family doctor again; pride forbids it. Therapy is for mad people, hysterical people, people who can't cope.

I'll cope. I'll be fine. Fine.

Hah!

SINS OF THE FLESH

My heart writhes within me,
  the terrors of death come upon me,
fear and trembling overwhelm me,
  and shuddering grips me.
And I say,
'Who will give me wings like a dove,
  to fly away and find rest?'

from Psalm 55

Herein lies the final fling. This. The last round. End of the line. Rock bottom.

It began like this.
Smoke is curling from a freshly lit cigarette Rachel holds in her right hand. It rises from the glowing tip, curls around her fingers and floats through the airless room from where she sits on the end of Ruby's bed: shoulders hunched, stomach slack, head drooping. Small marks dot the back of her left hand, which hangs flaccidly between her knees.

Are these marks chicken pox, open wounds that have been scratched by an irritated sufferer?

The sores are not chicken pox. They are burns, which form a cluster of small red holes, angry little pools of exposed tissue rimmed with shrivelled black skin and ash.

Rachel did not cry out when she burnt herself. She clenched her teeth, held the cigarette against her skin until she could bear

bar
254

the pain no longer. Then found another spot, and another, and burnt herself again.

Six times.

This occurred next.
Cold, clammy sweat burst through her skin; diaphragm muscles contracted. Metallic-tasting saliva flooded her mouth.

The charge of vomit was too quick; Rachel leaned forward and threw up, spurting the contents of her stomach onto the carpet. Pieces of it splashed the tops of her exposed feet and her suede shoes. When her stomach was emptied, she retched, dry, tight heaves that expanded her rib cage to near bursting, caused veins to stand out on her forehead.

I make myself sick.

She looked around the room hoping to find a glass with some water in it, a cup containing remnants of cold tea or coffee. Anything would do; nothing was there.

Tears welled in her eyes, whether from weeping or the rheuminess that follows vomiting, she neither knew nor cared. Pulling a corner of the sheet from beneath the quilt, she used it to dab the corners of her eyes, wipe her mouth.

What is to become of you? Mewling, puking, weeping. What has become of your dignity?

The stink from the puddle was awful. Rachel waved her hand in front of her face in an attempt to move the foul air away. A futile gesture. She looked around for a tissue—*Is there never anything in this room when I need it?*—then flipped her feet, trying to shake away the speckles of vomit that had stuck there; obdurate, they held fast to her skin. With her left foot she pushed her right shoe off, then, with the big toe of her right foot, eased off the left shoe. It bounced backwards on the thick woollen carpet, right into the pool of sick.

Was that it? Was that the last straw?
Patience.

Rachel howled, a long, bay-at-the-moon howl, plaintive, despairing.

There is a cry, a shrill warble, made by African women. They waggle their tongues to manipulate a single note. Ululation. A single, piercing note. A trill at the high end of the tonal range. If I knew how, I would trill that high-pitched wail and never stop.

Ul-u-la-tion.

I don't know how.

Pain crept up her arm. She cradled her damaged hand on top of the other, which she had curved into a platform, and rested both on her lap.

Then came this.

Her howling brought Jerry running from the back of the house.

'What's the matter?'

'Nothing', she snarled, refusing to look at him. 'I'm fine. Go away.'

She is ashamed.

He came to a halt in the doorway and took in the scene, recoiled from the smell.

'Are you ill? What has happened to your hand?'

Rachel whipped her hand behind her back.

Anger darkened Jerry's face. He stepped into the room and grabbed Rachel's wrist from behind her back.

That hurt.

'What have you done? Rachel?'

His voice was harsh, his look disbelieving.

'Nothing', she replied, petulant.

Why can't he leave me alone?

'What have you done?' he repeated, enunciating each word, roaring now. 'Tell me, Rachel, what is this? Cigarette burns? Is that what they are? Have you gone completely fucking mad?'

Have I? Gone mad? Completely fucking mad?

Revulsion and horror widened his eyes. He let go of her hand. Rachel, her eyes still to the floor, saw his feet move back from her.

'Yes,' she conceded, 'that's what this is.'

So what? Belligerent, defensive.

Rachel pushed her bare feet into the carpet, wishing the pile were deep enough to hide her entire body in, wishing that she was not the object of his disgust, and her own.

'Stop that', Jerry ordered. 'Stop it! Go and dress that hand. At once. I'll clean up this mess. Then we are going to talk. This cannot continue, Rachel.'

'Not now, Jerry. Please', she beseeched. 'We'll talk later.'

'No, now. Stop that bleating. This is not about Ruby any more, if it ever was. Go. Fix your hand.'

Decisive, resolute.

It was unlike Jerry to be so commanding. Rachel had grown accustomed to his resignation, his mute frustration in the face of her interminable depression and self-destructive behaviour. Because it was rare for Jerry to speak this way, Rachel became fearful.

He will leave me for another woman—younger, of course— a woman with whom he could have children. New ones. Children of his own. Bright, fresh children. Clean-slate children. Perfect new children who would never use drugs.

Rachel was afraid of life without Jerry, so she stood up and went obediently down the hall to the bathroom to dress her wound, just as he had ordered her to.

Good girl, Rachel.

Followed by this.

They sat opposite each other in the livingroom.

'What has happened to you, Rachel?'

'I ask myself the same question.'

Her voice was flat. Weary could not begin to describe the tiredness she felt.

'And?'

'I don't have any answers.'

'No answers! Not one bloody answer?'

His gaze, settled on her now, was piercing as he waited for her reply. When it came, it was so softly spoken that he found it difficult to hear, so he leaned in closer in an attempt to catch her words.

'No', she whispered, shaking her head. 'Ruby . . . I so wanted the program to work for Ruby. I can't help worrying about her since she left the rehab. If only—'

'Enough!' he cried out. 'Enough about Ruby. I am not talking about the past few weeks. I am not talking about Ruby. I'm talking about you. You, Rachel.'

'Why can't she get well? I feel so helpless.'

'Is that reason enough to mutilate yourself? Is it? Why should

you feel helpless? Whether or not Ruby gets well is out of your
control. So are her comings and goings at the rehab.'

He paused for a response; none was forthcoming.

'Where in hell did you get the idea that you had to try and
fix this on your own? You never ask for help. You and your
family, you're all the same. You like to think of it as indepen-
dence! I call it pig-headed pride.'

'This has nothing to do with them!'

'Aha! She speaks, addressing, as usual, the point of least sig-
nificance. Nothing, as usual, about why she's gone off the rails,'
he sneered, 'or, as bloody usual, about why our marriage has
become so hellish that I can hardly stand to be here any more.
Or how painful it is for her to let her children get on with their
lives. Or how much she misses them. Talk about the real problems? Oh no. That would be too much to ask.'

'How can I talk to you? I don't know myself why I'm miserable all the time.'

His lips curled with scorn.

'Even you don't believe that, Rachel.'

She ignored that one.

'Why should I ask for your support?' she said. 'Whenever I tell
you I'm concerned about Ruby, you tell me to leave her alone,
that she'll be all right. I can't abandon her.'

Jerry stood up; he paced the floor in front of her as he spoke.
Back and forth. Back and forth. Back and forth.

'There you go again, Rachel. You deliberately misconstrue my
remarks. Not once have I suggested you abandon her. That
would be unthinkable. How many times do I have to tell you
that there is nothing more you can do for Ruby? Love her, yes,
let her know you love her. But you will not get her clean. Getting well is something she has to do herself. Do you understand?
She will only get clean when she is ready to want it and to work
at it. Work damn hard. When she can't stand the life a minute
longer and is ready to trade it in for something better.'

She glared at him.

'You find it impossible to say no to her because you're afraid
she will disapprove of you. More particularly, that she'll die. Oh
yes, you think I don't know about that, don't you? Well, maybe
she wants you to say no. Did that ever occur to you?'

It never had.

Jerry took a deep breath to calm himself.

'Rachel, Rachel, your life is out of control. If you can't cope with your own pain, how can you expect to manage hers?'

'What are you talking about?'

'I think you know', he said. 'You think you're a failure. When you realised that Ruby was using you slid . . . no, not slid, that would be too quick. What happened to you has been slow and protracted.'

He stopped pacing and drew a chair up close to her.

'If Ruby is using and unhappy, so goes Rachel. If Ruby has a job, if she is glowing in love this week, if she's been working on her art, if she's clean and of good cheer, so goes Rachel. Ruby has become all you seem to care about.'

'That's not true!' she protested.

'If it's not true, then what else *do* you care about, Rachel? Tell me.'

'The garden. The nursery. Eli.'

The absence of his name from her list passed unremarked.

'Eli!' he scoffed. 'When was the last time you heard from him? He got so fed up with listening to you rant about Ruby, fret about Ruby, wonder what Ruby might be up to, that he stuck you at the end of a forty foot pole and only reels you in when he feels strong enough to withstand the onslaught of another of your outpourings.'

'He does not! How do you know that?'

'Some members of this family talk to each other, Rachel.'

She was furious.

'The nursery? The nursery is your chore, another of your obsessive burdens. It's rote for you now. Rote and isolation. A bit of small talk with the customers to keep you from becoming a complete isolate, but not enough to intrude on your most pressing thoughts. Your Ruby thoughts. The garden? It is a beautiful garden, a work of art, but you don't do anything else. When was the last time we went to the pictures? I'll bet you can't even remember. I certainly can't. What about the last time we had a leisurely meal out? Months. We either don't go or we bolt down our food and race home in case the phone rings. Do you think I'm blind?

'Your life exists between the garden and the nursery, with a phone close at hand. That's it. Can you remember the last gallery you spent an afternoon in? How many years since you did a painting or sat down to draw?'

'The garden is my painting.'

'You have been working on that one painting for years and years and years, Rachel. Perfecting and perfecting. You can't let that go either. There has been little done in that garden but maintenance for longer than I care to remember. You once told me you would be finished when it was perfect. Remember? Well, it's perfect. Your perfect, finished painting has become your unfinished obsession. It is your cloister, the place where you hide from life.'

No argument with that. Didn't I say the same to Esther oh so long ago? 'This is where I hide, Essie.'

'It gave me such pleasure to watch you create it. I was envious of your talent. The way you chose colour and form and texture. It was a delight to watch it take shape. I used to love how it fed us. Now . . .' He shrugged.

This has never been part of the discourse.

'Have you thought,' he said carefully, 'about getting help? Professional help? Counselling of some sort?' He cleared his throat. 'A therapist. Someone like that.'

Caught her by surprise, that one.

This was uncharacteristic advice; Jerry was mistrustful of therapies. He must be worried. Still, she shook her head slowly.

'I don't need that. I'll be all right.'

'You won't be all right, you know. You can't go on like this. I can't go on like this, Rachel. You must do something, if not for us, then for yourself.'

'Are you threatening to leave me?'

'Not this week.' Jerry managed a feeble smile. 'Don't think it hasn't crossed my mind. You have to work out a way to get your life back. But first,' he sighed, 'you have to want to get it back. Do you want to, Rachel? Do you want your life back?'

Then this.

Rachel did not reply. Leaning forward, her chin cupped in the unwounded hand, she stared through the window into the garden, fixing her eyes on the pendulous clusters of mauve wisteria draped across the pergola.

Will she desist?

If this conversation were to follow the pattern of the many that preceded it, soon she would be off and running with her fantasies for Ruby's life—'If only . . .', 'What if . . .'—lamenting it as a life wasted, expressing her fears for her daughter's safety. She would say nothing further about herself. Or their marriage.

Soon after commencing her monologue, she would lose him: his eyes would become lifeless, he would settle them on a spot in the space over her shoulder into which he would stare until he could stand the sound of her voice no longer. Then he would leave the room.

Can she refrain?

That's how it was with them. That's what it had become. It was a sickness with her, like kleptomania, like compulsive gambling. Like heroin addiction.

In the early days, Jerry used to hold her in his arms, comfort her, ask if he could help with what was troubling her, or if she wanted to talk about it. These days he comforted infrequently, enquired rarely. He had become withdrawn, frustrated with her misery, irritated by the main topic of her conversation.

And why would he not be? Wasn't she tired of it herself?

'Do you?' he asked again, more insistent.

'I don't know,' Rachel shrugged, indifferent.

'That is pathetic. Truly pathetic, Rachel. Is that your answer?'

'I don't know how to want to', she whispered.

'Does that mean you want to?'

'Yes,' she shouted, 'it means I want to,' and whispered again, 'but I'm afraid.'

At last. The nub. The truth.

This next.

Jerry sat beside her on the couch.

'Rachel, Rachel', he murmured.

Gently, oh so gently, he lifted her swaddled hand and held it. Bending over the dazzling white gauze, he placed there the softest kiss, so soft that his lips barely touched the dressing. Then, to her astonishment, he pulled her to him and kissed her passionately on the mouth. He held her face in both his hands, nibbled her lips, kissed her again and put his tongue in her mouth; he sucked her tongue.

As light as butterflies, his hands fluttered over her breasts. Nuzzling into her, he sucked her nipples, then kissed her chin and her throat and the space between her breasts. He kissed her cheeks and the expanse of her forehead. He ran the tip of his tongue over her closed eyelids then kissed her on the mouth again, softly.

Heat—unexpected, immensely pleasurable—of a kind not recently experienced, infused her. Rachel allowed herself to succumb, she allowed herself his touch. Her eyelids became heavy, her breasts swelled with desire, her face flushed; fiery heat kindled between her thighs.

Almost as suddenly as he had begun, he ceased, resting his forehead against her own. It was then she realised he was crying. His tears fell between their faces, dropped from their chins and splashed through the cotton fabric of her dress.

He sat back and said, his voice grown cold, 'Do something about it. Find someone who can help you. Whatever it takes. I cannot go on like this any longer.'

Rachel closed her eyes and sighed as she drew him to her, stroked his head. She jiggled a handkerchief from his trouser pocket.

And, finally, this.

I wonder, she thought as she dabbed at his cheeks and stroked his head, if the burns will leave any scars? I wonder where Ruby is right now?

That's what did it. That last thought. Yes, that. Seven words. Nothing special about them at all. 'I wonder where Ruby is right now?' That was the moment she had had enough of hearing them, of saying them, thinking them. She had had enough of wondering.

She was sick of asking the question.

She was sick of what her life had become.

The trigger. The last round. End of the line.

Iz genug.
Rock bottom.

Change was coming. Rachel was trepidatious about change. Fear, sorrow, martyrdom, these feelings were an integral part of her life, as lovingly worn as a favourite scarf, a beloved T-shirt, old and faded, soft and loose.

Comfortable.

Familiar.

How difficult it would be to discard them. And in exchange for what?

Terra incognita.

She shivered.

Could the changes be worse than what she knew? Before too long she would be fifty. Rachel knew she did not want to live the remainder of her life a woman weeping, waiting. Waiting for—what? For her life to happen? For something, someone, to fill her up?

She was so tired. So tired of being tired.

Voices whispered, not the squealing voices, the demonic fast-backwards, demonic voices. Not them. These were new voices: they were gentle, encouraging, kindly, though not without urgency.

Rachel paid attention to their urgency; she followed these urgent voices to their source.

They came from within her.

Rachel is ready. She hadn't realised quite how ready she was.

KINDRED SPIRIT

How many sorrows do you try to hide
In a world of illusion that's covering your mind
I'll show you something . . .

Annie Lennox/David A. Stewart,
'The Miracle of Love'

Kath Deutscher, a Saturday-morning regular at Coffee Lounge, was sitting alone at a table for four.

'Good morning, Kath.'

Kath looked up from her newspaper.

'Hello, Rachel. Come and join me.'

'Thanks.'

The Deutschers were neighbourhood people. Their children and the Brigg children had attended the same primary school, then the Deutchers kids were sent to private schools. Acquaintances rather than friends, Rachel and Kath liked each other well enough to have an occasional coffee together on the weekends they happened to be in Coffee Lounge at the same time.

'How are you?'

'So-so. How about you?' Rachel removed her coat and gloves, then set her bundle of newspapers on a vacant chair. She noticed Kath Deutscher's face was pale, her lips pinched. In the fingers of her right hand she twirled a match, a miniature cheerleader's baton, around and around and around.

'I'm okay.' Kath hesitated. 'How's Jerry?'

Rachel shrugged. 'He's gone to the football. You look a bit down in the mouth, Kath.'

'I am. There's been a bit of drama at our place.' Again she hesitated. 'We kicked Liz out yesterday.'

'Liz? What on earth for?'

I know! I know what she's going to say.

Kath composed herself.

'Liz is a drug addict, Rachel.'

Twirl. Twirl. Twirl.

'No! Not Liz!' Rachel cried out in disbelief. Two or three patrons looked in their direction. Rachel lowered her voice. 'Not Liz.'

Liz Deutscher. Oldest of the three Deutscher kids. University student—medicine. Or was it dentistry? Bright, from all reports. Won a prize in a debating competition when she was seventeen. A bit sporty, too.

'Yes, Liz. Frankly, Rachel, I find it hard to believe you didn't know. Everyone else does', Kath replied bitterly.

'I didn't know. What happened?'

Twirl. Twirl.

'We tried everything: understanding, patience, sympathy. It was hopeless. If we expressed disapproval or became angry, she burst into tears and said we didn't love her.' Kath shook her head. 'We thought if we withheld her weekly allowance she wouldn't have enough money to buy it. Jesus,' she laughed, 'how naive can you get? She just kept using that damned stuff. Kept on.' Kath sighed.

Twirl. Twirl. Twirl.

Rachel listened to Kath's well-modulated voice, her rounded vowels, took in her expensive clothes and tried to make sense of what she heard. How could this be?

Kath and Karl Deutscher were, as far as Rachel knew, a happily married couple. Kath had a well-paid job in academe, Karl was a senior partner in a stockbroking firm. Their children, like their parents, were high achievers. A charming home, a comfortable, ramshackle holiday house (west coast, nothing too ostentatious), two pets (a pedigree dog of unusual breed, a Persian cat), two cars (solid, European models, updated every two years) parked in their double garage: the Deutschers were the sort of family that was . . . well, they were a picturebook, fairy tale family. A perfect television family. How could one of their children possibly be an addict? It didn't make sense. Heroin addiction didn't happen in families like this one.

If Kath's revelation was puzzling, her forthrightness was shocking. Rachel was stunned by the frankness of Kath's disclosure and, more particularly, her apparent lack of shame. 'Liz is a junkie.' *Punkt.* Straight up, just like that.

'The arguments were exhausting. Karl and I were so sick of being yelled at, or being ignored. What's more . . .' Kath paused to pluck an imaginary piece of lint from her skirt, '. . . she became so damned slovenly.'

Kath Deutscher rolled her eyes, pulled her mouth into a rueful grimace. Clearly, it was beyond the pale for a Deutscher daughter to deport herself in whatever manner was considered shabby in *that* household. Words tumbled from Kath's mouth; she was unstoppable. The twirling gathered momentum.

Would I be like this were I to let go? Would I babble like a brook, my words the water flowing over the pebbles and rocks of my sorrow?

'. . . Helen's brooch,' Kath was saying, ' . . . last straw.'

Twirl. Twirl. Twirl.

'Brooch?'

'Yes. A beautiful piece, marcasite, with garnets in the centre. Karl's mother left it to her.'

'Garnets.'

Objects disappearing. Less money in your purse than you thought you had. I know about that.

Coffee Lounge was cosy, warmed by the newly installed combustion stove, yet Rachel shivered.

'What did you do when things were . . . went missing?'

'Karl suggested that Liz might be using drugs. I didn't want to believe it. Not one of my children.'

Twirl. Twirl. Twirl. Twirl.

'We had a family meeting to talk about what had been going on. Nigel and Helen confirmed it. It seems they'd known for some time. Everything suddenly became clear. Talk about denial!'

'Did you ask her to leave straight away?'

'No, not immediately. We had a talk with her first. We told her we knew she was using drugs and that she was stealing from us.'

'What did she say?'

'She was livid. "How can you say that?", "I told you I was sick", "You don't trust me", that sort of thing. Denied everything. It was pathetic, Rachel. A trapped rat scuttling for cover with no cover to be had.

'After a lot of shouting and weeping, accusation and counter-accusation, she finally admitted she'd been using heroin for almost a year. A year! We were devastated.'

Twirl. Twirl. Twirl. Twirl.

'We insisted she seek treatment. We offered to help her find an appropriate place. Karl said we would pay for it.'

'Did she agree to go?'

Can you see me changing before your eyes, Kath, transmogrifying into an enormous sea sponge, all the better to soak up the spillage of your story?

'She did at first, then she became reticent. "If you are not prepared to enter a rehabilitation program," Karl said, "we cannot permit you to stay here. Not until you stop using drugs completely." Karl sounded firm when he said it, but I know it distressed him terribly. I don't know if he would have been able to stick to his resolve. I would have found it very difficult. Fortunately, she agreed to go. We made arrangements with a centre . . .'

Which one? Where is it? Is there a waiting list? How much does it cost? Can anyone go? How long does it take before they get well?

'. . . there a few weeks before she came home. "Everything's okay now. I'm clean. I haven't used for five weeks", was what she said. We thought five weeks was marvellous at the time.' She shook her head. 'God, how little we knew.

'Life did seem settled for a while. Liz went for a run each morning, she caught up with her university work and re-enrolled, helped around the house, got on well with Helen and Nigel. All that sort of thing. We assumed she was better, that life had returned to normal.

'Before long—two, three weeks—she was up to her old tricks.'

Twirl, twirl, twirl. Faster. Faster. Around and around went the little baton. Around. Rachel was mesmerised.

'One night I heard Helen crying in her room. "What's the matter?" I asked her. It took some doing, but eventually I dragged it out of her. Liz had misplaced the brooch.' Kath stilled the match long enough to curl her index fingers into inverted commas around the word 'misplaced'. Then she began the twirling again.

'That was the last straw.'

Snap! The match splintered in two.

'Helen and Nigel brought the whole thing to a head. "Either Liz goes, or we're going", they said. To tell you the truth, Rachel,' Kath shook her head, 'Karl and I were pretty sick of it by then. Nothing we did seemed to be of any use, so we agreed to ask her to leave.'

Rachel sipped her coffee, which had gone cold. She didn't dare look directly at Kath, who was dabbing the corners of her eyes with a paper serviette. 'Anyway, that's enough of my miseries. How are things with you?'

Rachel heard the background murmur of voices. The slap of a winning hand of cards onto a Laminex table made her jump.

'Me? I'm fine, thanks Kath.'

'How about your kids? Are they okay?'

'Yes. They're in good form.'

'Ruby?'

Why did she ask that?

'Oh yes, Ruby's fine.'

Rachel ventured a question.

'Do you feel guilty?'

'Guilty?'

'Yes. Do you blame yourself for her using? Aren't you scared?'

Two questions. Watch it, Rachel, you'll give yourself away.

Rachel struggled—successfully—not to lower her eyes from Kath's quizzical stare.

'No, I do not feel guilty,' Kath replied in a calm, slow voice. 'I feel responsible on occasion. How could I not? I feel sad and, yes, I do feel frightened. Yet, you know, Rachel, I thought I was a good parent. Karl, too. We are good parents. We gave our children everything. Did we do enough? Was what we did for the best? How can we know?'

Does she mean 'we' her family, 'we' mothers? Perhaps she means the 'we' of our generation of parents, our only instruction the teachings of our own fallible mothers and the now discredited child-rearing theories of our day.

'I don't know either, Kath.'

'We have two other children. Karl and I have lives of our own. We couldn't sacrifice everyone.' Kath peered at Rachel. 'Are you all right, Rachel?'

'Yes, thanks.' She forced her lips to smile. 'It's sad to hear about Liz.'

Kath didn't take her eyes from Rachel's face.

Does she know? She probably knows. Tell her. Talk to her. She would not judge you.

Rachel was confused. She wanted time to think about Kath's outpouring.

'I must get going. Nice to see you again, Kath. Give my regards to Karl and the kids.'

'Thank you, Rachel. It was nice to see you, too.'

'I hope things work out with Liz.'

Kath shrugged: there's nothing more I can do.

— o —

Grace came to visit.

'I saw Kath Deutscher on Saturday,' Rachel said.

'Yes. Liz is an addict, too.'

Grace is not mincing her words tonight!

'Who told you about Liz?'

'Rachel, everybody's known about Liz for ages. People notice things and wonder. They talk, ask questions; they tell one another. You may well be the only person around here who didn't know.'

'Do they talk about me, Grace? About Ruby?'

'Yes.'

'Oh, no', Rachel moaned. 'Oh, this is awful.'

Grace embraced her friend, bringing Rachel's head to rest on her shoulder.

'Dear Rachel, why is it awful? Everyone has problems, you

know. If you weren't so busy condemning yourself, so engrossed with Ruby, you might be able to see a bit more of what's going on around you. You'd be appalled by how many kids are messing around with hard drugs.'

'Who, for example? No kids I know.'

'Yes, kids you know.'

Grace told her their names, and mentioned the names of two adults. Rachel was appalled.

'No one said anything to me.'

Grace arched an eyebrow.

'Who do you talk to?'

Rachel looked sheepish.

'You and Esther, sometimes Annalise. But . . .'

'But what? We're sworn to secrecy. You take a risk when you reveal a secret. You make yourself vulnerable, but if you're not prepared to be vulnerable, what are your friends to think? That you're coping? We know you're not.'

Rachel felt uncomfortable.

'You know how it goes. Someone, bursting with desperation, no longer able to keep her misery dammed up, divulges her secret. The secret is passed on in strictest confidence. The teller insists that it not be repeated. "Promise not to tell." Too late. The dam has been breached. It is no longer a secret. Is that so awful? With this first breaching comes a measure of relief, so she tells someone else, also in the strictest confidence.

'This seepage of telling, this dribble of pain and need, soon becomes a flood. The sympathetic recipient of the secret remains true—for a time. She is reluctant, at first, to convey her knowledge to the next person who asks what's the matter with so-and-so, who has been looking so unhappy, so tense, lately. But in the end, few are able to refrain. This is not idle gossip—'

'How can you say that, Grace?'

'All right, it is for some.'

'It's nobody's business!'

'Maybe so, maybe not. Your friends intend you no harm.'

'Are you saying that nothing's private?'

'No! Of course there must be privacy. And discretion. What I'm saying is that we give our own secrets away, sometimes more willingly than we'd care to admit. People observe, they listen. They wonder. They talk.'

'Do you leak my secrets, Grace?'

'Do you leak mine?'

The air between them snapped and crackled for a brief moment. In unison they said, 'Esther', then laughed.

'But not the special ones.' Grace shrugged. 'Ruby's condition was hardly a secret. Don't you remember when Shimon and Esther saw her at the pictures?'

'God. Eight years ago.'

They were quiet for a while. Rachel rocked slowly back and forth on the couch. Grace interrupted her thoughts.

'Esther phoned me that time. She needed to talk about what she'd seen and how to approach you. Nowadays we're as concerned about you as we are Ruby. The most troubling thing is how isolated you've become. You never leave the garden. Esther thinks you resent having to go inside to sleep.'

'Pair of bloody gossips.' Rachel smiled a half-smile, unsure whether she was annoyed with them or not. 'What do you say?'

'That you think Jerry is an encumbrance. He diverts you from your task of rescuing Ruby, which in turn diverts you from the task of living your own life.'

'Grace!'

'Is it true or not?'

Rachel did not respond to Grace's question, but said instead: 'The ever-so-respectable Deutschers! Crud doesn't happen in families like theirs.' She shook her head. 'What floored me was how frank she was. Kath Deutscher and I hardly know each other, yet she talked about it as if it were just another fact of life.'

'Drugs *are* a fact of life, Rachel.'

Rachel looked away from her.

Grace, at home in Rachel's kitchen, put on the kettle and prepared the cups for tea. Rachel remained on the couch, her chin resting in her palms.

'Addicts were other people's children, Grace, not mine, not the children of people I knew. My idea of addicts was down-and-outers, people from the wrong side of the tracks, artists and musicians whose lives had run out of control, prostitutes, people with scungy lives. Nothing like that could happen to my family. You know, nice middle-class Jewish girl, good job, nice home. A pair of respectable husbands.'

'Rachel,' Grace returned to the couch with their tea, 'you read newspapers, you know what goes on. It makes no difference where you come from or what you do to earn a living.'

'That's what Ruby said.'

'Claudine came from the same background as you. Jacob Rothberg's family is rich and powerful. Gully was once a sweet boy from the country. Try remembering that from time to time. As for the Deutschers . . . well, you couldn't get more respectable or more middle class than them!'

They sat quietly, sipping their tea.

Why this daughter and not another? Why those two sons and not their sister? Why in this family and not the one next door? Why did some get clean, others not? Some die, others not? It seemed so random. Was it simply the luck of the draw?

Rachel's thoughts kept returning to Kath. It puzzled her that Kath didn't seem to feel responsible for her daughter's addiction, though Kath and Karl could well be more upset than Kath had let on. Even so, the Deutschers had made a decision to let Liz go on with her drugging so the other members of their family could get on with their lives. Rachel admired that.

'I wish I had the courage to take the stand the Deutschers did.'

'When you want it badly enough, you will do it', Grace assured her. 'Soon, I hope. Well, Rachel dear, I have to go. Work tomorrow.'

'Me too. Thanks for coming over, Grace. It was good to see you.'

They walked up the hall to the front door. Jerry was turning his key in the lock.

'Hello, Grace. Leaving already?'

'It's after ten, Jerry. I've been here for two hours. How are you?'

'I'm well, thanks. Good evening, Rachel.' His greeting was restrained. 'I'll leave you two to it', he said and went inside. Rachel heard the football crowd's roar coming from the television.

The night air was clear and crisp. In the morning car

windscreens would be covered with frost, puddles turned to ice; frozen grass would crunch underfoot.

'Think about having a talk to Kath, Rachel. Ease up on yourself.' Grace smiled. 'Coffee on Saturday?'

'Yes. I'd like that.'

'I'll let Esther know.'

Rachel warmed herself by the fire, glancing every few minutes at her watch. During a commercial break, she began to tell Jerry about her conversations with Kath Deutscher and Grace. He sat quietly, his eyes fixed on the television as she spoke. After five minutes he said, in a flat, uninterested voice, 'That's interesting', and went to bed.

Rachel remained by the fire. She smoked a cigarette and thought more about her conversation with Grace. Fifteen minutes elapsed. She drank the last of her now cold tea and set the cup on the table. Then she opened the Teledex at the Ds and dialled.

'Hello, Karl. It's Rachel Grinblatt. Fine, thanks. You? That's good. I hope this isn't too late to call. Is Kath still up?'

PROGRESS

The clouds pass and the rain does its work,
and all individual beings flow into their forms.

I Ching

Part 1

Grace puts Rachel in touch with her friend Felicity, a counsellor at a drug and alcohol rehabilitation centre. Rachel has a session where she yanks at the lever and opens the floodgate, a voluntary act.

This session, Felicity tells her, is the commencement of facing her guilt. She has begun the process—'It *is* a process, Rachel'—of coming to terms with her sorrow.

Rachel is inconsolable.

'I'm always angry, always afraid. I feel as though I am bound in plastic wrap', she sobs. 'It is all that's holding me together. If I peel it away I'll disintegrate. I shall never stop weeping.'

'What are you afraid of?'

'I'm afraid she will die.'

'It is unlikely she will die. Possible, but not too likely.'

Rachel hopes it is very unlikely. Entirely improbable.

Felicity cites figures. Few die, she explains. Most, tired of the life by the time they're thirty, seek help.

'If she were to die, it will not be your fault. She is old enough to choose to give up drugs or continue using and face the risk of dying. You are not responsible for her using, nor for the consequences of it in her life.'

Will I wake up one morning and believe that?

Rachel describes the hope she invests in Ruby's attempts to get clean, her disappointment when she busts.

'Getting clean and staying clean is difficult, Rachel', Felicity explains, reminding Rachel of the telephone conversation with Annie. 'Recovery is uneven. Many try often before they succeed. However, that's Ruby's life. You need to make some choices about your life, Rachel.'

The rehab has a self-help group for parents of addicts. Why not attend?

Self-conscious, uncomfortable, determined, Rachel attends.

The group facilitator supplies the three attendees with sheets of paper containing empirical data about drug addiction and alcoholism. The information is illuminating; it calms her.

'In the drama of addiction, life becomes a series of manipulations. How much more difficult it would be for them to continue drugging and drinking if you were to withdraw your support. Hmm? Each party in this relationship is needy; each blames the other for their miserable lives, each seeks absolution from their guilt. Yet disentanglement seems impossible. This,' the facilitator is pleased to pronounce, 'is what we call codependence.'

'But I love my daughter', Rachel protests. The others nod: they love their children, too.

'This has nothing to do with love. Nothing. Your relationships have become a game of dependency. No one says what's really on their minds. None of you are able to behave like adults.'

Some tools are provided to assist Rachel and the others to grow up.

— o —

Ruby asks to borrow money for rent.

Rachel's heart is pumping so hard she thinks it's going to burst from her chest and fly across the room when she hears herself reply, 'I'm sorry, Ruby, I am not prepared to give you any more money.'

So astonished is Rachel with her own daring that she looks over her shoulder to see where the voice has come from that spoke these words. She is surprised further when Ruby grins and says, 'Fair enough.'

Rachel grins too.

When Ruby asks again the following week, they fight. Acrimonious, spiteful, loud. Ruby leaves the house, slamming doors as she goes. Rachel is terrified; she regrets not giving Ruby the money and lacerates herself fiercely. Later that night, Ruby phones. Her tone is accusing, her words slurred.

'I've had a hit', she says.

Rachel's heart has slowed. She speaks with a new firmness.

'That was your choice, Ruby.'

There is silence, until Ruby says, 'I suppose it was.'

It is a victory—for both of them.

— o —

The other two parents leave. The group founders. Two new women join. The facilitator starts the process from the beginning.

The restlessness of dissatisfaction propels Rachel in search of something more substantial.

Part 2

Esther prescribes the walking cure. She is enthusiastic in her praise of it.

'Walking is the best antidote for anxiety.'

'Walking?' Rachel is sceptical.

'If something's bothering me, I walk. It never fails. We'll go together after dinner tonight.'

Esther suggests a route along Park Street following the disused railway line west to Princes Park where, she proposes, they shall take a brisk turn around the perimeter of the Carlton football oval.

Rachel's sigh is heavy with resignation.

— o —

The night is quiet and foggy; they speak little as they go. Though she is hot and damp with sweat, and a blister bulges on the pad of her right foot by the time they return to her street, Rachel is glad she did it.

'Nu?'

'I enjoyed the sense of moving across the landscape. I don't feel so anxious.'

Esther is triumphant.

'What did I tell you? Walking cures everything.'

Rachel sleeps soundly. When she awakes in the morning she is smiling, though she remembers not one detail of the dream she knows has filled her night.

Before long, walking becomes part of the rhythm of her day, a need. When she doesn't walk her sleep is restless and peppered with bad dreams. Sluggish days ensue; her anxiety returns.

An idea.

She phones Mickey to ask if he would like a regular day's work. A frisson of pleasure ripples through her body at the sound of his voice. Sadly Mickey is unavailable. He recommends a competent woman in her neighbourhood who he knows is looking for part-time gardening work. The woman relieves Rachel of the nursery on Tuesdays, enabling her to walk further afield and in the daytime.

Fitzroy, Carlton, through the Exhibition Gardens to the city, to Chinatown, along St Kilda Road, south along the banks of the Yarra to the Botanic Gardens, further south to Fawkner Park. She takes trams to St Kilda, to South or Port. From Port she cuts a clip along the promenade that follows the curve of Port Phillip Bay from Port Melbourne to Brighton. No matter what the weather. The wild, windy days of September and October are particularly appealing, as are the sunsets of autumn.

There are times when the punishing thoughts join her. Uninvited and unwelcome, they intrude at their leisure and refuse to leave.

Part 3

Rachel opens the door to the church hall. An Al-Anon meeting. There follows a rush of panic, the instinct to flee, a tidal wave of self-consciousness. Seated in a semicircle, facing the front of the hall, are sixteen people, most of them women, all but two strangers. The two who are not—Kath Deutscher and her daughter, Helen.

Those nearest the door turn towards her as she enters the cosy room.

'Welcome', they mouth, not wishing to disturb the speaker. Rachel is puzzled. Who are these women? They seem to recognise her.

Of course they recognise her. She is one of them.

Helen's shy smile is a greeting. Kath smiles too, a wry half-smile, as she pats the chair next to her.

At the front of the gathering, a smartly dressed woman of cheerful countenance describes her isolation and frustration during the long years she attempted to control her husband's drinking, and to control him. She describes the despair of those years, the futility of her endeavours. Attendance at these meetings changed her life. Rachel folds herself inside her overcoat and hopes she will not be called upon to speak

For the next hour Rachel listens while people share their stories. They are Rachel's stories.

There are tales of madness brought on by feelings of ineptitude and the inability to rescue.

This one bought trolley loads of goods from convenience stores that she neither enjoyed nor needed. That one filled her house—filled it—with miniature china ornaments, animals and cupid-like children, endlessly dusting, washing and rearranging them. So depressed was another, she did not leave her house for weeks at a time, while yet another deliberately burnt herself with the iron.

There was deception and the assumption of responsibility that was rightfully another's.

From wherever they could raise the money, they paid their husbands' tabs at the pub and went hungry for their efforts. They phoned in excuses to the boss in the hope their bingeing spouses, wouldn't lose their jobs.

There was terror and loss.

They watched the family home disappear through the bottom of whisky bottles and lines of coke, fled with their children to shelters to avoid their husbands' drunken beatings.

Mention of children brings a sombre mood to the meeting. A film of sadness descends.

There is pain, excruciating pain.

A woman weeps for the daughter who died in her arms, drunk, pilled. One describes the grief of finally having to ask her son to leave home and her fear of not knowing what would become of him, a violent alcoholic and speed addict. A woman younger than many others tells of a brother who works the streets to support his heroin habit; when he doesn't have enough money for drugs, he drinks himself into oblivion. When he drinks, he phones her from Broome, Caloundra, Port Pirie, Darwin, asking for the bus fare to get home. He has no idea how he reached these towns, or when he arrived. Among those gathered, there is more than one who has lived through the slow demise or the suicide of a child, a sibling, a lover or a spouse.

Of modest means and well-to-do, all have been martyred to the cause of rescuing. Their efforts were fruitless. When they could no longer tolerate what their lives had become, when they realised their devotion to their beloved alcoholic or addict could never fill the empty spaces in their own lives, they walked through these doors.

Hearing their stories—of lives benighted by death, mental illness, and terminally estranged relationships—Rachel is aghast. For the first time in many years, she weeps for someone other than herself or Ruby.

The formal meeting ends. They stand in a circle and join hands.

God, grant me the serenity
To accept the things I cannot change
Courage to change the things I can
And the wisdom to know the difference.

Rachel chokes on the word 'God'. For the rest, she reads from a card standing on the table and appreciates the commonsense of the words.

— o —

Tea and teddy bear biscuits follow. Women gather around her, the new girl. They listen quietly as she reveals snippets of her story, comfort her when she cries. Words of encouragement fall about her like fairy dust.

Of all the homilies they offer—there are many—Rachel thinks her biggest test will be to 'Keep it simple'.

Oh, to slow the racing of her mind.

Little by little, the plastic wrap begins to fall away. Instead of oozing all over the floor as she anticipated, Rachel journeys towards peace.

'Keep coming back; it works.'

It does.

Part 4

Jerry accepts the offer of a six-month transfer to the London office of his firm. A good career move, he tells her.

'It will do us good to spend some time apart', he says.

Rachel recognises a soft option when she hears one. She does not protest.

'Perhaps when I'm settled you could come over for a while.'

His invitation is offered with little enthusiasm.

Rachel replies, 'We'll see.'

They go out to dinner.

She says: 'I thought things were improving between us.'

He says: 'We have become civil, Rachel. You don't talk about Ruby as much as you used to. But . . .' He shrugs but does not finish the sentence.

She says: 'I thought with the meetings . . .'

He says: 'Ah, yes, the meetings. Your new life.' He stares into a space over her shoulder, silent for a moment. 'I'm sorry, Rachel.'

She says: 'I'm sorry too, Jerry.' She doesn't know if she is or not, or exactly what for. Her madness? That she pushed him out of her life? His leave-taking? Perhaps all of it. Possibly none.

She is still unravelling answers. Still working out the questions.

She says: 'I have thought for some time that you would leave me.'

He says: 'Why didn't you do something about it?'

She says: 'I was unable then. Now I can.'

He says: 'It's too late. It has been too late for a long time.'

They have nothing further to say.

Two weeks later he has gone. He leaves behind two items: his once loved hippie vest—multicoloured and gold threaded—which hangs for many months in the wardrobe in the front room, and a recently dated letter, fussy handwriting on pink paper, neatly folded into a scented envelope, which is postmarked 'London'.

Following his departure, Jerry and Rachel communicate but twice: Four months after arriving in London Jerry sends a fax to say he would appreciate it if she would file for divorce; Rachel writes to ask him to sell her his share of the house.

Each accommodates the other's request without rancour; it is too late for that, too.

Soon after the divorce, Jerry remarries. Rachel hears on the grapevine that his wife—Maureen—is expecting a child. It will be the first of two: bright, fresh children. Clean-slate children.

Rachel considers what she might do with the rest of her life.

Part 5
Eli phones.

'I am going overseas', he tells her. 'I'm going to buy a 1960s convertible and travel around America. Would you like some company for a while before I leave?'

'You want to come and live with me?'

'Sure. Why not?'

'Because we've hardly seen each other. We haven't spoken in weeks.' A momentary pause. 'I thought you'd never want to live with me again after . . .' The sentence is left dangling.

'Just because I don't speak to you every day or see you every week doesn't mean I don't think about you or care about you. I've got a life, Rachel. You know I get around there when I can.'

It is never as often as she would like. How could it be?

He is twenty-five. Does she want his company? Since Jerry's departure, she has discovered that she enjoys living alone. Will they argue? Will he impinge on her space? She on his? Will she be able to refrain from treating him like a child?

What am I thinking? Of course I want him to stay.

Eli guesses her thoughts.

'I'm at work all day. I won't get in your way. If you get in mine, I'll let you know. No mucking around. If you behave,' he teases, 'I'll bring you breakfast in bed.'

He moves in two days later.

That night, over dinner, she apologises.

'What for?'

'I don't think I made a very good job of being a mother.'

It is said without self-pity.

'You were okay. You were a good mother.'

'Aren't all your memories awful?'

'When are you going to give up that crap, Rachel? My memories are mixed. Bitter-sweet. Like most people's and much better than many others'. I always liked us.'

He watches to see if she remembers that conversation.

She is smiling; she remembers.

'What I hated was seeing you throw your life away when you became obsessed with Ruby. After that there wasn't room for anything or anyone else in your life.

'Ruby was the same, except she filled her life with dope. It wasn't that I didn't care about Ruby or what happened to her; I did. But we drifted apart.' He shrugged. 'Junk does that to people. Nothing I could do. She had to get well herself.'

'Jerry always said that. What makes you so wise?'

'We talked about it when the two of you were driving the two of us nuts. I knew from people my age, my own friends, too.' He nods. 'One of my girlfriends was a user. I didn't realise until one night she OD'd. She turned blue and I had to walk her so she wouldn't die. It was terrible.

'Do you remember when I was working at that dance club? How you never knew why I quit all of a sudden? It was because it became so tedious seeing idiots doped or pissed out of their brains and thinking they were genius kings and queens of the world every Friday and Saturday night when all they were was loud and stupid and rude. Drunks were the worst. Drunks and speedsters. They got pretty ugly sometimes.'

'You don't approve of people using drugs or drinking?'

'I'm not that prudish! Not everyone who drinks or uses drugs is an alcoholic or an addict, Rachel. Besides, if people want to do it, they're going to do it. I can only make decisions for myself and I've never been interested.'

'Never?'

'Never.'

'I always loved you, you know.'

He laughs.

'I knew that. It wasn't an issue.'

'That's hard to believe.'

'You never want to believe the good stuff, do you? It wasn't an issue. I knew you loved me. You were preoccupied, that's all.'

Ouch.

Rachel discerns no bitterness in his remark. She walks around the table to where he sits. Standing behind him, she hugs him, a great big bear hug.

'Welcome home, Eli.'

He raises his arms over his shoulders and places them, backwards, around her neck and returns her hug with matching ferocity.

Next day, before leaving for work, he brings her breakfast in bed: a perfectly poached egg (the albumen and half the yolk firm, the centre of the yolk runny), the toast on the side topped with a puddle of butter. Coffee. In the corner of the tray, the pepper grinder and, in a tall, slender vase, a single Appeldoorn tulip.

— o —

Eli declines her offer to drive him to the airport.

'Nah, I hate airport goodbyes. Too mushy', he says.

'Will you write?'

'Rachel,' he grins, 'you know better than that. Probably not. All right,' he relents, amused by the disappointment she fails to conceal, 'maybe a postcard from time to time. But that's it. If I have enough money I'll phone you.'

'You won't. You never have enough money.'

'No, I probably won't. But I'll be thinking about you.'

They laugh.

She stands on the footpath as he tosses his cases into the boot of the taxi. When his luggage is stowed and the boot lid closed, he returns to where she is standing and kisses her goodbye.

'I love you Eli. I enjoyed having you stay.'

'I love you, Rachel. Look after yourself.' He wags a finger at her. 'Get out a bit, have a good time. Get back into painting. Have some *fun!*'

As she watches the taxi's tail lights disappearing down the street, Rachel is reminded of other departures.

She does not cry.

Eli twists in his seat to blow her a kiss and wave her a last goodbye through the rear window.

Ah, Eli, I'll miss you.

She bends to pick a bunch of flowers. Clutching the posy to her breasts, she walks inside and quietly closes the door behind her.

— o —

Eli writes a brief letter from New York, a postcard from St Louis, Missouri, another from Mendecino. He phones from Seattle, where, he says, he could imagine himself living. He loves America. There is—already!—a girlfriend in Seattle and the offer of a job. He will try for an upgrade of his visa status. If his application is successful, he will stay.

'Oh no! Seattle?' Rachel groans to Esther. 'Why did it have to be Seattle? Couldn't he find a girlfriend or a job in New York?'

'New York. Seattle. What's the difference?'

'Seattle is so far away!'

Esther laughs so hard that she is barely able to speak.

'From what? New York isn't far away?' she gasps. 'New York is further away.'

'If he were in New York I could visit him. What's in Seattle that I would want to go there?'

Which remark brings on another round of laughter from Esther.

'Rachel, you old darling, you never get it, do you?'

Rachel gets it.

They laugh and laugh. They are unable to stop.

Part 6

Ruby phones.

'I've been accepted into a long-term rehab.' She names a country town in another state. 'The rules are tough. No contact for the first two months. Not even letters. I won't see you for a long time. I'm allowed to stay for up to a year. I'm going to give it a go.'

'I wish you all the best, Ruby. I hope it works for you.'

'Thank you Mama.' There is a pause. 'I'll miss you.'

'I will miss you too.' Now Rachel pauses. 'I'm so proud of you, Rube', she says.

'Proud?'

'Yes. I admire the fact that you keep trying. It must be very difficult.'

'Thank you. It is, for me.'

'I love you, Ruby.'

'I love you, Mama.'

Ruby stays five months in the long-term rehab. Not bad. Not bad at all. When she returns to Melbourne she does not ask if she can stay with Rachel. A household of friends—clean and sober—takes her in.

Ruby is almost twenty-seven years old.

Part 7
Rachel is forty-nine.

The meetings have become rote. From Annalise she obtains the name of a therapist.

The therapist sits at a respectful distance from her in a separate armchair. Rachel feels safe. She relaxes into her armchair.

This therapist is not an anonymous, silent ear; they converse. He neither admires her clothes nor comments on her hairstyle—or her weight. He is punctual. She thinks of him as a workmate. They are doing a job together. She has rarely felt so succoured.

She describes her fantasy family. To her astonishment—and delight—he remarks that television and Hollywood have a lot to answer for.

The interpretation of dreams excites her. Once again she feels she is moving across a landscape, the terrain on this occasion her inner life.

Is it appropriate to suggest that the interpretation of that which arises from the unconscious—from dreams—makes sense?

She brings the therapist a dream in which her serene self stands in a garden surrounded by an exquisite sunset.

'Why don't you paint it?' he suggests.

Subdued by his suggestion, she says, 'I haven't picked up a brush in years.'

To which he replies, 'Something to think about?'

And so she begins again.

She buys the requisite equipment and drives to Aireys Inlet where she spends a day sitting in the sand, painting her dream. The result pleases her.

— o —

Their time together draws to an end. He foreshadows their separation.

She panics but mildly.

A few weeks later he enquires if she has given their separation any thought.

She tells him she is no longer afraid of the prospect.

They set a date two months hence and talk, in the interim, about the difficulty of separation.

'No one finds it easy, Rachel', he says.

She stares out the window at the buttery yellow roses trailing along the cast-iron latticework affixed to his verandah.

— o —

The day of the last session arrives.

'You have done well', he says.

'I shall miss these sessions', she replies. She would like to say, 'I shall miss you', but she is too shy.

He smiles and shakes her hand, a firm, congratulatory handshake.

'All the best, Rachel.'

Rachel's only regret is in the rules of the game. She wishes they could be friends: the rules forbid it, and in truth, she senses that were they to meet in a social setting she would feel uncomfortable.

She turns and leaves his room for the last time.

He sometimes appears in her dreams.

Part 8

A Friday night. Rachel stands in the back row of a synagogue, singing a prayer, the melody and words of which she thought she had forgotten.

When the rabbi opens the ark to remove the Torah, tears of joy run down her cheeks: a homecoming.

Baruch ata, Adonai
Eloheinu, melech ha-olam
asher kideshanu bemitsvotav
vetsivanu lehadlik neir shel Shabbat.

People shake her hand and bid her '*Shabbat shalom*'—Sabbath peace.
Sabbath peace.
The service is followed by *Kiddush*. Congregants are served wine and grape juice in tiny glasses. They gather around a table laden with food where, led by the rabbi and the kantors, they sing blessings over the candles; they sing praises for the gift of the wine and the *challah*, sweet plaited bread of her childhood. When the blessings are completed, the rabbi breaks the warmed bread into small pieces. All partake.

The singing, the rich voices of the kantors, the sweet and aching melancholy of the music, touch her soul.
She is drawn by the ritual.
She is drawn by community.
She grieves for what she has lost in having abandoned them. Rachel does not become devout; belief remains ambivalent, yet in this place she senses a presence. She calls it life and accepts its mystery.

Part 9
The garden is as perfect as it is ever going to be. There is little left to do but maintenance. It is time to move on. Rachel puts the house and nursery on the market.

Part 10
Ruby?
Felicity's caution proves correct: the path is uneven. Ruby does her recovery hard.
There are weeks, months, when she is clean, others not. She visits Rachel only when she is clean, or not stoned. That's the rule. Ruby respects it.
They continue to meet in their favourite haunts for coffee or

lunch, they walk along the beach, in parks. Once a month they spend a day together going to galleries. When Ruby comes to the house she works with Rachel in the garden and the potting shed, helping her maintain the plants until the property changes hands. Together they go through cupboards and drawers in preparation for Rachel's departure from the house. Rachel is pleased to have her there to share the memories.

'This is a good thing, Mama, selling the house.'

'I thought you'd be more sentimental than that, Ruby.'

'Just because I think selling is a good idea doesn't mean I won't miss it. I'll miss this garden too.' She looks around the livingroom, through the window to the garden. 'We had some good times here, didn't we? What about you? Will you miss it?'

'I'll miss what it represents. Family life, whatever its short-comings.'

'That was yesterday. This part of your life is over. Now it's time for you to move on, see what the rest of your life has in store for you. It's time for Rachel's big adventure.'

My children continue to surprise me.

— o —

There is a memorable evening with lipstick.

Rachel visits Ruby at her share house. The walls of her room are decorated with her art, the piece Caroline gave her, and one piece of Rachel's. On her dresser, among the *tshatshkes*, is a collection of lipsticks, neatly arranged in columns.

Ruby notices Rachel looking.

'Mum, you old beatnik!' she exclaims, dragging a chair in front of the mirror. 'Why don't you try on some lipstick?'

She observes Rachel's hesitation.

'Come on, let's play.'

She opens one tube after another, holds each against Rachel's cheek.

'Too pink. Too purple. This one's good. Hmmm, bit dark. This one. Oooh, this would look gorgeous!'

And so on, until a selection of four is separated from the rest.

'Head up a bit. Stretch your lower lip. That's the way.'

Rachel is happy to succumb. Ruby steps aside to allow her to inspect herself in the mirror. Rachel is uncertain what she thinks of the unfamiliar image of her face with darkened lips. It has been a long time.

'It's too pink.'

Ruby hands Rachel a tissue.

'Get rid of it. We'll try this one.'

The texture is drier, the colour richer, more earthy.

'You look beautiful. Lipstick suits you.'

They pass an hour. One colour after another. Two colours together. Smeared on, wiped off. They joke and laugh. Ruby refuses to make coffee until the lipstick game is over.

'Now we do eyes', she announces.

'No, no, no! I'm happy with my eyes the way they are!'

'Yes, yes, yes! Just try. You'll love it.'

Ruby gathers in shadows, brushes and liners, mascara and kohl. When Rachel is permitted to look in the mirror, she sees a Kewpie doll.

'No, Ruby! It's lurid. Quick, quick,' she shrieks, 'another tissue!'

'It looks great.' Ruby steps back to admire her handiwork. 'Honest. You're just not used to it.'

She withholds the tissues from Rachel's reach. Rachel tries to be stern.

'Ruby, give them to me at once.'

Ruby dances away with them, laughing.

Rachel hides her eyes behind her hand.

'Didn't you learn about less is more at art school, Ruby? Pass me a tissue.'

Eventually, Ruby acquiesces. She puts a finishing gloss on Rachel's lipstick, touches up her own. Making pouty lips and laughing, they go to the kitchen where Ruby prepares coffee and supper. They settle in for a round or two of canasta, coffee and cake. And Bonnie. And Ry.

— o —

Ruby's life is not always the life Rachel would wish for her, but if Rachel has learnt anything it is this: Ruby's life is her own.

There are times when twenty questions come close to bursting from her mouth: What are you . . .?, Did you . . .?, Why don't you . . .?, How are you going to . . .?, Who . . .?

She desists.

Sometimes Ruby asks for the loan of money; sometimes Rachel lends it, but only in small amounts. Sometimes it is returned.

She wonders if Ruby continues to struggle against the seduction of heroin and wonders too if there are times when the desire for the drug overcomes her ability to resist.

She never asks. It is not her business. She does not want to know.

Ruby volunteers the information, weeping, fearful she will be drawn into the life again (a phrase, Rachel realises, which is unintentionally ironic, given that, by the time one is hooked, it seems to be not much of a life at all).

When Ruby is irritated by Rachel's suggestion of therapy or counselling—'This is not your business, Mama. It's something for me to decide'—Rachel remembers that her daughter comes from a tribe of stiff-necked people, and from a long line of women who wear a stripe of martyrdom as their badge.

'I don't need that', she says. 'I'll manage.'

And so, Ruby gets on with her life.

Rachel gets on with hers.

LITTLE RICHARD

Rachel is walking along the floor of a deep valley, so deep it is almost a ravine. The surrounds are lush—dense green forest, grasses of many hues and textures, few flowers. A humid mist surrounds her.

Faces peer through portholes set into the valley's left wall. Impassive, they watch Rachel as she walks through. When she begins to talk to one of them they seem unable to hear her.

A resonant voice (not from a porthole) fills the valley. She is on the wrong side, it tells her. If she wants to talk to the people behind the portholes, they must be on the other side of her.

Puzzled, Rachel stands still. At first she tries to work out how to get the people on the other side of her, then realises that all she has to do is turn herself around and her relationship to the others will be changed.

She turns around and begins walking the other way. The sun bursts through the mist and shines brightly.

— o —

A benign evening: clear sky, warm air, the faintest hint of chill. Dappled light filtered through the trees onto the street and the bonnets of parked cars; it fell on Rachel's face and shoulders in large golden freckles as she passed.

Perfect autumn.

As ever, Rachel was seduced by the colours of the season: reds and russets, golds and oranges, the caramel-browns that mingle with the evergreens and the blue-green of eucalypts. In one garden a prunus was growing alongside a scarlet Japanese maple.

Hanging across the fence from the garden next door, yellow leaves of a silver birch fluttered in the evening breeze. Another house, white, was adorned with an ornamental grape vine.

At the corner of Rae Street and Stewarts Lane, Rachel was startled to see legs, spread wide on the bluestone paving blocks. The clothes identified an approximate age of the person sprawled against the fence of the corner house: jeans, flannelette cowboy shirt, red and white sneakers. They gave no clue to gender.

Homeless? Drunk? Overdosed?

Rachel hurried past the lane, stopped, walked a few hesitant paces back, turned again and continued quickly on her way, north along Rae Street, past four houses, then stopped once more.

What if this were Ruby? What if people left her lying in the street, not knowing whether she was dead or alive? If she were treated like a pariah? What if this kid's sick, not stoned?

Rachel's fear evaporated. Pushing her shoulder bag behind her—just in case—she returned to Stewarts Lane and she squatted alongside the sprawled figure.

'Hello', she called. 'Can you hear me?'

'Mmmph.'

Alive!

'Do you need help?'

If someone overdoses, make them walk to get their circulation going. It could save them from dying. But how long after a hit is one in danger of dying? A minute? Two? Longer?

'Are you stoned?'

The mumble sounded like 'No'.

'Stand up. Let's walk for a while.'

Make them talk. Isn't that one of the things you do?

'Come on, talk to me. What's your name? Talk to me, sweetheart.' Her tone was firmer, her voice louder. 'What's your name?'

'Rishd.'

'Richard?'

He peeped at her with the eye that wasn't draped with hair.

'Rishud.' He gave a single emphatic nod and sat upright—after a fashion.

It's a boy! You could have fooled me.

Richard was as pretty as a girl: sensuous red lips and lobelia-blue eyes that were surrounded by enviable lashes, thick and long. He had the smoothest skin she'd ever seen. His lustrous brown hair, which grew beyond his shoulders, gave off a faint smell of patchouli oil.

'Hello Richard.'

'Woss your name?'

'Rachel.'

'Hiya Rayshell. Goddasigret?'

Rachel removed two from her packet, lit up and placed one between Richard's lips. Then she made herself comfortable, seating herself cross-legged beside him. The bluestone blocks, heated by the sun, warmed her buttocks.

'Good stuff', Richard said appreciatively, taking a long drag. He turned his face to the setting sun, chin high; his eyelids drooped over his beautiful eyes.

Settled now, and calm, Rachel turned to look at him. He had nodded off again. His jaw was slack; dribble ran from his drooping lower lip. The cigarette hung loosely in his fingers, about to drop onto his jeans.

'Richard. Wake up, Richard. Come on. Open your eyes, Richard.'

Maybe he's okay and I am spoiling his high. Perhaps he just wants to sleep.

Unsure, still afraid he might die, she persisted.

'Wake up, Richard.'

'I'm 'wake.' His head lolled; he lifted the cigarette with a heavy arm. 'Rayshell!' he beamed.

'How are you feeling?'

'Thirsty. Gotta drink?'

'No, but I have an orange. Would you like some?'

'Orange. Nah. Donwannanorange. Got any grog?'

Did Ruby ever sit in gutters like this? Did strangers—possibly people who knew her—walk past? Did they keep her alive, give her cigarettes, oranges, cups of tea?

Sitting in the lane with Richard, Rachel felt light-headed. She sensed herself to be on the brink of release from the remnants of an enormous burden.

Pay attention, Rachel.

People passing looked at them with distaste or contempt. They averted their eyes and hurried on. Not so long ago Rachel would have been one of them, hurrying past, her eyes filled with disgust. Filled with fear.

Juice spritzed into Richard's face when she split the orange in half.

'Fuckin' 'ell!' He dragged his shirtsleeve across his cheek.

Rachel laughed as she held a half out to him.

Richard licked his dry lips.

'Yeah. Maybe I will.' He sucked greedily. 'Got any more?'

'No. That's it.'

He closed his eyes.

'Why did you stop?' he asked suddenly.

Because I know you, Richard. I recognise you.

'You looked like you might need help.'

Richard didn't speak for a while. Then:

'Yeah? Why else?'

'My daughter's an addict. I'd hate to think she was left lying in a gutter, possibly dying, with people walking past, their eyes front and their noses in the air.'

'Yeah?' He was incredulous. 'Your daughter?'

'Yes. Her name is Ruby.'

'Ruby. Man, that's cool.' Richard grinned, then became serious. 'I'm not an addict', he insisted. 'No way. I can stop any time I want to.'

His wide-eyed innocence made Rachel laugh.

'People say that, then one day they wake up and discover it's too late.'

'No, really. I could stop if I wanted to. Any time.'

Does he believe his own earnest declaration?

'Why don't you?'

'Don't want to, that's why.'

'Why not?'

'It's great. It's fantastic. The best. I love it.' He squinted at her. 'You ever tried it?'

No point telling him about the opium, or that time with Spike.

'No, I haven't. I don't want the kind of life that goes with using it.'

Does anyone want that kind of life?

'You can stop any time you want to. Smack's grouse.'

'My daughter thought like you. She was hooked for years. Other people I knew. Some died.'

'How old is she?'

'Twenty-nine.'

'How long's she been using?'

'Eight or nine years. Possibly longer.'

'Didn't you ever try anything?'

'Grass. I used to smoke a lot of hash. I still have a joint from time to time. I like hash. I tried cocaine.'

Aha, here was something.

'See! You did! Did you like it?

'Yes, Richard,' she smiled, 'I did like it.'

'Do you still do it?'

'No.'

'Are you sad about your daughter?'

'Is that why you use, Richard? Because you're sad?'

This is an old Jewish trick, Richard: answer a question with a question. Deflect enquiry.

'I use because I love it. It blocks out everything. *Everything.*' His smile was beatific, the spread of his arms expansive. 'Everything. All the shit, all the crap you get from people.'

'What people?'

'Everyone. My mum, my old man, everyone.' The smile slipped off his face; his eyes became dark, his brow furrowed. Apparently reminded of an incident—or someone—unpleasant, he scowled.

Rachel suppressed a wild desire to laugh at him. He seemed so pathetic, so babyish, so sorry for himself.

Did Ruby talk like this? Did she whine about me? Does she still?

She assumed so, but the thought wasn't painful.

'How old are you, Richard?'

'Eighteen. D'ya think that's too young?'

'For what?'

Richard didn't answer. He fossicked in his pockets until he found his own cigarettes, lit one, then offered Rachel the packet. Rachel shook her head.

'My backside's getting sore sitting here,' she said. 'Let's walk. Which way are you heading?'

'Clauscen Street. Let's stay here. We could stay all night. Just you and me.'

'No, I'm going. You can stay here if you want to. If you want to walk together, let's go. I have to get home.'

'You married?'

'No.'

That wasn't painful either.

They scrambled to their feet. Richard almost tumbled into her with the effort of standing. Rachel caught him, straightened him out and they set off. He was shorter than she expected.

'You're the kindest person I've ever met. I wish you were my mum.' He danced a clumsy little jig up the street. 'You got a drink?'

'What rubbish. And no drink. Remember?'

'I hate my mum and dad.'

You are becoming irritating, Richard.

'Everyone hates their mum and dad sometimes.'

'Yeah? Well, I hate mine all the time. They never leave me alone. They always want to know what I'm doing, where I'm going. They don't like any of my mates. They give me the shits. You've got no idea.'

Oh yes I have, Little Richard.

'Well, they're probably concerned for you. Parents worry.'

'Bullshit. They couldn't care less about me. They spy on me all the time. They never leave me alone.'

'Do you live with them?'

'Sometimes, but if I had enough money I'd move out for good.'

Rachel couldn't resist.

'If you spent less money on drugs, you might be able to afford to leave home.'

'Bull*shit*.'

'Why do you keep saying that?'

'Just bullshit.' Now he was petulant. 'I really wish you were my mum.'

'Try talking to yours. And your dad.'

Oh, very good advice, Rachel. Excellent.

'No way. I told you. They're fuckin' hopeless. Real straight. I can't talk to them about anything. I can talk to you, though.'

Yes, Richard, you can. Just as I can talk to you. And this, precisely, was Annie's point. 'This may be painful for you to accept,' Annie had said, 'but you are not the one who is going to help her.' It is because we are strangers, Richard, you and I. There is no history between us. We have not had time to find each other wanting or to see our expectations of each other fall short. We have not weathered the difficult time of adolescence together, Richard.

Don't we all—in some measure, at some time—want our parents to be ignorant of us, believe they are unworldly in the ways of our lives? Are they? Perhaps so. But not so ignorant, so unsophisticated, as we would have ourselves believe. Even the least worldly of them.

Still, we are more inclined to find a different confidant. An aunt (familial or so-called), a friend, a friend's mother, the hairdresser, a doctor, a teacher, a therapist. A candlestick maker. A good thing, too, that there is someone. The remove is often easier; we are more apt to listen to what the one outside the family circle has to say, and they to us.

Mama and Papa, we say, they wouldn't understand. They're too old, too straight, too square, too dumb. They would freak out. What would they know?

They know plenty. They understand more than we realise.

Another dimension. Consider this.

Not only do we think our parents won't understand (no matter our age), but we also wish to present them with the person we want them to see us as, believing them to be too fragile to see our weaknesses, our failures, our sorrows.

As if, in loving us, they did not see them, and love us anyway.

And this. Pay attention, Richard.

Withholding parts of ourselves is a natural part of the game plan we call our lives. It is an act which separates us from our parents on the road to adulthood.

Richard trudged along beside her, morose, silent.

Would you comprehend any of this, Richard, were I to say it aloud?

'I'm going to leave you, Richard. This is where I turn off.'

'I'll come with you.'

'No, I don't think that's a good idea.'

Crestfallen, he pouted, 'Why not?'

Rachel employed one of the tools from the parents' group of years ago.

'I don't want you to come.'

'Oh well, suit yourself.'

I'm trying to.

'I enjoyed meeting you, Richard. I hope your life works out.'

'Yeah. See ya, Rachel.'

'Goodbye, Richard.'

Rachel walked the short distance to her house, looking twice over her shoulder to make sure Richard wasn't following. Though the sun had set, it wasn't yet dark. The double-storey Victorian-era shops at the western end of the street were as shadows, black against the evening sky, their soft Mediterranean pastels faded for the night. Fluorescent lights glowed in their windows; neon lit their signs. Along the outline of their rooftops, the last remnant of the sun's rays glowed, a gleaming stripe, a golden farewell to the day.

POSTLUDE

Rachel soars high in the sky on filigreed wings fashioned from Russian gold. The wings shimmer in a flaming sunset. The sparkling blue of the sky above her dissolves into translucent yellow on the horizon.

Swoop, glide, swoop, all the while surveying a desert landscape below. Then she soars again

A graceful figure approaches. It is the poet Leonard Cohen, who is wearing the robes of a Buddhist monk. Draped around his neck is a tallit, a white silk shawl worn by Jews at prayer.

'Hello, Leonard.' Rachel, smiles at him. 'What are you doing here?'

'Hello, Rachel. I'm looking for the lyrics to my song.'

'Which song?'

'"Tacoma Trailer".'

'Leonard,' she chuckles, 'there are no lyrics. "Tacoma Trailer" is the second movement of your piano concerto.'

'Oh', he replies, nonplussed. 'What will I do now?'

Rachel executes a swoop then glides back to where Leonard hovers in the sky, confused.

'Write the third movement.'

'A third movement?'

'Yes.'

From a pouch secreted in the sleeve of his robe, Leonard removes a silkbound notebook and a fountain pen. As Rachel glides and swoops, he begins to compose the third movement of the Tacoma Trailer Concerto, a piece for solo piano.

— o —

The house and nursery are sold. Everything but two suitcases of clothes, a box of books and a selection of compact discs is placed in storage. Before moving out of the house, Rachel fills a hand-ful of buff-coloured envelopes with seed from her favourite flowers—all are her favourites—removes some bulbs and rhizomes, pots up cuttings of the roses. She leaves them in Rivka's safekeeping.

She phones Eli, resident of Seattle, to tell him she has bought a stationwagon—a solid, second-hand, European model—and that she is going travelling. He is excited for her.

'Are you going to the desert? If you go to the desert, always take water supplies and let someone know where you're heading. If the car conks out, don't go wandering off.'

She smiles.

'I won't always know where I'm heading, Eli.'

'I know what you mean. Not knowing is a good way to be.'

He smiles, too.

Eli provides her with enough details of his life to keep her happy: his job is interesting, he loves his girlfriend and she him, there are probably worse places in the world to live than Seat-tle (which means he is enjoying being there) and he is in good health. He has joined a local baseball team. They like his style. His workmates and fellow members of the baseball team now greet each other with 'G'day'. He is teaching them how to use 'good on ya'.

No, he has no idea when he will return to Australia. He may never.

She says she will write to him from pinpricks on the map. Once in a while she will phone.

They wish each other well.

Both say 'I love you' before hanging up.

— o —

Rachel and Ruby meet at Mario's in Fitzroy. Hospitable, cheer-ful Mario leads them to a large, round table.

'Have you set a date for your departure?' Ruby asks.

'Two weeks.'

'Where will you go?'

'I'll drive to the Grampians first. I want to see the wildflowers. Then I think I'll wander west. After that, I don't know.'

'You don't always have to know your destination. Sometimes it's more important just to be on the road.'

'That's what Eli said!'

'See, we told you that you raised us right.'

Ruby is excited for her too. Rachel is relieved.

They order meals and drink their coffees, content in each other's company. Rachel is about to bite a forkful of pasta when she senses Ruby looking at her. She looks up.

'What?'

Ruby holds her head to one side and looks at her mother, appraising her. When she speaks her voice is quiet.

'You never understood about me and Claudine, did you? You had no idea why I defied your ban.'

'It was because you were so fond of her.'

Ruby gives a slight shrug. 'Yes, that. You know, apart from Dad leaving, it was the most painful thing that had happened to me.'

Ruby crosses one leg over the other and rearranges her short-skirted printed cotton dress, incongruously worn with a pair of walking boots and socks. She lights a cigarette and inhales deeply, continuing to speak through slowly exhaled smoke.

'I wanted to save her, though in those days I hardly knew what I was saving her from. Mostly I thought she was sick in some awful, indescribably painful way.' She looks into Rachel's eyes. 'Soul painful, not physical.'

Rachel nods. Ruby's rollie has gone out. She lights up again and continues talking. 'Parents—adults—like to think teenagers don't know what goes on in the world. We know all right. You seem to think that by remaining silent about things that frighten you, you'll protect us, as if your silence will keep us innocent.' She displays the best of her wicked grins. 'No way. Even if we're not doing any of the things adults are terrified we're doing, we still know. Mind you,' her grin broadens, 'we were often busy trying it. All of it.' She whoops. Patrons turn to stare, then look away. From behind the bar, Mario grins and points to the coffee machine.

Yes, Rachel nods, bring more coffee.

'A couple of days after you imposed your ban, I went over after school and asked her what was wrong. She was so direct. I asked her if she could die from using heroin and she said maybe. I was desperately upset by that, and frightened, but I remember being more upset by how ratty she looked, how sad. So damn sad. Her house—remember how lovely it used to be? The house looked like a shitheap. Piles of beautiful Italian clothes lying everywhere, dirty, rumpled. The sniffing made me want to scream.'

Ruby picks breadcrumbs from the tablecloth and rolls them around in her fingers.

'I went one day a week, every week, after school.'

'Every week? Weren't you afraid?'

'Of what? Ah, that I'd find her dead. Yes', Ruby replies, solemn. 'My heart always pounded as I approached the gate, but I couldn't not go in. I'd let myself in. She wasn't always home. If she was she'd be flaked out in bed or on the couch. It was as if I'd entered a house that had been abandoned, yet it still had people living in it. Sometimes the television was on; picture, no sound. I cleaned the house.'

'Ruby, what a generous thing to do!'

Ruby shrugs. 'She was my dearest friend. I loved her better than any of my friends at school in those days, even better than Rhea.'

'What else did you do there?'

'Not much. Each week I put aside some of the money from that job I had at the art supplies shop and bought her something to eat, usually chocolate mint biscuits. She adored them. Remember?' Ruby's smile is wistful. 'I'd buy her a couple of apples, a bread roll. If I could afford it, I'd get two dollars' worth of her favourite cheese. Was it Stilton? I think so. They were her favourite foods.

'I never had enough money to buy flowers, so I pinched them from gardens along the way.' Ruby sighs, ruffles her hennaed hair. 'If she was awake I made her a cup of tea or coffee, fixed up the food I bought. She rarely ate it.

'After the cleaning was done, I'd sit with her and read her an essay I'd written that week, or a chapter of my English Lit text, sometimes we'd talk. Then I'd come home.' She laughs. 'And there you'd be, worry and anger all over your face, some kitchen or gardening implement poised, and off we'd go, doing battle over whether or not I'd been there and how I wasn't allowed to visit her, and if you ever found out . . . blah blah blah.'

Ruby sits back in her chair.

'I was afraid for you. Once I knew she was using, I didn't think you should be going there but, other than insisting that you obey my rules, I didn't know how to stop you. Grounding you wouldn't have done any good.'

'No, it wouldn't. I was aware you were afraid, but apart from your insistence, you never talked to us about it. All you said was—and I remember this very clearly—you said, "I don't want you around that *stuff*, ever". You were hysterical.'

'Would you have obeyed me if I'd been less hysterical?'

'Probably not. Claudine was my friend, independent of you. Going there, looking after her, it was my secret, something I refused to share with you.

'It was as though I was the last vestige of her connection with the world that had nothing to do with smack. I'm sure that wasn't true, but that's how I felt at the time. She seemed content just to allow me to minister to her domestic needs.' Again Ruby sighs. 'But each week she looked worse. I became more and more worried about her.

'I know you always wondered what I got up to there. I have wanted to tell you for years. The time never seemed right.' Ruby puts out her cigarette and reaches across the table to hold Rachel's hand. 'I feel I owe you this part of the explanation, too: I never did drugs with her. She never offered, not once, and I was never interested. In fact, the day I asked her about heroin she gave me a long and stern talking-to, to warn me off, made me promise her I would never touch it. She didn't yell, or get hysterical. She just talked. "Look at me," she said. "Is this how you want to end up?" She gripped my chin between her fingers so tight it hurt. She made me look at her.

'So, bound up with every other shitty feeling I had about myself using was that I'd betrayed Claudine.' She squeezes Rachel's hand, then lets go. 'Claudine didn't turn me on to drugs, Mama. Using drugs had nothing to do with why I went there. I wanted to save her, simple as that.'

Both women remain quiet for a long time. Mid-afternoon sunlight pours in through Mario's window. Traffic sounds penetrate the plate-glass window: cars, motorbikes, trucks, trams. They roar and snarl and rattle, a background music to their conversation.

'It was as if I knew I was saying goodbye to an important time in my life. Even if I was unable to comprehend it completely, somewhere inside me I knew that she was dying because she didn't want to live any more, and that this special friendship was almost over. Once she died, when it was over, I could never be a child again. There would never be a special relationship with someone like Claudine again because I would no longer be a child. Do you understand?'

'I think so.'

'Later, when I was using, I thought a lot about those days.' She wipes a single glassy tear from the corner of her eye.

'Why did it end?' Rachel asks gently.

'Do you remember that day I came home from school crying my eyes out?'

'Yes, I'll never forget. I'd never seen you so upset.'

'I went around as usual and she told me to piss off. No shouting, no screaming. Cold as ice. She wouldn't let me read to her, wouldn't allow me to clean. When I handed her the chocolate biscuits, she dropped them onto the floor and pulverised them with the heel of her shoe, very, very slowly, never once taking her eyes off me. I was stunned. I kept saying, "Claudine, what's wrong? What's the matter? Did I do something to upset you?" Over and over. I was crying like mad. "Get out, you irritating little bitch", she said. "Get the fuck out of here." Then she stepped right up close to me, almost nose to nose, and said, "What do you think you're doing, coming around here, poking around, taking over my house? You think you're going to save me, is that it?" They were her exact words. I've never forgotten them. She laughed at me then.' Ruby shivers. 'It was such a creepy laugh. I'd never heard her laugh like that. I was really scared.'

'It must have been awful for you.'

Ruby ignores Rachel's interruption.

'She said, "You little Goody Two-shoes, take your fucking

chocolate biscuits and your pissy little stories and get out of my house and never come back." Then she went to the door and held it open for me to leave. Wide open. So I left.'

'Ay, Ruby, you poor darling.'

Ruby rolls another cigarette; she drags deep. 'I wanted to die that day.'

Their silence is contemplative; sadness fills the space between them. Ruby speaks first.

'Years later, after I got over the worst of the pain and I'd grown up a bit, I wondered if what she did that day was the only way she knew how to get rid of me. She knew I wouldn't abandon her. I wondered if she was ashamed of me seeing her like that.'

'Perhaps so, but even now it seems very cruel.'

'Ah, Mama, Claudine was a junkie. She was sick and sorrowful and on her way out of this world, even if it did take years for her to die. By the time we saw the last of her, all of us, we knew that.'

They are quiet again. Rachel casts her eyes around the cafe.

Who are these people? What sort of families do they have? Who among them uses? What is their pain? What are their joys, their passions, their dreams?

Rachel turns to Ruby and asks a question whose form she learnt in her twelve-stepping days. 'How are you travelling?'

Ruby shakes away the memory of Claudine and laughs.

'You know how it is. Some days smooth, others rough.'

'Today looks like a good day.'

'It is. Just for today, I'm clean. I have a part-time job and,' she blushes, shy, 'I'm seeing someone. He's a nice man.' Then grins. 'There, that should keep your wheels oiled for a while.'

Old habits—in their myriad varieties—die hard.

Questions rattle around in Rachel's head: Do you go to meetings? Is your man an addict? Is he clean? Where did you meet him? Do you see a therapist? Did you go on methadone? Do you get tempted back into the life? Does the temptation get the better of you—do you use? Is the place you work a good place, not a dive? Do they pay you well? Will you return to art school? She says:

'I'm very happy for you, Ruby.'

'No big deal. My job is in a cafe like this. Very respectable. The pay's so-so, but the tips are good. You want more?'

She is playing.

'No. It's all right.'

'Yes you do! We've been together four months. He's not an addict. He's a teacher. History. He knows about me. No secrets. Will we make it? Who knows? You must have heard how difficult it is for an addict to have a relationship and stay clean, especially in the early days. First sign of angst, we want to run for a spoonful of loving comfort.' She shrugs. 'We're working on it. And, in case you're wondering, no, I'm not going back to art school.' In response to Rachel's obvious disappointment, Ruby says: 'Being an artist was your dream, Mum, it's always been yours. It's true I have some talent, but painting's not my dream. I'm not sure yet what I'll do, so many years lost to junk. I have some ideas . . . When I've been clean for long enough to have worked it out I'll let you know. Now,' she laughs, 'that's all you get, Nosy Parker.'

'I am not.'

'You are so.'

'I'm interested in what happens in your life. I want you to be happy.'

'Mama, Mama,' Ruby's sigh is loud. 'I can't be happy all the time. No one can. No one is. If I were happy all the time, how would I know what happy is?'

She takes Rachel's hand in both her own; she is still smiling.

'I know. But you're my little girl. You will always be my little girl and I will always want you to be happy.'

They laugh so hard that when they stand to leave, one of them bumps into the table, knocking a coffee cup to the terrazzo floor. Over Rachel's protests, Ruby pays for their meals. When she offers to pay for the broken cup, Mario says, 'Don't worry about it', and waves them on their way.

They stand on Brunswick Street.

'I have to be at work soon', Ruby says, looking at her watch. 'Where are you staying?'

'With Esther and Shimon.'

'I'll call you.'

Rachel puts an arm around her.

'I wanted to say this to you before I left.'

Wary, Ruby takes a step back.

'What?'

'I always loved you, Rube.'

'You did?'

'Yes. I never stopped.'

'Despite everything I did?'

'Yes. Always. I didn't always like what you did, or how you behaved. I was often angry, always afraid, but I never stopped loving you. I know now that my love must have been suffocating at times.'

'I always loved you too, even though you drove me crazy.'

'I often wondered.'

'Of course I loved you, and I never blamed you for the life I led. You must have known that. I told you often enough.'

'Oh, Ruby, come on.'

Rachel knows she will never completely believe it.

'No, I didn't.' Ruby grows testy. 'The choice to pick up was mine, even if I didn't want to admit that until I'd done a few meetings. Quite a few.' Her mouth sets in a determined line. 'Look, heroin was something else to try, along with all the other things I tried. I could bleat on about you and Dad breaking up, the heartbreak of Claudine, Gully, you and Jerry fighting, my own messed-up relationships. Anything. But I always had choices. There were other things I could have done instead of smoothing it all out with hammer. I just loved it too much.

'Remember Liz Deutscher from high school? She was so bad her parents kicked her out of home.' Ruby grins, then sobers. 'Liz died. Did you know about that?' Rachel nods: yes.

'Rhea tried it, you know. So did Josh. Lots of kids I knew tried it a few times and never touched it again. Others dabbled on and off for years. You'd be amazed. They never got hooked. Me? I got hooked. Do you ever wonder about that?'

'All the time. I had so many conversations with Esther and Grace and Jerry about it. Hell, I even got brave enough to talk to Eli about it once.'

Ruby smiles at her. She raises a enquiring eyebrow and points at the outdoor tables.

'Won't you be late for work?' Rachel asks.

'Mama,' Ruby warns, 'don't you think I know how to read a watch or use a phone?'

'Sorry.' Rachel blushes. They sit down again and order another round of coffees. People bustle by, a blur of colour and voices and smells. A red heeler makes itself comfortable at their feet.

Ruby strokes Rachel's cheek. Rachel leans into her palm, and sighs. 'I'm sorry if I made life difficult for you.'

'Thanks, Mum.' Ruby removes her hand and drinks her coffee. 'Me, too. But it wasn't all difficult. We had many great times, so much fun, even if you did embarrass me with that mouldy green birthday cake!' She replaces the coffee glass on its shiny black saucer. 'I want to thank you too for your faith in my ability to get clean. It never seems to waver.'

'There were times when it did, and when my fear that you would die overrode everything.'

'Ah, I was curious about that. I wondered if you always felt in your heart, as strongly as you said, that I would make it.' She laughs softly. 'Still?'

'Sometimes.'

'Hmm. Well, don't think I always appreciate your unwavering faith.' In response to Rachel's perplexed look, she explains: 'If I don't have faith in myself, how can I accept it from you?'

'I thought if I could support you in any attempt you were prepared to make to give it up, it might encourage you. It might compensate for my having been so flawed a mother.'

'Have you got over that nonsense yet?'

'I'm working on it.'

They smile at each other, stand, and prepare to leave. An unexpected question spills from Rachel's lips.

'Do you ever think about having children?'

'From time to time.'

'And?'

'It makes me nervous. What if I fuck up? What are you grinning at?'

'We all say that.'

Ruby takes a step closer and tweaks her mother's ear. 'Well, whatever I get wrong, it won't be the same things you got wrong.'

We all say that, too.
'I have to go, Mama. I love you.'
'I love you too, Ruby.'
Ruby hugs her. Unable to say anything further, she kisses Rachel and leaves.

— o —

They arrange to meet three more times before Rachel's departure. Ruby shows up twice, phones to apologise for the appointment she will be unable to keep.

At a final, unscheduled meeting, Ruby gives her mother a going away present, a lipstick.

'Even in the desert, Mum, a girl should look her best.'

Ay, Ruby, dear daughter, I will miss you.

— o —

Esther, Annalise and Grace take Rachel out to dinner. Their evening is spent in laughter. Each friend brings a gift.

Rachel gets misty eyed, tries to make a speech. Emulating their children, her three friends hoot in unison: 'No mush! No mush!'

After they arrive home, Rachel and Esther lounge around talking until three in the morning.

Esther promises to keep in touch with Ruby.

Rachel spends her last night in Melbourne in deep and satisfying sleep, dreaming of the poet Leonard Cohen.

— o —

Rachel drives her way across the country. There is little order to her travelling: she chooses locations based on factors as random as the pleasure she derives from the sound of a town's name, its proximity to a river, a creek or the sea, something she has read of it in a book, how much petrol there is in the tank, or how hungry she is for a shop-bought meal and cup of coffee.

As she drives, she plays her music loud; it seems appropriate in such vast spaces.

She drives hundreds of kilometres when the only music she listens to is the hum of tyres on the highway.

At night there is peace, and a Milky Way of millions of stars so brilliant, so close, that she feels herself cloaked in a diaphanous blanket of light.

Stretched out in the back of the stationwagon, she falls asleep listening to the chirruping and clicking of beetles and crickets, the whine of mosquitoes, the whirr of moths and other flying creatures. There is the yowling of dingoes and foxes, the snuffling of kangaroos.

Along the road and on its verges, she sees dead possums, rabbits, wallabies. There is much blood; the sight of it does not cause her to shudder.

She meets people along the way.

Days pass not meeting anyone.

She is rarely lonely.

Some time is spent painting, drawing, though less than anticipated. Deeper gratification is gained from observation, contemplation and reading.

From pinpricks on the map and from larger towns she writes to Eli, Ruby, her parents and friends. They respond care of post offices in locations where she tells them she will eventually be. When she needs to hear their voices, she phones.

— o —

There are the days and nights when the madness returns, when she is unable to rid herself of guilty memories, of fear, of wondering if Ruby is all right. If Ruby is alive. Then she drives to the nearest town and attends a meeting of whatever twelve-step program is available there. Al-Anon, Alcoholics Anonymous. It doesn't matter. After the meeting she accepts an invitation to have coffee or a meal then continues on her way, at peace with herself once more—or not.

— o —

Five months after leaving Melbourne, she returns.

'What's next?' Esther asks.

'It may be too late, but I am going to see if I have any talent left to be an artist. I've been accepted into art school. I have money enough to live off for three years if I'm careful. I'll look for a space in Williamstown that can double as a studio and a place to live. It's cheaper over there. I'd like to be near the beach.'

A friend of a friend of a friend knows someone . . .

A large old warehouse—seven metres by twelve, high ceilings, sunny, inexpensive, two blocks from the beach—is available. It has an adequate kitchen, and a bathroom which, she is overjoyed to discover, has a bathtub.

There is a garden, of sorts: two narrow strips either side of a small bluestone courtyard. It will suffice.

Of her many household goods in storage—the collected clutter of two marriages and thirty years of domesticity—there are few items she requires or wants. Travelling has taught her the pleasures of a simpler life. She spends a day at the removalist's sorting through her cartons, from which she removes her minimum requirements: a small selection of Japanese and Chinese crockery, cutlery, some furniture, the CD player, Manchester and a food processor. Three vases. One of Ruby's paintings, two of her own.

She brings a large box of books and two boxes containing compact discs. Lastly, three manila folders, each one full to bursting with photographs of family and friends. The remaining thirty boxes she leaves in storage at the removalist's and pays their modest rent.

She arranges the bed, diamond-like, in a corner of the room.

Two days after moving in, Rachel is driving down Williamstown Road when she spies a Japanese screen and a pair of shoji lamps in the window of a second-hand shop; they are in almost perfect condition. The screen hides her unmade bed. She places the lamps on her bedside tables, which stand angled at forty-five degrees to the bedhead.

In the opposite corner, near the large window, she sets up her easel and paints.

Rachel scours the local second-hand shops for a selection of cheap frames in which to mount the twenty-five photographs she has selected from the folder. In the linear arrangement she first gives them, each photograph appears isolated from the rest. The effect of the high ceiling and the length of the wall compounds their isolation, making each appear lost, diminished. She tries again, reorganising them in a close cluster of rectangles, squares and an oval or two: Ruby and Eli together, individually or with friends, Rivka and Nate together, on their own, with Rachel, Eli and Ruby. There are photos of Rachel with and without husbands, with and without children, with and without parents. A number with friends. There are photos of the adults as children, children as adults. Photos of previous generations—her grandparents—are found a place. Moods vary.

Every possible permutation is represented.

Grouped together in this manner—their different shapes and sizes, the multifarious combinations of people—the lost look vanishes. Grouped together, the composition appears a little cluttered, a little messy, yet it is not without harmony. The arrangement has appeal.

Grouped together, they look more like a family.

— o —

By week's end, Rachel is ready to commence work.

ACKNOWLEDGMENTS

The author would like to thank the following for permission to reproduce: lyrics from 'Slip Slidin' Away', words and music by Paul Simon, © 1977 Paul Simon, all rights reserved; extract from *La Vie Matérielle* by Marguerite Duras, © P.O.L., 1987; extract from *I Ching*, © 1950 by Bollinger Foundation Inc., New York, NY, new material © 1967 by Bollinger Foundation, renewed 1977 by Princeton University Press; extract from *Beloved* by Toni Morrison © 1987 and Alfred A. Knopf, reprinted by permission of International Creative Management, Inc; extract from *The Fire Next Time* by James Baldwin, Penguin, 1990; lyrics from 'The Miracle of Love' (Annie Lennox/David A. Stewart) © 1986 D'N'A Limited, reprinted with kind permission of BMG Music Publishing Limited; lyrics from 'Ballerina', words and music by Van Morrison, reproduced by permission of Warner/Chappell Music Australia Pty Ltd., unauthorised reproduction is illegal; lyrics from 'The Tower of Song', written and composed by Leonard Cohen, courtesy of Sony/ATV Music Publishing Australia.